# THE
# LETTER

Josephine Cox was born in Blackburn, one of ten children. She never forgot her own childhood experience of hardship and strongly believed in education as a way out of poverty. Josephine had a long and happy marriage to her husband Ken and was immensely proud of her family and her grandchildren. She passed away in 2020.

Her books have sold over twenty million copies worldwide and she is amongst the most borrowed writers from libraries, of which she was a vocal supporter. Josephine said of her books, 'I could never imagine a single day without writing. It's been that way since as far back as I can remember.'

Her legacy lives on through Gilly Middleton who has co-authored with Josephine Cox for many years and feels very privileged to have worked with her. Gilly lives in Sussex, where she likes to go to the theatre and to watch cricket.

## Also by Josephine Cox

# JOSEPHINE COX

with GILLY MIDDLETON

# THE LETTER

HarperCollins*Publishers*

HarperCollins*Publishers*
1 London Bridge Street,
London SE1 9GF

www.harpercollins.co.uk

HarperCollins*Publishers*
Macken House,
39/40 Mayor Street Upper,
Dublin 1
D01 C9W8
Ireland

First published by HarperCollins*Publishers* 2023
This edition published 2023
1

A catalogue record for this book
is available from the British Library

ISBN: 978-0-00-812864-7 (PB)

Typeset in ITC New Baskerville Std by
Palimpsest Book Production Ltd, Falkirk, Stirlingshire

Printed and bound in the UK using 100% Renewable
Electricity by CPI Group (UK) Ltd

# PROLOGUE

'M UM, CAN I go—'
Nanette seemed not to hear her daughter but carried on talking. '. . . And then, Harry, I thought we could stop at St Ives on the way back. The light is so special there, even at this time of year.'

'Good idea,' said Harry. 'I'll put my gear in the back of the car.'

'Mum, Dad, can I—'

'Yes, but let's keep it simple. No easels or half a ton of paints.'

'When did I ever take half a ton of anything?' Harry pretended to look indignant, but his eyes were twinkling.

'When did you ever not? Sometimes with you, preparing for a day out is more like packing for a three-week expedition. Like a trip to . . . to *the Alps*.'

'Such drama, my love! And not true!'

'The honest truth,' laughed Nanette. 'If you have the backseat for your stuff, I'll take the boot, but if any of your things get in my space, I swear I shall chuck them into the road! Now, give me half an hour to do my face and put on a nice frock, and we'll be on our way.'

'A whole half-hour, when you already look ravishing?'

Nanette, rising from the table, beamed at her husband and grabbed his hand, giving it an affectionate squeeze. 'I'm right excited about our day out.'

'*Right excited*, eh?'

'Dad, Mum! Please! Can I come, too?'

'What?' Nanette, now halfway to the door, stopped and turned as if surprised to see her daughter sitting at the breakfast table. 'Oh, Millie . . .' she said vaguely. 'I thought you said summat about going to Sarah's.'

'No, Mum. It was *you* who said about Sarah's. I want to come with you. Please let me. You know I love St Ives.'

'But, Millie,' said Harry, 'we're not going straight there. We're off to see Jane and Donald, talk about Mum painting some flowers on their living-room walls, have something nice to eat . . . Probably something nice to drink, too.' He turned to look up at Nanette with a wink. 'Grown-ups' day out. No children allowed. You'd only be bored, anyway.'

'I wouldn't, Dad. I like Jane and Donald, and they never make me feel like a little child . . . like a left-over . . . like I'm *not wanted*.' Millie could feel the familiar heat of resentment gathering and taking control of her.

'Leftover? Not wanted?' said Nanette, giving Millie a

hug. 'Really, Millie, you don't half talk soft sometimes. Jane and Donald are always very kind, but they've invited just your dad and me today.'

'But why didn't they ask me, too?'

'Because I told them you would be seeing your friend Sarah.'

'No, Mum, it was *you* who said—'

'Millie, please, stop being a baby,' said Harry, mildly. 'Mum and I are going to see our friends, and you are going to see your friend. Makes perfect sense to me.'

Millie flung her head down on her folded arms at the table. Her parents knew just how to twist situations to suit themselves, often leaving her to kick her heels alone or offloading her on their friends and neighbours while they had all the fun together, just the two of them.

'But I don't want to,' she insisted. 'I want to go with you. Sarah's all right, but her mum talks to me as if . . . as if she feels sorry for me. And she keeps on about me going to school. I'd rather go to Jane and Donald's and see what you're going to paint, Mum.' She felt angry tears threatening. 'It's not fair! I want to go to St Ives!'

'Millie, love, you sound just like a toddler, not a child of fourteen,' said Nanette, reaching for her cigarettes on the dresser. 'Life isn't fair – it's tough. I know that as much as anyone.' As she stretched up for her matches, as if to emphasise her words, her sleeve fell back, showing an old, deep scar on the pale skin of her forearm.

'If you don't want to go to Sarah's, you can stay here and amuse yourself. Just so me and Dad can have a precious day together.'

'But you have lots of days together. Are they more precious if I'm not there? It's as if you don't want me. As if you'd prefer me not to be here. I bet you wish I'd never been born!'

'And now you're being silly,' said Harry. 'And where did you learn to put on the drama? From your mother, I bet.' He turned to wink at Nanette to show he was trying to jolly Millie out of her mood.

'Don't be mean,' said Nanette, giving his arm a gentle slap as she passed him. 'Right, I'm going to get ready.' She left, trailing cigarette smoke and leaving the kitchen door open.

'And I'm going to gather my painting things. Do you want to help me, Millie?'

'No.'

'Suit yourself.'

'If I suited myself, I'd be coming with you.'

'Darling, it's not all about you all the time,' said Harry, and he headed off to look out some paints and canvases from the big, light room where he and Nanette worked. It was very large and could accommodate both without any cause for them to argue about their own spaces, even though they frequently did.

Millie got up only to slam the kitchen door as hard as she could behind her father. She listened, but there was no reaction to this. It was as if her parents were already mentally on their way and unbothered by her anger at being left behind.

'I hate you!' she yelled as loudly as she could. 'I wish you were dead!'

The sound of the car engine faded. They were gone, with hugs and kisses – as if they minded that she was not going, too; as if they hadn't excluded her on purpose.

'Millie, love, you have a lovely day. Mebbe go and see Mags if you don't want to go to Sarah's,' Nanette had said with a big smile as she'd arranged her coat around her in the passenger seat. Her dark curls were tied back with a jolly red and white spotted scarf, the red the exact same shade as her lipstick. She looked gorgeous. 'We'll see you later.'

'Yes, yes, off you go,' Millie had snapped. 'And don't hurry back,' she'd added viciously.

Now she put on her coat and went to let the half-dozen pert little hens out into the garden, then, shoulders hunched, mooched over to see if there were any eggs in the nesting boxes. There weren't. She knew there were things to eat in the pantry, but she was in the mood to feel she had been left to starve now there were no eggs. Then she wandered around the garden in the wet grass, kicking the decayed remains of fallen apples and stoking the fire of her resentment at being left behind – again.

Eventually she went down the lane to see Mags, an old lady who was a potter. But Mags's cottage was silent, and there was a pencilled note stuck with a drawing pin to the door, easy enough for Millie to read: *Daisy, I'll be back by four.* Who was Daisy? Millie felt excluded again.

Perhaps she should go to Sarah's after all, but by now she was too fed up to want company. She would stay here, by herself. She would go and occupy her parents' studio, and paint a really big picture on one of their canvases, using a lot of their paint, and making a huge mess. That would serve them right for abandoning her.

In the studio, she lavishly squeezed paint from several tubes onto a palette, then set a large blank canvas on her father's easel, first removing a half-finished painting of her mother that he was working on and propping it against the wall. She'd start with images of her parents – Mum all pretty with a lipsticky smile, and Dad looking handsome and smart with one of his brightly coloured scarves, which he liked to wear instead of a conventional tie.

Colourful clothes, cigarettes, smiling faces – soon, there they were, looking as they had when they had set off a few hours before. The resemblance was striking.

Millie knew she had a gift for painting, even now, at fourteen, and she had learned many of her parents' techniques, sitting quietly here, just looking, then copying. When the mood took them, Nanette and Harry were happy to share their knowledge, and these rare times were very precious to their daughter.

It was just a shame that they so seldom wanted to be

bothered about her at all! Like now! Setting out so smiley and happy, and leaving her behind and not caring. It was all right doing exactly what you wanted some of the time, but sometimes it would be nice if Mum and Dad organised her days, showed they minded even a little bit about what she did.

The trouble was, there was little room in her parents' lives for anyone except themselves and each other. Millie thought it significant that she was an only child: they'd given child-rearing a try and decided that it was not for them. They were not like other parents, so far as she could see: they didn't insist on her going to school, or wearing particular clothes at certain times or brushing her hair. They didn't mind what she did so long as she didn't bother them, except on their own terms. If their friends came here, she joined in the fun: the gossip, the dancing to gramophone records, or playing casual games of tennis in the garden. But if Mum and Dad went out and left her, she just went for walks in the woods or on the beach, observing the colours and the changes in the sky, picking the wild flowers. Sometimes she made dens in the garden, where she ate picnics – usually just bars of chocolate – either alone or with Sarah, if Sarah wasn't at school. Sometimes she went to see Mags, who liked Millie to help her decorate her pots and who fed her soup made out of home-grown vegetables.

Millie felt another dark wave of ill-temper rising. If only Mum and Dad were as caring as Mags. But they didn't care at all. They really didn't!

As rage rose and took possession of Millie, she made a violent sweep across the canvas, a broad gash of vivid red seeming to scar the surface over the neat depictions of Nanette and Harry. Scarlet rivulets ran down from it, partially obliterating the figures. Millie's anger increased, and she flung her arm towards the canvas, the paintbrush like a wand, emitting not sparks but a violent spatter of paint, which flicked out and stained wildly all around the figures.

*Good! I hate them, I hate them.*

Next she stabbed the brush into black and white and blue, then swirled it over the surface, creating threatening clouds that resembled a strangely low-lying thunderstorm, or billowing smoke.

She stood back, panting. There was paint on the floor, on her clothes; red paint, like blood, on her hands.

Millie's heart was hammering, and she tried to be calm, to gather herself. She looked at the canvas. The image was terrible, chaotic and bloody, burning with rage. It was no longer a picture of her parents, but a depiction of her own fury, horrible and frightening.

It had grown dark, and Millie's parents had not returned. It had been a long day, alone. She'd locked up the hens for the night, and now she was waiting. She had returned her father's portrait of her mother to the easel – Mum looked so beautiful, her slim figure half turned away, but smiling over one shoulder – and propped her own depiction of anger with its face to the wall. It betrayed the violence of her jealousy, her momentary hatred, and she was ashamed. She didn't know how she would explain it to her parents. Even so, it was getting late, and she wished they would hurry up and come home.

She cut herself a doorstep sandwich of cheese and Branston Pickle, and was just wondering whether a tiny measure of cider, a bottle of which was open on the shelf in the pantry, would help it down and blunt her worries, when there was a knock at the door.

There was Mags, crying. Millie had never seen her cry before, and for a moment she was so distracted by this that she didn't notice the other figure: a policeman.

'Oh, my pet lamb,' crooned the old lady, enveloping Millie in her arms. 'Such a terrible thing 'as 'appened to your poor ma and pa. Oh, my darlin', I don't quite know how to tell you . . .'

# CHAPTER ONE

'MILLIE BOYD, JUST do as I tell you, for once in your life,' Mona Marchant snapped. 'Go and change out of those school clothes, wash your hands and then come down and help me.'

Millie gave an exaggerated sigh and got up heavily, as if her legs would hardly hold her. 'I will do. In a minute . . . when I'm ready.'

'Do it now. Why do you always have to be so difficult?'

'Because I know you'll have me peeling potatoes or sweeping out the hearth or some other horrible job. It's like slavery, living here. First having to go to school – work, work, work – and then chores when I come back. I never get a moment to myself without you nagging me to help with stupid tasks: do this, do that. Mum and Dad never treated me like a slave. They never asked me to do anything.'

'Slavery, indeed! Don't be ridiculous. I reckon your parents spoiling you is the root of your whole problem.

"Spare the rod and spoil the child" is what I always say. If Frank and I had known that you'd been so badly brought up, well, we would have thought twice about offering you a home with us, that's for sure.'

'And maybe that would have suited me as well.'

'Enough of your backchat, you ungrateful hussy. It's little enough I ask of you in return for your board and lodging.'

'Yes, Aunt, board and lodging. That's what this house is like: a soulless boarding house. A comfortless place of nothing but bricks and . . .' Millie cast her eyes around the sitting room, at the overstuffed armchairs with shiny antimacassars, the plump cushions that she was forbidden to sit on, a row of fussy ornaments along the mantelpiece. '. . . bricks and bric-a-brac.'

With a sudden rise of temper, she snatched up a little pottery donkey wearing a sombrero with, inexplicably, *A Present from Morecambe* painted on the side of its Spanish-style pannier, and hurled it into the hearth, where it shattered beyond repair.

'Ooh, you little witch! How dare you break my lovely things?'

'I dare because I hate you,' lashed out Millie.

'Well, just think how I must feel about you,' snarled Mona, grabbing Millie tightly by the arm, deliberately pinching her hard. 'I offer you a home out of the goodness of my heart, and look how you repay me.' She turned a woebegone face to gaze at the sorry fragments of the donkey. 'It isn't as if you're even related to *me* at all.' She pulled Millie roughly towards her and hissed into her face. 'I wish now I'd hardened my heart when your parents were killed and I'd insisted your uncle Frank put you in an orphanage. You've been nowt but trouble since that dreadful day we went down to London to meet you off the train with that potter woman—'

'Mags was Mum's dearest friend. If she'd known she was delivering me into the hands of someone like you, she'd have taken me straight back to Cornwall with her. At least she loved my mother and father; you didn't even like them.'

'*Someone like me?*' Mona let go of Millie and fluttered her hands around her face as if she were about to swoon. 'I can't imagine what you mean by that. And as for your parents, I hardly knew them. Nanette was your uncle Frank's sister, not mine, and we saw nowt of her. Not only did she choose to live in remote parts, but she never got on with Frank. But I'd learned enough about her and your dad to know that they weren't my kind of folk – artistic types, not steady like your uncle . . . *bohemians*, I think they call that sort – and how I wish I'd followed my instincts. You will never fit in here. I can see that now.'

'I'll take that as a compliment,' said Millie, and ran out, slamming the door.

Later that afternoon, wearing two cardigans and her coat over her frock, Millie went out to sit on the dustbin in the walled yard behind her aunt and uncle's terraced house. It was very cold and already nearly dark, but the damp, sooty Blackburn air was preferable to the stiflingly tense atmosphere inside the house.

Millie allowed herself a few tears, thinking of her beautiful parents: Mum, with her huge smile, her bright clothes, her red lipstick and pretty curls, her love of life and her special talent to see the fun in every situation; Dad, so tall and tanned and good looking, so generous with presents and with praise. They had adored each other – even when they were having cross words, they were clearly only seconds away from falling into each other's arms. They *had* loved her, even though they probably loved themselves and each other more. They had done their best in their own way. Perhaps they even thought their way *was* the best way, that a child needed freedom above discipline. *They* hadn't shouted at her – ever. *They* hadn't minded whether she went to school or stayed at home, or what she did. *They* had just let her do as she liked, while they painted. She had basked in their encouragement and praise as she'd learned to paint, too, and had begun to develop her own style.

Millie closed her eyes at the memory of that last afternoon, that awful painting she had done, depicting – and, yes, foretelling – her parents' deaths. She did not want to think what she might have conjured, what part she might have played in their end in a way that was beyond understanding. If she did, her guilt would consume her . . .

How quickly her life had changed since then. Alarmingly, it was becoming harder and harder to remember Mum and Dad's smiling faces in sharp detail, although they had been dead for only three months. In the sad chaos of her life following their deaths in a car crash, Millie had left Cornwall without even a photograph of them. It was an oversight she deeply regretted.

Who was she without them? Where was her place in the world? Who cared? Did anyone?

Was this what she would be like from now: cold, angry, and alone, sitting on a dustbin in a dreary, darkening grey yard, behind the soot-blackened house of her uncle and aunt? Uncle Frank and Aunt Mona looked exactly what they were, in their grey clothes, with their pasty, sun-starved features beneath their greying hair, their expressions permanently sour: grim and joyless.

I *have* to get away, Millie thought; I *have* to, before I become like them. But what could she do? She felt powerless: just an unwanted orphan, a burden.

Suddenly, for the second time that day, Millie felt her anger rising up like lava in a volcano, burning hot and growing instantly out of control. With a shriek of rage, she picked up a loose brick from the top of the wall and hurled it at the scullery window, which shattered with a loud crack. She heard the brittle tinkle of the glass falling onto the yard outside, and into the sink within. A scream went up from Aunt Mona. Millie knew there would be punishment now, but it would be worth it. The sound of that pane smashing had been the best thing about today.

'Millie Boyd, come here now!' It was Uncle Frank, standing by the back door, flexing his vicious whippy ruler, his regular weapon of choice, chosen for its sharp sting.

'No!'

'If you don't come here now, I shall drag you off that dustbin and give you a hiding you'll never forget.'

Millie swallowed; she could well believe it. Better to face the ruler and get it over with. She slid to the ground and went to receive her punishment, trying to think of brave martyrs who had gone before, who had featured in her picture books: Joan of Arc; Mary, Queen of Scots . . .

Uncle Frank closed the back door and loomed over Millie. He was a heavy man with a big head and prominent beaky nose. She was small for her age and slight. One to one, she felt outnumbered.

Aunt Mona had disappeared to recover from her shock at having a brick through her window. It had missed her by several feet, but even that was too close for her nerves. Now she came back, breathing heavily, her lips pursed, and shakily took a seat to observe the punishment.

'Hand out.'

Without a word, Millie put out her hand. *In ten, this would be over.* She started counting silently.

*Whack!* went the ruler on the palm of her hand.

There were five of those.

'Now turn over your hand,' Uncle Frank said. He sounded almost cheerful now.

'Do as you're told, girl,' chimed in Aunt Mona, 'or I'll be boxing your ears at the same time.'

*Whack!* Five more.

*. . . nine, ten.* Millie managed to get by without without crying to the end. She knew they would be happier if she cried, and she wanted to deny them that satisfaction. *Oh, thank goodness that's over . . .*

'Now stand there and hold onto the back of that chair.'

'What? No! It was only a broken window. I won't do it again.'

'Too right you won't,' said Aunt Mona. 'Now do as Frank says. If you can't take the punishment, you shouldn't do the crime.'

'Crime?'

'Vandalism! And I could have been killed.'

*I wish you had, you hateful old baggage.*

Mona pulled Millie's hands onto the chair back, where she held on while Frank hit her with the ruler as hard as he could, three strikes on each leg.

'Let that be a lesson to you,' he said, unable to hide a smile, his eyes bright with sadistic pleasure. 'Now off you go. We don't want to see you until it's time for school tomorrow. There'll be no tea for you this evening.'

Millie limped away. There was nothing she could say that would not bring more punishment, and she had no dignity left, now that tears were running down her face, and one hand and both legs were burning with the ruler's sting. At least she was spared having to sit and eat with the monstrous pair. It was that thought that kept her on her feet until she got to her room and threw herself down, trying to howl silently.

Later, lying in bed, hugging her red and stinging hand and trying to find a cool place on which to rest her legs, Millie was filled with hatred for her aunt and uncle. Being sent to bed without any dinner had sharpened her mind and, having dried her tears, she lay awake, gathering herself, channelling the energy of her hatred to some purpose. She became focused and intent: ruthless.

She would pay her aunt and uncle back for this.

Her mother had rarely spoken of her brothers, but Millie had learned enough to piece together something of Nanette's unhappy childhood. Grandma Marchant, widowed young, had worked long hours in a mill and was often exhausted with the work and her poor health. She left her younger two children in the 'care' of Frank, her eldest, much of the time. But Frank had been a bully then, just as he was a bully now. Uncle Thomas had been too weak and too cowardly to stand up for their younger sister, Nanette, and Frank had delighted in tormenting them both. Mum had had that scar on her arm where Uncle Frank had burned her with a poker, and another on her leg where he had lashed her with his belt as a punishment for trying to run away when she could bear it no longer. It was Uncle Thomas, the one who should have been her ally, who had betrayed her escape plan, and Frank who had dragged her back home.

Millie had thought never to meet these two uncles, but her parents' deaths had taken her to London, where she had briefly met Uncle Thomas and her cousins, Alice and Bella, and Uncle Frank and Aunt Mona, who had taken her back with them to Blackburn. Uncle Thomas and his daughters lived in the next county, by the sea.

Now, lying in her hard bed in the dark, Millie saw that here was the chance to pay her aunt and uncle back for the way they had treated her mother. Maybe that would go some way towards proving how sorry she was that she had painted that terrible scene, so full of anger. That violent painting had put her rage out into the world, and perhaps rage was like a wild animal: once set free, it could wreak havoc and destroy.

This time she would resist the temptation to lash out. She needed to be patient, disciplined, but she would not forgive Uncle Frank and Aunt Mona for today and all the other days on which they'd hit her, and she would not forget. She'd like to see for herself that they were punished.

By the time she fell asleep, she had plotted a very neat and fitting revenge on Frank and Mona. That, however, would have to wait. The first thing was to save herself and get out of here.

# CHAPTER TWO

'I T'S A PITY I can't just take the babies' arms off. That would make dressing them so much easier,' said Bella Marchant, threading one fat little limb through the armhole of a tiny hand-knitted vest. 'Their heads are enormous, too. I'd never get this on at all without the shoulder opening. Do real babies ever have heads so huge on such tiny shoulders?'

'Fortunately, not usually,' said Mrs Warminster, with feeling. 'Toby was quite a neat little baby, although you do hear of some poor mothers . . . Well, never mind. An unmarried young woman like you doesn't need to know.'

She broke off abruptly to serve a lady who wanted to buy a teddy for her granddaughter. Weekdays were generally quiet in the toyshop at this time of year, except in the hour after school finished for the day, when the place could get very lively indeed.

'Not unmarried for very much longer,' beamed Bella

when the lady had gone, taking a teddy with her. 'I'm thinking about the autumn for the wedding. After the holiday season. September's a good time; often nice weather – I've got my dress all planned – and between the busyness of the summer and the beginning of the Christmas trade.'

'You're a good lass, Bella. It's so like you to think of us at the shop. What does Sidney say?' Cassie Warminster went over to rearrange some wooden soldiers in a fort, letting Bella continue to dress a whole row of baby dolls.

Bella remembered Sidney's noncommittal shrug when she'd tried to discuss with him her ideas for their wedding. Maybe he had just been tired, what with his important job in Planning at the town hall. He hadn't really been listening at all, she knew – so, rather than waste her breath, she'd changed the subject to the football match he would be playing in at the weekend. Then he had snapped out of his weariness and was eager to talk at length about the chances of his team, Theddleton Town – known as The Seafarers – against Baybury, their old rivals from up the coast. Sidney liked to talk about football – his skills, his expectations of displaying them in the coming match, his past glories . . . And, after all, it was only February – there were months until September – and it wasn't as if Bella had in mind a big and extravagant wedding, with elaborate arrangements to put in place. No, it would be quite a small do, she thought. In fact, it would *have* to be: the church, her father and her sister, Alice . . . Sidney's mother, of course . . . Vera and Iris and a few other friends – oh Lord, but would Sidney want to invite the entire football team? – and then a tea afterwards, something dainty and delicious, with an iced wedding cake, and perhaps even wine for the toasts . . . Would Dad be able to afford that? It seemed so little, really. Maybe the reception could be in the room that could be hired at the town hall. Bella had briefly considered enquiring about the dining room at the Imperial Hotel but decided that would be pretentious. And expensive. If dreams were to come true, she knew, they had to be firmly rooted in reality.

Bella realised Mrs Warminster was still waiting for an answer.

'Sidney and I haven't really discussed it properly yet,' said Bella. 'There's still time, though. I expect he'll have some ideas as the weeks go on.'

Cassie looked at her carefully. 'Perhaps he's letting you do as you choose, love,' she suggested kindly. 'Leaving the big decisions up to you. Men aren't always bothered about wedding details.'

'Yes . . . yes, I expect that'll be it.'

'Alfred left all the arrangements to me . . . well, to me and my mother, who definitely had a view. Perhaps Alice could give you a hand, as you're without your mam.'

Bella laughed, looking up from buttoning a knitted jacket on a baby doll. 'I don't know as Alice would be keen to help with my wedding – anyone's wedding. And can you imagine Alice in a fancy bridesmaid dress? She'll probably turn up on the day wearing a pair of trousers and that coat she's fond of with the big pockets, with some dog-eared book stuffed inside in case she finds the whole thing too boring and needs a distraction.'

Cassie shook her head in mock bafflement at Alice's very individual style and character. 'Yes, you and your sister are cut from different cloth, I reckon, for all you get on so well and look quite similar.'

'So folk say. Right, I'll just finish dressing this last baby, have a quick tidy of that shelf of games, and then I'll begin stitching those boots for the Edwardian ladies.'

'Alfred's painting roofs and might want some help, but make sure you keep away from that side if you are sewing.'

'Will do, Mrs Warminster. Give me a call if it gets busy and you need me here.'

The shop doorbell jangled then, announcing a woman with a toddler, and Cassie went round to attend to them while Bella quickly finished dressing the doll, then arranged it carefully on a shelf so that it sat appearing to observe the little girl and her mother.

Then she quickly neatened the pile of board games in brightly coloured boxes and went into the workroom behind the shop, where Alfred Warminster was applying dark red paint to the roof of a doll's house on his work-table. Three similar models, their roofs already drying, stood on a paint-splattered sheet to one side. The other side of the room was strictly out of bounds for painting. It was furnished with a cutting table, drawers of fabrics and threads, with a treadle sewing machine and straight-backed chair situated under the window.

'Bella, love, would you care to give me a hand with those window frames? Your eyes are sharper than mine for the very fine work.'

'Of course. Yellow?'

'Yes, please.' Alfred grinned. The canary-yellow window frames were a feature of the famous Warminster doll's houses.

Bella put on a very large brown overall that completely covered her plaid frock and warm cardigan. She rolled back the over-long sleeves and then, with a screwdriver, levered the lid off a little pot of yellow paint and took up a fine brush. Carefully she began painting the miniature window frames of the house's front and two sides, which were laid out flat along the bench to the rear of Alfred's work area. It was an intricate job, but it allowed her time to think and to daydream.

Perhaps she and Sidney would have a house this pretty one day. Not to start with, of course; they would have to save up. Sidney had suggested they would be living with his mother after the wedding. Bella wasn't at all keen on this, afraid she'd feel like a guest – or even an intruder – in what was Mrs Bennett's long-established home. She really wanted somewhere to call her own at the outset, but Sidney said his mother had it all arranged and would be terribly offended if Bella rejected her kind offer. Oh dear, Mrs Bennett was a bit of a one for taking offence, although Bella always went out of her way to try to please her future mother-in-law . . .

This delightful model of doll's house was called 'The Mock-Tudor', with interesting gables and a sort of half-timbered effect on the upper storey; it was the kind of house established families might live in, in real life. The blue front door was smart and cheerful – blue door, yellow window frames, red roof . . . so eye-catching and attractive, a dream home. Actually, this model was of a house far grander than the cottage where Bella and Alice lived with their father.

As if the thought of her father had been spoken aloud, Alfred took up the subject.

'So how is your dad getting on at the Three-Mile, Bella? Suits him, does it?'

Bella gave a lop-sided smile. 'I don't know yet, Mr Warminster. He's hardly been there a fortnight and hasn't said much about it – but I'm hoping so. I really want Dad to find some job he likes after all this time.'

'Well, Thomas has tried a fair few since your mother passed away, that can't be denied, but the right one will turn up, I'm sure.'

'Shop work, office work, various seasonal jobs, a waiter at the Imperial, crewing a fishing boat, even . . . Those are just some of the ones I can remember. None of them lasted. But I hope he can stick with this one for a while, for all it's easy work and the pay's not much,' she said, before realising that last remark might be for family ears only.

'Potman, isn't he?'

'That's right. I don't mind what he does, just so long as he's happy with it. But,' she sighed, 'I wish he'd stick to a job and not give up so easily. It's as if he's searching for summat, and nowt he tries seems to be the answer.'

'I expect he still misses your mam and that's making him unsettled.'

Bella thought about this as she straightened up and carefully wiped her brush against the rim of the paint tin. 'I can understand that, but Mam's been dead for years now.'

'There's no time limit on grief, love.'

'No . . . of course, you're right. But if Dad just found summat he was truly interested in doing, then I think that would help him settle. It's as if he's marking time, waiting for a purpose, one that will set him on a new path. But I'm beginning to worry he'll wait for ever.'

Alfred stopped painting and looked up. 'Mebbe looking forward to your wedding will give him a purpose,' he suggested kindly.

'Mm, mebbe . . . At least Alice is happy at the book-shop. She's the opposite of Dad – it suits her so well that I think she'll never leave there.'

'Never's a long time,' said Alfred lightly.

'True, but I can't imagine her wanting to go anywhere else. Gets on well with Mr Patterson.'

'And Miss Patterson?'

'She doesn't say.' Bella knew better than to utter an indiscretion about anyone in the small community.

'Hmm.'

They worked on in companionable silence for a while, until the noise in the shop grew around mid-afternoon and Bella went to help Cassie. There was always a demand when school was over for pocket-money toys like Snap cards and marbles, and then shelves to tidy when little hands had been exploring them.

At the end of the day, just as Bella was cleaning her brush for the final time, Cassie came through, announcing that she was about to close up and it was time for Bella to go home.

'I lost all track, Mrs Warminster,' Bella said, taking off her overall and hanging it behind the workroom door.

She put on her coat and hat, gathered up her handbag and the bit of shopping she'd nipped out for at lunchtime, bid the Warminsters a good evening and let herself out onto Theddleton High Street.

The second-hand bookshop where Alice worked was a short way along, nearer the seafront, and there was Alice, right on time, walking towards Bella, hands in her pockets, yet still managing to look poised and slightly regal. Bella admired her elder sister's style and wished she could achieve something similar herself, but Alice's tailoring just looked like dressing-up clothes on Bella, as if she wasn't really wearing the garments with conviction. Besides, although they looked alike, with distinctive green eyes and long dark hair, Alice was taller, which Bella thought gave her an advantage.

'Good day?' Alice asked.

'Fun. Sometimes it's almost as good as playing with the dolls and the houses.'

Alice smiled. 'Reading books, playing with dolls . . . aren't we the lucky ones!'

'Let's never grow up.'

'I think I might already have done, even if you haven't, little sister!'

'Well, old woman, you certainly smell of dust.'

Alice gave a hollow laugh. 'Hardly surprising. The dust in that window is starting to breed, I'm convinced. I can't think why Miss Patterson won't let me tackle it. The longer it's left, the bigger job it will be. I suspect it's already too big for her to want to face the disruption of clearing it.'

'Perhaps she hopes the fairies will see about it.'

Alice rolled her eyes. 'Mebbe . . . provided she doesn't have to pay them.'

They linked arms, strolling home in the fast-fading light to the little cottage where they lived with their father, well beyond the inland end of the High Street, in the narrow lanes where the Theddleton residents lived whose lives did not revolve around the seaside location – away from the hotel and the guesthouses. Visitors to the little town never ventured this far from the seafront and its modest attractions. The High Street shops had many visiting strangers, but here the Marchant girls knew everyone, having lived their entire lives at number 8 Chapel Lane, where the row of cottages stretched along one side behind their neat front gardens, overlooking a meadow of what was currently very wet grass beyond a fence on the other.

Alice produced her key first and opened the door, bending to gather the post off the doormat. It didn't look as if the girls' father was home yet.

'Dad?' she called, but there was no answer.

'Must still be busy at the Three-Mile,' said Bella. 'What's the post?'

'Looks like a bill – Dad *will* be pleased – and a letter addressed to both of us. Strange. I don't recognise the hand, either.' She showed it to Bella as she stepped inside and closed the door.

Bella shrugged. 'Mebbe a child's writing: awkward.' She half remembered giving their address to their cousin, Millie Boyd, but this did not look like the writing of someone as old as her.

Alice put the post on the little hall table while she took off her knitted hat and her coat and hung them on a peg near the door, then took off her lace-up shoes. Bella did the same and then took the letters through to the sitting room.

'Here, you open it while I get the tea on.' She went into the scullery to wash her hands.

When she came back, Alice was sitting staring at a sheet of lined paper, which looked as if it had been torn from a school exercise book.

'Tell me.'

'It's from our cousin, Millie.'

'Why is she writing to us? I thought she was all settled with Uncle Frank and Aunt Mona since they took her on after that awful accident.'

'Not settled, it seems. She doesn't sound at all happy with them.'

'Let me see.'

Alice handed the untidily written and misspelled letter to Bella, who slowly lowered herself onto the sofa as she read it.

*Dear Alice and Bella,*

*It is orfull here. Please, you must come and rescew me. Uncle Frank + aunt Moaner are to strict and I am so unhappy. They never even let me speak. Aunt Moaner says children should be seen and not herd. Spare the rod and spoill the child. Uncle Frank beets me and they send me to bed without my dinner.*

*I miss Mum + Dad so much. Please save me before I die of beeting or starve to death.*

*With love from Millie Boyd xxx*

'Crikey, Alice, that sounds terrible. Poor Millie.'

Alice frowned, saying nothing.

'Bad enough her parents are dead – it was only last November and she's grieving for them still – but to be treated so cruelly . . . What?'

'If it's true,' Alice said quietly. She looked anxious.

'Are you saying it's lies? Why would Millie lie to us? She doesn't even know us. She's clearly sent this note in desperation, crying out to be rescued. Oh, the poor child. You know how, er, strict Uncle Frank and Aunt Mona are. They're not exactly known for having fun, are they? It's plainly too much for Millie to bear.' Bella got up and started pacing about the room, clutching the scrappy letter.

'Bella, do sit down. I'm not saying it's lies, exactly, but p'raps there's been a falling-out, or she's been naughty and has sent this to us in a temper, as a kind of revenge for her punishment.'

'Punishment? Outrageous! What is she – about fifteen? I seem to recall she's quite small for her age, too. Uncle Frank is such a huge man, and he's got neither patience nor a good temper.'

'Yes, just fifteen, I think. But, listen, what if she *was* naughty, as I said?'

'Alice, she's been beaten and starved, if this is to be believed! I can't bear the thought. Did Dad ever hit us? Did Mam?'

'No, of course not, but lots of people do smack their children,' Alice pointed out, 'especially as they get older, if they're cheeky.'

'Lots of people beat defenceless animals, but that doesn't make it right. It's cruel – worse, it's unforgivable!'

'Yes, I agree, Bella, but please calm down. We can't just take this as the truth. We need to find out more. If you remember, Uncle Frank and Aunt Mona said they were only too pleased to step in and take Millie. They were childless, and here was an orphan in need of a home – and not just any orphan, either, but their own niece. They were delighted to have her. Well, p'raps not delighted exactly – it's hard to think of them being delighted about owt – but you know what I mean.'

'But, from what Millie says, they're certainly not delighted to have her now. Seen and not heard, indeed! Spare the rod and spoil the child – a bully's charter, if ever I heard one. It sounds like some nonsense from last century. No one brings up a child like that now. If they wanted a silent house, they shouldn't have invited Millie into it. If you remember, we suspected things weren't going smoothly when Aunt Mona wrote at Christmas, saying Millie was "a real handful", or summat of the sort. They clearly haven't a clue how to look after a bereaved child.'

'Yes, yes, all right, Bella.' Alice leaned back in her chair and closed her eyes, thinking. 'Let's see what Dad says. Aunt Nanette was his sister and, for all they don't get on, Uncle Frank is his brother, after all. Then we can decide.'

'You're right, of course,' said Bella, her anger subsiding a little. Then she added fiercely, 'But we're not doing nowt.'

'I didn't say we were.'


Thomas Marchant slowly cycled the short distance home in the dark. The Three-Mile Bottom, the inn where he currently worked, was just outside Theddleton, on a flat, straight stretch of the main road that bypassed the town. It catered mainly to travellers who weren't wanting to stop at the pretty little seaside place, but were passing by on the way to somewhere else. Thomas worked mornings, serving breakfasts and generally helping out, and at lunchtimes, serving drinks and clearing in the bar. It was unusual for him to be there after mid-afternoon, but today being a Friday and the weather good, the Three-Mile had been busy. The landlord, Mr Fairbanks, had asked him to stay on for a few extra hours, and Thomas had been willing to do so, to earn a little more.

The money would be more than useful. Lottie had been given a generous amount by her parents when she and Thomas had married, and that had been a big help, especially when he was struggling so badly after her death, but it was nearly all gone now. There was Bella's wedding to pay for and, although she was planning a modest celebration, Thomas didn't want her to have to rein in even those thrifty ideas. He did not doubt that, secretly, she was dreaming far bigger than she was letting on, but she wasn't spoiled or selfish and would make the best of what he could afford and what she herself was carefully saving towards. Bella would make a beautiful bride . . .

Lulled by his own slow, rhythmic pedalling along the flat road, Thomas fell into a daydream, but soon realised he was remembering Lottie as she had looked on that wonderful day when she had married him. Fashions had moved on in the quarter-century since then, and Bella would not want a dress in the style that her mother had worn. Why, Alice was so modern that she wore trousers, although not to work any more – not since that sour-faced Eileen Patterson had 'had a word'.

Alice was so like Lottie that sometimes, seeing her poise, that straight back and long neck, as if she was balancing a crown, he would feel his heart flip over. Bella, at twenty, was growing into that same dark beauty, for all she was shorter, less willowy.

Lottie had died giving birth to a longed-for third child – a daughter, Jenny, who also died. That's when Thomas had become cast adrift, unable to anchor his life to any plan or pattern for very long. Even now, years later, he still felt as if he was marking time, waiting for something, or someone, unable to find his own way forward without her hand to lead him.

Mebbe this job at the Three-Mile is one I can stick with for a while, he thought. Perhaps this is what I've been looking for . . . for all it's not exactly interesting, and Mr Fairbanks is not what I'd call considerate . . . or even likeable. Quite unpleasant, in fact. But if I can just try to settle into it, then I'll be better able to face Bella getting married and leaving home to go to live with Sidney Bennett and his mother. At least I'll still have Alice with me. I don't think I could bear it if Alice left, too . . . How would I cope then? What would I do, alone, just a sad old man by himself?

Thomas drew up at his front garden gate, dismounted

from his bike and wheeled it through and round the house side, then let himself in at the front, making a conscious effort to snap out of his self-pitying mood.

'Dad!' It was Bella calling from the kitchen. 'You're late.'

'Hello, love. Hello, Alice.' Thomas hung up his cap and jacket, and sat down on the stairs to unlace his boots. 'Busy at the Three-Mile. Quite a few travellers heading south for the weekend.' He came through and briefly hugged Alice, who was setting the table, then Bella, who held up a greasy spatula to ward him off.

'Hurry up and wash your hands, Dad. Your tea's nearly ready – egg and chips – and . . .'

'What?'

'No, it's all right – it'll keep.' Bella was bursting to tell him about the letter from Millie, but she had promised Alice she'd keep quiet about it until their father had had time to sit and eat his tea in peace.

'Right, Bella, that was lovely, but can you please tell me what the news is that's so obviously nearly making you explode?' Thomas asked, pushing his empty plate away.

Alice drew the badly addressed envelope out of her skirt pocket and handed it to him. Thomas scanned the handwriting, extracted the letter and read it carefully. Then he read it again.

'Well, now,' he said. 'What are we going to do about this?'

'We *have* to find out if any of it's true,' said Bella.

'It could just have been written in a moment's temper, and even now she's regretting sending it,' reasoned Alice.

Thomas nodded. 'My thoughts exactly. But I don't think we can assume that. If young Millie's very unhappy, it would be cruel to dismiss it.'

The memory of Nanette, attempting to run away from home with some lad she was friends with, passed through his mind. That had not ended well. It was Thomas who had found out, who knew the young fella was a bad 'un, and he had told Frank. He'd meant it for the best, but Frank had turned very nasty. Thomas would never forget Nanette's scream when Frank burned her arm with the poker. Then he had given her the hiding of her life with his belt. That was when the rift between the Marchant siblings had become too deep ever to be healed, although Thomas was an appeaser by nature and had done his best. He understood Nanette had not kept in touch with Frank once she'd left home for good. And now she was dead, and her only child was begging his daughters for help . . .

'Mebbe Uncle Frank and Aunt Mona are finding it difficult to manage Millie, as they're not used to children,' Alice ventured, not wanting to criticise her father's brother and his wife openly.

Thomas gave her a look that said he understood what she wasn't saying.

'What if they can't cope at all, as Aunt Mona hinted when she wrote at Christmas, and Uncle Frank's got in one of his tempers, and Aunt Mona can't bear to have Millie making her house untidy, and they've resorted to punishments? And poor Millie is desperate and trapped there, all alone and grieving for her parents,' Bella said, her eyes round as she imagined the sorry scene.

'But if the arrangement there isn't a success and we bring Millie here, will *we* be able to manage?' said Alice. 'We're all at work most days.'

'We'll sort summat out,' said Bella. 'She's not a little child who will need constant looking after, is she? How difficult can it be?'

'Let's not get ahead of ourselves, Bella,' said Thomas. 'I think Millie is cleverer than you might think. She didn't write to me, did she? She appealed to her two cousins, whose young female hearts may be soft and their heads easily persuaded by the plight of a poor orphan. She might well think that her elderly uncle – don't laugh, girls; fifty seems ancient when you're only fifteen – is probably cut from the same cloth as his brother and sister-in-law—'

'Never! Oh, Dad!' his daughters denied on cue.

'And indeed, you are both kind enough not to turn the other cheek.'

'I'm going to write to Aunt Mona—'

'No, Bella, you know you can never disguise what you're thinking. You'll only go stirring things up when there may be nowt to get worked up about. *I'll* write to Aunt Mona,' said Alice. 'I'll take a moderate tone, say we'd like to come to visit them in Blackburn, see how she and Uncle Frank are. Leave it at that. What do you think, Dad? Shall I suggest Saturday next week? We'll have to ask for time off work . . .'

'Yes, please. You write, Alice, and arrange a visit.'

'I reckon that's the only thing to do,' said Bella. 'We *have* to find out what's going on.'

# CHAPTER THREE

'I WONDER, MR Patterson,' said Alice to her employer at E. & G. Patterson Books, the following morning, 'if it would be possible for me to have next Saturday off, please?'

She had written to her aunt and uncle to propose a visit: *It would be so lovely to see you.* The letter was on the sideboard at home, ready to post, but it seemed tempting fate to send it before finding out if any of them would be allowed the time off work to go. Both Alice and Bella thought it unlikely that their father would be able to take a day's holiday. He wasn't saying much about his new job, which implied it was not a success, but he'd been at the Three-Mile only a couple of weeks, and weekends were busy there.

'A holiday – I don't see why not,' Godfrey Patterson replied. He glanced around the bookshop, as far as he could see, which admittedly was not far, as the shop comprised a maze of small rooms. There was not a single customer in sight from where he stood behind the counter in the main room. 'Not exactly busy most days, are we?'

Alice looked carefully at him. He'd spoken lightly but his face appeared despondent, his frown deep.

'I'm sure trade will pick up once the visitors start arriving,' she said. 'I've been thinking: what about having some seasonal window displays this year, make them really eye-catching so people stop to look? Do you think that would attract customers? We needn't wait – we could start now, if you think that would work.'

Godfrey smiled. 'I admire your enthusiasm, Alice, but it is only February, too early for seaside-holiday reading.'

'But not for curling up by the fire with a gripping novel. Or thinking about planting the garden for the summer. Or cooking some warming stews. The volumes in the window aren't really displayed at all, are they? With so many different titles and subjects, and the window never changing, it's possible people just walk past and don't look at the piles of books at all.'

'Well, Eileen's always looked after the window, as you know. I really don't think we should interfere with it,' said Godfrey, looking more anxious.

'Not interfere, exactly,' lied Alice. 'But there's nowt lost in trying a new approach. If passers-by notice an interesting window display, they might decide to come in. Once we've got them in, I'm sure we can find them some books to buy that they'd enjoy reading.'

'Yes, nothing lost . . . quite right. I'll ask Eileen.'

'Ask me what?' Eileen Patterson appeared silently, like an apparition. She was a grey-haired, grey-clothed little woman, but there was nothing colourless about her opinions.

'Oh, Eileen, there you are. Alice has just had an idea about the window.'

'What's wrong with the window?'

'Nowt,' said Alice, 'but we – I mean, you – haven't had many customers lately, and I just thought if the window had a bright new look, it might catch the eyes of passers-by.'

'Did you, indeed? But we sell second-hand books, and those are what are in the window.' Eileen spoke slowly, as if Alice must be too stupid to have grasped this.

'Yes, of course, but what about, say, a window display made up exclusively of novels that people might like to read beside their fires on these cold evenings? Or one of cookery books, or gardening? Or children's books when it gets near the Easter holidays?'

'Hmm, it sounds like a lot of work, moving all those books about.'

'But I could do it. It might be fun, dressing the window in new ways, making an appealing scene, like a theatre set.'

'*Fun? Dressing the window?* Oh, I don't think we want to go in for anything fancy, Alice. And it will cost, too.'

'It needn't,' said Alice, getting into her stride. 'You could borrow props from the other shops—'

'Borrow props? What are you talking about?' Eileen sounded affronted, but Alice was determined to get her idea across.

'Well, I just meant you could, for instance, borrow a chair from Mr Wilkinson's shop to suggest a cosy sitting room, or—'

'His furniture in my shop window!'

'Only as a scene-setter for the books. It could benefit both businesses.'

'You've got some very strange ideas, Alice,' said Eileen, shaking her head in exaggerated sadness at her employee's foolishness. 'Now, those books that woman from Baybury brought over are still in boxes in the back room upstairs. Do you think you could sort them for Godfrey and me to price up? Perhaps that will help take your mind off those bizarre ideas.'

'Yes, of course, Miss Patterson,' said Alice, knowing when she was beaten, at least for the moment.

As Alice sorted through the boxes, she wondered whether Miss Patterson would eventually come round to the window-display idea. Eileen Patterson was like an ocean liner – she took a long time to change direction. Perhaps her brother would redirect her, as he sometimes had in the past, smoothing and flattering her so that in the end a new idea became her own and therefore acceptable to her. Alice saw the necessity of this tactic, which was usually the only way anything ever got changed. The business side of the bookshop was nothing to do with her, but she worried that the obvious lack of customers was becoming a serious problem, and that was bad news for all of them. At the moment, there were definitely more books coming in than going out. Something needed to be done.

Still, at least she had a day out on the horizon: the following Saturday off work to go to see her aunt and uncle, and to get to the root of her cousin, Millie's, letter. She was fairly confident that the kindly Warminsters would grant Bella a day's holiday, too.

As both Bella and Alice had predicted, Mr Fairbanks, the landlord at the Three-Mile Bottom, was not pleased at all that his new potman was asking for time off already, so Thomas had chosen, for once, to oblige his employer and keep his job.

'Do you think this means Dad's found a job he likes?' asked Bella quietly that evening, as Thomas went outside to polish his boots, a long-suffering look on his face, and the girls washed up. 'There have been times in the past when he's just walked out when summat didn't suit him.'

'I doubt it,' Alice replied. 'Mr Fairbanks hasn't a reputation for being sympathetic – quite the opposite – although I notice Dad's keeping quiet about him. Anyway, it'll be just the two of us.'

'I'm so pleased we're going together. I didn't fancy facing Uncle Frank and Aunt Mona on my own.'

'Let's just go and see what we find, keep our minds open . . .'

'Yes, Alice,' said Bella, mock-seriously, 'I promise to stay calm and reasonable.'

'There are enough folk with narrow minds,' Alice muttered quietly.

Bella, up to her elbows in suds, turned to look directly at her sister. 'That sounded heartfelt.'

'Oh, ignore me. I'm just a bit fed up today. I thought up an idea for the shop window but, as always when I suggest owt, it was batted away by Miss Patterson. It isn't as if the business is thriving – how can it be when there's hardly ever anyone in the shop?'

'Are you worried about your job?'

'A bit. It does suit me there, pottering around among the bookshelves, although I wouldn't mind actually selling a few and getting customers interested in the books I love. The whole place needs an overhaul and a rethink if it is to continue – starting with that dreary window display – but Miss P is too obstinate and too proud to consider any of my ideas, solely because they *are* my ideas.'

'I think you mean, solely because they're not hers. Infuriating!'

'But, Bella, never mind about the bookshop, look at the time! Didn't you say you were meeting Sidney?'

'Oh Lord, I did. I'll have to go now, this very moment, if I'm not to be late.'

Bella hurriedly dried her hands, rushed into the hall to comb her hair in front of the mirror there, and snatched up her handbag and coat.

'Don't run. You'll only arrive with a glowing face,' advised Alice. 'And make sure Sidney walks you back afterwards.'

'Yes, of course. Bye, Alice. Bye, Dad.' Bella raised her voice in the direction of the back door.

'Bella, wait,' called Alice, as her sister trotted off down the lane, her coat unbuttoned, her torch in her hand to light the way. 'You're still wearing your pinny!'

Bella waved her thanks, laughing over her shoulder, then reached to untie her pinafore, pulling it over her head and stuffing it into her bag as she hurried on her way.

The 'do' at the town hall was a dance to a jazz band of local musicians, with a prize draw and a tombola to raise funds for the construction of a floral clock, which the council hoped would be a visitor attraction. Bella wasn't bothered about a floral clock – 'What does it do that the church clock doesn't, apart from need weeding?' – but Sidney had asked her to go, and she was keen to dance with him to the jazz music.

Sidney Bennett was waiting for her at the door to the function room, clutching the pair of tickets he had bought in advance and looking tall, dark, and handsome. Bella's heart did a little flip, as it always did, when she saw him.

'Hello, love. I'm so sorry I'm late,' Bella said breathlessly. 'Alice and I were chatting over the washing up, and I lost track of time.'

'You and your sister – like a pair of gossipy old women,' said Sidney. It was unclear to Bella whether he was being indulgent or unkind.

'Well, it wasn't gossip. You see—'

'Look, there's Colin and Muriel over there – shall we join them?'

'Well, all right, if you want to.' Colin had already seen them and was waving, so Bella could hardly say otherwise. She hadn't been friends with Muriel Chalfont – whose family owned the Imperial, the only hotel in Theddleton – when they'd been in the same class at school, and she didn't like her any better now. Colin Wilkinson, who worked for his father at the family furniture shop on the High Street, was always friendly, however.

Sidney, cutting quite a dash in his double-breasted suit, and sporting a very bright tie, which Bella thought must be new, led the way to a table. It was covered with a rather creased cloth, embroidered at the corners with crinoline ladies in pastel colours. It had been cold outside, but Bella felt herself suddenly growing hot with her hurrying, now she was in the crowded room.

'Hello, Bella, Sid,' said Colin. 'You're looking well, Bella.'

'He means you look a bit overheated,' laughed Muriel, which made Bella's face feel hotter.

'No, I didn't,' said Colin quietly.

'I'm fine, thank you, just had to hurry,' Bella said, sitting down and slipping her coat onto the back of the chair. She wished she'd made more effort with her dress, which was very pretty but old and home-made, and her hair, which was damp from the evening air. Muriel was looking at her disdainfully.

'Let's get these girls some drinks,' said Sidney. 'What would you like, Bella?'

'A glass of lemonade, please.'

'And I'll have a gin and lime,' said Muriel daringly.

'C'mon, Colin,' prompted Sidney, and the two young men headed to the end of the room where a trestle table was set up as a bar.

Bella felt her nose starting to run as her cold face grew warmer, and she reached into her bag for her handkerchief, but, oh no, there was her pinafore, stuffed untidily in the top. She tried to push it further down, out of sight, but Muriel, who had a sixth sense for an awkward situation, noticed what she was doing and pounced.

'What's this you've brought?' She was bold enough to reach into Bella's bag and pull out the pinafore, which she held up so that the people at the tables to either side could not fail to see it. 'I didn't realise you've come to help in the kitchen.' She laughed.

Bella made a grab for it. 'I just forgot to take it off until after I'd left home.'

'Oh dear, do you have to do your own housework?' said Muriel. 'Poor you! We have a girl living in to do ours.'

'How nice for you,' Bella said, wishing Sidney and Colin would hurry up and return with the drinks. She pitied the poor skivvy, whom Muriel had not referred to by name. Probably she hadn't even made the effort to learn it.

Sidney and Colin returned then, each carrying a pint for himself and a drink for his partner. As they set them down on the table, Muriel loudly told the men that Bella had nearly turned up wearing a pinafore 'like a charwoman', and there was more laughter, which Bella had no other option than to join in with, while adopting a 'silly me' expression. The alternative was just to sit there being laughed at.

'Don't worry, Bella,' said Colin. 'I'm always forgetting stuff at the shop. I've taken to making a list. If I have any new ideas, I write them down or they just fly straight out of my head again.'

'Yes, but it's very different for you,' said Muriel. 'Your father owns the shop, and you're an important person there, with lots of responsibility, whereas Bella . . .' She shrugged.

'Whereas Bella what?' asked Bella fiercely, her patience at an end.

Muriel looked taken aback to be challenged. 'I only meant . . .'

'What did you *only* mean?'

'Bella?' said Sidney, taking her hand. 'I don't suppose Muriel intended owt to cause an upset.'

'Don't you indeed?' muttered Bella, so that only he heard. How could he not see that Muriel was trying to put her down all the time? She turned back to Muriel. 'I work in a toyshop, Muriel,' she said, 'and my employers are the kindest people you could ever meet. You might want to come by the shop one day and see if a little of their kindness rubs off on you.'

Everyone looked down in silence for a few moments.

Colin cleared his throat. 'Right, shall we dance?' he asked Muriel, who was now looking sulky. The band had started up at the opposite end of the room from the bar, and the music was surprisingly skilfully played, considering the musicians were all local amateurs.

Colin led Muriel away to dance; several other couples were already crowding enthusiastically into the cleared space in the centre of the room. Muriel tossed her blonde hair and made much of smoothing down her fashionable dress as she went.

'Bella, that wasn't very nice,' said Sidney.

'It's Muriel who's not very nice. You reckon I should just sit here and take it, do you?' Bella retorted.

'Take what?'

'Her bullying, of course. Bullies need to be faced down, Sidney. I'm old enough to have worked that out now. She was the class bully at school – I'm surprised you don't remember – with her mean group of hangers-on, picking on the younger girls and the ones who were different from the herd, and generally making herself unpleasant. It's a shame she hasn't grown out of it.'

'Ah, leave it, Bella. You just don't get on with her, that's all. She's not so bad.'

'Well, perhaps she's got the message,' said Bella. 'Now, shall we have a go at that tombola?'

'Depends what the prizes are,' Sidney replied. 'If it's

all bath salts and old-lady stuff, I think we should give it a miss.'

Bella agreed, but they went to look anyway. The prizes were generally unappealing to anyone youthful, but there was a bunch of snowdrops in a tiny vase, which Bella thought was pretty, and a box of chocolate peppermints, which Sidney said he'd like to win for her.

They bought five tickets each but won nothing.

'Never mind, it all raises funds for this floral thingy,' said Sidney, as they went back to their table. 'Mam's on the Committee to see about it.'

'Oh, I didn't realise. Is she here?' Bella looked around. 'I haven't seen her.'

'No, she doesn't like jazz music. She got out-voted over the band so she decided to stay away altogether.'

'Oh dear . . .'

'But speaking of Mam reminds me. She asked me if you could come and have tea at our house next Saturday, and I said you'd love to.'

'I'm sorry, but I'm already busy then, Sidney.'

'Doing what?' He looked suddenly suspicious, as if he thought she might be up to no good just because he wasn't a party to her arrangement.

'I'm hoping to visit my aunt and uncle in Blackburn. Alice is going with me. We might be late back.'

'Oh, yes? It's all arranged, is it?' He sat back, taking a sip of his pint.

'Alice has written to them to ask if we might go.'

'So not arranged, then?'

'Well, it is if they agree to our visit.'

'Can't you go on Sunday instead?'

'No. We're going on the train, which has a very poor service on Sundays, so we might not be able to get back then at all.'

'But Mam's already asked for you to come to tea, and I've told her yes.'

'Well, I'm afraid you'll have to tell her no, Sidney. The Blackburn visit is all in hand, the day off work booked and everything, and we can't change it. Please thank your mam for the invitation. Tell her I'm already busy but I'd love to come another time.'

'I suppose I'll have to, won't I?' he said crossly.

'It's only that one Saturday. I can manage most weeks. But please, next time, check with me first before you tell your mother what you've decided I'm doing.'

Sidney didn't look appeased, and Bella squeezed his arm.

'Sorry, Sidney, but there'll be another time.'

'Yes, you're right, of course. I just hope Mam won't be too disappointed.'

'Oh, I expect she'll get over it,' Bella said innocently. 'Now, shall we dance?'

While she and Sidney danced together, Bella had an idea.

'Sidney, what do you think of the band?'

'They're excellent. Why?'

'Well, I reckon they are, too, and I'm wondering about

having them play at our wedding reception. They're amateurs, so I'm hoping they won't be too expensive.'

Sidney frowned. 'I don't think so . . . I've already told you my mother doesn't like this kind of music.'

'But we do, and it's our wedding, not your mother's, so it's our decision, isn't it?'

'Bella,' said Sidney, guiding her to the side of the room, 'I hope you wouldn't say owt as rude as that to Mam. Not her wedding, indeed! She'd be so insulted if she heard what you were implying.'

'What? No, Sidney, you've misunderstood. I wasn't implying owt about your mother. I'm very much aware she's a respectable widow, and no one would doubt that for a moment, but surely we are allowed to choose the music when it's our wedding? All I said was that I'd like some nice music like this played at our reception, and I asked you what you thought—'

'And I said no.'

Bella closed her mouth and took several deep breaths while she fought down a number of replies that sprang to mind. First Muriel Chalfont and now Sidney – what had got into everyone this evening?

*All right, better to just forget that exchange. Move on with dignity – that's what Alice would do. You don't have to sort out the music now, this evening. It can wait . . .*

'Well, are we dancing, Bella, or do you want to sit this one out?' asked Sidney, possibly deciding on the same course of action.

'We're dancing, of course,' Bella replied, seeing that

Muriel was seated back at the table, preening herself in her compact mirror.

Sidney was a good dancer, a considerate partner, and Bella had a very enjoyable time twirling in the arms of her gorgeous fiancé, the best-looking man in the room. After several lively numbers had been played, the musicians had a break and it was time for the prize draw.

The numbers for the draw were on the admission tickets to the event, so everyone had one, and the anticipation in the hot room was palpable as each searched for his or her number. The prizes were generous and ranged from one-off events supplied by local businesses, such as a pair of tickets for the theatre at Baybury, and a tea for two at the seafront tearoom, to fancy goods and presents to take home that evening. The Warminsters had donated one of their Edwardian lady dolls, which Bella was desperately hoping not to win because she'd made the doll's elaborate outfit herself, including the hat and the parasol, and she didn't want to be the recipient of her own handiwork. Muriel was at pains to let everyone in hearing distance know that her father had donated the prize of a lunch for two in the Imperial Hotel dining room.

The draw went on for a while, with the bar open, so people were continually wandering around getting drinks, and the numbers had to be repeated if no one claimed a winning ticket straight away.

Sidney was buying more drinks when Bella's number was called out, and she went to the front and was given a slip of paper that said she'd won a ride along the coast in a fancy car. There was a name and a telephone number to call: *B. Reeves, Baybury 361.*

She went back to the table feeling deflated.

'Never mind,' said Muriel. 'I think all the best prizes have already gone.'

Bella shrugged, folded the paper and tucked it into her handbag.

Sidney came back with the drinks, then got distracted by someone he knew from work on the next table, and then Muriel's number was called. She sashayed up to collect her prize in a self-conscious way, flicking her hair and smiling, just like the stars at film premieres that Bella had seen on the newsreels at the cinema.

But when she came back, she was looking tragic and clutching a voucher to spend at Cathy's, a dress shop in the High Street.

'What did you win?' asked Colin eagerly.

Muriel showed him.

'Well, that's great,' he said. 'Cathy is such a nice woman – a friend of Mam's – she'll fix you up with summat lovely.'

'I doubt it,' pouted Muriel. 'Her dresses are more for the likes of your mother than me. The sizes in the window are always huge, and the styles so old-fashioned.' As if she hadn't been rude enough already, she leaned over to Bella with a patronising smile. 'Here, Bella, you take it. Get yourself summat new. I'm sure the clothes at Cathy's are right up your street.'

For a moment, Bella felt her face flaming at the calculated insult, but she was determined not to be Muriel's victim, and she also thought she should stick up for Colin's mother, who had been insulted in passing. Colin was looking as if he couldn't quite believe what he'd heard, while Sidney was now sitting back with his drink, watching the tickets being drawn and taking no notice of any of them. If he'd heard the insults, they hadn't registered.

Muriel Chalfont is ridiculous, Bella thought, starting to laugh at the young woman's absurd pretentions, and soon Colin joined in. Muriel frowned, clearly trying to work out what was funny when she'd so deliberately aimed to hurt.

'Oh dear,' chortled Bella, wiping her eyes, 'what a corker, a real Muriel Chalfont special! You never fail, do you, Muriel? You should write down your cattiest remarks and make them into a book – *The Muriel Chalfont Book of Insults*. I'm sure it will sell well to the kind of people who are nasty enough to want to spoil someone else's evening.'

Muriel went very pink, obviously unused to having her arrows deflected with outright laughter and some home truths. 'I think I want to go home now, Colin,' she said.

'Oh, come on, Muriel, you only got what you deserved,' he said. 'If you're going to be rude to folk, you have to be prepared for them to slap you down. Now stop behaving like a spoiled baby and let's stay until the end of the draw. Sid and I might yet have our numbers called. Mebbe I'll win a prize for you,' he said, trying to jolly her out of her sulk.

'Do as you like,' said Muriel. 'I'm going to powder my nose.' And she picked up her bag – and her coat, Bella noticed – and stalked off.

'Sorry,' said Colin quietly to Bella. 'I don't know what's got into her this evening. She's usually such good fun.'

Bella wouldn't have recognised Muriel from that description, but she nodded and then said, 'I think she's intending to leave, Colin. She's taken her coat.'

'I'd better go after her,' he said, standing up. 'I'll see her home safely. Thanks for your company, both of you. Sorry she spoiled your evening,' he added quietly to Bella.

'Don't worry.' She smiled.

'Bye, Col,' said Sidney, and raised his glass to Colin as he sidled past.

'What was all that about?' he asked as soon as Colin had gone.

'No idea,' said Bella. 'Are you ready to go, too?'

'Yes, all right.'

They collected up their belongings.

'Here,' said Sidney, picking something up from the table, 'is this yours?' It was the dress shop voucher that Muriel had rejected.

'So it is. Thank you,' said Bella, pocketing it. Well, you never knew . . .

\* \* \*

'I thought that was a right good evening,' said Sidney as they started to walk towards Chapel Lane, down the High Street, which was fortunate enough to have street-lights.

'Did you?' asked Bella, wondering in what way it could possibly be described as 'good'. Although the dancing had been fun, apart from the disagreement because the music wasn't to his mother's taste, Muriel Chalfont's mean remarks had cast a shadow over the evening for Bella, and Sidney had not even noticed.

'Yes, lively music, lots of punters – which will please Mam and her Committee. You won that shop voucher, the drinks weren't too dear, and the company was charming.'

'Thanks, Sidney.'

'That Muriel is quite a looker, isn't she?' he went on, as if it was Muriel he had been thinking of. 'Knows it, of course, but I expect people tell her how lovely she is all the time.'

'*Lovely?*' Was the man deranged? Yes, she was pretty enough, but five minutes in her company revealed her to be a very nasty piece of work.

'Blonde hair, dresses well, such style . . .'

'Perhaps you should take Muriel to the next town hall fundraiser,' suggested Bella icily.

'Don't be silly, love. I just meant she's got style.'

'Well, it's a shame her charm is all about her appearance and not her personality,' said Bella. 'Now, how was the match this morning?' she went on, abruptly drawing a line under the evening, and prepared to pretend to listen while Sidney delivered a full report of Theddleton Town's success and his own vital role in it.

While he talked on, sometimes demonstrating a particularly skilful move, Bella thought about the following Saturday, hoping that her aunt and uncle would agree to her and Alice's visit. A part of her was dreading going, but that was silly and cowardly, she berated herself. She'd given Muriel Chalfont a verbal facer, and she and Alice together were more than a match for Uncle Frank and Aunt Mona, if it came to an argument. But she hoped it would not come to that!

It would be good to see Millie again. It would be better still if what lay behind that letter, begging to be rescued, was a simple falling-out, now over and done with and forgotten. Somehow, though, Bella doubted that.

It had been three months since Millie had travelled up from Cornwall, heartbroken at the loss of her parents. She had been accompanied by a good friend of Nanette's, Mags, who'd been kind enough to bring the girl as far as London on the train. Millie, clutching her one suitcase and looking thin and tragic, had been met at Paddington Station by Thomas, Bella and Alice, and by Frank and Mona, and then handed over to the Blackburn Marchants, so keen to take her in, they said. Frank and Mona had soon whisked Millie away to catch the train north from Euston Station, not even stopping for a cup of tea.

'So noisy in London, and ridiculously expensive, and

we have a long journey ahead. We can't be hanging around chatting,' Mona had said. She and Frank had treated the whole business as nothing but a nuisance to themselves, for which they were taking on the roles of martyrs, Bella thought. That was very strange when they had kept insisting how pleased they were to offer Millie a home.

Millie had been silent and sullen, which was understandable. As her relatives led her away to get their train, Bella had slipped her address into her young cousin's hand.

'Just so you know where we are if you need us, Millie,' she had whispered.

Thomas, Bella and Alice had bought Mags lunch in a café near the station and then saw her onto a train back to Cornwall, reimbursing her expenses, although she was reluctant to take the money, insisting she was glad to do the right thing for Nanette and Harry's orphaned daughter. Thomas and his daughters very much appreciated Mags's kindness, aware that she had spared them a lengthy journey from Yorkshire to Cornwall and back.

Now, outside the gate to Bella's home, Sidney tenderly kissed her good night.

'I'll see you safely inside, Bel,' he said. He was always attentive about her safety and welfare, and his attention now instantly made Bella forgive him over his lack of interest in her earlier and in planning their wedding generally.

She went up the path, put her key in the door and turned to smile at him as he shone his torch on her from the blackness of this out-of-town lane. The street-lights didn't extend this far beyond the High Street and the Promenade.

'You look beautiful by torchlight,' he said, and blew her another kiss.

'So do you.' She laughed, pretending to reach up and snatch the kiss out of the air.

Never mind about the jazz band. What did it matter? There were more important things to look forward to in their future together than the music at their wedding reception.

# CHAPTER FOUR

'MILLIE, COME IN here. I've had a letter from your cousin Alice,' said Mona, when Millie, home from school, tried to sneak up to her room unnoticed.

She came into the kitchen unwillingly, flung herself down tiredly at the table and lowered her head onto her arms.

School was exhausting. Millie was bottom of her class in every subject except art, and this shaming position came with the taunts and ridicule of her fellow pupils. There was, of course, name-calling. 'Millie Minus', one wit called her, 'because you always get minus summat out of ten, ha ha.' 'Thicko' and 'daft' were the insults hurled by rough boys and catty girls. School, for Millie, was not a happy place at all.

After giving it a chance for a few weeks and finding nothing good in it – except the art classes, in which she excelled and had nothing to learn from the teacher – Millie had started simply leaving at first break, escaping stealthily through the gates and spending most days wandering around town, keeping warm in the shops. She became adept at passing unnoticed. She found she had a talent for being invisible.

Loitering around King William Street one day, she had happened to see something very interesting indeed. A little follow-up, a few questions asked, and she knew she had struck gold. She was keeping this to herself for the time being. The knowledge made her feel powerful but, like an unexploded bomb, it could only be used once. She'd know when the time was right. She was prepared to wait.

Her truancy had stopped when Aunt Mona had received a letter reminding her of her legal requirement to send Millie to school. The woman had been furious and fearful for her reputation – 'What if the neighbours think I've deliberately kept you away? What will people say if I get fined, like a common criminal? How will I be able to face folk in the street?' – and Uncle Frank had made liberal use of his switchy ruler on Millie's hand and the backs of her legs, with the promise of more if she played truant again.

Today had been as dismal as any other schoolday, but news of the letter from Alice raised Millie's hopes. Please, please, let it be good news, she silently begged.

'It seems Alice and her sister, Bella, want to visit,' Mona went on. 'Alice makes a point of saying how nice it will be to see us. I can't think why they should want to come now, and I certainly don't need the expense and the bother of some kind of tea party, but I suppose I'd better agree to the visit. I'm not really surprised your uncle Thomas isn't coming, too. He's always been a bit funny with Frank. Jealous of the big brother, I've always thought, Frank being such a pillar of the community, with his job at the bank and everything, although it may well go back further than that. Whereas Thomas . . . oh dear, such a waste. Anyway, no doubt we shall see what it's all about when those young women turn up on Saturday.'

'Saturday?' said Millie, looking up, then quickly composing her face to a more moderate expression of pleasure.

This was good news indeed. At last, hope was on the horizon. When she'd posted her letter – the stamp and envelope stolen from the sideboard, the paper torn from her school essays book – she hadn't been entirely optimistic. Her cousins might be slow to respond and do nothing for weeks or months, or even not bother to reply at all, although Millie didn't think this was likely. It was, after all, Bella who had given her the precious piece of paper with their address on, discreetly, almost as if it was a secret between them. And she'd sounded kind and concerned, as if she guessed Millie might need to be in touch with her. Millie's whole escape plan rested on her cousins responding, and it seemed that Alice had been very swift to do so, while keeping quiet that Millie had written to her, too. On Saturday, she would be out of this awful prison at last. She could hold out until then: just four days. She'd be counting the hours. Then it would be goodbye to these two awful bullies and hello to a new life by the sea in Yorkshire. It had to be better than this!

Millie was unsure how her uncle Thomas fitted in with her future plans. He had sneaked on Nanette when she had tried to run away, and then Frank had really hurt her so that she had the scars for ever after. Was Thomas still weak and not to be trusted? But it didn't sound as if Thomas and Frank got on well together even now, from what Aunt Mona said. Millie decided she would wait and see how things were. At least if she went to live with him and her cousins, she would be in the right place to mete out whatever she felt he deserved.

'That's right, Saturday,' Mona was saying. 'I only hope you'll be able to behave yourself while they're here. It would be better if you didn't say owt to them . . . about owt. Just be polite – I'm sure you can manage that for a few hours if you try hard. If they speak to you, just smile and say summat nice.'

'Summat nice . . .' imitated Millie. 'Like what, Aunt?'

'You daft girl, what do you think?'

'I really can't imagine,' said Millie. 'I haven't heard anything nice since I got here.'

Mona slapped out at Millie's head, not too hard, but as a reminder of what could follow. 'Then I suggest on Saturday you stay in your room if you can't be polite to your cousins. Alice and Bella will have a long way to travel – and I really *can't* think why they're bothering – and they don't want to be looking at your miserable face, pouting and sulking and telling lies.'

'No, Aunt,' said Millie. 'You're right. Don't worry, they won't hear any lies from me.'

Mona looked uncomfortable, as if she wasn't sure she wanted agreement on this. Then she said, 'Now, don't sit there taking up space and making the place untidy. Go and take off those outdoor shoes at once – what have I told you? And if you've no homework, you can give me a hand with preparing these faggots for tea.'

'Actually, Aunt Mona, I have a lot of homework today,' said Millie. 'I'll go up and get on with it now.'

'Off you go then,' said Mona, thwarted. 'And change your shoes, otherwise I'll have you sweeping that stair carpet!'

Millie yanked off her shoes as she passed through the narrow hall, chucking them into a corner, then raced upstairs and shut her room door. A huge smile broke out on her face as she flung open her wardrobe and started to gather her few clothes together to pack her suitcase. On second thoughts, she must give her aunt and uncle no clue that she was expecting to leave. She put her things back, but in neat piles, ready just to pick up on Saturday morning. She did not doubt for one minute that the end of her residence at number 20 Beaucroft Road was in sight. In the meantime, she'd have to work at hiding her gleeful anticipation and composing her face into its usual lines of discontent.

\* \* \*

Bella and Alice came out of Blackburn Station into a cold, wet, February Saturday. How sooty and grey the air was here compared to the bracing freshness of Theddleton. They put up their umbrellas and set off walking towards their aunt and uncle's house.

The girls had left home in the dark of early morning and already it seemed like the train journey, with two changes, had taken days. The contrast between Theddleton, which was little more than an overgrown village, and Blackburn, with its long industrial history, streets of terraced houses and general air of bustle and busyness, added to their feeling of having left their familiar world behind long ago.

The sisters walked into the centre of the town, and then on through a park with flowerbeds, where early spring bulbs were beginning to show in the wet earth, and wide paths lined with grass and shrubs brought a measure of freshness and quiet, in contrast to the busy streets. A gate at the far side brought them out to a residential area, and a little further on, slowing, they tried to recall the way in the only vaguely familiar neighbourhood.

'There,' said Bella, pointing to the road name, 'Beaucroft Road.' She found her steps slowing.

Alice took her arm. 'Come on, we came to do the right thing and we're here now.'

'Yes . . .' Bella straightened her back and gathered her courage – this was just her family, after all, so how bad could it be? – but she was glad Alice was beside her.

They walked along to the house, a terrace of the better sort, with a patch of garden in front and a tiled path leading straight to the front door with a brass number 20 shining from it. Alice lifted the knocker – also very shiny – and rapped the door loudly.

After a few moments, Frank Marchant appeared. He was much bigger and heavier than Thomas, with a heavy jaw and a distinctive large, hooked nose. Considering it was a Saturday, a day off from his job in a bank, he was surprisingly formally dressed, with a stiff collar to his shirt and a tightly knotted tie. Did the man ever relax?

'Good morning, Alice and Bella,' he said. 'Please come in.'

He opened the front door wide to allow them past him into a narrow hallway, in which there were two pegs, one with a man's brimmed hat and a large grey mackintosh on it, and the other with a brown winter coat, over which hung Millie's pretty green coat, which Bella and Alice remembered her wearing at Paddington Station in November, and a rather severe flowerpot hat of brown felt on top, obviously Aunt Mona's.

The tiled floor was very shiny indeed, and the busy floral wallpaper clashed with its geometric pattern.

'Mona, Alice and Bella are here,' called Frank, although Bella thought her aunt would surely have heard their knock.

Aunt Mona came out of the front room – she must have actually seen them arrive, too – and offered a heavily powdered cheek to be kissed. She was of a similar build to her husband, and also strangely overdressed for a Saturday morning in her own home, in a shiny brown rayon dress that had an upholstered look to it.

'How nice to see you again, Alice and Bella,' she said, not looking as if she thought it 'nice' at all. 'Please put those wet umbrellas in the corner where they won't drip on owt. And please leave your shoes on the mat before you tread outside in, and put your coats on the hooks.'

She stood over them while they did this, leaving their fashionable young women's shoes next to three other pairs, two large and one smaller and slimmer, then beckoned them into the front room where a tea set, which had the shine of infrequent use, was laid out on a low table, with some Rich Tea biscuits on a plate.

'Sit yourselves down and I'll just go and make the tea,' said Mona, and went to do so, leaving them alone. Frank had disappeared, too.

Bella and Alice sat down on the hard and shiny horsehair-padded sofa and looked at each other. The house felt cold – there was no fire in the grate – and Bella shivered in her stockinged feet, thinking she had felt more at home in a dentist's waiting room. Her relatives hadn't even asked how the journey had been.

'I wonder where Millie is,' she said. She lowered her voice. 'It's not very . . . homely, is it? Apart from the coat and shoes, I don't see any sign of Millie's things, either – no games or books. It's almost as if she doesn't exist.'

Alice was looking unhappy. 'It feels all wrong,' she

said. 'I think I'll go and have a little chat, see what I can find out. You could have a quick nose around while I do that.'

She got up and went out, leaving Bella looking about the room, searching for any evidence that her young cousin lived in this unwelcoming place.

Above the mantelpiece, on which stood two moulded glass vases and a hideous pottery figure of a fat cherub, was a text embroidered in cross-stitch, the kind of thing Bella had learned to do at school when she was hardly more than an infant, although hers had been a joyful undertaking, a neatly embroidered alphabet, in bright colours, ringed with garlands of flowers. This was quite different from that. *He that covereth his sins shall not prosper*, read the black stitching within a heavy frame. Just the kind of proverb to cast a dampener over a tea party, thought Bella, turning back to the obviously 'best' china. Her stomach rumbled – it had been hours since breakfast – and she wondered if she could just take one of the dry biscuits now, but she felt sure helping herself uninvited would be regarded as stealing, and for that sin she wouldn't prosper.

She padded out to the cold tiles of the hallway to try to hear what was going on. The muffled sound of voices came from behind the closed door at the end, obviously the kitchen. Bella could hear Alice's tone, even and reasoned, but not her actual words. Alice was not one to back down, even if outnumbered.

Suddenly Bella knew what she must do. Silently she

ran up the stairs. At the top were two bedrooms, the doors closed. She guessed Millie's room would be the one at the back. She tapped on the door.

'Millie?' she called as quietly as she could. 'Millie? It's Bella. Alice and I are here to see you. We got your letter. Are you coming down? You're not ill, are you?'

She heard the sound of feet stomping across the floor to the door. Then a voice just the other side said, 'No. But I can't get out. I'm locked in.'

Bella saw the key in the lock then, turned it and opened the door. There was Millie, standing with a mixture of anger and defiance on her face. She was thin and pale, as if she hadn't begun to fill out, and small for her age, the strongest-looking thing about her the determination in her face. She was dressed in an odd combination of what looked like a slightly too-short pink summer dress with a frill at the hem, with black stockings beneath, and two black cardigans, both too big, over the top. Her long dark hair was awry, as if it had been tied back and she'd roughly pulled it loose.

The room was cold, the daylight dim and bleak through the small window, but sufficient for Bella to see that her young cousin had her suitcase standing beside her bed.

'Millie, what's happened?' asked Bella. 'Are you all right? Why were you locked in? Have you done summat you shouldn't have?'

'Yes, I have,' said Millie. 'But you see, I wanted the money – I *needed* it, for today – and they don't give me pocket money, so in the end I just helped myself. I had no choice. It wasn't very much, but I had to have the train fare. I couldn't be sure you and Alice would have enough for my ticket, you see. I hoped Aunt Moaner wouldn't miss it, but she jolly well did and got in the most awful rage. Of course, I couldn't tell her why I'd really taken it, so instead I said I wanted to buy some sweets, and she went a bit mad.'

'Crikey,' said Bella. This was a lot to take in. She felt as if she was watching a film but had arrived late and missed the first hour. 'So you took Aunt Mona's money for the train fare to go home with Alice and me?'

'Yes! I thought I'd ruined the plan at the last moment, getting locked in, and it was all going so well up until then.'

'Plan?'

'To escape, with you. I wrote, and here you are, and now we're going to escape.'

Millie had no trace of a northern accent, for all her mother was Thomas and Frank's sister, but then she had been brought up largely in Cornwall and her father had been from London. She had hardly spoken when she was brought to London, so Bella had not noticed this before.

'We did get your letter,' Bella said again, 'and we've come to see what's happening. Come down with me and let's hear all about it.'

'They won't let me tell you what it's like here,' said Millie. 'If I try to, they'll just say I'm a liar and give their

71

own version. *That* will be the lies. And if you question them or disagree, they'll just ride roughshod over you. But I've got my case packed – see? – and now you're here, and you've unlocked the door, I'm ready to go. It was all going well until Aunt Moaner discovered the missing money and locked me in my room. I did think about escaping out of the window, but it's too high and there's nothing to break my fall.'

'Good grief, Millie, I'm glad you didn't attempt that,' said Bella, her stomach turning at the thought.

For a moment, Bella was torn between the madness of making a run for it with Millie, and doing the sensible, grown-up thing of finding out exactly what had happened. Sensible Bella won out, of course: there was Alice to consider, possibly still in reasoned debate with their aunt and uncle in the kitchen. She would never abandon Alice, and she ought not to believe everything that Millie said when there was, perhaps, another version of events to consider. Certainly, it had been wrong to try to steal the money, but the girl must have been desperate.

'Come on,' said Bella. 'Let's go and find Alice, hear what they've said to her.' Already, she noticed, she had slipped into referring to her aunt and uncle as 'they', like Millie had done.

'All right, then, if we must. I'll bring the suitcase,' said Millie, and hefted it through the doorway, where Bella took it from her and carried it downstairs.

By now, Alice, Frank and Mona were back in the front

room. Bella deposited the case in the hall near the front door and ushered Millie before her. Mona was pouring tea into the precious china cups and Alice was sitting on the hard sofa again, opposite her uncle.

'Here's Millie,' Bella said brightly, leading the child to the sofa to sit down between Alice and herself. 'She's come down to say hello.'

'What are you doing down here, young madam?' said Mona. 'I told you, you would stay in your room until I came to let you out. Bella, this is your doing, isn't it?'

'Yes, of course it was me, Aunt Mona,' said Bella. 'We came to see Millie, too, and I found her imprisoned in her room.'

Alice silently put out a hand to hush her sister's impassioned words, but it was too late.

'Imprisoned!' gasped Mona, affronted. 'That child needs some discipline. She should reflect upon the error of her ways, or she'll surely end up in prison, all right!'

'I gather there was some money stolen . . . for sweets. I'm sure Millie is sorry.'

'I'm sure she isn't, the lip she was giving me,' retorted Mona. 'And it was a lot more than just pennies she took, too.'

'You had no right to undermine us, Bella, or to wander about our home uninvited,' said Frank angrily. 'Millie's a wicked girl, and she was being punished as she deserved. We told her of your visit, but she still couldn't behave herself, and so she has to forgo the treat.'

'*Wicked? Punished?* Those are strong words to apply to

a child,' said Alice evenly. 'What else has Millie done to deserve them?'

'I'll tell you what she's done, young woman,' said Mona. 'She broke a window in the scullery. She broke it *on purpose.*'

'Did you see her breaking it deliberately?' asked Alice.

'No . . . but I know she did because she admitted it. I could have been injured by the flying glass. It was a dreadful mess.'

'But you weren't injured?' asked Bella.

'That's hardly the point,' snapped Frank. 'We took in this child to bring her up as our own, and now we find it's too late. She's gone to the bad already. She lacks discipline and respect; she steals and lies.'

'She's all cheek and backchat,' Mona added. 'And then there's her refusal to help with the chores and her moping in her room.'

'I expect she's feeling sad because she misses her parents,' ventured Alice. 'The accident . . . the sudden-ness of it . . . such a big and awful thing for her to have to cope with, especially when she's so young.'

'What do you know?' said Mona, completely forgetting that Alice and Bella knew all too well what it was like to lose an adored parent. 'Anyway, that was months ago,' she went on. 'She's made no effort to fit in with us at all.'

Bella had never liked her aunt and uncle very much, and she was liking them less with every passing minute. Were they really so stupid? She looked again around the horrible room and wondered if it had occurred to them that Millie would need someone to cuddle her, to mop her tears and to listen to her memories of Nanette and Harry. No wonder Millie had plotted to escape from here.

'Perhaps your expectations of Millie are a bit, er, unrealistic. She is still little more than a child and has been through such a lot in her life already,' said Alice with quiet dignity, clearly thinking exactly the same as Bella.

'Well, we have to start as we mean to go on,' said Frank. 'No point spoiling her and then trying to impose discipline when it's too late.'

'But who does Millie play with, and where are her things?' asked Bella.

'Things?'

'Her games and books? She must have some things of her own to amuse herself with, and some friends to share her spare time.'

'We don't like the children who live around here very much,' said Mona, a look of distaste on her face. 'They're not really "our sort", if you know what I mean.'

Bella opened her mouth to reply, but Alice's hand shot out again and grabbed her arm in warning.

'So no friends. And no things with which to amuse herself either?' asked Alice.

'I kindly lent her one of my own books, but she hardly made any effort to read it,' said Frank. 'So I took it back, only to find she'd drawn and coloured a picture on the blank pages at the back.'

'Then you do have coloured pencils, Millie?' asked Bella, deliberately missing the point.

'I didn't, so I borrowed some from school and they didn't miss them,' Millie said.

'Stole them, you mean, you wicked child!' said Frank, and with surprising speed for such a big man he stood, reached over the tea things, and delivered a stinging cuff to Millie's ear.

'Ow!'

At once, Bella was on her feet. 'Stop that! It's not right to hit people. And Millie's far smaller than you.'

'Don't you take that tone with me, Bella Marchant,' Frank snarled, while Alice hugged Millie to her, cradling her red ear. 'Or you'll find yourself on the end of summat similar.'

'You will not threaten us,' said Alice. She did not raise her voice but her eyes flashed with fury.

'You've got far too much cheek, the pair of you,' shrilled Mona, 'coming here, telling us what to do. Bella, sit down and be quiet.'

'They hit me all the time – they're always beating me and locking me up,' said Millie, her lower lip trembling. 'Look what they did to me.' She pulled the cardigans off one shoulder and displayed a large purple bruise at the top of her arm.

Bella gasped and turned back angrily to her aunt and uncle. 'This looks awful. How could you assault Millie like that?'

'We don't have to answer to—' yelled Frank.

'And starved me, too,' interrupted Millie, holding up her skinny bruised arm.

'Oh, poor sweetheart,' said Bella, pulling the cardigans back over Millie's thin, sleeveless dress.

'Now look here . . .' Frank said.

'We're trying our best, but that child is a bad 'un and I doubt anyone could control her,' Mona said.

'I blame Nanette and that husband of hers,' said Frank. 'She was far too flighty, far too lax. Too busy gallivanting about, never a proper day's work between the pair of them, to bring that young hoyden up respectably. The child has been allowed to go wild and now *we're* reaping the consequences.'

'My mum and dad were good people,' said Millie, suddenly tearful. 'It's you who are the bad ones – starving and beating, shouting and locking—'

'You see what we have to put up with?' said Mona. 'Backchat, lies and impudence.'

'Right,' said Bella, 'I've heard enough.'

'How dare—'

'I dare, Aunt, because I see how things are. I wanted to believe all was well with Millie, but now I see that's far from the case. Come on, Alice, we're leaving.'

Both sisters stood up to go.

'Don't leave me!' shrieked Millie desperately, grabbing Bella round her middle.

'Of course not.' Bella freed herself from Millie's arms and sidled out from behind the table of tea things, taking Millie's hand to bring her out, too. 'Go and put your coat and shoes on. Quickly!'

Millie ran out to the hallway to do as she was told.

'We've tried our very best,' said Frank. 'That child needs discipline. Her bad behaviour would try anyone's patience. Why can't she just sit down and be quiet? Why can't she behave herself? Because she's never been taught, that's why. It's too late now. She's spoiled for good and if you take her home with you, you'll rue the day. You'll see what we've had to put up with. You'll be here again before a month is up, begging Mona and me to take her back, you'll see.'

'She's sly and untruthful,' spat Mona. 'We took her in out of the goodness of our hearts, and look where it's got us: vandalism, petty crime, rudeness . . . We even had the police round once! They had found her wandering around town in the dark one evening when we thought she was in her room. I nearly died of embarrassment. There had never been any trouble here before Millie came. We're respectable folk, with some standing in the neighbourhood.'

'Well, Aunt, you may comfort yourself that there will be no more near-fatal embarrassment for you,' said Alice, following Bella out of the room.

By then, Millie had her coat and outdoor shoes on, her suitcase in her hand, and was waiting on the front step.

Frank and Mona crowded into the front-room doorway, continuing to berate their nieces as they pulled on their shoes and coats, not bothering to button them in their hurry to leave, and grabbed their umbrellas.

'You'll learn . . .'

'Not just naughtiness, but wickedness . . .'

'Mark my words, you'll be sorry . . .'

'Goodbye,' said Bella, following Alice and Millie out, and she pulled the front door to behind her. She half expected her aunt and uncle to wrench it open and continue their tirade, but the door remained shut and the quietness of the street, and the gentle rain, fell around them like a blessing. Bella had noticed, as she took down her coat, that the crown of Aunt Mona's hat had been stoved in, but she decided to keep that observation to herself.

'Here, give me your case,' she said, relieving Millie of it. 'Come on, let's go and get the train home.'

'Yes,' said Millie. 'I'm so glad you came for me. They're so strict and cross all the time – they don't know any other way. There's no fun in that horrible house. Living there . . . well, it couldn't be less like it was with Mum and Dad.'

Bella and Alice looked at each other over Millie's head. Oh, but that whole visit had been awful. Bella could see that Alice was upset but trying to fight it down, and she knew her own face showed the same.

She took a deep breath to steady herself. 'Well, Millie, Alice and I aren't generally very cross about things, so I expect we'll get along all right,' she replied, making a huge effort to put the last half-hour behind her and sound carefree. 'And our father, your uncle Thomas, is not a man for moods either . . . or at least not angry ones.'

'In that case, I'm twice as glad to get away from those two,' Millie said. 'With my parents . . . with them gone, it feels like I have no home and no place in the world. I don't belong anywhere now.'

'No, you're wrong about that, Millie,' said Bella. 'You've got us.' She made an effort to smile, trying to put all thought of that horrible confrontation out of her mind. 'And we've got you.'

'I'm so pleased you believed my letter and came for me so quickly. I wasn't sure you would.'

'Well, we couldn't do nowt, could we? And, don't worry, we've got the money for your train fare home.'

Alice, too, was making an effort to gather herself. She reached out to squeeze Millie's hand in reassurance. 'Cold hands and no gloves,' she said. 'Or hat.' She removed her own knitted beret and gave it to her cousin. 'Here, I've got the umbrella so you have the hat.' But she held the umbrella over them both.

# CHAPTER FIVE

It was, Thomas thought, rather odd that Millie should look so very much like his own girls. Their colouring of dark hair and green eyes resembled Lottie's far more than it did his own. He had noticed this same colouring in his niece when he had briefly seen her in London, of course, and now here she was, living in his house, where he had the chance to observe her at length. It wasn't just her features; in the way she turned her head, held herself, even in the shrug of her shoulders, she could easily pass for Alice and Bella's younger sister. Such a strange thing, really, now he thought about it . . .

Thomas considered this as he cycled to the Three-Mile Bottom early on Sunday morning. It was still dark as he set off. Bella, a cheerful early riser, was up to wave him goodbye, her backlit figure silhouetted at the front door. Dear Bella, his brave, determined girl . . . How he wished he could live up to her courage, to be the father she and Alice deserved.

There was no sign of Millie yet this morning. Perhaps, like Alice, she wasn't keen to start her day early. There was much to learn about Nanette's child. So far she was quiet, her look hooded and watchful, as if she didn't really trust him. Perhaps she thought he was like his brother, Frank. Well, she'd soon learn that this household was run on altogether different lines. He meant to make it up to Millie. He should not have allowed Frank and Mona to take her without even challenging them. What a mistake . . . another mistake. He had let down Nanette all those years ago, and then, so recently, he'd let down her daughter as well. He vowed it would not happen again.

This morning, Thomas wished his journey was longer, his slow, rhythmic pedalling conducive to allowing his thoughts to wander before he arrived at work. Before long, he would be running back and forth with racks of toast and pots of tea, while Mr Fairbanks chivvied his staff, yelling orders and creating tension and discontent. It was tempting just to keep riding along that long flat straight road on which the inn lay, passing by the Three-Mile without stopping.

*Why* had Frank insisted on taking in Millie? It was, Thomas realised, a plan doomed to fail. How could the daughter of free-spirited, lively, funny, spontaneous Nanette ever have fitted in with the unimaginative, self-righteous and joyless Frank and Mona?

Frank had always been a bully, and it was clear from what Bella and Alice had said that he hadn't improved over the years. Why could I not have stood up to them that day Millie arrived from Cornwall with Nanette's friend, Thomas asked himself. He wished that he'd had the strength of character to acknowledge what he had known in his heart at the time and intervene by taking Millie home with him then, instead of just going along with Frank and Mona.

Of course, Millie was fifteen now – had been since the beginning of the year – and could leave school at Easter, if she wanted.

For a moment, Thomas slowed to a wobble on the quiet main road. Fifteen! And it was fifteen years since Lottie had died . . . and the baby, Jenny. Had they lived, how different his life would have been. And yet here was a child . . . of fifteen. It was just one of those odd coincidences in life: Nanette had given birth to a healthy girl, while, in the same year, Lottie and baby Jenny had died.

Thomas felt the heavy black cloud of fifteen years of sadness shift and settle within him like a physical presence. He struggled to resist its hold, knowing it could set him on a downward spiral to the kind of dark mood that had been known to overwhelm him.

*Stupid man. Will you ever learn? The tragedy couldn't be helped then, and it can't be helped now. Self-pity – so easy to indulge in if you don't snap out of it directly.*

It was possible that Millie need not go to school at all now, being fifteen already and with just weeks until the end of term at Easter. It would hardly be worth buying the uniform. But she would have to find a job. Not that he was rushing the child to pay her own way, but if she didn't go to school, she should look for work before long. The Marchants weren't well off and couldn't afford to be idle. Thomas remembered how thrilled Alice and Bella had been to secure employment at the bookshop and the toyshop, how grown up they had felt to be earning. He wondered what Millie would like to do. It was always better to find a job you were interested in, he mused. That, of course, was one of the problems with his own numerous attempts to settle into employment. It was difficult to get up any enthusiasm for repetitive, boring or largely unappreciated work.

It had been early in the war when Lottie and Jenny died, leaving Thomas to bring up his two girls. He had been features editor of the local newspaper and, with his young daughters to care for, and the struggle he was having to keep his head above the water of despair, he was exempt from call-up when that time came. Iris Cook, his friend and neighbour, and a mother herself, helped out by looking after Alice and Bella after school. Looking back, Thomas could not remember very much of that time. His life was just a blur, a grey emptiness, in which he avoided his colleagues as much as he could because he could not face their sympathy while, at the same time, he felt a terrible pressure to pull himself together while the whole country faced jeopardy. He just wanted to gather his daughters to him and never let them out of his sight.

Eventually he left the newspaper, and started working at whatever he could find, seeking anonymity, feeling aimless, searching for the resolution of his grief. But he just wasn't that interested in any of the jobs he took – not really, or at least not for long – and that had made him restless and unhappy each time until he packed it in – or was asked to leave – and he started over with something new, something he hoped would suit him better. The trouble was, so far nothing had, and after all these years, this itinerant life had become a habit. Lottie's money had enabled him to live that way, and then the girls grew up and started earning, but – he must face it – money was now increasingly tight. There was Bella's wedding to pay for . . . In the meantime, there were four of them living at the cottage. He would have to stick with the potman's job at the Three-Mile for now. At least it was paid work.

'What would you like to do today, Millie?' asked Bella, passing her cousin a plate of toast.

'I'd like to go to the beach,' said Millie. 'I really love the sea.'

'Good idea, then, but only if you don't mind the cold.'

''Course not. Being beside the sea is rather the point of Theddleton, isn't it?'

'Completely the point,' said Alice, pouring herself some tea and then sitting down to snuggle into her dressing gown, pulling the sleeves down over her hands.

It was a handsome brocade garment bought second-hand and originally made for a man, altered by Bella to fit her sister.

'Shall we take a picnic?' asked Bella, her eyes sparkling.

Alice smiled. 'Of course.'

Millie looked unsure. 'Isn't it a little bit *too* cold for that?'

'Not at all. Not when you know the *very best place* for a picnic, which Alice and I do. Eat that toast and get some warm clothes on while I pack up the food. Alice, you'd better hurry up and get dressed.'

Alice took her tea upstairs, while Millie spooned extra marmalade onto her toast when Bella's back was turned, wolfed it down and then went to fetch her cardigans, and Bella packed up a wicker shopping basket with whatever she could find that would make a good lunch, plus a flask for hot drinks.

They set off down the lane, Bella carrying the basket, Millie looking around, taking in everything, asking her cousins who lived in that house, and that one.

Eventually they got to the High Street.

'This is where I work,' said Bella, proudly, when they reached Warminster's Toys.

Millie looked in at the eye-catching window display. The floor of the window was laid out like a dolls' picnic, with a tiny tea set in the centre and the dolls and teddies all sitting up around it.

'It looks babyish,' she said. She sounded as if she were trying the idea out, unsure what her twenty-year-old cousin was doing involved with little children's toys and not minding.

'No, it isn't,' Bella replied indignantly. 'Just because I work in a toyshop doesn't mean it isn't a proper job. Not only do I help serve the customers and tidy up after children have been in, but I make the dolls' outfits and help paint the houses. The houses are quite famous – people come from miles away to buy them – and Mr and Mrs Warminster have a lot of orders, especially at Christmas. And they're such nice people to work for, very kind. I love working here.'

Millie shrugged and walked on. She clearly thought anything to do with little children's toys was beneath her dignity. Bella and Alice exchanged looks: *Oh, well . . .*

Soon, they came to E. & G. Patterson Books.

'This is where I work,' said Alice.

'Is it a junk shop?' asked Millie. 'It looks all dirty and old.'

Even Alice, with her own poor opinion of the window display, felt a little defensive at such bold criticism.

'It's a second-hand bookshop, and it's nicer inside,' she said. 'Folk who are interested in books can wander round the little rooms and search out summat they like the look of.'

'Are there lots of rooms, then?' Millie pressed her nose to the glass, trying to see beyond the dusty heaps.

'It's like a maze. You could get lost, with rooms on all different levels, and little flights of stairs and passages linking them. Sometimes customers emerge into the main part looking relieved and say they've been trying to find the way out.'

'It's my opinion,' said Bella, 'that occasionally the rooms like to rearrange themselves magically to catch people out.'

Millie laughed. 'The shop sounds more interesting than the books. Perhaps I could come here to see if I can get lost and then find my way out.'

Alice thought of Eileen Patterson. 'I don't think the lady who owns the shop would like you just to explore the layout. She'd prefer it if you at least acted like a potential customer.'

Millie looked disappointed. 'I don't really like books,' she said, 'but I like the sound of a shop like a maze.'

'If you don't like books, it's only because you haven't found the right one to interest you yet,' Alice pointed out. 'There's a book for everyone, but sometimes it can take a while to find it.'

'I think I might like books more if I was better at reading,' said Millie, almost shyly.

'Is that why you didn't like it at school, Millie?' asked Bella, gently, remembering the poorly spelled and worded letter. 'Because you find the reading hard?'

Millie nodded. 'The teacher made me sit at the back in the school in Blackburn, and the others said I was stupid.'

'Which clearly you aren't,' said Bella.

'Mebbe we can help,' offered Alice, 'but only if you want us to and are prepared to work. It might just be a case of more practice.'

'But let's not worry about that now,' said Bella, 'because . . . I can smell the sea!'

'Oh, so can I. Come on.' Millie set off quickly down the street, leaving her cousins to keep up as best they could.

The High Street came to an end at the Promenade, a wide path edged with railings overlooking the beach on the far side. On the corner where the two roads met was the Imperial Hotel, with steps up to glazed double doors under a pillared portico. It was the only building of any grandeur in the entire town, which tended towards higgledy-piggledy cottages painted in marshmallow colours and guesthouses behind brightly painted railings. The Imperial looked as if it had been picked up by alien forces, from somewhere much bigger and a lot more pompous than modest Theddleton, and set down at this breezy corner.

'What's this place?' said Millie, staring up at the doorman, who wore a green coat with brass buttons and a peaked cap.

'Ah, the Imperial. It's a hotel that knows its own importance,' said Alice, keeping her voice low.

'What does that man in the cap do?'

'Opens the door for people,' said Bella.

'What, all day? Just stands there until someone comes, and then opens the door?' Millie looked as if she could barely believe it.

'I expect he carries their bags, if they have any,' said Bella.

'I could do that,' said Millie. 'And if it's supposed to be work, they'd pay me for it, too, wouldn't they?'

'I'm sure they would, although possibly not a great deal.'

'Mm, I wonder if all the work in the hotel is that easy,' said Millie. 'They must employ an awful lot of people if they even have a man just to open the door.'

'Commissionaire,' said Alice. 'That's the word for him. No doubt that's the word the Chalfonts use when they refer to him.' She caught Bella's eye, and they both grinned.

'Who are the Chalfonts?' asked Millie.

'Local business folk,' said Alice, as they crossed the road to the side overlooking the beach. 'Mr Chalfont owns the hotel.'

'Oh, I understand,' said Millie. 'You're trying to be polite, but they're stuck up and self-important, like that building.'

Bella laughed loudly. 'You could well be right,' she said, leading the way through a gap in the railings and down some wooden steps, like slats, onto the beach.

The beach was a mix of sand and shingle. Millie immediately crunched her way down to the sea and her cousins followed more slowly. Close to the water, they felt the breeze keenly as it blew their long hair around their shoulders, although all three wore hats knitted by Bella, Millie's borrowed.

'I'm going to wear this one. It's by far the prettiest,' Millie had announced as they'd donned warm clothes for the walk, commandeering Bella's own favourite beret, a complicated Fair Isle pattern that had taken her many evenings to knit.

By now, the late winter sun was well risen and was shining a dazzling white trail across the grey sea. The tide had turned, leaving a crown of seaweed high up on a bank of shingle, the waves lapping gently in and then retreating with a *shush* like a whisper a few yards further down.

'There's more sand when the tide's gone out completely,' said Bella. 'I expect you think you're too old for a bucket and spade, but it's lovely to come down here for the air and the walk.'

'Well, I hope I'll have time for that,' said Millie, 'but there will be other things I have to do now.'

They started to walk north, the sea on their right, the sun on their backs, and Baybury ahead.

'What do you have to do, Millie?' Alice asked seriously. 'You're allowed a little time to get over your parents' accident and . . . just *be*. I reckon that's what you need, and perhaps Aunt Mona and Uncle Frank didn't understand. They didn't give you time.'

'They are horrible people, mean and . . . violent, and I don't even want to speak about them again,' Millie retorted.

'Then we won't,' said Bella. 'But tell us what it is you have to do.'

Millie stopped walking and turned to gaze out over the sea, as if gathering her thoughts. When she turned back, she looked very serious. 'I have to find out how I can make my way in life. It's a bit scary not being able to see the way forward. I'm nobody, just a girl without parents now . . . cast adrift. I don't even know how to begin.'

'It's all right to let us help you, you know,' said Alice, thoughtfully. 'That's what families are for: to look out for each other and help each other along. You've got us now.'

Millie shrugged, and her face assumed a closed look. 'Perhaps. But only if you want the same things. People only help you if they want the same things. If you start moving in a different direction, or they don't agree or understand, they become less helpful. Sometimes they even stand in the way. Mum taught me that.'

'That's true, I suppose, but really, they're just offering advice. It doesn't mean they don't want the best for you,' Bella said. 'We certainly do. That's why we rescued you. And that's why we're walking along this freezing cold beach on a Sunday morning with a basket full of nice things to eat, and sharing with you our favourite picnic spot in all the world.'

'Where? Where is it?' asked Millie, casting off her sombre mood. She looked up and down the beach but could see nowhere obviously suitable.

'You'll see in a minute.'

They walked on further, and then Bella led the way up some steps to the very end of the Promenade. Above the beach here, the road curved inland, but the coastal path continued on to Baybury. Beside it was a little row of beach huts, all painted different colours, although none of them looked as if it had seen any new paint in recent years.

'Ooh, like tiny houses,' said Millie. 'Can we go in one?'

'We certainly can,' said Alice. 'We can go in . . . *this* one.' She stopped outside one painted blue and white, and produced a key from her coat pocket.

'Really? This is yours?'

'It belonged to our mother and now it belongs to Bella and me.' Alice put the key in the padlock on the door.

'I can't wait to see.' As Alice opened the door, Millie rushed in. 'Oh, it's lovely,' she said, looking round appreciatively, her eyes huge. 'I wish I could live here and it could be my very own little house.'

'Well, we love it, but even we admit it would be perishing cold to live here all winter, and very dark at night, as there is no electricity,' said Alice. 'It's only for use during the day. And if you lived here, you'd have to sleep in one of the deck chairs, which wouldn't be at all comfy or cosy. And there's not very much room, unless you open the doors and extend outside.'

Millie looked around at the once-white, now slightly mildewed interior, the deck chairs folded and leaning up against one wall, the tea-stained butler's tray, its stand showing rust at the hinges, and the blue and white gingham curtains held against the long, narrow front windows by taut wires. She sniffed, inhaling the pervading smell of damp.

'Well, it could be a *bit* nicer, I suppose,' she said, 'but it will be lovely for the picnic.'

'Exactly,' said Bella, putting down the basket. 'It's a Marchant family tradition to picnic here. Come on, hook the doors back and help me to set up these deck chairs while Alice unpacks the food.'

They sat outside on the wide path in front of the beach hut, huddled into the deck chairs, their coat collars raised, their hats pulled low, their faces turned towards the sea. Bella and Alice were pleased to see that Millie appreciated the simple pleasure of a winter picnic. She polished off two sausage rolls, an apple, and by far the largest part of a bar of Fry's Chocolate Cream, which Bella was reluctantly sharing as a treat. All this was washed down with Camp Coffee from the flask.

'Tell us what you like about the sea, Millie,' suggested Alice.

'Well, it goes right round the world, so you can go anywhere if you set sail. You just need to have the courage to go.'

'I suppose you do. And where would you go if you "set sail"?' asked Bella, smiling.

'Well, Mum and Dad lived in Cornwall when they . . . when I . . .'

'Yes, we know, love, and we're very sorry that such an awful thing happened. What did they do in Cornwall?' asked Bella. She and Alice knew only that their aunt

Nanette and their uncle Harry lived artistic lives, no details. They couldn't even remember meeting them. Aunt Mona had been dismissive and condemning of the Boyds as 'bohemians', but then, thought Bella, what value was there in Aunt Mona's view?

'They sat around smoking and painting. They often had their friends visiting.'

Bella laughed. 'Smoking and painting? Did they do that for a living?'

'Not the smoking,' corrected Millie, sighing in exasperation, as if she thought Bella was being silly. 'When Dad painted, Mum used to pose for him. He said he'd paint me one day, but he never did. Most of his paintings were of Mum, wearing different outfits, even costumes, like in the films, and looking pretty, although sometimes he painted her wearing nothing at all. And Mum painted pictures of where we lived: the village and the house, which she and Dad rented, and the garden with tall, wild flowers, some fat little hens and some apple trees.'

Bella widened her eyes at Alice. *Heavens, what a world away from Aunt Mona and Uncle Frank! What a world away from Theddleton . . .*

'It sounds lovely. Were they good paintings?'

'Of course they were! They were *brilliant*, especially the ones Dad did of Mum. But he never wanted to sell them, and they would argue about that because Mum said we had to eat and pay the rent for the house, and buy more paint and things, and she couldn't afford to keep us from the sale of her paintings alone.'

'So what happened?' Bella had to ask, although she hoped she wasn't leading Millie into the kind of conversation she really shouldn't be having.

'One time – a couple of years ago, I can't really remember – Dad went off to visit a friend, and while he was gone, Mum put all his paintings of her in the car, all piled up so that there was hardly room for me – I don't think she'd have taken me with her, except she said she needed me to help unload at the other end – and I had to sit with some of the canvases on my knee. I couldn't even see out of the windows. Then she drove off somewhere to see a man she knew, and he bought all the paintings.'

'I hope she got a good deal,' said Alice encouragingly.

'At first, on the face of it, it was a disaster!' said Millie. 'Dad flew into a terrible rage, and he did a lot of shouting, although not at me, of course. I don't think either of them even noticed I was there when they were arguing. Then Mum got angry with *him* and threw some plates, and then, after a bit, they made up and it was all kissing for days.' She shrugged, suddenly fighting back tears. 'That's what they were like. I didn't really mind the rows because I knew they didn't mean any of what they said, and I was lucky to have such special parents, but, well, sometimes I wished they would notice a bit more that there were three of us. I just used to go off to see Mags or mess about somewhere outside until I was hungry.'

Bella could imagine the sun-dappled garden, a run-down house brimming with life, the easy come-and-go attitude of Millie's parents, with their colourful life of painting and socialising, their too-casual attitude to their daughter's upbringing and education, the showy drama of their rows and the passion of their reconciliations. In sharp contrast to all this colour and sunshine and generous emotion for each other – and, Bella was beginning to suspect, selfish neglect of their daughter – was Uncle Frank and Aunt Mona's buttoned-up chilliness; the high-tension comforts of their spotless, silent, cold house; their stiff clothes and the restricted lives they'd made for themselves, Mona always minding what their neighbours thought of them; their utter lack of imagination and empathy for a girl who had lost her parents . . . their anger. No wonder Millie had wanted to escape from them. She no more fitted into Frank and Mona's lives than her uncle and aunt would have got on in the artists' chaotic house in Cornwall.

Bella leaned over in her deck chair and put an arm around Millie's shoulders. 'I'm sorry,' she murmured. 'It's a pity it's not one little bit like a hot, sunny day in Cornwall now, so you can feel more at home here. At least we managed the picnic.'

Millie hugged Bella tightly for a moment. Then they all gazed out to sea for a minute or two.

'It's really good here in summer,' said Bella eventually, 'because you can change into your bathers inside the hut, and then it's just a few yards down to the beach. When you've done your swimming, you have the luxury of being able to get dried properly and put your clothes on in private, whereas other swimmers have to wrap themselves in towels and struggle to dress under them on the beach, with all the danger of sand where they don't want it and accidentally showing their bottoms.'

Millie giggled, as Bella had hoped she would.

'Hello. Here's a surprise,' said a man's voice, and there was Sidney Bennett, who'd approached from the Baybury end of the path.

'Sidney, how nice,' said Bella enthusiastically, squinting up at him from her deck chair. 'I didn't expect to see you today. We were just having a picnic. You would have been welcome to join us if you'd come by earlier.'

'Thanks, but I think you must be mad in this temperature.' Sidney laughed. He turned his attention to Millie. 'Who's this, then? Looks like another Marchant sister. Don't tell me your father's got a secret love child.'

Even Bella, who knew only too well that Sidney didn't always think before speaking, looked taken aback.

'Not funny,' said Alice. 'Just in very poor taste.'

'Whoops, I can see I've spoken out of turn, Lady Alice. No offence meant.'

'None taken, Sidney. We all know what you're like,' Alice said evenly, coolly raising an eyebrow at him. She got up. 'Millie, shall we go back down to the beach, see if we can find some shells?'

Millie nodded, but she continued to eye Sidney in silence from her deck chair.

'This is Millie Boyd, our cousin,' said Bella. 'Millie,

this is Sidney Bennett, who is a good friend of mine. In fact, Sidney and I are engaged to be married.'

'Hello.' Millie gave him an assessing look. She didn't smile.

'Where did you spring from?' Sidney asked. 'No, let me guess – you belong to Bella's aunt and uncle in Blackburn, and you're just here for the weekend.'

'No!' yelled Millie. 'I do *not* belong to them. I will *not* go back to live with Frank and Moaner. Ever, ever, ever!'

She leaped out of the deck chair and raced towards the steps down to the beach.

'Oh Lord,' said Alice, 'I'd better go after her.' She got up and quickly followed.

'What was all that about?' asked Sidney, sinking into Alice's deck chair. 'Seemed to have touched a nerve there. Bit old for a toddler tantrum, isn't she?'

'Well, I was going to tell you . . .'

Bella outlined her and Alice's visit to Blackburn and how they had left with their cousin, although she avoided lingering on the unpleasant details.

'. . . and it's plain that she misses her parents so much. Uncle Frank and Aunt Mona just aren't in the same mould at all. They haven't the first idea about looking after a bereaved child or even the most basic things, like having fun. Millie wasn't happy there, so we've brought her to live with us.'

'Live with you? What, for ever?'

'Why not?'

Sidney raised his hands in an exaggerated gesture of

astonishment. 'Heck, Bella, that's such a big thing. Are you sure you've thought it all through, love? I know what you can be like, rushing into things.'

'I don't think that's quite fair,' said Bella. 'And of course, we've all agreed.' Bella was aware that none of them at home had discussed the possibility of Millie living with them *quite* as much as they might have done before the Blackburn visit. Really, the rescue had been finally decided there and then for Bella, in Beaucroft Road, when Millie had emerged from her room with her suitcase. When she had pulled down her cardigan sleeves and shown her bruised arm, that had been the clincher for Alice. Bella would not tell Sidney this, however.

'So what are you going to do with her?'

'Put her to work scrubbing floors, of course – honestly, Sidney, what's the problem? She'll be like a little sister: the little sister Alice and I would have had if she had survived. I told you about Mam and the baby, and that's why your "secret love child" remark was so unfunny. I thought you might have remembered. Millie is going to live with us at home.'

'But you're not expecting to be there for very much longer.'

'Then Dad and Alice will look after her. I don't see the difficulty. Lots of people have younger siblings.'

'I don't.'

'I'm very much aware that you're an only child, Sidney,' said Bella, deadpan, 'but not everyone is.

What are you saying? Millie won't make any difference to us. We'll still be getting married in the autumn, won't we?'

'Of course. But . . . I just want to be sure, that's all. We can hardly start our married life at Mam's with your orphaned cousin in tow.'

'Really, Sidney, do stop talking nonsense. Millie's presence in Chapel Lane is nowt to do with you – with *us*.'

'As I said, I'm just making sure.'

He leaned back in the deck chair, gazing out to sea, oblivious to the cross look Bella was giving him. An apology would have been nice, but she realised as the silence went on that he wasn't aware that he'd been rude.

'So where have you been this morning?' she asked after a minute or two. 'I wish I'd known you were passing this way. As I said, you'd have been welcome to join us.'

'Oh, I wouldn't want to intrude on your packed lunch,' Sidney said. 'Besides, Mam's got one of her roast dinners on, and you know what a wonderful cook she is. No, I only came out to stretch my legs.'

'All alone? You must have been ahead of us. We've been down on the beach.'

'You didn't see me, then?'

'No, I sort of just said that. We were on the beach and must have missed you.'

'Right . . . good . . .' Sidney rubbed his hands together. 'Well, I must be off home.'

'Yes, don't let your lovely roast dinner spoil.' Bella

smiled. 'Give my regards to your mother and I'll see you soon.'

Sidney got up, kissed her briefly and went off along the Promenade.

Alone with the deck chairs and the picnic debris, Bella wondered what had got into Sidney. He hadn't been at all sympathetic about Millie and was very keen that her presence in Theddleton shouldn't encroach on him in any way. The whole encounter had been a bit odd, now she came to think of it. Well, let him take his solitary walk – wherever it was he had been – and think what he liked. He would soon see that Millie made no difference to their plans for the future at all.

# CHAPTER SIX

'MILLIE! MILLIE, COME back,' called Alice, seeing Millie racing across the wet sand as fast as her spindly legs would carry her. Alice negotiated the low shingle bank, sinking into the stones, then picked up speed and caught up with Millie as she sped along the shoreline. Thankfully, Millie stopped running then, and turned defiantly to face Alice.

'I'm not going back to live with Frank and Moaner. I *told* you. I'd rather die! But maybe that will serve me right!'

'Millie, please! Enough drama,' panted Alice. 'That was just a silly misunderstanding. You are stopping with us – we've *told* you that. It's been decided. We all want you here.'

'I don't think that man does – what was he called? – who Bella says she's going to marry.'

'Sidney Bennett. Well, I wouldn't take any notice of him if I were you. It's nowt to do with him. He doesn't

103

mean any harm – he's just thoughtless. You do believe me, don't you?'

Millie considered this, frowning. 'Yes,' she said eventually. 'I think you're telling me the truth. If you were lying, you'd also pretend that you like Sidney Bennett, but it sounds to me as if you don't.'

'He's nowt to do with me.'

'So you *don't* like him.'

'I didn't say that, and we're not talking about him. We're talking about you, stopping with us and finding out what you want to do in life, remember?'

Millie nodded. But she said, 'When is Bella going to marry him?'

'In the autumn, she's thinking.'

'So she's going away then?'

'Yes, but not far. Sidney wants them to live at his mother's house, which is just over there, behind the Promenade, although Bella would rather have a home of her own.'

'What is his mother like?'

'Like him.'

'Thoughtless?'

Alice had had enough of this conversation. 'Why are you so interested in Sidney Bennett, Millie? He's Bella's choice, and she can marry whom she chooses. It's not for the rest of us to judge. The important thing is that there will still be Dad and me at the cottage with you. By then, who knows? You might be settled in Theddleton, doing summat you love, and already starting to see the direction you want to be heading in.'

Eventually Millie nodded.

'Good. Now, why don't we throw some stones in the sea, use up some spare energy, and get rid of all that crossness?'

'Yes, all right. Sometimes, when I feel really furious, it helps to throw things.'

'I understand. I feel the same, although the only throwing I do is of stones in the sea.'

The stone-throwing started off with little pieces of shingle, which Millie hurled into the sea, where they spattered and disbursed like shrapnel, but soon she was lobbing ever bigger stones as far as she could. Alice watched the determination with which she launched the stones, as if propelling them by the power of her grief and anger, watching the loud sploshes they made in the sea with grim satisfaction.

'Millie, is this how you felt when you broke Aunt Mona's window? I'm not angry – I'm just interested to know.'

'I did. I knew they would smack me – Uncle Frank's got a very whacky ruler that hurts a lot – but I really, really wanted to hear the sound of that window breaking. At the time, it seemed worth the punishment. Sometimes, when I miss Mum and Dad so much that I think I'm going to explode, only a great big smash will do.'

Alice looked at Millie, now bending to extract a big stone, which she launched like a pint-sized shot-putter towards the lapping waves.

*Poor little girl.*

'Let's do some stone-skimming,' Alice suggested, and with a swift side throw she skimmed a stone out to sea, where it bounced three times before disappearing.

'That was good. Show me again.'

'I'm surprised you don't know about it. You have to have the right shape of stone: flat, not like those great things you've been digging out. Let's see what we can find . . .'

When Bella appeared with the picnic basket and, thankfully, without Sidney Bennett, Alice was instructing Millie in the skilful and controlled art of stone-skimming.

'Well done,' said Bella quietly when Millie had wandered off to replenish her arsenal of flat stones. 'Sorry about Sidney. He can be such a chump at times, but he means no harm.'

'I just wish he'd engage his brain before opening his mouth,' Alice replied.

'I'm working on him. His mother's just the same, of course,' said Bella, tolerantly. 'But he seemed oddly bothered about Millie living with us. I can't think why.'

'Me neither. When you're married to Sidney, Millie will be with Dad and me instead of with the three of us. And that will make no difference to you and Sidney at all.'

That evening, getting her things ready to go to work the next day, Bella saw that her handbag was looking shapeless. It was getting heavy, too. She tipped it out on the sofa to sort through the detritus and found, among the toffee papers, receipts and crumpled hand-kerchiefs, the folded slip of paper detailing the car ride she'd won at the fundraising do. She had forgotten all about it; she wasn't interested in a ride in a big fancy car all by herself. She wouldn't have minded going with Sidney, but the prize was just for one. But perhaps Thomas would like to go.

'Here, Dad, how about swapping your bike for a car ride?' Bella handed it to him and explained where it had come from.

'Thank you, love, but I'm not bothered,' he said. 'What would it be for? I don't need a ride out with a stranger in his . . .' He glanced more closely at the paper. '. . . his Rolls-Royce.' He handed it back and returned to the newspaper he was reading.

'What about you, Alice?' Bella asked.

'I'm not sure. The car ride sounds a treat, but who is "B. Reeves"? Has anyone heard of him? Would it be safe to get into a car alone with a man I don't know?'

'He might have a chauffeur to drive you both, as it's such a posh car. And we'd know who you'd gone with. It's a Baybury telephone number, so he must be fairly local. Phone him up and see if you like the sound of him. You can always say you'll have to call back later if you want to get out of it.'

'I think you should telephone, Alice, and arrange the ride,' said Millie. Her eyes sparkled mischievously. 'After all, he might turn out to be really lovely, and he thinks you are, too, and he falls madly in love with you and you get to ride in his Rolls-Royce anytime you want.'

Everyone laughed, and Alice rolled her eyes. 'Millie, I do believe you are a hopeless romantic, just like Bella. It's more likely he'll turn out to be some ancient ex-army type with five middle-aged unmarried daughters at home, fiercely guarding the fortune that bought his Rolls-Royce and keeping him from falling for bookshop assistants a fraction of his age.'

'And who could blame them?' said Thomas.

'Still, I suppose I'll never know if I don't do owt about it,' said Alice.

'Go on, then,' said Bella. 'Ask Mr Patterson if you can use the shop telephone when Miss Patterson is out. I'm sure he'll let you.'

'I'll see,' said Alice noncommittally. 'Right, Millie, what are your plans for tomorrow? Dad's at home on Mondays, as you know.'

'Well, I thought I might see if there's any work at the hotel,' said Millie. 'If they pay a man just to open the door, then there are bound to be masses of other jobs to do. That will start me off earning some money.'

The others looked surprised.

'You don't have to rush into employment, love,' said Thomas. ''Course, it's good you want to work—'

'Well, I'm not going to school any more, that's for certain,' said Millie with a petulant little stamp of her foot.

'No, you're old enough to leave at Easter anyway. I

think if you found work then no one would expect you to go to school now. I'm just saying, take your time.'

'But I need to earn some money. I'd like to buy some paints and paper.'

'Oh, sweetheart,' said Bella, 'of course you need some things of your own. And it's good that you're so keen to have a regular job.' She couldn't resist casting a quick, meaningful glance at her father. 'After we've eaten, I'll look out what drawing things Alice and I have kept that you can use. Would that do to be going on with?'

'I don't know,' said Millie, the daughter of professional artists. 'Depends what you've got.'

Bella found some old coloured pencils, all different lengths, the red especially short, and a notebook of plain paper for Millie to sketch and colour on.

'I'm afraid it's not proper drawing paper, but at least it isn't lined,' she said. 'Here, rest on this tea tray if you want.'

'Thank you, Bella,' said Millie, looking only moderately pleased, and sat back in one of the comfy chairs in the sitting room, the tray on her knees, to examine the finds.

'Are you ready to tell us a story, Dad?' asked Alice.

'I am.'

Millie looked up, scowling, at Thomas. 'A story? What, like a bedtime story? But we're not little children.'

'And why would we not want a story whatever age we are?' asked Bella. 'Dad's the best storyteller in the whole world. We've been listening to his stories on a Sunday evening since we were little, and we will never be too old to enjoy them.'

'But what about when you're married to Sidney Bennett and living at his mother's?' asked Millie innocently, seeming to relish mentioning Sidney's mother for some reason Bella couldn't fathom.

'Oh, I expect I'll come back here every Sunday to see Dad and you and Alice, and stay until I've heard the story.' Bella smiled.

'You don't have to listen if you don't want to, Millie,' Alice said. 'You can go and sit at the kitchen table to do your drawing in peace – we don't mind.'

Millie shrugged. 'No, I'll stay.'

'All right,' said Thomas, and leaned back in his chair. 'Once upon a time—'

'Honestly, we're not babies!' Millie huffed, rolling her eyes. 'This sounds like a story for tiny little children.'

'Millie, will you please be quiet and not spoil it for us?' said Bella. 'Dad's stories always start with those wonderful, magical words, and if you don't want to listen, Alice has already told you what you can do. Now, please, stay and be quiet or go.'

Millie stayed. Once the story was underway, she started to sketch in the notebook and then coloured quietly with the pencils, while Alice and Bella sat still, relishing this time of family togetherness, a years-old ritual of which they would never tire.

\* \* \*

'. . . and all that was left was a little pool of bright golden sunlight in the forest,' finished Thomas.

Millie looked up from her sketchbook. 'But what happened to the beautiful lady who lived among the trees?'

Bella and Alice looked at each other, smiling, and Bella winked at her sister.

'We'll never know,' said Thomas. 'I think she melted away in the sunlight, but you might have a different idea.'

'It was a far better story than I thought it would be,' Millie admitted grudgingly.

'Thank you,' Thomas replied modestly. 'I'm glad you liked it.'

'Are you going to show us your picture?' asked Bella. 'You were very busy while we were listening.'

'But I was listening, too,' said Millie. 'It was impossible not to, somehow, like being caught in the lady's magic spell.' She looked very carefully at the picture herself, then turned the notebook to Bella. 'That's the magical lady, and this is the lost traveller.'

'Good heavens,' gasped Bella. 'That is so good. It's brilliant! And that's exactly how I was imagining the traveller, even down to his hat and boots.'

'How strange,' said Alice quietly, getting up to have a closer look. 'I thought he looked like this, too, and she looks somehow familiar. Her hair is . . . well, it's the very image that was in my head. It's a really beautiful drawing. How clever you are, Millie. Anyone can see that you have a special talent. What do you think, Dad?' Alice took the notebook from Millie and passed it to her father.

Thomas gazed in silence at the sketch for several seconds, and suddenly tears welled in his eyes. He put the notebook aside, his hand to his mouth as if in shock.

'Dad?' asked Bella gently, filled with concern. 'What is it? Please don't be upset.'

Thomas shook his head and wiped his eyes. 'Such a strange thing,' he said. 'The lady in Millie's drawing is the very image of my mother – the shape of her face, and her hair piled up just so. So lovely.'

'Perhaps Millie noticed the photograph of Grandma in the other room, and that's what sprang to mind,' said Bella, who had never met her grandmother at all. 'That will be it, won't it, Millie?'

The picture didn't resemble the photograph exactly, but clearly Thomas had seen something that only he knew of his mother in Millie's drawing.

'I expect so,' Millie said quietly, after a pause.

There was an unsettled atmosphere in the room now, not at all like it usually was after one of Thomas's stories.

Alice cleared her throat. 'Right, Millie, time for bed, do you think?'

'Yes, all right. But I'm going to take the pencils and notebook up with me.'

'As you like.'

When Millie had gone up to the little attic room that had hurriedly been made pretty and comfortable for her after her arrival the previous day, and Alice had gone to make some cocoa to take up to her, Bella went to kneel down beside Thomas's chair.

'Don't be upset, Dad. It was such a good story that, somehow, she couldn't help imagining what you were thinking. She clearly is astonishingly talented, and none of us knew that until now.'

'Yes, love, I reckon you're right,' Thomas agreed. 'That's the only explanation, isn't it? She's got a very vivid imagination.'

It was sad that people traditionally hated the prospect of going to work on Mondays, Bella thought as she and Alice walked to the High Street. The wind coming off the sea could blow the smile off your face this morning, but Bella knew there would be a warm welcome at the toyshop and a pot of tea brewing.

'Odd about Millie's drawing,' she remarked. 'I can't stop thinking about it, how the lady looked like Grandma, especially to Dad.'

'Yes, strange. I could tell Dad was quite unsettled after Millie had gone up to bed. But as we can't explain it, there's no use dwelling on it. Don't forget, Grandma Marchant was Millie's grandma, too. Mebbe Aunt Nanette had a photo of her mother and Millie was remembering that. Or mebbe the knowledge is just . . . I don't know, in her bones or summat.'

'She didn't say so. You don't think she was trying to . . . upset Dad by knowingly drawing such a lovely picture of Grandma and not saying? Some mischief that went further than she knew? I've noticed she's sometimes a bit . . . hostile towards Dad.'

'Oh, Bella, she's just a child,' said Alice with certainty. 'Whatever's wrong in all this, it isn't Millie. She's just the innocent we had to rescue.'

'I'm sure you're right, Alice. Oh, do you see who's coming?'

'Mrs Bennett. Lucky you. Right, I'd better be getting on. See you later.'

Alice strode purposefully down the High Street towards the bookshop, acknowledging Nancy Bennett with a friendly wave as she hurried past her without breaking her stride.

'Mrs Bennett, good morning,' said Bella, approaching more slowly, then stopping to greet her future mother-in-law.

'Is it?' said Mrs Bennett. 'A good morning, I mean. Seems to me it's a rough 'un with that wind. Nearly blew me off my feet. I'm only out this early 'cos I wanted to get to the butcher before he's out of kidneys. But these cold blasts are playing merry hell with my rheumatics.'

'I'm sorry to hear that.'

'That's easily said. You wouldn't know owt about it, Bella, being so young. But you'll not be young all your life, you know. You'll learn.'

'Er, I expect so. Anyway, I'm sorry I couldn't take up your kind invitation to come to tea on Saturday, Mrs Bennett.'

'Oh, aye?'

'Sidney said you'd invited me, but I was already busy.'

'So I heard. Summat to do with a young cousin of yours. Sidney told me all about her when he came back from his walk yesterday. Said she's a bit of a one for flying off the handle.'

'Did he? Well, I'm not sure how Sidney can say that, Mrs Bennett, as he's hardly met her. Millie's parents are dead, and she needs a loving family around her, to help her get over that and to look after her now she's without them.'

'So a problem child?'

'No, not at all. Just a young girl in need of some love and kindness.'

Mrs Bennett sniffed, and Bella remembered how certain the woman always was of the rightness of her own opinion.

'Well, I expect you'll get to meet her before long, Mrs Bennett, Theddleton being such a small place,' Bella said.

'I'll make a point of meeting her,' said Nancy, as if Millie passing muster with her was essential to the girl's staying in Theddleton. 'I should expect to meet her if you're going to be marrying my Sidney.'

'Well, yes, I *am* going to be marrying Sidney,' Bella said with a smile. There was no 'if' about it, despite then having to have Nancy Bennett as her mother-in-law. Still, you couldn't choose your in-laws.

*Come on, Bella. She's only this side out because her rheumatics are giving her gyp.*

'Right, Mrs Bennett, I'd best be off to work. I hope your rheumatics are better soon.'

'I'd be amazed if they were. They're a life sentence, lass.'

'Perhaps a nice warm stay in bed with a hot-water bottle—'

'I'm not one for stopping in bed, and I hope you're not either, Bella Marchant. I can't abide folk lazing about when there's owt they could be up and at. If you're coming to live at mine, there'll be no lying in bed of a morning, I'll tell you that now.'

'No, of course not. I just meant . . . well, never mind. You go carefully in this rough wind, and I'll see you soon. Bye, Mrs Bennett.' Bella turned away, she hoped not too hastily for good manners, and made for the toyshop.

Why on earth was Sidney's mother out at this hour if all she was going to do was grumble? The woman really was a mystery.

Bella walked the last few yards to the toyshop and went in.

'Bella, good morning,' chorused Cassie and Alfred.

'Bright and early, and there's tea in the pot, love,' added Cassie, beaming. 'Now tell me, how did you get on in Blackburn on Saturday . . . ?'

Monday being Thomas's day off from the inn, he saw Bella and Alice leave to go to their work and then pottered around in the little garden behind the cottage, where he was a keen grower of flowers and vegetables.

Already there were daffodils and primroses showing, their cheerful yellows brightening the wintery plot.

Millie came out to find him, then bent to smell the fragrant daffodils.

'I think I might go to the Imperial now and ask about some work,' she announced.

'So soon? I told you, lass, there's no hurry.'

'But I need to earn some money so I can buy some proper artist's materials. At school in Blackburn, they said I'd "never come to owt", but I mean to prove them wrong.'

'Of course they're wrong, Millie. Forget about them. It's easy enough to feel lost and directionless in this life, without listening to other people putting you down, especially when you've things to be sad about already.'

Yes, thought Millie, you're right. Frank and Moaner would never even have thought that, never mind said it to me.

'But I don't want you going down to the hotel and finding they're too busy to see you, or they have no jobs going and you're disappointed,' Thomas went on. 'Tell you what, why don't I go along with you? While we're out, we can get the *Theddleton Informer* and see who's advertising work in that. And, in the meantime, you can be thinking about what you can do and what kind of job you would like to try.'

'All right.' Millie thought her uncle might not be much of an asset as far as job hunting went, but at least he cared and was being kind.

'Perhaps you need some new clothes, too – the kind of things women wear to work. The girls can help you with that. Your pink frock isn't "serious" enough for work in some places. It's important to dress the part.'

'I'll ask them. Thank you,' she added quietly.

Millie was struggling with her long-held opinion of her uncle, gathered from what her mother had told her. She could see that he was a bit sad, a daydreamer, his life run by Alice and Bella, while, she gathered, he wandered from job to job, but his story the previous evening had, surprisingly, been the best tale she had ever heard: clever, funny, and exciting. And he wasn't weaselly or sly, as she had thought he might be. Already he was being thoughtful and considerate, treating her as if she were one of his daughters. She felt caught off guard.

They set off, stopping at the newsagent's, where Thomas bought the *Informer* to read later, and then they walked along towards the sea. Millie shoved her hands in her pockets and shrugged her coat collar up, to protect her face against the wind and to save her having to talk to her uncle. She wasn't ready to be won over yet.

'Right,' said Thomas, when they got to the end of the High Street where the hotel was, 'I suppose you could just go in and ask if there's owt you could do – as we're here.'

'I could do his job,' said Millie, indicating the commissionaire.

'Of course you could – until someone turned up with half a ton of luggage.' Thomas laughed.

'I can't help being small,' snapped Millie.

'Well, there's only one direction to grow in,' Thomas answered mildly.

They went up the steps, and the doorman opened the door for them with a slightly supercilious expression on his face.

In the foyer, where the murmur of conversation was hushed by the depth of the plush carpet, Thomas pointed out the reception desk to Millie. 'Now, go over there and ask the receptionist if Housekeeping need anyone. That means laundry and cleaning jobs. Not exciting, I know, but you have to start at the bottom for your first job, and it'll earn you a bit to buy your paints. I'll wait here for you.' He went to sit on a deep sofa in the corner, looking surprisingly at home.

Millie did as he suggested. At least he was taking seriously her wish to earn money to buy paints. The receptionist was dismissive of her at first, hardly looking up from what he was doing, but the air of assurance Millie assumed soon made him pay her more attention. He noted down her details and said he'd be in touch if there were any suitable jobs available.

Millie went back to Thomas, not feeling very hopeful. The commissionaire had by now moved casually into the foyer, away from the door, Thomas noticed, as if he wanted to avoid showing deference to people so ordinary-looking a second time. Thomas and Millie saw themselves out.

As they emerged outside onto the steps, some visitors

were just arriving: an old lady in a coat with a fur collar and a white-haired gentleman with very smart shoes.

'Good morning,' said Millie, opening the door wide for them and smiling charmingly.

'Good morning,' replied the elderly couple, and the man pressed a coin into Millie's hand as he passed into the hotel.

Thomas was laughing loudly by the time he and Millie reached the pavement.

'What a kind man – generous, but terrible eyesight,' he said. 'I think he mistook your green coat for a commissionaire's uniform.'

'There's nothing to this doorwoman lark,' giggled Millie. 'I could walk straight into that job if that commissionaire thinks himself too grand to treat everyone alike. After all, it's only opening the door, isn't it? What's he got to be so stuck up about?'

'Quite,' said Thomas. 'How much did the gentleman tip you?'

Millie opened her hand and showed him a shiny sixpence.

'Heavens, that was decent of him.'

'My first pay,' said Millie, delightedly holding the coin up to catch the sunlight. 'And I haven't even done any work yet.'

Eileen Patterson had decided to visit a friend of hers in Scarborough and had left the bookshop for the station halfway through the morning. This gave Alice the opportunity to ask Godfrey if she could use the shop telephone.

'Of course you may, Alice,' he said. 'I'm excited to think you have won such an imaginative prize in a draw.'

'Well, I've no idea who this Mr Reeves is but, as Bella said, if I don't like the sound of him, I can always pretend I have to go and then not ring back.'

'Oh, come now, it will be wonderful,' said Godfrey enthusiastically, and went into one of the other rooms while Alice made her call.

'Baybury three six one,' announced a woman in clipped tones.

'Good morning,' said Alice. 'Please may I speak to Mr Reeves?'

'I'm afraid he's not here at the moment. Who's calling, please? Can I help – or take a message?'

'My name is Alice Marchant, and I won the ride along the coast in the floral clock fundraiser draw.'

'Ah, excellent,' said the woman. 'I'd almost given up on anyone coming forward to claim it. Now, when would you like to go?'

'Oh, on Sunday, please, if that would be all right?'

'Ten thirty suit you?'

'Yes . . . that would be fine, thank you.'

'I hope it will be – fine, that is. Always better along the coast when it isn't shrouded in fog or raining sideways. Where would you like to be picked up from?'

Alice was about to say the Imperial Hotel, a place everyone around here knew, but it occurred to her it would be better if Bella and Millie saw this Mr Reeves, whoever he was. If she was abducted or something equally awful, at least they would be able to describe him to the police.

*And whatever am I thinking? Ridiculous, neurotic idea. This woman is perfectly friendly.*

'Oh, er, Chapel Lane, Theddleton. Number eight.' Alice briefly gave directions from the High Street.

'Got it,' said the woman efficiently.

'Thank you, Mrs . . . Miss . . . ?'

'Reeves,' said the woman. 'Goodbye, Miss Marchant.'

'Goodbye.'

Alice put down the receiver. The woman must be this Mr Reeves's wife. She seemed to know all about the prize, anyway. That was good: Alice thought she'd be perfectly safe if the man's wife knew all the arrangements.

She felt excited to have an outing lined up, even though it was with someone she hadn't even met. It would make a change from staying in with Thomas, spending the time reading or going for walks or attending book discussion groups and classical concerts at the town hall with Vera and her brother, Mike, friends she had known all her life.

'All organised?' asked Godfrey, coming back in, smiling with expectation in a way that made Alice suspect he'd been listening.

'Yes, thank you. Funnily enough, I wasn't that bothered about the prize until I telephoned. Now I'm rather looking forward to it.'

# CHAPTER SEVEN

LATER THAT WEEK, with everyone else at work, Millie was feeling at a loose end. Alice had looked out some books for her to read, with a promise to hear her reading them and to help her with any difficult words, as she did every evening now, but Millie was bored with this. She preferred drawing to reading. She decided to take the notebook and coloured pencils and go to the beach hut. She hadn't asked to take the key, but she'd seen where Alice had put it back the previous Sunday and she saw no reason not to help herself.

There was much for her to think about: her uncle Thomas, for a start. Far from being mean and sly, the kind of person who would split on his sister and allow her to be thrashed, he was kind, mild-mannered, tolerant. Bella and Alice, although sometimes exasperated by him, clearly loved him dearly. This went against everything Millie had imagined before she came here, but she had had vague thoughts of revenge on her uncle

Thomas for his betrayal of her mother for so long that it was difficult to set those aside so soon. It was early days for forgiving and forgetting.

Then there was Bella and Sidney Bennett. Millie could see that he was very handsome, but even having met him only briefly, she realised that he was not clever, but rather the kind of person who spoke out of turn because he was too dim to know that he was being inconsiderate, or perhaps too dim to care. Obviously Bella saw something more in him, but it would be such a shame if she were to marry someone so far below what she deserved. Would she be able to see this before it was too late?

And Alice: the sensible grown-up. She was more reserved, more considered, than Bella. She had friends in Theddleton and Baybury, yet she seemed to have no one special in her life, which was a surprise . . . Millie tried to concentrate, to think really hard, in the hope of being able to imagine what was ahead for Alice, but failed to find an answer.

Millie knew that sometimes the pictures she drew or painted were hard to explain. Uncle Thomas had been upset that she had drawn Grandma Marchant, as if she were playing a trick on him, but the image had just flown into her mind. It was a kind of gift, but one she could not explain. More complicated, more worrying were the pictures she made that were fuelled by her anger. It was as if her rage had the power to shape events. That horrible picture she had painted on the day Mum and Dad had been killed . . . how she wished with all her heart that she had not allowed that stupid, hateful, throwaway thought to have entered her head: *I wish you were dead.* Now she had to live with the consequences, the terrible suspicion that she might actually have killed them herself, just by allowing that brief, mad, angry thought loose into the world.

Sitting at the kitchen table, having finished her breakfast, Millie put her hands to her mouth, anguish shooting into her heart. It had been only a stupid, petulant, momentary lashing out before her parents had set off that last morning without her – *I wish you were dead* – but even a flash of a wish could be dangerous if you had this frightening and strange gift – or curse – to make a picture full of significance.

She dashed away threatening tears and turned her thoughts back to her cousins, hoping to foresee happiness, not only because she wanted that for them, but also to offset the guilt she felt for the horrible end she had so angrily conjured for her parents.

She tried to think what to do about Bella and Sidney Bennett, to see how that might play out, but her mind was a blank, as it was over Alice. This power was not something that could ever be controlled or exercised to order.

Feeling she was wasting the morning, Millie packed up the basket with a picnic, including some chocolate from Bella's supposedly secret stash in a Cadbury's tin in the sideboard, and put the notebook and coloured pencils in, too.

She had just let herself out of the cottage when she saw a woman come out of the house next door. She was wearing a pair of wellingtons, and her skirt and jacket were well worn and crumpled. Her hair was tied up in a woollen headscarf, and she had big leather gloves on her hands: work gloves, not fine ones. She had a comfortable, motherly look and a kind face.

'Hello,' she called. 'You must be Millie. Your uncle Thomas told me about you, love.'

Millie racked her brain to try to remember whether she'd been told the woman's name.

'Mrs Cook,' said the neighbour, as if she knew what Millie was thinking. 'I've been a friend of your uncle's for years – and the girls', of course. I'm just going to the allotments – do you want to come with me, or are you off somewhere particular?'

Millie decided that the friendly Mrs Cook might be a useful person to know, so she put her picnic basket in the little front porch, out of sight, and said she'd come along.

'They're only just over there,' said Mrs Cook, 'down that ginnel.' She pointed to a narrow path down the side of the meadow opposite the cottages.

They set off in single file, due to the width of the path, Mrs Cook chatting over her shoulder about her numerous children.

'You must get to know our Edwin,' she said. 'He's not much older than you. He works at the bakery on the High Street – gets up very early, but then he's free for most of the afternoon. I don't know how he has the energy, but he just seems to manage a longer day than most folk. Now, here we are.'

There was a gate and, beyond, a large plot of land divided up into rectangles, each with its own layout and character. Many had funny little sheds at one end, some standing on a slant, clearly made out of old doors or even kitchen cupboards.

'This one is mine, over here in the corner,' said Mrs Cook.

Her allotment was very neat, although her shed was as ramshackle as any of the others. She unlocked it to show tools hung up on hooks, string and labels in a box on the floor, and a wheelbarrow upended.

'Now, I have some weeding to do and I need to mark out a seed bed for some cabbages. Do you want to give me a hand?'

'All right,' said Millie, 'if you show me what to do.'

They chatted as they worked, and Millie told Iris Cook about the garden at the house in Cornwall, with the fat little hens in the orchard.

'I wouldn't mind summat like that,' said Mrs Cook. 'The eggs would be useful. Now, Millie, if you'd like to take the weeds over to the compost – over there, look – that'd be a help while I pack up.'

Millie set off with the wheelbarrow, weaving and wobbling between the plots to get to the far side. The communal compost heap was enormous, a series of smaller heaps making up a mountain range over six foot tall in places. She couldn't tip the barrow high enough to add the weeds to the top, and in the end she had to deposit them at the foot of the vast stack.

She was about to turn away to wheel the barrow back when a huge man, grizzled and unkempt, with tramp-like clothes, his trousers held up with twine and his jacket worn through at the elbows, suddenly sprang out from behind the heap. He was armed with a broad shovel, which he hefted with menace and brought crashing down with lightning speed just where Millie had been standing only a second before.

'Aah!' Millie fell back into the barrow in shock, from where she struggled to escape, kicking her legs and screaming.

'Got you, you little bugger,' yelled the wild man, raising his shovel again.

As he smashed the shovel down a second time, Millie, struggling like an upturned turtle in the barrow, realised, despite her panic and her screaming, that he had no intention of hitting her.

He bent down and picked up a huge brown rat by the tail, its bloody and oozing head horribly crushed, and displayed it proudly to Millie. He was grinning widely, and Millie saw that his gappy teeth were dis-coloured with decay. She didn't know which was worse: the gory sight of the murdered rat or the man's repellent smile.

'Got it first time,' he said slowly. 'Second was just to make sure, like.'

Alerted by Millie's screams, Mrs Cook came panting up as fast as she could.

'William, what on earth are you doing frightening the lass like that?' she said, helping Millie out of the barrow.

'Sorry, missus,' he said, hanging his head. 'Meant no harm.'

'I should think not, indeed. Not to Millie, anyway. That rat looks like it won't be bothering anyone again, though.'

'Got it first time,' William said again, showing his ghastly grin.

'That's grand, William,' Mrs Cook said. 'Now, put that shovel down – yes, and the rat, too – and say hello to my new neighbour, Millie.'

'How do, Millie?' he said, woodenly extending his filthy hand, the same hand that had held up the dead rat.

'Millie, this is William Gladstone,' said Mrs Cook. 'William looks after the compost heap for us here at the allotments and keeps the rats down. He's also a mole-catcher and the scourge of slugs and snails.'

'Hello, William,' said Millie, eyeing him carefully, her hands behind her back.

'Right, now, let's get this barrow put away and then we can be off home,' said Mrs Cook bracingly. 'Goodbye, William.'

'Bye, missus. Bye, M . . .'

As she helped tidy Iris Cook's tools away, Millie kept glancing over at the compost heap, trying to keep an eye on where William Gladstone had got to. He wasn't the kind of person she wanted creeping up behind her.

'It's all right, love,' said Mrs Cook. 'He's harmless unless you're a pest to the allotments. He *claims* his name is William Gladstone, but I have my doubts. Maybe he is called Gladstone and was then named after the prime minister of the time he was born, when I reckon he was dropped on his head. But it's just as likely he's heard the name and thinks it makes him sound important. Mostly you'll hear him called Slow William. He's pretty quick with that shovel, though, I'll give him that.'

'What's he doing here? Seems an odd sort of a job,' said Millie.

'The Allotment Committee employ him to keep away the pests. He comes and goes as he wishes, but he seems to do a very good job.'

'Who are the Allotment Committee?' asked Millie.

'Well, it's me, mostly, but there's a couple of others to keep me in check.' Iris Cook laughed to show she meant this as a joke. 'Now, Millie, love, I'll pull you some of those leeks and you can take 'em home. I know your Bella's pretty handy in the kitchen.'

'Thank you, Mrs Cook.'

On the way back up the path, Mrs Cook continued to chat about her family and her 'old man', by which, Millie soon realised, she meant her husband, not Slow William.

'There's the boat moored at the jetty, down the far

end of the beach,' she said. 'You might want to ask our Edwin to take you out in it one day.'

'A boat of his own?'

'Of *my* own,' corrected the head of the Allotment Committee. 'My old man gave it to me for my birthday the year I turned thirty. He had come into a bit of brass, saved up on top of that, and bought it for me. I'd always had a fancy for a boat, for all it's just a hobby, sailing up to Baybury and back, mostly. Had it made specially, so I was able to choose the name.'

'What did you choose?' asked Millie.

'She's called the *Hope and Peace*. It was just when Mr Chamberlain was declaring he'd secured "peace for our time" and so I thought that was fitting. Fat lot of use that turned out to be – Neville Chamberlain, I mean.'

Millie nodded, which Mrs Cook, ahead of her, couldn't have seen, but it didn't seem to matter. She was talking about her elder daughters, Cath and Joan, now, but Millie wasn't really listening, thinking instead about the boat and also about that strange man William Gladstone.

Millie waved goodbye to Mrs Cook at the gate of number 8, went inside, left the leeks unwashed on the draining board, then collected the basket from the porch as she came out again. The key to the beach hut was safely in her pocket.

Along the High Street, she inspected the shops as she passed them for various opportunities. At the greengrocer's, she helped herself to an apple, hardly breaking her stride as she slipped it into the basket. At another shop, there was a card in the window asking for an assistant, but she saw the place was a chemist's, with a very unpleasant diagram of a foot with bunions in the window and a display of verruca ointment. She didn't even want to think about those things.

The fishmonger was also advertising for an assistant, but Millie looked at the gutted creatures in the window, ice dripping all around them, and knew she couldn't face the glazed look in their dead eyes, nor dealing with their insides.

It was a shame there wasn't an art shop or a place that sold flowers or fat little hens. These were the kinds of things she felt she could happily work with. It was very little, she realised, as she passed the bookshop where Alice worked, and looked in at the piles of dusty books, some titles of which she didn't even know how to pronounce. She had to face it: she couldn't do very much at all. She was out of her depth. She felt anger at her parents igniting again: why hadn't they insisted she was educated and prepared for life?

When she reached the Imperial Hotel, Millie saw the commissionaire was on duty, smiling smarmily at arriving visitors and pocketing tips. She dealt him a fierce look, wishing ill on him as she passed. She bet she could do that job far better than he could.

Sullen with discontent, Millie arrived at the beach hut and let herself in. Without the excitement of the shared picnic and Bella and Alice's enthusiasm for the place that was linked forever in their minds with their mother, the hut felt more desolate than it had on Sunday. Its interior was notably sad-looking today. It really could do with a coat of paint.

Millie set up a deck chair just outside and placed the basket beside her. She took out the notebook and began sketching the view, the railings in the foreground and, beyond them, the strand and the sea. Further along the beach, a young child and his mother were flying a kite with a long tail of coloured paper bows. Millie brought them into her sketch, pleased to add some bright colours in contrast to the grey of the wintry sea. Her bad mood was evaporating now she was working on this view.

'What an excellent picture,' said a female voice, and Millie looked up, realising she'd been concentrating so hard that she hadn't even heard the woman arriving at the neighbouring beach hut.

'Thank you,' she replied.

The woman looked quite old – perhaps fifty, Millie thought – with fair hair peeping out from under her felt hat. Her clothes, in keeping with her voice, were smart: a navy-blue coat with deep patch pockets and a pretty woven scarf around her neck, very like the colourful silky ones that Nanette had liked to buy when she could afford to.

'I don't think I've seen you before, but I'm guessing you're related to Bella and Alice Marchant,' the woman said, speaking a little too loudly. 'Same look about you – very pretty.'

'Yes, they're my cousins. I'm Millie Boyd, and I live with them now.'

'How wonderful,' said the woman, which Millie thought was exactly the right reaction. Clearly this lady knew Bella and Alice well. 'I'm Rosemary Hailsham. I live along there, towards Baybury' – she indicated further along the coastal path with a casual wave of her hand – 'and I've just come to see how the old hut is. I haven't been down over the winter and, actually, Millie, I rather dread to think what I might find.' Already, Mrs Hailsham was adopting a confiding tone, as if she and Millie were friends, not people who had met just this minute.

Mrs Hailsham dug around in one of her deep pockets and produced a key. Then she bent close to the padlock and, after a struggle to insert it, managed to get the lock undone and extracted from the hasp. She carefully opened one door, bending down with difficulty to fasten it back with its hook. For a moment, she stumbled. Millie was on her feet and reaching to help her, but Mrs Hailsham didn't seem to notice and managed the second door more easily.

'Right, nothing for it but to have a look,' she said, taking a deep breath like a swimmer about to dive into cold water, playing up the drama.

By now, Millie was all ready to lend support if the hut was rotting or had had a flood, but when she looked over Mrs Hailsham's shoulder, she saw the interior was no worse than that of Bella and Alice's hut. There were a couple of folded deck chairs and a tiny painted wooden table with tall legs, a grubby-looking glass on it. Standing on the floor by the wall were a couple of empty bottles.

'Oh, dear me,' muttered Mrs Hailsham, peering in at her hut, looking around carefully. Her eyes alighted on the bottles. 'Just as I feared – empties.'

'It's no worse than Bella and Alice's,' Millie said, hoping to prevent Mrs Hailsham getting upset. Why was she so anxious? Bella and Alice hadn't been very bothered about the state of theirs. 'Perhaps it just needs a coat of paint.'

'Paint? Mm, you may well be right, Millie, dear.' The woman's tone was affectionate already, and she turned and looked right at Millie, smiling. 'What colour do you think I should have it painted?'

'What colour would you like it to be?' *And why are you asking me?*

'Oh, wallpaper would be nice, don't you think? Something floral and pretty.' She laughed loudly, almost as if she knew she was being charmingly silly.

'I don't think wallpaper would work well in a beach hut, Mrs Hailsham,' Millie said seriously. 'It would soon fall off the walls with the damp.'

'Yes, yes, I think I might be thinking along the wrong lines there . . .' she said vaguely. 'But a little home from home would be nice, don't you think? Somewhere I can come to get away from . . . prying eyes.'

Then Millie had an idea – a very brilliant one, she thought.

'If you really want flowers, you could have them painted on the walls. I could do that for you, if you like?'

'Goodness! What a marvellous idea. I do believe you're a genius,' gushed Mrs Hailsham. 'But could you really make it *lovely* for me?'

'Oh, yes. It just needs preparing, and then I can do it in a few days,' said Millie, who had seen her mother do something similar. Nanette had had several commissions from her friends once word had gone round of her talent for painting murals. 'All you have to do is choose the colours and buy the paint, and I'll do the rest. My terms are quite reasonable,' she added, so Mrs Hailsham should be in no doubt that this was a commercial transaction, not a favour.

'Splendid.' Rosemary Hailsham beamed. 'You really are a life-saver.'

Millie didn't understand in what way this could possibly be true, but by now it was clear the lady had an exaggerated style of talking that was all her own.

'I charge, er, two shillings an hour, and I think it will take me three days,' said Millie, determined to keep on the subject of her terms, and hoping this sounded about right.

Mrs Hailsham looked as if she was trying to decide if this was fair, and Millie held her breath. She hardly knew if it was reasonable herself; she'd just pulled the figure out of thin air.

'Very well,' said the lady. 'But do you have any references at all? The names of some people who can tell me what a truly marvellous painter of beach huts you are?'

'No, I'm afraid not,' said Millie, now fearing Mrs Hailsham had got her measure and was laughing at her. But she was determined not to let control of the situation slip away from her altogether. 'I'm new here, you see. I used to live . . . and work . . . I used to work in Cornwall where my parents were well-known artists. They taught me their techniques, and I painted murals on the walls in their house. I did the whole house last summer. I painted their friends' houses, too.'

'Indeed? That sounds delightful. But, oh dear, I fear it must be a bit of a come-down for you to be painting a mere beach hut.'

'I don't mind,' said Millie, deciding she'd better not add anything else to her stories in case she got carried away and then couldn't remember later what she'd said. 'When would you like me to start?'

'How about on Monday morning?'

Millie pretended to give this some thought. 'Yes, I can manage that,' she said.

'Splendid,' beamed Mrs Hailsham. 'I shall see you here then.'

She locked up her hut, taking exaggerated care, gave a little sigh and, with a wave to Millie, meandered off up the path towards Baybury.

Millie hugged herself, grinning. A job, just like that! And at two shillings an hour! Perhaps, when she'd painted the beach hut, Rosemary Hailsham would recommend her to her friends and there would be lots more work, just as had happened with Mum.

Millie decided she would stay here and work on some more sketches. It was possible that someone who owned one of the other huts would come by and admire her work and that might lead to another painting job, if today was her lucky day.

Having eaten her picnic, including both the chocolate Flakes she'd pilfered from Bella's tin, Millie decided to plan her design. After all, she had to look professional. She had a feeling she had teetered on the brink of being found out to be . . . exaggerating her experience already. It wasn't, strictly speaking, lies, she reasoned, just a different version of the truth, some of which had yet to happen.

She was sketching out a pretty wild-flower-meadow design when she happened to glance up and see, beyond the railings, a figure she thought she recognised, walking along the beach. As she had met few people until today, this seemed unlikely, and she leaned forward to get a better look.

It was a tall man, slightly flashily dressed in an overcoat with a curly fur collar, and highly polished shoes. Millie saw as he came nearer that without a doubt it was Sidney Bennett, the man Bella was going to marry. And walking beside him, talking and laughing in a flirty kind of way, was a woman who most definitely was not Bella.

The woman was also quite showily dressed, wearing a hat with a big bow on the front of it. She had a pretty face, and her hair was blonde.

As quickly as she could, Millie packed up her things, locked the beach hut door and set off along the Promenade, keeping the pair in sight. She was behind them now and could see only their backs, but they were clearly talking, their heads close together. At one set of steps, they came up onto the Promenade ahead of Millie, then stood together, talking a little more. Millie slowed down, knowing she would not get close enough to hear anything without their noticing her.

Then, with a wave and a smile, the woman walked on, and Sidney Bennett crossed over the road and went down the street that ran parallel to the High Street, whistling, his hands in his pockets. A signpost at the road end indicated it was the way to the town hall and the station.

Which of them to follow? Maybe this was an innocent encounter after all. They hadn't kissed on parting. Perhaps Sidney Bennett had a sister, although their colouring was not alike, and the woman had had quite a familiar manner, leaning into him and clutching his arm. Millie decided to follow her. Even if she was noticed, the woman would not recognise Millie, of course.

The blonde woman soon crossed the road and went up the steps to the hotel. Millie was close behind her now. The commissionaire opened the door very promptly to her and said, 'Good afternoon, Miss Chalfont,' with exaggerated deference.

Chalfont – Millie racked her brain to remember where she'd heard the name. Hadn't Bella or Alice told her that the Chalfonts owned the hotel? So that explained why the doorman had been even smarmier than usual, and why the woman had swept into the hotel with such confidence.

There was no reason why this Chalfont woman should not be a friend of Sidney Bennett's, of course, but from the way Bella had joked about the pretensions of the Chalfonts, Millie doubted whether Bella was a friend of the Chalfont woman.

That evening, Millie was keen to share the news about the prospect of her first paid work. While Bella made Mrs Cook's leeks into soup, and Alice and Thomas read their post, and everyone drank tea, Millie told them about it, although she didn't volunteer her hourly rate. She still wasn't sure if she'd made a mistake about that.

'For Mrs Hailsham, you say?' queried Bella, turning from her pan to look at Millie properly.

'Yes, I told you. She mentioned your names when she came to open up her beach hut.'

'And how did you find the lady?' asked Thomas.

'Nice, though a bit . . . dramatic. It's the way she has of talking.'

'It's the way she has of living,' said Alice. 'Major Hailsham was killed in the war, and poor Mrs Hailsham has found it . . . hard to cope. Their daughter lives with her and looks after her. Mrs Hailsham would be lost without her.'

'Hard to cope' sounded worrying.

'So is she struggling – I mean, to make ends meet?' asked Millie, anxious about her two shillings an hour, although the lady *had* agreed to it.

'Not financially, so far as I know,' said Alice. 'It's no business of mine, but I gather she's rather well off.'

'It's life she's having more of a struggle with, I think,' said Bella, using a tone that implied there were things she wasn't saying. 'Everything is always . . . a big drama to her, as if she's always on the brink of disaster, even with everyday things.'

'But she isn't?' asked Millie.

'Oh, no, the daughter sees to everything for her. It's just Mrs Hailsham's perception that things are so difficult. Perhaps they are, for her. She's a nice woman, very charming, but I wouldn't want to be her very best friend or her daughter – far too much hard work.'

'I see,' said Millie, relieved that her job was safe after all. 'Rather well off' at least meant Mrs Hailsham would pay up, which was the whole point of the work, of course.

'Anyway, well done about your decorating commission. You've got off to a flying start,' said Thomas.

Alice raised her teacup in a toast to Millie, and Bella gave her a warm hug and whispered, 'Well done, sweetheart.'

Millie put her worries aside.

'I met Sidney as I was coming out of the shop,' said Bella, tasting the soup then adding salt.

'How is he?' asked Thomas.

'Hard at work on town hall business – I don't know

what. He says Planning is very busy and he's barely looked up from his desk there all day. Mr Penrose has been cracking the whip and has been running all his subordinates ragged, apparently. Sidney's mother has invited me to tea again on Saturday, and I've said I'll go. I'll make her a cake and take some flowers.'

'That's kind,' said Thomas. 'I hope she'll be kind in return.'

'Well, I'm hoping the presents will win her over.'

'Honestly, Bella, what's the matter with the woman?' asked Alice crossly. 'You're going to marry her son and she should be pleased and proud, not need "winning over". She should be able to see what an asset you are. Sidney is a very lucky man.'

'Thank you, Alice. She'll come round in the end,' said Bella. 'I'm quite determined about it. After all, she wants us to live with her, Sidney says, and she wouldn't want that if she didn't like me. I think mebbe she lacks charm – the opposite of Mrs Hailsham.'

'I hope at least she *likes* you, even if she isn't much good at showing it,' said Thomas. 'You know, you could wait to marry and save up a while longer for a house of your own.'

'But I do want to be married to Sidney as soon as we can. September will be lovely, and I've got my dress pattern – I've just got to save up to buy the fabric – and I'm thinking about the reception and everything. It's just living with Mrs Bennett that I'm worried I might find a bit difficult. Mebbe it won't be for very long.

Sidney's doing well in Planning, and he's got an eye on promotion.'

'Up to you, Bella,' said Alice, putting spoons on the table. 'You have to think what your choices are: marry in the autumn and live at Mrs B's, or wait to marry until you've saved up a deposit for your own place.'

'But there's also Sidney's wishes to take into consideration,' said Bella. 'He's quite keen we should live at his mother's, and he says he doesn't want her to be offended by our not taking up her kind offer.'

'Well, he would say that,' said Alice. 'He's her only child, and she makes a huge fuss of him – of course he wants that to continue. I expect he's looking forward to having both you and his mother fussing around him.'

'Oh, I don't think so,' said Bella, frowning. 'I think he also wants us to marry as soon as we can, and that's really lovely and romantic. He's pleased his mother's made this generous offer to accommodate us so we can be married sooner rather than later.'

Millie saw Alice catch Thomas's eye and shake her head in an exasperated fashion.

Millie thought Sidney Bennett's mother sounded like a real old baggage if she was going out of her way to be awkward with Bella. She thought about the blonde woman, Chalfont, flirting with Sidney on the beach, the way she'd strode into the hotel as if she owned the place, which possibly she did, and that doorman bowing to her as if she were royalty. And Sidney Bennett certainly hadn't been at his desk all day; he had lied to Bella about that. Bella should know about this, but Millie decided it was better to tell her alone. It wasn't always a good idea just to blurt things out, she was learning.

Wednesday was half-day closing in Theddleton, which meant Alice and Bella were not at work. Alice went to see their friend Vera Hoskins in Baybury. Bella offered to look in her wardrobe to see if there was anything she could alter to fit Millie, who had very few warm clothes, but when she brought out the garments she hadn't worn lately, they looked threadbare and tired.

'I'm sorry. I can't expect you to wear any of these. Honestly, Millie, I think we could all do with new clothes.' Bella sighed. 'Perhaps I'll have to try one of those competitions in the newspapers to win a cash prize. That would help with the wedding, too. Even Alice's lovely coat is looking a little shiny at the elbows.'

'Perhaps when I've started my job at Mrs Hailsham's beach hut, people will come by and see it, and I'll get lots more work,' said Millie hopefully. She was so looking forward to having some money in her pocket and was already making plans about how she would spend it. Obviously, she'd have to give some to Alice, who did the household accounts, for her keep, but now it seemed that everyone needed new clothes, not just herself. It was easy to see why most people never had enough money.

Her parents had spent their money when they had it: the rent and painting materials first, of course, but then nice food, entertaining their friends, visits to interesting places, gramophone records, wine and cider and cigarettes. When the money ran out, they had just reined in their spending again until they had some more. In contrast, the Blackburn Marchants never admitted to allowing themselves any fun at all. Or, at least, that was the impression they both liked to give.

'It would be lovely if Mrs Hailsham's beach hut did lead to lots more work, sweetheart, but I wouldn't bet on it,' said Bella. 'However good the mural – and I'm sure it will be beautiful – you'll need potential clients not only to see it but also to want to have their huts done as well, and to be able to afford that. Not everyone is as well off as I believe Mrs Hailsham is. And it will be hard for you to make a go of it as a painter, you being so very young and none of us knowing the kind of people who want paintings.'

'Well, perhaps she'd like me to decorate her house when I've done the beach hut.'

'You could always ask her. She does live in a big house; it's further along the path to Baybury. I think it belonged to Major Hailsham's family, but she's got it now, and all the inheritance, so the story goes.'

This all sounded very hopeful for future commissions, Millie decided.

Bella, sitting on her bed amid a pile of disappointing clothes, suddenly leaped to her feet and ran from the room, calling, 'I've just had the most brilliant idea, Millie.'

Millie heard Bella's feet drumming on the stairs as she rushed down, then, almost immediately, came back up more slowly.

'I'd put this behind the clock and only remembered it just now.' She handed Millie the voucher for Cathy's dress shop, which Muriel Chalfont had won at the fund-raising do.

Millie looked carefully at it. The text was easy enough for her to read without hesitation, and she was plummeted into disappointment.

'Cathy's? But that's the place on the High Street with old-fashioned clothes in the window, and the things look as if they're for quite large women, too.'

'True, Millie, but this is the idea. How about we use the voucher to buy the biggest frock we can find? It will need to be in a nice colour, of course, something you want to wear, but the style doesn't matter. In fact, the more tent-like, the better. More fabric, see? And I'll just rip out the seams, lay it all flat and use the fabric to make you something new that fits. If it's really huge I could make you a couple of dresses, or a jacket and skirt. What do you reckon?'

'Brilliant! Thank you, Bella. But promise you won't make me wear anything old-lady brown or dull old-lady blue?' Millie was thinking of Aunt Mona, but she wouldn't say the name aloud.

'No, I told you. And if you choose something not too fancy, it can make some smart, everyday sort of clothes for you: a pinafore dress you can wear different blouses underneath, or a gathered skirt. I'll make it nice and you can choose your favourite colours.'

'I'd like a coat like Alice's, with those long seams and big pockets.'

'So would I, Millie, but I think you and I are going to have to dream on where that is concerned. Promise me one thing, though, and this is really serious.'

'What?' said Millie suspiciously, thinking she might have to do something disagreeable in return.

'Just be polite and respectful to Cathy in the shop. Let me do the talking, and on no account be rude about the clothes and the sizes. Cathy is a really kind lady and, though her shop may not be to our tastes, Cathy is clever enough to know who her customers are and what they want, all right?'

'All right,' Millie agreed. 'I'll button my lip.'

'You do that, sweetheart.'

'But, Bella, there is one thing I can't button my lip about.'

'What's that?' Bella looked anxious, picking up Millie's tone.

'It was after I met Mrs Hailsham. I saw Sidney walking on the beach with a pretty lady, blonde, flirty. She went in the hotel, and I think I heard her being called Miss Chalfont.'

Bella opened her eyes wide in surprise. 'But I saw Sidney later, and he said he'd been hard at work at the town hall all day. I even said I was sorry for him, Mr Penrose being so strict a boss.'

'Exactly. That's why I'm telling you, Bella. I absolutely promise I'm not lying that I saw them.'

The way Millie said this made Bella think that her young cousin did tell lies, but this wasn't one of those times.

'Mm, I'll just have to ask him,' she said. 'I'm sure there's a good explanation.'

But, just at that moment, she couldn't think what it could possibly be.

By the Friday evening, Bella had spent every minute of her free time sewing for Millie and had turned a very large dress with a wide skirt and long sleeves, in a pretty blue and violet print, into two skirts in different styles and a matching jacket for Millie. In addition, she'd altered an old blouse of her own to fit Millie – 'I know it's a bit worn, but don't worry, no one will see under the jacket' – and made Millie a painting smock out of an old shirt of Thomas's.

'Now you'll look the part when you start work on the beach hut on Monday.'

'Thank you, Bella,' said Millie, as pleased with the smock as she was with the skirts and jacket.

She hugged Bella and secretly vowed to replace the chocolate she'd stolen from Bella's tin, spending the tip she had been given by mistake at the door to the hotel. She'd better do that straight away, before Bella discovered the theft. The longer she lived at number 8, the more Millie realised that the Marchants really didn't have a lot of anything to share, apart from love. Bella and Alice, on the face of it, were very generous with their affection. Thomas, too. But, Millie reminded herself, she had been here only two weeks. It was too early yet to overlook Thomas's betrayal of her mother. The point about betrayal was that you didn't see it coming.

# CHAPTER EIGHT

ELLA KNOCKED ON the door of Mrs Bennett's
house at number 14 Wellington Road. All the
curtains were closed and the place had a locked-up look
about it. In Bella's hand was a bouquet of spring flowers
– a few daffodils from the greengrocer's, supplemented
by a special variety that Thomas was growing in the back
garden, all tied up prettily with a ribbon around them.
She also carried, in a string bag, a tin containing a very
light sponge cake, sandwiched with buttercream and
apricot jam. Sponges were Bella's speciality, and she was
pleased to present to Mrs Bennett something home-
made that she thought her future mother-in-law would
like and over which she'd taken great care.

Soon, the door curtains were drawn back so that the hall
light showed through the fanlight and, after much fiddling
with the lock, Mrs Bennett opened the door a crack and
peered out. It didn't look as if she was expecting anyone,
and Bella was suddenly unsure if she had got the right day.

150

'Hello, Bella. Come in and let's get the door closed. There's an awful draught off the sea, and it's doing my rheumatics no good at all,' said Mrs Bennett, opening the door barely wide enough for Bella to squeeze inside.

'Thank you for asking me round, Mrs Bennett,' said Bella, trying not to catch her feet in the curtains, then handing over the flowers. 'I hope you like daffodils. Dad grew most of them.'

'Oh, aye? Yellow,' said Mrs Bennett with a sigh, but she did not explain. She took them from Bella in a disappointed way.

'I've made you a cake,' said Bella, offering the tin and hoping the apricot jam would not be too 'yellow' for Mrs Bennett. *Thank goodness I didn't sandwich it with lemon curd.*

'We've got cake, thank you, Bella. I'm hoping my cake will be good enough for you.'

'But of course. No, this is for *you*, for another time – save you baking when . . . whenever you were next going to . . .' said Bella, smiling sweetly, but now anxious she'd inadvertently caused offence. 'I wasn't expecting you'd want to eat it today. It's a present.'

'Oh. Right-o then, Bella. I'll have a look at it later.' Mrs Bennett took the tin and carried it into her kitchen, giving the impression that the gift of a cake was a burden she could do without.

Oh dear, that had not gone down well.

She came back and hung Bella's coat up for her, then leaned into the stairwell with her head back and shouted, 'Sid-neeey!' at astonishing volume. Nancy Bennett was a short, thin woman, quite birdlike, and although Bella had heard this particular summons before, she was surprised every time that someone so insubstantial-looking could make so raucous a noise.

'All right, Mam!' yelled Sidney, equally loudly, coming downstairs.

'Hello, Bella.' He kissed her cheek in the brotherly way he always did when at home, as if shy of showing her any romantic affection at all in his mother's presence. 'Come and sit down, take the weight off.'

With all the dressmaking, Bella hadn't seen Sidney to ask him about his walk with Muriel when he said he'd been at the office all day, but she could hardly demand an explanation now.

'Glad you could come *this week*, Bella,' said Mrs Bennett, following them into the dining room with a teapot. 'I was right put out you rejected my invitation last time.'

'Oh, no, it wasn't a rejection at all,' said Bella. 'As I said the other day, I had already arranged to go to see my relatives in Blackburn.'

'Ah, yes, Lancashire,' muttered Mrs Bennett with a sniff of disdain. 'Well, never mind, you're here now.'

There was a pause.

'This all looks lovely,' said Bella, admiring the tea table. 'You've obviously gone to a great deal of trouble to make it all so nice. Thank you.'

'I like to make an effort,' said Mrs Bennett, sounding martyred.

'Mam always puts on a grand spread, don't you, Mam?'

'I have my standards. Now, Bella, let me pour you a cup of tea and you can tell me about your visit to Lancashire. Genteel kind of folk, are they, your relatives? Help yourself to milk.'

*What a strange question.* 'Not so you'd notice, Mrs Bennett. I don't know as anyone I'm related to is what you might call "genteel".'

'That's a shame, but, well, I thought p'raps not. I'm just wondering how that young cousin of yours is fitting in, like.'

'Millie, she's called, and so far she fits in very well, thank you,' said Bella, determined to be charming. 'Her parents were killed in a car accident a few months ago, a terrible tragedy, and now Millie lives with us – me and Dad and Alice.'

'I'm sorry to hear that,' said Mrs Bennett ambiguously, passing Bella a plate of slices of tongue. 'There's a lot of it about – car accidents; folk driving too fast.'

'I don't know what happened,' said Bella, taking a piece of tongue and hoping her tone of finality would curtail this line of conversation.

'Here, Bella, have some lettuce with that,' said Sidney, passing a bowl of salad. He turned to his mother. 'But, Mam, I did tell you, Bella says this Millie is stopping with her dad and her sister when we're married.'

'Is that right, Bella, love? Only, I need to be sure. I can't be doing with anyone else coming with you. We're not a hotel, and space is a bit limited.'

'Yes, of course,' said Bella.

By now, Bella was wondering what had got into Sidney and his mother. First he, and now she, seemed very keen to know that Millie would not be encroaching on their lives.

'Please be assured, Mrs Bennett, that when I marry Sidney in September, I will not be bringing Millie to your house with me.'

'Well, that's a relief,' said Mrs Bennett, and she did indeed look relieved.

She had evidently been worrying, and Bella suddenly felt a bit sorry for her. She'd lived here with Sidney, just the two of them, for many years now, and it was under-standable that she wanted as little disruption as possible in her well-established pattern of life. She'd generously offered to accommodate the newly-weds, and the possi-bility of a young cousin coming too would, of course, have made her anxious.

'And it's September for the wedding?' said Mrs Bennett, sounding surprised as she passed round a plate of bread and margarine. 'Seems very soon to me. You don't want to rush into these things. Better to take your time.'

'September's the plan,' smiled Bella. 'Didn't Sidney tell you? It fits in nicely with the shop.'

'The *shop*?'

'Well . . . yes. Mr and Mrs Warminster are busy in the summer season, with all the visitors, and very busy in the run-up to Christmas. I want to avoid getting married when they really need me there.'

'My son's wedding, planned to fit in with a toyshop? I see! And what about us?' said Mrs Bennett, looking affronted. 'I like to go to my sister's in Birmingham in September. What about fitting in with me?'

For a moment, Bella didn't know what to say that was not a snappy retort – surely, as the bride, her own wishes came first – but she swallowed down her anger and took a deep breath.

'Well, I'm sure Sidney's aunt is to be invited to the wedding,' she said. 'It will be lovely to meet her. You can spend time with your sister, and you can both enjoy the wedding.'

'Well, of course, if it *must* be September, she'll want to be here, instead of me going there, like I reckoned to do. But where's she supposed to stay?'

By now, Bella was wishing she was at home with her dad and Alice and Millie, exchanging news about their day at the shops and the inn, and looking at the excellent sketches Millie was doing every day at the seafront in the hope of catching the eye of someone else who would employ her, in addition to Mrs Hailsham.

'. . . of course,' Sidney was saying. Bella, distracted, hadn't heard the first part. 'Or even at the Imperial. She's not short of a bob or two, from what I've seen, and mebbe the hotel would suit her better.'

'You could have a word with *Muriel Chalfont*, see if she can get you a special rate for your auntie Beverley, if it comes to that,' said Mrs Bennett, emphasising Muriel's name in a clanger of a name-drop, and looking to see if Bella was impressed.

'I didn't know you knew Muriel Chalfont well enough to be asking favours of her, Sidney,' said Bella, lightly. 'Although didn't you see her earlier in the week – a walk along the beach, wasn't it?'

Sidney looked flabbergasted for a moment. Then he said, 'But we both know Muriel, don't we, Bella? Since school.'

'Yes, *know* her, but not as a friend. It's just that I thought you said you'd been too busy to leave your desk.'

'Well, if Sidney said that, it must have been right,' said Mrs Bennett.

At the same time, Sidney, looking relieved, said, 'Oh, I know what it was. One day I was on a site visit, and that must have been when I saw Muriel. On the way back to the office.'

Not everything about this added up to Bella, but she could hardly pursue it and start an argument.

'Anyway,' said Sidney, looking embarrassed, 'I've mentioned the Chalfonts once or twice, to do with some planning applications at work, and I reckon Mam's got the idea that I know them better than I do.' He looked at his mother very hard.

'Oh, I just thought—' began Mrs Bennett.

'Perhaps Auntie Beverley would be happier at one of the guesthouses,' Sidney interrupted. 'Bella, you could choose your favourite, someone you know, and reserve some rooms for our guests, couldn't you?'

'Of course,' said Bella. 'There's the one belonging to Mrs Edwards, Mr Warminster's sister.'

'There you are, then, Mam. All organised,' said Sidney, rubbing his hands together as if he was about to get stuck into a heavy task.

'Let me have your sister's address, Mrs Bennett, and I'll be sure she has an invitation,' said Bella.

'I'll warn her,' said Mrs Bennett. 'Now, Bella, would you like some more bread and marg, or some salad cream on that lettuce . . . ?'

After tea, Sidney and Bella cleared the table, and Bella suggested the two of them could wash up while Mrs Bennett had a sit-down, but Sidney's mother was having none of that.

'Oh, no. Sidney was playing football this morning and must be absolutely worn out,' she said, sounding as if she thought Bella had overstepped the mark, suggesting who was to do the chores in her house. 'You sit and read the paper, Sidney, love, and Bella can wash while I dry.'

Bella had been at the shop all day, which was often heaving with noisy children on a Saturday, but she was too polite to mention that.

It soon became apparent why Nancy Bennett wanted to get Bella alone.

'You know, there's no rush to be married, Bella,' she said, drying her salad bowl while Bella rinsed the soap suds off the teacups. 'Perhaps you could wait until next year. After all, it would be even more convenient for the shop in the autumn, wouldn't it, if you were never absent at all?'

Bella turned to look at her carefully, trying to work out what it was she wasn't saying.

'And it isn't as if my Sidney's even bought you a ring yet, is it?'

'He's saving up for a nice one,' said Bella, on the back foot. Now she thought about it, Sidney did seem to have plenty of smart new clothes – his bright ties, that nice winter coat with the astrakhan collar – but his saving up for the ring had been going on for months, with no end in sight, so far as Bella knew. He was never mean with her when they went out – was very generous, in fact – and he mentioned his intention to buy her a ring from time to time but so far had not done so.

'Without a ring, no one even knows for sure you're engaged.'

Bella felt a sudden chill in her stomach. Was Sidney's mother trying to back him out of marrying her? It was clear now that, for whatever reason, Mrs Bennett wasn't keen for the wedding to go ahead, not just in September, but possibly ever.

'Sidney and I know,' said Bella, 'and that's what matters.'

'Ah well, you'll have to see how it works out, won't you?' said the reluctant future mother-in-law. 'But I don't see there's any need to hurry.'

* * *

'Oh, Alice, I don't know what she was getting at. It sounded like she didn't want me to marry Sidney at all,' said Bella, telling her sister all about it the next morning, after Thomas had gone to work; Millie hadn't yet put in an appearance. 'It was a horrible tea in every way, and I really wish I hadn't gone.'

'Awful woman. But isn't she always rude?' asked Alice. 'She's the type to boast she "calls a spade a spade", using it as an excuse to trample thoughtlessly all over other people's feelings, while being "offended" at the slightest thing, real or imagined, coming her way.'

'Mm, that does about sum her up. I thought I was winning her round, and now she seems to have turned against me, and I don't even know why.'

'Nowt to do with owt you've done,' said Alice with certainty.

'It was very odd, but she asked if my Blackburn relatives were "genteel". Who asks that sort of thing? When I'd got over my surprise, obviously I said they weren't, and then the next thing I know it's as if I'm suddenly not good enough for Sidney. She was making up all kinds of reasons for us not to be married as soon as September.'

'You're the same sweet, kind, lovely Bella that you've always been,' said Alice, 'and, as I said the other day, if Mrs B is too stupid to appreciate what a treasure you are – how completely fortunate Sidney is to be going to marry you – then more fool her. She's certainly nowt to be snobbish about, ridiculous woman.'

'Mm, you're right about that. She *is* ridiculous. Genteel, indeed! I wonder if Mrs Bennett and Aunt Mona don't have summat in common.'

Alice laughed. 'Probably.'

'How could *I* have relatives anyone would describe as "genteel"?'

'Slander! There's me, for a start.'

They both started giggling, and Millie appeared then, brushing her hair and wearing her cardigans over her nightie.

'But not Millie, brushing her hair in the kitchen,' said Alice.

'What about me?'

'Not genteel.'

'Heavens, I should hope not,' said Millie, sounding so assured and grown-up that she set the sisters off laughing again. 'That's just what Mum used to say,' she explained.

'I think she must have been a very wise woman,' said Alice.

'Only in some ways,' said Millie.

'Anyway, whatever Mrs Bennett says, I still want to marry Sidney,' said Bella, pouring a cup of tea for Millie, and putting some bread to toast under the grill. 'It's just . . .'

'I know, Bella,' said Alice. 'As we said the other day, you could always put off the wedding for a few months, save up for your own place and have as little to do with Mrs B as possible. Dad isn't keen to get rid of you, and

Millie's only just found you. Even I could put up with you for a while longer, as I don't think I'm going anywhere.' She grinned.

'Well, you're going for a ride along the coast today,' said Bella, 'and I'm all ready to note down the description of Mr Reeves to help the police with their inquiries if you don't return.'

'You may mock, but it's as well to be careful,' said Alice. 'His telephone number is behind the clock, if you need it.'

'Daft thing – you'll have a lovely time. And you do look very nice in that green frock. Millie, will you put some clothes on when you've had this toast, please? I don't want Mr Reeves turning up and seeing you in your nightie.'

'I'm practising not being genteel,' said Millie, laughing.

How quickly their cousin had become one of them – or almost, Bella thought.

It was just a feeling she had, but there was something a little bit wild, a little bit unknown, about Millie still, like a young cat that wasn't really tame, and might equally well turn with a snarl and bared claws as purr on your knee.

At half past ten, a primrose-yellow and black Rolls-Royce drew up outside number 8 Chapel Lane, looking very polished and quite the grandest thing any of the girls had ever seen. Alice was out of the cottage in a trice, with Bella and Millie close behind, ready to be sure they had seen Mr Reeves and would be able to describe him to the police in the event of Alice's abduction, as if the car wasn't enough to identify him. Bella was taking this only half seriously, and Millie wasn't taking it seriously at all. The atmosphere, so down and unpromising to start with that morning, had taken on the air of a holiday with Alice's outing now underway.

But the person who got out of the driver's seat and came round to meet them was definitely not *Mr* Reeves. It was a tall and strikingly beautiful blonde woman in her late twenties, wearing a dark-blue velvet coat that exactly matched the colour of her eyes.

'Good morning. I'm Bobbie Reeves,' she said, extending her hand first to Alice, the one obviously dressed for an outing.

'Oh . . . I hadn't expected you. Good morning, Mrs Reeves. I think we spoke on the telephone. I was expecting Mr Reeves – I don't quite know why.'

'I hope you're not disappointed,' Bobbie Reeves said, 'but my father doesn't get around very easily these days, so he lets me drive his car. And it's *Miss* Reeves.'

'Miss Reeves, I am Alice Marchant. This is my sister, Bella, and my cousin, Millie.'

'We just came to see you off,' said Bella, treading on Millie's foot because she just *knew* she was about to disclose the reason for the reception party. 'I hope you have a lovely ride, Alice.'

Alice looked completely delighted not to have to worry about getting into the car with a strange man. Bobbie

Reeves opened the front passenger door for her and then carefully tucked the skirt of her coat inside when she was seated on the gorgeous fawn leather.

Bobbie Reeves turned the car with only a little difficulty in the narrow gateway to the meadow opposite and drove off, Alice beaming and waving from her seat.

'Crikey,' said Bella. 'I wasn't expecting that.'

'At least we don't have to worry about Alice being abducted,' said Millie.

The outing was a huge success, and Alice returned in a very good mood, giving her account of the day as they all sat down to their dinner. Bella had cooked the food with Millie's help, which she felt had been more of a hindrance. Millie would keep adding ingredients to the pans without asking, taking a free-spirited approach to the cooking and explaining that this was what her parents liked to do. They seemed to have got through an unusually large amount of butter since Millie's arrival.

'Bobbie is such a good driver. I can't think how she manages so huge a car, but she drives with such confidence. I doubt I could ever do that,' Alice said.

'I doubt you'll get the chance,' said Thomas. 'Where did she take you?'

'Oh, up past Baybury, towards Scarborough. The views were amazing. We stopped for a picnic on the way, then a cup of tea on the way back. She made the whole day a lovely treat. Thank you for giving me your prize, Bella.'

'That's all right,' Bella said. 'I'm glad you had a nice time.'

She hadn't imagined she'd won more than a run up just beyond Baybury and back in a showy car, but an entire day out was far more generous, and she tried not to mind that she would, in fact, have enjoyed the outing herself, had she wanted to go alone. Well, she could have done, and the fact that she hadn't was her own fault. No use lamenting over it.

'What did you have to eat?' asked Millie, always interested in food.

Alice enthusiastically described the many delicious-sounding dishes that had emerged from a vast hamper in the boot of the car.

'You'll think our picnics at the beach hut are quite a come-down,' said Bella.

'Never!' said Alice. 'This was a one-off occasion and doubtless I shall soon forget all about it. Our beach-hut picnics are always special because Mam left the hut to us, and we used to have picnics with her there when we were very little. Nowt can be better than that precious memory.'

Bella was so pleased to hear Alice say that. She'd feared for a moment that Alice's head might have been turned by game pie and fresh pickles and white wine and other fancy stuff that Bella had never tasted. It would be a terrible shame if the simple pleasure of a sausage roll washed down with Camp Coffee were over-shadowed for all time.

'And what was Miss Reeves like?' she asked.

'Nice. Kind. Determined that the prize should be a special treat for me. She didn't need to go to so much trouble, but she was very generous, what with her time and the picnic.'

'What does she do?' asked Thomas.

'I'm not quite sure,' said Alice. 'The car belongs to her father, who's got a gammy leg – from the war, she said – so now she drives it, but I don't think she takes it out all that often. She's not one to talk all about herself, and I didn't like to ask too many questions in case I sounded rude. I think she's some kind of book-keeper.'

'A career woman,' said Thomas.

'Honestly, Dad, what's odd about that? Lots of unmarried woman have to support themselves these days.'

Some of us have to support our father, too, thought Bella, then mentally slapped herself down for being mean-minded.

'Nowt odd at all, love. Just saying,' said Thomas. 'Just trying to place her, that's all.'

'Well, it doesn't matter really whether you can place her or not,' said Alice. 'I've had a special day, but it was one lovely outing and that's the beginning and end of it.'

Bella hoped it wasn't entirely the end of it, though. It was a long time since she had seen Alice looking so . . . sparkly.

# CHAPTER NINE

MILLIE REALISED SHE hadn't arranged a specific time to meet Mrs Hailsham at the beach hut, but, no matter; if she got there by nine o'clock in the morning, she very much doubted she would miss the lady.

It was a cold day with a very stiff breeze blowing in from the sea. Millie opened up Bella and Alice's hut and hooked back one of the doors. It was too cold to set up a deck chair outside on the wide path and wait there for Mrs Hailsham, so she sat just inside, huddled into her coat, Bella's Fair Isle beret pulled down over her ears, and waited. And waited.

She had brought her notebook and coloured pencils, ready to show Mrs Hailsham her wild-flower design, and a couple of alternatives she'd dreamed up, but she was soon distracted by the wait. How much longer was Mrs Hailsham going to be? After an hour and a half, she had lost all concentration for any further sketching.

What had happened to Mrs Hailsham? Perhaps she

was ill. But she lived with her daughter, so the daughter could have come here with the paint and explained. The job wouldn't *not* go ahead just because Mrs Hailsham had a cold or something, surely?

It couldn't be that Mrs Hailsham had simply forgotten, could it? But they had had an entire conversation about it. It had seemed important to her last week, so what had happened between then and now? It just didn't make sense.

As the hands on her watch ticked round to eleven thirty, Millie realised she'd made a mistake overlooking fixing a time to meet, but she had a sinking feeling about the whole enterprise, too. This job, which meant so much to her – her first paid work in Theddleton, and the start of her brilliant painting career – just wasn't going to happen. She must face it: the longer she waited, the longer she would wait. No one was coming.

Mrs Hailsham had said she lived 'along there', and had indicated the path in the direction of Baybury. She had seemed to have arrived at her beach hut on foot, so probably she lived quite nearby. Millie closed the door, locked it, and marched off up the path, determined to find out what was going on.

The row of beach huts seemed to mark the edge of Theddleton. After them, the seafront path narrowed and there was an expanse of tough-looking grass blowing alongside it. At the other side of that now ran a road parallel to the footpath, serving the houses along the further side of it. Millie veered off across the grass to look at the houses. They faced the sea but stood well back, with long front gardens.

The first one had huge gates and was rather grand, with big windows. So was the next one and the third. Maybe one of these was Mrs Hailsham's house, but, if so, which one?

Millie was just about to go to ask at the first house when a postman came down the road towards her on his bicycle. That was a piece of luck.

'Excuse me, please,' said Millie, when he had drawn to a halt and dismounted, 'I need to speak to Mrs Hailsham – do you know if she lives nearby?'

'I do,' said the man. 'She lives in this house here.' He indicated the middle one of the three. 'I have some post for her now.'

'I can give it to her, if you like,' said Millie.

'No, thank you. It's my job to make sure it gets to her house myself,' said the postman. He opened a small gate to one side of the front hedge and Millie followed him in, quite pleased to have the moral support his presence lent as she approached the imposing house. No, she would not be overawed by the place or the people who lived there, she resolved. Her mother would just have walked up and said her piece, and Millie would, too.

The postman put some envelopes through the letter box in the door and wished Millie good morning, before crunching his way back down the gravel path to the gate. Millie heard the gate clang shut. She took a couple of deep breaths, reminded herself who she was and why she was here, and then banged the knocker on the front door of the house.

After a minute or two, a woman who looked about the same age as Bobbie Reeves, but tired and plain, opened the door. In her hand she held the letters the postman had just delivered.

'Yes?' She didn't sound friendly.

'May I speak to Mrs Hailsham, please?' Millie asked.

The woman looked suspicious. 'May I ask what it's about?'

'The beach hut.'

'What's happened to the beach hut?'

'Nothing,' said Millie. 'That's the problem. Mrs Hailsham asked me to paint the beach hut, and we agreed I was to start this morning. She was to meet me there with the paint, but she hasn't appeared and . . . I'm worried she might be ill.'

'Ill? How do you mean, ill?' asked the woman, suddenly indignant.

Millie wondered what on earth she couldn't understand about that. The word 'ill' seemed to have made her very cross.

'I meant she might have a cold or something. Just not well.' Then she had an idea. 'If she's bought the paint, I can take some of it, borrow the beach hut key, and begin now. I've sketched a design that I'm hoping Mrs Hailsham will love. She seemed very disappointed when she saw the inside of her hut looking a bit shabby.'

'The inside? You're going to paint the *inside*?'

Oh dear, why didn't this woman, who Millie thought must be Mrs Hailsham's daughter, know anything about the commission? This didn't bode well at all. Millie felt what remained of her optimism slipping away. There was no job, and there would be no pay. She felt a surge of anger rising hot and fierce within her.

'This is not right at all,' she declared. 'It's not fair to say you'll employ people and then just leave them in the lurch, wasting their time. I would have been working for someone else this morning, I'll have you know, but Mrs Hailsham asked me most particularly to work for her, and I've spent a long time designing a beautiful mural for her beach hut, just because *she said she wanted flowers*! So I've spent time, and I've turned down other work, and now I'm out of pocket. What are you going to do about it? That's what I want to know.'

Some of this line of argument had once been used by her father when there had been a misunderstanding over a portrait commission, and it had flown into Millie's mind alongside her fury. However, it did not have the desired effect.

'How dare you take that tone with me? Coming here, claiming my mother has employed you. I think you're nothing but some whippersnapper hoping to take advantage. I don't believe a word you say. Now remove yourself from my doorstep at once. Go on, off you go.'

'No!' shouted Millie. 'I will not! It's you who is taking advantage. You wait, I'll have everyone in Theddleton know that Mrs Hailsham said she was going to employ me and then she let me down. Then they'll know what kind of person she really is. Unreliable!'

Unexpectedly, this last word seemed to pull up Miss Hailsham with almost magical speed. She stood huffing for a few seconds, and then she visibly gathered herself. When she spoke next, her voice trembled but it was quieter, calmer.

'I think you had better wait here – what's your name?'

'Millie Boyd.'

'Miss Boyd, I shall go and speak to my mother. I shall return directly.'

She turned and retreated quickly down the hall to a door at the far end, her heels tapping loudly on the parquet floor.

Millie, left on the doorstep, peered into the house. The hall was very large but furnished in a homely way, with coats and hats hanging up, and books and news- papers lying on console tables, a couple of glasses and a sherry bottle on a tray on top of one of the piles of books. The place looked lived in and a little neglected. She glanced about to see if there was anything she could quickly pocket as compensation, as the commission looked to be a non-starter, but there was nothing she wanted, and anyway, nothing she could take that would go unnoticed about her person by Miss Hailsham when she returned.

After a couple of minutes Miss Hailsham reappeared, her face set in angry lines.

'I'm afraid there's been a misunderstanding. My

mother has forgotten all about asking you to paint the beach hut. She isn't expecting it to be done now. I'm sorry, but there it is.'

'What? But we had a long talk about it. She was buying the paint, and I am supposed to start today. She agreed to pay me two shillings an hour.'

At once, Millie saw that mentioning the money had been unwise. Miss Hailsham's face darkened.

'Two shillings an hour? That's absolutely outrageous! It's perfectly obvious that you tricked my mother into agreeing, if agree she did. Which I doubt. Why would she pay you so much, and you hardly out of school?'

'Because she *agreed* to it,' persisted Millie. 'I said that is my rate, and she agreed. Now, please may I speak to Mrs Hailsham? I know she will remember when I tell her what we said.'

'No, you may not. My mother is indisposed this morning and not available to casual callers.'

'But I'm not a casual caller.'

'Well, I haven't asked you to come here.'

'I've told you, I'm the person she is employing to paint flowers on the walls of her beach hut.' Millie's voice rose in fury. 'She particularly asked for flowers. She suggested wallpaper, but I told her it wouldn't stay on and I'd paint her some flowers instead.'

'Wallpaper! What a bizarre idea. I think you're making the whole thing up. No one wallpapers the inside of a beach hut. The whole notion is ridiculous. Please leave at once. I've heard enough nonsense.'

But Millie would not just turn and go without another word. She put her hands to her face, but she wasn't crying; she was gathering her inner strength.

After a few moments, she lowered her hands and looked fiercely at the older woman, who took a step back at such blatant hostility. 'I think, Miss Hailsham, that you will regret the way you and your mother have treated me,' she said. 'I intend that you should.'

'A-are you threatening me?' gasped Miss Hailsham.

'What threat could I be to you? You said I am "a whippersnapper hoping to take advantage" – why would you have anything to fear from me?'

'Fear?' Miss Hailsham picked up on the word. But even saying it, she looked fearful.

Millie said nothing, just raised an eyebrow. The two regarded each other with dislike, and the late morning air seemed to buzz and vibrate with the intensity of Millie's hostility. She channelled all her anger about being let down and dismissed into that fierce stare. Miss Hailsham was the first to look away, paling visibly.

'J-just go,' she said, sounding thoroughly unnerved, her voice trembling. She closed the front door then, but gently, as if she did not dare show her own displeasure again in the face of such a powerful force of anger; as if she felt defeated, despite getting what she wanted in the argument.

Millie stood for a moment, radiating ill-will towards the Hailshams with all the power she could muster, then turned and walked slowly back down the path to the side gate. She went out through the gate and banged it closed behind her as hard as she could.

It was Thomas's day off work, and he was standing gazing out to sea, thinking about those dear women who were lost to him: his beautiful mother, whom Millie had portrayed as a magical being in a strangely remarkable likeness when she had been inspired to illustrate his story; Nanette, his dear sister, determined, mischievous, and so much larger than life – he would regret to the end of his days the rift between them that had never healed; Lottie, his darling wife, the very best of whom he felt privileged to glimpse every day in Alice's intelligence and poise, and in Bella's kindness and passion for fairness.

Today, he felt hollow inside, despite his pride in his daughters. A familiar grey gloom had settled on him.

Where was his life going? Was he wasting it, marking time, just being but never achieving? The girls thought so, but it was very hard to see the way forward for him.

His girls were grown up, and Bella would soon be married. He wished Bella would just wait to marry until she could have a home of her own, but he understood that she was a romantic young soul, in love with a handsome man, and when you were young, you didn't want to wait for anything. He wished, too, that he could afford to help her with buying a house, but that was out of the question. He could barely afford to save up to pay for the wedding. What kind of father was he? A pathetic one, he knew.

Maybe Alice would marry, too. And why not? She was a lovely woman, blessed with beauty and brains. Any sensible man should be proud to call her his wife.

What then? More years of life wasted in stupid, meaningless jobs he wasn't interested in doing and only tolerated because they were paid work. What was the point of it all, making just enough to pay the bills, while sacrificing any proper enjoyment of his life?

Now he had Millie to support, too. She was a good girl, though. She had got a painting commission already, all through her own talent. It was possible that Millie was so gifted she wouldn't need him in just a few years. She would be doing well, whereas he might just be a burden on her, a silly old codger needing support, useless and pathetic . . .

He became aware of someone standing nearby, radiating a powerful force of negative energy, so that he could feel the air vibrating. He turned to look, fearful, almost expecting to see a miasma around this person, so strong were the dark feelings.

It was Millie, also staring out to sea.

'Hello, Millie, love,' said Thomas gently, almost timidly. 'What's the matter?'

Millie did not answer. She possibly didn't even hear. She was gazing intently at the grey sea, grinding her teeth, a look of concentrated anger setting her face in an ugly line.

'Millie?' Thomas put out a hand and gently touched her arm, and the strange cloud of negativity faded as if it were carried away on the breeze. 'How's Mrs Hailsham's beach hut?' Thomas asked. His own dark mood was as nothing compared to what he saw in Millie's face and, with an effort, he shrugged it off, seeing the girl needed kind words of encouragement. 'How's it all going?'

Millie looked round then, and for a second, Thomas thought he saw an intense light, like fire, in her eyes. Then that, too, faded, and she assumed her usual, pretty face but looking disappointed.

'What?'

'The beach hut – you've not finished already?'

'Oh . . . that. Not started. She forgot all about it.'

'That's disappointing. Can't you start it tomorrow instead?'

'No, it's not going to happen now. When Mrs Hailsham didn't turn up with the paint she was supposed to choose, I went to her house. I thought she might be ill. I never even got to speak to her. Her daughter accused me of trying to cheat them, said I'd made the whole thing up and didn't believe me at all.'

'Well, I believe you, love. Shall I go and speak up for you?'

Millie was surprised he was offering. From what she knew of him, he wasn't a battler.

'No, Uncle Thomas, thank you. I spoke up for myself. The commission is never going to happen.'

'I'm sorry, but I reckon you know you're right about it being off, love.'

They stood side by side, cast down and miserable, watching the waves break roughly on the shingle.

'I think I'll have to tell you, Millie,' said Thomas after a little while of silence between them. 'The girls and I don't like to gossip, and we thought when you met Mrs Hailsham and she asked you to paint her hut that everything would be straightforward and there'd be nowt to concern you. But Mrs Hailsham – well, she's known to be a drinker. And I do hear that Marjory, her daughter, is living on her nerves due to the stress of coping with the mother. Marjory's known to be bad-tempered and shrill. I'm sorry I didn't warn you – I can see now that we should have done, that *I* should have done – but, as I say, I thought it was all going to be all right and you'd be spared having to know about that.'

Millie thought about Mrs Hailsham's overbright laughter, her silly idea of wallpapering the beach hut, her difficulty getting the key in the lock, and her stumble when she had bent down to hook back the door. There had been empty bottles and a glass in the beach hut – had she hoped to find a bottle that wasn't empty? Was that what she had been disappointed about, and not the décor at all?

Millie nodded. 'Yes, I can see that now. I should have realised.'

'No, love, why should you know the signs, a young girl like you? I should have warned you but, as I say, I hoped it wouldn't be necessary.'

'Not your fault, Uncle Thomas. It's theirs.'

'I don't know as we can even blame them, Millie. Major Hailsham was killed, and Mrs Hailsham can't cope with that. Now her daughter has the burden of coping with her mother not being able to manage. It's a sad business.'

'Well, I'll just have to put it behind me and find another job,' said Millie, with a sigh.

'You're a good girl,' said Thomas, giving her shoulders an encouraging squeeze. 'Come on, let's go home and get ourselves summat to eat. Then this afternoon, mebbe we can make a plan for you.'

As they walked along the beach towards the High Street and their turn for home, Millie said, 'But what about a plan for you, Uncle Thomas? I think you need a plan of your own – you really do.'

'Why, bless you, love, I think I'm too old for a plan. I'll just have to go on as I am.'

'But what a waste of your life that would be,' said Millie boldly. 'Everyone needs a plan, something to aim for. Otherwise, how do you know where you're going in life?'

'It's easier when you're young and you've got talent,' said Thomas. 'Not so easy when you're old and useless.'

'Uncle Thomas, I do wish you'd buck up and stop wasting your life with self-pity and no purpose,' Millie said crossly. 'You just need to decide what you want to do. Then you need to set out to do it. I'd have thought you'd have decided by now, but you're not too old to change and make an effort!'

Thomas was taken aback at being spoken to so fiercely by someone a fraction of his age, although he could hardly argue.

'It's not so easy, Millie,' he said eventually. 'You've got a talent for drawing and painting, just like your mam, but I'm not up to much on any front.'

'I don't believe that,' she said more gently. 'When I said I don't like reading books, Alice said it was just because I haven't found the right one yet – that there's a book for everyone. Perhaps it's like that with what you can do: you just have to find it, but you won't if you don't make an effort to steer onto the path where it's likely to be found. And I don't think that's at the Three-Mile Bottom.'

'Mebbe, lass. You're a good, kind girl. I know that.'

'Only sometimes,' said Millie. Then she gave a bitter-sounding laugh, as if she had remembered some dark irony.

That afternoon, Thomas and Millie sat down, each wearing a couple of cardigans – the fire would not be lit until everyone was at home – and thought about what Millie could do now that she wasn't working on Mrs Hailsham's beach hut after all.

'You could always paint Alice and Bella's hut instead,' suggested Thomas. 'The only trouble is that we'd have to buy the paint, and we couldn't afford to pay you – especially at two shillings an hour, did you say? – but at least you'd have your work to show off to potential employers.'

'Yes, I wondered about that, too, but I didn't want you to have any expense, especially if Alice and Bella don't actually *want* their hut painted. They like it as it is, because it is how it was when they went there with their mum. I can understand that.'

'So can I,' said Thomas. 'But I've seen your design for Mrs Hailsham's beach hut, and it's brilliant. I believe you can make summat of your talent, but what you really need, as an artist . . .' He smiled at Millie, who acknowledged the title with a little nod. '. . . is a patron: someone who has the means to pay you and has influence. Of course, you're very young and have much to prove, and that might take a few years. I'm afraid, Millie, you might have to find summat else to do in the meantime, before you get established. But once you do find a foothold, it could all take off. Your mam would have known what I mean. Did your mam and dad work for anyone in particular, and that meant that person's friends and acquaintances saw the work, and that led to more commissions?'

'Yes, of course. Mum did some lovely murals in our house, and then some friends saw them, and then Mum did their house, and then *their* friends' houses, too. But the problem is we don't know anyone who wants murals on their walls. We don't know anyone who can afford that, do we? I had hopes of Mrs Hailsham but look how that went, her daughter almost throwing me off the doorstep.'

'You're right about that, Millie.'

'I only hope I can find *someone* who will be interested in commissioning me to paint a mural or a picture, otherwise I'm sunk.'

'So do I, love.'

They fell silent for a few moments and then Millie said, 'Uncle Thomas, about Mum . . .'

'Yes, love?'

'You know the reason why she didn't keep in touch with you much and not with Uncle Frank at all?'

'Of course.'

'She blamed you as well as him. She told me that you betrayed her, and if you hadn't sneaked to Uncle Frank she'd have succeeded in running away, escaping his temper and his bullying. Those scars she had on her arm and on her leg – she said you were partly to blame.'

'No, Millie! It was Frank. It was all down to Frank. No one forced him to behave like he did. That's why Nanette wanted to get away. Yes, I told on her, but it might have been even worse if I hadn't. And I mean for her, not me.'

'Why? Tell me what happened.'

'I found Nanette packing some of her things to run away from home. She said she was meeting some young lad she was friends with at the time and going to London with him. Of course, she was my little sister, and I was scared for her. I knew if she went, anything might happen, and this lad hadn't got the best reputation for being reliable. She'd have been ruined, and besides, I reckoned she knew nowt of London, or anywhere else but Blackburn. Our mam was ill with TB and worn down with hard work, and I feared if Nanette went, Mam's heart would break and hasten her end.'

Millie's eyes were round. She hadn't heard any other version of this but her mother's. 'So what happened? I know what she *said*, but you tell me, Uncle Thomas.'

'I tried to stop her, begged her to stay and just put up with Frank and his ways until she was older, but she wouldn't be told. She was never one for putting up with owt. She made off with the lad, but Frank came home from work soon after – it's a wonder he hadn't seen Nanette leaving – and I was too frightened to hide what I knew when he demanded to know where she was. Let's just say that Frank knew how to get what he wanted and, having given me a thrashing, he set off after Nanette and the lad in a wild fury, armed with one of the fire irons. He soon caught up with them, gave the young fella a hiding and dragged Nanette home for her share. He was merciless, love. I tried to stop him, but Frank was a big lad, and strong, and neither your mam nor I stood a chance against him. She never forgave either of us, and the family was fractured for good after that. Our mam's heart was broken anyway, so it was about as bad as it could be.'

'Then why did you let Uncle Frank and Aunt Moaner take me home with them?' demanded Millie.

'Oh, Millie, love, I thought time had changed Frank. I thought his bullying was the idiocy of youth – an overgrown lad with more strength and temper than wisdom – and he'd be a reformed character now. I was taken in by him having his responsible job at the bank, his dull life and his duller wife. Or mebbe I just hoped that was the case. I'm sorry for it.'

'He's no different,' said Millie. 'He's a horrible, brutal bully, and I hate him. I hate Aunt Moaner, too.'

Thomas felt tears threatening at the thought of his mistake: that he had allowed this lovely girl to be subjected to Frank's terrible temper and physical punishments.

'I'm sorry, love,' he said again. 'Can you forgive me?'

Millie's face was bleak. 'All this time, I thought you were a sneak and a coward, and Mum was the only one with courage. But Uncle Frank is a terrible man, and you were both his victims.'

'I was younger then than you are now, Millie. I wish I'd been older and wiser. I wish I could have done things differently.' Thomas looked desolate.

Millie lowered her head and single tear trickled down her face. She thought about her parents, selfish, irresponsible in many ways, neglectful of her but so happy together. With Dad, Mum had found the happiness she deserved.

'I wish I had, too,' she said, fighting back tears.

When Bella and Alice got home from work that evening, they heard the whole sorry tale of Millie's visit to the Hailshams'.

'I wish I'd warned you about Mrs Hailsham properly,'

said Bella. 'I feel I've let you down by not preparing you for the chance of disappointment, but I just hoped you wouldn't even have to know about Mrs Hailsham's problems.'

'It's her fault, not yours, Bella,' said Millie.

'Just forget about her and start again,' said Alice. 'It's a setback, I know, but it's all you can do.'

'Well, we'll see,' said Millie. 'Somehow I doubt I shall see Mrs Hailsham at the beach huts again. In the meantime, I have to find someone else who wants me to paint for them, and Uncle Thomas needs to find a job that suits him at last.'

Bella looked at Thomas in surprise. 'Is that right, Dad? You're going to make an effort and stop marking time, getting nowhere?'

'Well, Millie says so . . .' said Thomas weakly.

'But Bella and I have been saying this to you for ages,' said Alice.

'I know, love. I shall just have to have a think what it is I might want to do and then I'll get to it.'

'Oh, Dad,' sighed Bella. 'I really want to believe you will do that, but it doesn't sound as if you're ready to move forward yet.' She looked at Alice and shook her head sadly.

# CHAPTER TEN

'HOW WAS YOUR day, love?' Nancy Bennett asked Sidney as he came into the house and hung up his coat and hat. 'You look tired.'

'Yes, I've been quite busy, Mam. It's all go in Planning.'

'Sit down, love, and let me pour you a cup of tea,' said Nancy, going ahead of him to plump the cushion in his favourite chair. He knew she often felt lonely during the day, when he was at work, especially if she hadn't got one of her committee meetings, and it suited them both that she made a fuss of him when he came home.

She disappeared quickly to the kitchen, then came back with a tray containing two cups of tea and one chocolate digestive on a plate, which she put on a little table in front of him. She took her own tea, sat down, and imparted the news that she'd obviously been bursting to tell.

'I saw Muriel Chalfont in the queue at the butcher's

this morning,' she said, emphasising the young woman's name to make sure he heard.

'Oh, yes?'

Trying to play it cool while wanting to know what Muriel had said to his mother, Sidney reached out for the *Theddleton Informer* and, putting it across his knees, opened it at the sports pages.

'Yes. She was right in front of me and made a point of turning to speak, like. I saw folk were noticing, too.'

'Well, I expect she was just being friendly,' prompted Sidney.

'More than friendly, love. She invited me to have a cup of tea with her at the hotel.'

Sidney, who did not generally show much interest in his mother's daily life, except where it impacted on his own comfort and well-being, was all ears now.

'And was there a purpose to this tea party?' he asked.

'It wasn't a party as such,' said Nancy, 'there being just the two of us, but it was very nice. Anyway, it turns out her father – him that owns the hotel, you know—'

'Yes, I do know, Mam.'

'He's thinking of sponsoring the floral clock outright.'

'Let me stop you there, Mam. I know this because Mr Chalfont has written to us at the town hall, and we're considering it. Plus, I have *just happened* to bump into Muriel occasionally, as you know, and she has mentioned it, too.'

'You've seen Muriel Chalfont again?' Nancy asked.

'Well, she does live in Theddleton, Mam,' Sidney answered evasively. 'It's not that big a place.'

'So what did she say to you?'

'Well, er . . . nowt, really, nowt that I didn't already know. She mentioned that her dad was keen to sponsor the floral clock entirely, but he wants it to be bigger – much bigger – than was originally planned, and to have the crest of the Imperial Hotel on it, plus a sign up saying it is sponsored by him.'

'That sounds reasonable, if he's putting up the money, Sidney. You don't put up the brass and expect nowt in return.'

'Well, you might if you were a philanthropist, but I think Mr Chalfont sees this as a good business opportunity. The name of the hotel will be right outside the station, where visitors will see the advertisement, in the shape of a floral clock, the moment they arrive in Theddleton.'

'You reckon so?'

'Without a doubt. I can hardly blame him, but Mr Penrose sees it differently. He says it's a case of deciding whether we want to make over quite so much public land to summat that some might view as almost entirely for the benefit of Mr Chalfont and his hotel, as weighed against the benefits for Theddleton generally and the people who live here.'

'But you're in favour, love?'

Sidney thought it unwise to confide in his mother anything about him working on persuading other members of the Planning Committee to come round to Mr Chalfont's way of thinking.

'That's none of your business, Mam. When we've considered it, we'll let Mr Chalfont know our conclusions,' he said pompously.

Nancy frowned. 'There's no need to be rude, Sidney. None of my business, indeed! Muriel Chalfont obviously thought I would be interested to know about it.'

'Well, it's for us in Planning to make the decision, not the Fundraising Committee.'

'But if Mr Chalfont sponsors the clock,' said Nancy, clearly shrugging off her hurt feelings, 'it'll be maintained for good at no cost to the folk of Theddleton, and very nice it will be, too, with that smart-looking crown that is the crest of the Imperial Hotel. It's almost like they're part of the Royal Family.'

Sidney, rolling his eyes, put down his cup and saucer and looked directly at his mother with a sigh. 'Mam, why are *you* so keen on Mr Chalfont having his way? I can't see what you have to gain by it.'

'I'm not,' said Nancy, 'but Muriel is a grand girl and, well, she was very friendly – not just tea at the hotel, but teacakes, too. And the waiter was very polite, even more so than the time I was there for the fundraisers' meeting.'

'Well, of course he was. Muriel is Joseph Chalfont's daughter – she's always going to be treated grand at the hotel.'

'But she didn't have to ask me to tea. She's really

chatty, once you get talking to her. Well, you know that, of course. I wonder, now she's made the first move, whether we could be friends, for all there's a few years' difference in age between us.'

Sidney laughed. 'Mam, Muriel Chalfont is my age – that's more than a few years.'

'Well, perhaps she's being friendly with me because she wants to get to know you better.'

'She's always very nice whenever I see her,' Sidney said carefully. He'd met up with Muriel a few times in the afternoons, when he'd been on site visits and had finished early. She was a looker and a flirt, always delighted to see him. At first he had thought her interest was only in the planning application for the floral clock, but she had been so very charming that he had come round to thinking she was quite keen on being friends – or perhaps something more. He wasn't telling his mother this, however.

'Don't sell yourself short, love,' said Nancy. 'You're doing well at the town hall, and I reckon you could become head of Planning if you continue to work hard. Not everyone gets on with that Mr Penrose, I gather. You'd be mixing in the right circles then.'

'Aye, mebbe . . .'

'It's always useful to know the right people, Sidney. The Chalfonts are the right sort in Theddleton. You could be aiming a lot higher than you are, you know, lad. Muriel is such a nice girl. Pretty, too. You'd be wise to get to know her better.'

'Mam, I'm engaged to Bella.' Sidney felt he had to remind his mother. And himself. But already there was the worm of an idea burrowing through his mind that, of the two, Muriel was undoubtedly the more glamorous, the more influential, and the wealthier.

'Oh, aye, but you can still be friends with Muriel . . . see where that takes you. And, you know, it's not too late to change your mind about marrying Bella Marchant.'

How strange that his mother had picked up on that very private and secret thought. That gave it validity: his mother definitely had his best interests at heart, and she was right about most things on which she expressed her opinion.

'You want a wife who matches you for ambition and *social standing*,' Nancy went on, when Sidney didn't reply, primping her permed hair and brushing an invisible crumb off her pleated skirt, 'not someone who's as much a child as an adult, working in a toyshop, for goodness' sake. Home-made clothes, and her hair in a plait like a schoolgirl.'

'Give over, Mam. Bella's all right.' Inadvertently, his mother had reminded him of the things about Bella that were very much part of her unpretentious appeal.

'Oh, aye, she's all right, but do you want *all right*, my lad, or do you want better than that . . . the best? 'Cos I reckon as Muriel has worked out you're a young man who's going places, love, and she's got her eye on you. And, as I say, if you know folk with influence, they can help you get on in life, Sidney. You'd be wise to bear that in mind. Certainly, I intend to foster the friendship we struck up this morning.'

'Please, Mam, just don't interfere with owt to do with this floral clock. It'd be embarrassing if you, my mam, and on the Fundraising Committee, said one thing and it looked like some kind of promise, and the Planning Committee decided on summat else. Leave it to us, please.' He looked hard at his mother.

Nancy went a bit pink, and she looked away. 'No need to take that tone, Sidney. Embarrassing, indeed!'

'Oh, c'mon now, Mam. I only meant we have to make the decisions and I don't want you to be caught in any crossfire between Planning and Mr Chalfont, that's all. And I don't want to be caught in any crossfire myself.' He gave his mother a meaningful look.

'All right,' conceded Nancy. 'But I reckon Muriel Chalfont's a lovely lass.'

Having had the last word, she got up to take her cup to the kitchen and begin cooking their tea, but turned at the door as if a new thought had just at that moment occurred to her.

'You know, Sidney, love, you don't want to be rushing into that wedding Bella's so keen to be planning and find it was all a terrible mistake, do you?'

'Give over, Mam. I'm rushing into nowt.'

'You see, love, I know better than anyone how special you are – how *exceptional* – and I don't want you finding out you've not done as well as you might. I'm beginning to wonder if Bella Marchant is really right for you.'

Sidney opened his mouth to tell her he'd had enough of this conversation, but Nancy held up her hand as if she were stopping traffic and continued: 'Oh, I've tried to like the girl, but she's a gift for misjudging things. To organise your wedding around pleasing her employers at the toyshop, for instance. I ask you!'

Sidney's conscience was pricked by now, and he wasn't ready to give up on his fiancée completely. 'She is keen on September, right enough. But, Mam, you know what a good sort Bella is. She likes to oblige folk, which is to her credit, and she does get along grand with Mr and Mrs Warminster.'

'Well, I don't see her obliging me, and I'd have thought I'd come above anyone . . . except you, of course. And I'll tell you what else I'm bothered about, Sidney. Now she's got that young cousin of hers in tow, despite what Bella says, you could just find yourself supporting that lass as well as Bella. Keeping them both! She may have told you that this Millie, or whatever her name is, is stopping with her dad and that sister of hers, but what if the cousin has a different idea? Or Alice and their dad do? Or Bella changes her mind and wants to bring her with her? Bring her *here*. I reckon you'd be wise to hold off marrying for a bit, until you see how things shake down.'

She went to cook their dinner, with a look on her face that said she thought she'd made her point.

Sidney threw the newspaper onto the chair she had vacated and then sat staring into his tea. He'd better warn Muriel off trying to butter up his mother. Her interfering would only muddy the waters, and he was pretty confident that, if he was discreet, he could work the decision about the floral clock Mr Chalfont's way, which would be in his interests, too. Mr Chalfont had made that clear.

As for Bella and her cousin, Bella had been at pains to assure him that Millie would continue to live with Alice and their father, but what if Mam was right?

Bella was extremely disappointed that Mrs Hailsham had proved unreliable over her commission for Millie to paint her beach hut. Millie had been so excited, and she'd shown Bella her wild-flower design with such pride. Not only was it very beautiful, it was astonishingly accomplished. Millie had thought of all kinds of special little touches: ladybirds and bees among the flowers, and bindweed and dog roses trailing up around the windows. It was a very ambitious plan for so young an artist to have designed.

Bella was then torn between thinking she should help Millie by offering the Marchant beach hut up to her to use as a shop window for her skills, and not wanting it painted at all because it was so comforting to keep it exactly as it had been when she and Alice were little and they had first picnicked there with their mother.

Bella and Alice discussed what to do on their walk home from work together one evening.

'I love the beach hut for all its associations with Mam

and our childhoods, but it will still be ours, even if it's got a bright new look,' reasoned Alice. 'Mebbe it needs painting after all this time, and why wouldn't we let Millie do it if it helps her, too? It would be almost symbolic: we're sharing our hut with Millie now she's in our lives. And her design is very impressive.'

'Oh, now I feel mean,' sighed Bella, wringing her hands. 'I don't want to exclude Millie, but she didn't know Mam. Mam's hut was left to us – you and me – and it has a history and place in our lives that it never can have for Millie.'

'All right . . .' said Alice, slowly. 'It's no to the mural, then?'

Bella nodded sadly. 'I'm sorry. I know I'm probably standing in Millie's way when she needs some help, but I don't think I can bear to have the old white walls painted over with flowers Mam will never see, however pretty. Some things are too precious to be spruced up and made over.'

'Don't be sorry, Bella,' said Alice. 'You've made your feelings clear, and you've a right to your opinion. The hut stays as it is. You'll only be upset and regret it if Millie decorates it, however brilliant it looks, so let's think of summat else for Millie to do.'

'We'll go down on Sunday and see if anyone's around and wants their hut painted,' suggested Bella.

The Sunday visit, with picnic, proved to be another disappointment, however. When the girls arrived at their beach hut, they saw that the windows to Mrs Hailsham's, next to it, had been smashed and the wind had got in and rent the curtains, which were hanging raggedly, limp with damp sea air.

'Oh dear, I wonder if she knows,' said Bella. 'It's a shame if her hut is falling into disrepair and she isn't aware of it.'

'Also,' said Alice, practically, 'it does make the whole row look shabby. We may not be bright and new, but at least we're not derelict. I think I ought to go along and tell Marjory Hailsham, in case she isn't aware. We've never had a problem with vandalism before now, but I can't think what else would be the cause, or why it's just Mrs Hailsham's hut that is damaged.'

'Maybe some stones got blown up off the beach and it was just bad luck they broke the windows,' suggested Millie.

Alice gave her a long look. 'Millie, you don't know owt about it, do you?'

'Why should I?'

'Because you have a bit of a history with stones and windows, if I remember rightly.'

'If I want to throw stones, I skim them into the sea, like you showed me,' said Millie. 'If I want to make trouble for the Hailshams, I can think of bigger ways to do it than smashing up their stupid beach hut.'

Alice and Bella looked at each other. Millie was clearly still angry about Mrs Hailsham reneging on the painting commission.

'Don't be cross, sweetheart,' said Bella. 'No one wants

any trouble. Put it behind you and let's think of summat else for you to paint.'

As they set up the deck chairs on the wide path, Bella noticed how the blue paint was peeling on the door-frame, and she suddenly had an idea.

'Why didn't I think of it before? Millie, I know you like to create pictures and you're not a painter and decorator, but if you were to repaint the *outside* for us, matching the old colour of the stripes, it would be as it ever was, only better.'

'That's a good idea,' Alice agreed. 'It would be more weatherproof and summat for you to do that might very well lead to commissions, although probably not for the kind of painting you really want to undertake, I'm afraid. Still, it would keep you out of mischief as you seem not to be having any luck finding a job.' She looked at Millie carefully to see how she might take this remark, but Millie didn't react to it.

Instead, she brightened. She had been furious about Mrs Hailsham's 'betrayal', as she saw it.

'Thank you,' she said. 'It would do to be going on with. People will come past and see your hut is the best, and then they'll want theirs doing.'

'That's the idea,' said Bella, 'but there are no guarantees, remember, so don't get your hopes up too high.'

After they had eaten their picnic and sat gazing out at the sea and breathing the scent of spring on the fresh air, Alice said she'd go and see if Marjory Hailsham was at home.

Bella and Millie declined to go with her, and Millie became very absorbed in sketching the view over the beach.

Alice looked up at the imposing façade of Mrs Hailsham's house. The place really was huge for just two women to live in, although perhaps a little sad-looking, a little bit neglected, now Alice could look more closely.

She hoped she wasn't intruding, coming here on a Sunday afternoon, but Miss Hailsham needed to know about the damage to the hut. There was no sign of anyone about. At least, thought Alice, she probably wouldn't be interrupting the Hailshams entertaining visitors.

She knocked on the front door and stood back. After a minute or two, Miss Hailsham, looking pale and worn, opened the door a fraction, peering out nervously.

'Yes?'

'Good afternoon, Miss Hailsham. I'm Alice Marchant.'

'Oh . . . yes, of course. I recognise you, Miss Marchant.' Marjory Hailsham sounded very tired. She opened the door wider. 'How can I help you?'

'I notice Mrs Hailsham's beach hut has been damaged – the windows broken – and I thought you should know.'

The wan look on Miss Hailsham's face disappeared then, to be replaced by a mixture of both anger and anxiety. 'That wretched beach hut! It's been just one thing after another lately – in fact, since some urchin appeared here, claiming to have been asked to paint it.'

Alice stepped back. She was inclined to shrug off the

woman's rudeness and go. After all, she'd only come out of consideration to the Hailshams, and whatever was the matter here, it wasn't her fault. She understood 'some urchin' to be Millie, and she resented her cousin, who had been let down and disappointed by Mrs Hailsham's lack of focus, being referred to in this way. She turned to leave.

'Well, I'm sorry to have bothered—'

'It's an absolute nightmare. Since the very day of the mix-up about the beach hut, my mother's been claiming she's being visited by dead people in the night. She's terrified to go to sleep, and when she's awake she's so nervous, she's continually shaking. I can't seem to reason with her. She's become a complete nervous wreck.'

Alice backed away further in embarrassment. The woman was far from calm and obviously at the end of her tether, otherwise she would never be telling all this to a mere acquaintance. 'I'm sorry to hear Mrs Hailsham is ill, but—'

'And now I'm beginning to think it's catching. How can delusions be catching?'

With every passing moment, Alice was wishing more and more that she hadn't come here. She had nothing helpful to say, but Miss Hailsham seemed to be waiting for an answer.

'Er, I think, Miss Hailsham, that I had better go,' she said. 'I'm very sorry to have troubled—'

'I was sure there was someone – or something – with a lantern the other night, standing in the garden. Just standing there, waiting. I know it was just a trick of the light but, in those strange, dark hours, I was . . . well, I was frightened. Then, last night, I heard footsteps outside. There was someone coming to the house, slowly getting nearer and nearer. I distinctly heard their footsteps on the gravel. I hardly dared look – I was filled with dread – but when I did find the courage to peep out, there was no one.'

'Well, that's good, isn't it?' said Alice bracingly. 'You wouldn't want there to be anyone.'

'But I *heard* someone, I'm sure of it. Then, when the footsteps had abruptly stopped, right outside the door, where you're standing now, Mother suddenly started screaming. I nearly died of fright. It was just a bad dream, but . . . oh, Miss Marchant, I'm so tired, and Mother's getting worse. She has a little, er, fondness for a sherry sometimes, and I don't know if it's the' – she lowered her voice – 'the drink that's causing her madness or her madness that makes her drink. I don't know what to do . . .'

Marjory Hailsham started to sob noisily, her eyes red and her face contorted and ugly, and Alice gathered herself and decided she couldn't leave the woman like this, however much she wanted to.

'Right,' she said. 'I think what you need, Miss Hailsham, is a visit from the doctor. He's the person to help you and your mother. Would you like me to call him for you?' Alice had already noticed a telephone line running from a pole in the street to the house.

'Yes, please,' said Miss Hailsham in a broken little voice.

'And if he can come out to you straight away, I'll make you and Mrs Hailsham a pot of tea and wait here until he arrives. How does that sound?'

The distraught woman nodded. 'You're very kind, Miss Marchant.'

Oh, thank goodness, thought Alice. They were back on safe social grounds: a pot of tea and the doctor. She just hoped he was at home and would be able to visit at once.

'Alice, you've been ages. Were they in?' Bella asked, still sitting in her deck chair, knitting.

'They were in, all right. Both as mad as fish. Where's Millie?'

'Mrs Cook's lad, Edwin, came by and said hello. Millie's gone to look at his mother's boat with him.'

'Good. I'm glad she's not here to hear about the Hailshams. Oh, by the way, I've volunteered Dad to board up the broken windows tomorrow. Remind me to mention it, if I forget. It's no use expecting them to organise that.'

'I thought Miss Hailsham is someone who organises everything.'

'Well, she doesn't any more, Bella. Let me tell you what happened . . .'

Bella's eyes were huge with astonishment when Alice had finished the sorry tale of her visit to the Hailshams'.

'But I don't understand,' she said. 'Why would Marjory Hailsham associate all this lunacy with Millie's visit there?'

'I have really no idea, except for the timing, and that's just a coincidence. It seems to me that Mrs Hailsham's instability is at the root of her bad dreams, and mebbe it's the drink that's making her shake. Now Marjory is getting exhausted and starting to imagine things, too. Anyway, I waited while the doctor arrived and then fled. I've never been so glad to see anyone, I can tell you.'

'Oh dear, poor Mrs Hailsham. And poor Miss Hailsham. Mebbe they've been heading down this sad road for a while and have now arrived at this state at last. It can't possibly be owt to do with Millie.'

'No, of course not.'

'It was Millie who was the injured party in the business with their beach hut.'

'I said of course not,' snapped Alice. 'Oh, I'm sorry, Bella, I didn't mean to be short with you. It's just that it was horrible: weird and . . . unnerving. Marjory Hailsham was really frightened of what she thought she had seen and heard. I know it is far-fetched and ridiculous but, the way she described it, I almost believed her.'

# CHAPTER ELEVEN

E DWIN COOK MANOEUVRED the little boat back to the jetty at the southern end of Theddleton beach, tied it safely to the mooring and climbed up the short ladder onto the platform. He leaned down and offered his hand to Millie, but she was already clambering up onto the jetty unaided.

'Thank you for the trip out,' she said. 'That was fun. Your mother told me about the boat – is it really hers or does it belong to all of you?'

'Definitely hers,' said Edwin, pushing his overlong fringe out of his eyes, then shoving his hands in his pockets as he and Millie strolled back towards the Promenade. 'Dad bought it for her – she probably told you. I always ask if I want to use it.'

'Aren't you a bit old to be asking your mummy if you want to do something?' asked Millie, giggling.

'No,' said Edwin, not rising to the mockery one little bit. 'It's only right to ask permission to use other folk's things. Mam suggested this trip, anyway. She said, "If you see that cheeky scamp Millie, and she begs to be shown the boat, don't deny the poor child a chance to have a splash about." So I reckoned I'd take pity on you, you not having any relations quite as young as you are, and I did as she suggested.'

Millie laughed along with him. 'What's it like working at the bakery?' she asked then.

'Hard work, kneading the dough. Hot, with the ovens. Interesting, though. I'm learning a lot.'

'I'm looking for a job,' said Millie. 'Just to be going on with, until the painting takes off. I need to earn some money. If they want anyone at the bakery, you'd tell me, wouldn't you?'

'Well, I would, but would you want to work there? You'd have to get up very early, when most folk are still asleep, so a lot of the time it's dark. It's better in summer, when you can hear the birds singing as you go to work. Thing is, Millie' – he looked at her with a twinkle in his blue eyes – 'it doesn't sound as though you are committed to baking. Mr Harcourt – him that I work for – wouldn't want to be wasting time setting on a fly-by-night.'

'Ha, I've never been called that before,' said Millie. 'A fly-by-night. Is that like a witch that flies on a broomstick in the night? I like that. It sounds mysterious, with secret powers . . . Perhaps I *am* a fly-by-night.'

'It means someone not reliable, not in for the long haul, like,' Edwin explained. 'I'm not saying you are;

I'm just saying that *if* you are, Mr Harcourt wouldn't want to employ you.'

'Oh, I'm reliable all right,' said Millie. 'Probably not for baking, though, it's true. But if I set my mind on something, you can be sure I will see it through.'

Suddenly her tone was hard and her face set. Edwin looked at her, feeling a change in the atmosphere, the laughter and lightness of the afternoon dissipating, just as if the sun had gone behind a cloud on a sunny day. Although little more than a child, Millie sounded almost frightening. He had a feeling she wasn't thinking about a job in the bakery now, but something in the look on her face prevented him from asking her.

When they got home later that afternoon, Bella and Alice had plenty to tell Thomas. He listened to Alice's account of her visit to the Hailshams' house with a grave look on his face. She remembered to mention the broken windows in Mrs Hailsham's beach hut and that she'd said her father would board them over.

'I hope you don't mind me volunteering you, but they were both so completely hopeless that I knew neither of them would see to it being done. It passed through my mind that Millie might have broken the glass in a temper because Mrs Hailsham let her down, but when I asked her, she denied it.'

Even as she said it, Alice wondered if Millie *had* denied she'd broken the windows, but she couldn't quite remember what Millie had said.

'Our Millie, vandalising Mrs Hailsham's property! Surely not, love. I can't think she would behave like that. I know she had a hard time at Frank and Mona's, and that made her lash out a bit, but she's a good girl really. She's made a big effort to fit in here, she clearly loves you both, and she's determined to make her own way. She really wants this painting business to take off, but we've discussed the difficulties of getting up and running, and I reckon she's realistic about doing summat else for a while to earn some money. And look at how she's applied herself to the reading.'

'Yes, I'm so proud of her over that. Now she's putting in the effort, her reading has improved no end.'

'But I'm sorry you had such a horrible time at the Hailshams', Alice. I reckon Rosemary Hailsham's descending into lunacy and pulling down Marjory with her.'

'It was very strange. The whole place felt . . . wrong, as if it were haunted or summat. It was all right while I was on the doorstep, for all Miss Hailsham's drama, but when I went inside to telephone the doctor, it was sort of chilling. I kept looking behind me and expecting to find someone standing there, silent and menacing. I reckon Miss Hailsham had scared me with her daft talk.'

'Mebbe the bad atmosphere was created by the Hailshams themselves,' suggested Bella. 'If they've been frightened and upset by bad dreams, it would hardly feel light and cheery in their house, would it?'

'I agree,' said Thomas. 'You did your best, Alice, and

that's more than some would have done. I expect the doctor will have given them summat to help them sleep more peacefully. I reckon he'll know already about Mrs Hailsham's problem. I hope they get through this, though. I knew Major Hailsham in the old days and he was a good sort. And Mrs Hailsham is a nice woman, but one who's chosen her prop unwisely, although mebbe she can't help that.'

'Yes, I do hope the lady hasn't become too ill to recover,' said Bella, kindly.

'And so where has our Millie gone now?' asked Thomas. 'I've in mind a little story for this evening that I think she'll like.'

'She's messing about in Mrs Cook's boat with Edwin,' said Bella. 'We've told her she can paint the outside of our beach hut in the old blue and white stripes. We'll buy the paint and give her a bit of pocket money for doing it. I think we can just about afford that, but it'll have to be one coat only.'

'And not two shillings an hour to do it,' said Alice, smiling and rolling her eyes.

Thomas laughed. 'I reckon she didn't know what she was asking. If she makes a good job of it, one of the other owners is bound to want theirs done and she can negotiate a more realistic rate of pay.'

'It's lovely the way Millie looks forward to your stories, especially as she was so sceptical about the first one,' said Bella. 'Every day it's more and more as if Millie is our little sister.' She gave a sudden gasp at her thoughtlessness and clapped her hand over her mouth. 'Oh, Dad, I'm sorry. I hope you don't mind me saying that. I think we all feel the same, but I didn't mean to speak out of turn and upset you.'

'You haven't, love. I've been thinking much the same. And I'm so proud of you both, the way you've thought of so many ways to help Millie feel that she belongs here,' said Thomas.

They heard Millie arriving home then, calling goodbye to Edwin.

'Don't tell her about the Hailshams,' said Alice quietly. 'Let's just say no more about them.'

'How was the *Hope and Peace*?' asked Thomas, as Millie came into the kitchen.

'Fun,' said Millie. 'We rowed out to get started, and then Edwin showed me how to use the sail to catch the wind. We went all the way to Baybury and back. I wish it was my boat. I hope you've got a good story lined up for after dinner, Uncle Thomas, to round off a lovely day . . .'

After dinner, they all sat in their favourite chairs, and Thomas started his story with the traditional age-old incantation: 'Once upon a time . . .'

Bella and Alice leaned back, smiling in anticipation, and listened carefully, while Millie listened for a time with her eyes closed and then took up her coloured pencils and notebook and began to sketch. After that first week, when she had strangely conjured up a likeness to Thomas's mother, Millie had always done a drawing to illustrate the story, although none of them since then had contained any surprises.

'. . . and so, the princess thought at last, happiness is not always where you expect to find it.'

For a moment, there was complete quiet, and then Bella and Alice sat up, as if they'd been asleep and almost dreamed the story.

'Dad, that was lovely,' said Bella. 'That's one of the best so far.'

'I thought so, too,' said Alice.

'Thank you. This one's been in my mind all week, sort of brewing. Are we to have the pleasure of seeing it illustrated, Millie?' Thomas held out his hand for Millie's notebook, and she passed it to him without a word. 'Why, the princess looks just like Bella, I see,' he remarked happily. 'My thought exactly.'

'Let me see,' said Bella, then, 'Oh my goodness! Millie, how could you?' She looked suddenly angry and on the verge of tears.

'How could Millie what?' asked Alice, concerned. She jumped up from her chair and went to look over Bella's arm at the drawing. 'But that's really pretty. The princess does look like you, and her dress is beautiful.'

'But it's my *wedding dress*,' wailed Bella. 'It's the very dress I've been planning to make. I bought the pattern weeks ago and hid it away, and I've been saving up for the fabric. I didn't want any of you to see it until I was sewing it and couldn't keep it hidden any longer. You must have looked, Millie. You've been snooping in my room, haven't you?'

'No! Of course not, Bella,' said Millie. 'I wouldn't do that. And anyway, what do I care about your wedding dress? I saw you as the princess, and then my hand just drew what the princess looks like on her wedding day.'

'Then how did you know?' Bella snapped, looking daggers at her cousin.

'I don't know. I told you: my hand just kind of knew what to do, that's all.'

'But, even if that were so – and I can't really believe you – who's the bridegroom?' asked Bella, getting even crosser. 'Millie, if you were going to draw me as the bride, the bridegroom would be – must be – Sidney. Whoever that is, it certainly isn't him.' She looked at the drawing of a man she didn't recognise, her expression growing darker with every passing moment. 'That was a really mean thing to do. Millie, you know I'm going to marry Sidney; you should have made the King's robe-maker look like him. I know you could have done if you'd wanted. Instead, you chose to draw a picture of me marrying someone else! You even drew my *actual wedding dress*! That mischief is in very poor taste, and I'm surprised at you! How could you be so horrible to me?' Her face was red with fury as she fought back her tears.

'I think, Bella,' said Alice carefully, 'Millie just didn't realise that what she was drawing could be misinterpreted – isn't that right, Millie? You just wanted to make Bella the heroine of the story and couldn't remember what Sidney looks like.' She looked hard at Millie, willing her to agree and hoping no one raised the subject of the dress again.

'I suppose so,' Millie conceded eventually, not sounding as if she meant it at all. 'I didn't mean to upset you, Bella.'

'Well, you have. You've spoiled the whole story with your thoughtlessness and stupidity.'

Bella slapped the notebook down on the table, got up hurriedly and left the room, closing the door behind her rather more firmly than necessary.

'Oh dear . . .' sighed Alice.

'It's not like Bella to get in a bad temper,' said Thomas. 'Mebbe it wasn't the best choice of illustration, Millie. Bella's putting so much of herself into her wedding plans.'

'I'm sorry. I couldn't really help it,' said Millie.

'I think she's feeling a bit sensitive about the engagement,' said Alice in a low voice to her father. 'Sidney still hasn't bought her a ring, of course. He's supposed to be saving up for a fancy one, although he seems to have money to spend on himself while he's doing that. Bella hasn't been bothered about having a ring, but she told me that the last time she went there to tea, Mrs Bennett was implying that the engagement wasn't a real one without a ring – the troublemaker. Mrs B also suggested Bella might want to put the wedding off for a while. I'm afraid Bella is beginning to suspect Sidney's mother is hoping it will never happen at all.'

'Oh dear. Nancy Bennett is a woman very sure of the rightness of her own opinion, which is that no one is good enough for her Sidney,' said Thomas. 'She's always been like a ewe with one lamb, and he's always been a spoiled mammy's boy. But, of course, I do agree that Bella and Sidney would be better waiting until they've saved up for their own place. It's quite clear to me why that woman isn't welcoming to Bella, and she's only offering them a home because she doesn't want her darling boy to leave her by herself.'

'Perhaps it would be better if Bella didn't marry Sidney Bennett at all,' said Millie.

Alice turned to her angrily. She had almost forgotten Millie was still in the room. 'Don't ever say that to Bella, please, Millie. It's nowt to do with any of us, really. We shouldn't have said owt, so please forget it. It's between Bella and Sidney, all right?'

Millie nodded. Then she picked up her notebook, ripped out the drawing of Bella and her bridegroom, scrunched it into a ball and threw it on the fire.

'Now go and tell Bella that you're sorry, that you were just being thoughtless and you didn't mean to hurt her,' said Alice. 'And next time, perhaps you can think of summat to draw that doesn't cause an upset.'

'But I didn't really think of the picture – that is, decide and work it all out,' insisted Millie. 'That's what the drawings do sometimes: sort of draw themselves.'

'I don't understand, Millie. You can choose to set them down or not. And if it's summat that might upset someone, it's just better not to do it.'

Millie looked as if she was about to answer this, but

after a visible struggle with her mouth, she just nodded and went to apologise to Bella.

'What do you think she meant?' asked Thomas.

'I don't know, Dad. Uncle Frank and Aunt Mona said she'd drawn summat that upset them, but I didn't ask what it was, of course. I think our Millie's a child still in some ways and doesn't realise it's sometimes – often – better to keep quiet. As we should have done just now about Bella marrying Sidney Bennett. I just hope Millie doesn't repeat our opinions where she shouldn't, or, indeed, at all.'

'Ah, lass, you're a good girl with a kind heart. And you've the sense of your mother, I'm happy to say.'

'Oh, Dad, how I wish that were true.'


The following week, Bella went along to the bookshop to meet Alice from work. The evenings were lighter now, with Easter approaching.

'I thought we could go to see the beach hut,' Bella suggested. 'Millie said she'd be done today. She might still be there, finishing off, and I'm so excited about it, can't wait to see what she's done.'

Bella was not one to bear a grudge, and she had tried very hard to put the upset of the previous week behind her and restore affectionate relations with her young cousin. Sneaking a peek at a girl's wedding dress was a pretty mean trick, though, and Bella thought it wise to bear in mind that Millie wasn't entirely to be trusted – as if she hadn't already suspected that.

'Good idea. I can't wait either,' said Alice, and they set off towards the beach.

'I'm hoping I might see Sidney,' said Bella. 'I told him yesterday that I would probably go to the hut today after work. He's that busy at work just lately that he's been a bit distracted . . .'

'Well, then, keep an eye open for him,' said Alice.

What they both saw, however, as they neared that end of the beach, was a plume of grey smoke rising into the air and blowing gently inland on the breeze from the sea.

'That looks like a big bonfire,' said Alice. 'Gracious, the smoke is getting thicker by the moment. You don't think it's summat serious, do you, Bella?'

'I don't know. It's hard to tell exactly where it's coming from. C'mon, let's go up onto the path and see what's going on.'

They trudged along the beach, then hurried up the stairs, unconsciously growing faster. It was evident now, by the increasingly dense clouds of black smoke and the smell, that the fire was big and quickly getting bigger.

'It might be where the large houses are, on the road beyond the path,' said Alice. 'I think we should just go and see, in case . . .'

She didn't need to explain.

Neither gave a glance to the newly painted beach hut, but ran along the path that led towards Baybury. The smoke was even thicker now and the air full of the smell of it, smuts and ash blowing about. Soon, the girls could hear the crackle of flames and then the distant bells of approaching fire engines.

'Oh my goodness, it's Mrs Hailsham's house,' gasped Alice.

From their position on the footpath, out of the way of the action, Bella and Alice could see flames leaping up behind some of the top-floor windows. There was the sound of glass breaking as a window exploded outwards and the flames reached out, feeding on the fresh air, to engulf the frame and start to blacken the walls. More dense plumes of smoke billowed out. Even where they stood watching helplessly, the girls could feel the heat building and hear the roar of the fire consuming the house. Their eyes began to sting with the smoke, which also caught in their throats.

Three fire engines, the bells at their fronts being clanged rigorously, came down the road and drew up outside the Hailshams' house. Firemen leaped out and began their well-practised work with hydrants, hoses and ladders. By now, the Hailshams' neighbours at both sides had evacuated their own houses and were congregating on the wide verge between the seafront path, where Alice and Bella stood, and the road. A woman was crying and her husband was talking to one of the firemen, pointing to Mrs Hailsham's house and obviously telling him who lived there.

Bella and Alice continued to keep well back, unable to contribute anything, but mesmerised by the inferno.

It seemed uncaring to turn away when the fire was so very serious.

Soon, the roof was smoking and then flames began to break through. The firemen had their ladders up and were directing their hoses high, although the ferocious jets of water seemed to be making little difference.

'Can you see if anyone's going inside to rescue the Hailshams?' asked Bella, teetering on tiptoes and craning her neck but unable to see anything because of the fire engines.

'No, I can't see a thing. Let's just hope they're out and safe,' said Alice, looking distraught. 'Oh, Bella, it was only the other day that I was here and they were so . . . unhappy, so unsettled. And now this!' She wrung her hands. 'So many bad things . . .'

Bella had tears in her eyes, and not just from the smoke. 'Awful . . . awful . . .' she kept saying.

'I wish we could do summat,' said Alice. She looked round, taking in the scene. 'Oh, isn't that Muriel Chalfont? What's she doing here?'

'So it is. I think she lives in one of the other houses. She must have had to leave.'

'That's a bad job for her. It looks like her parents over there, too. I think we should go and see if we can do owt for them.'

'It would be mean not to,' said Bella. She didn't care for Muriel, but she wouldn't wish this situation on anyone.

Mrs Chalfont and Muriel were both visibly very upset, of course, but Mr Chalfont was taking his role as head of the household very seriously and being bossy and sensible.

'Thank you, Alice, but I reckon our home will escape the flames,' he said. 'It might be better if we stayed at the hotel tonight, though, what with the smoke, the smell, and the unfortunate situation. The fire brigade will be here a long while yet, too.'

'Do you know if the Hailshams were at home when the fire broke out?' Bella had to ask.

'I'm rather supposing so, although I don't know for sure. We'll have to leave it to the professionals to do their work, and trust it's not as bad as it might be,' Mr Chalfont said.

An ambulance arrived just at that moment and the two crew got out and rushed into the garden of the burning house with medical bags.

'Looks like they've found them,' said Mr Chalfont.

Alice and Bella glanced at each other with big round eyes.

'Are they dead? Oh, don't let me see!' cried Muriel, but craned her neck to look. 'Oh, it's too horrible to have people dying right next door to us.'

'Hush now, love. They might be alive,' said her mother.

'I think we should go,' said Alice, quietly. 'Useless spectators aren't helping and . . . well, there comes a point where it's just . . . better to go. C'mon, Bella.'

Bella, looking stricken, nodded.

'I'm so sorry you've been caught up in this. I hope you don't suffer any real damage,' said Alice to Mrs Chalfont.

'Thank you, Alice.' Mrs Chalfont patted her shoulder and then waved a sad little goodbye.

'Bye, you two,' said Muriel, her eyes still fixed on the ambulance so as not to miss a second of the unfolding tragedy.

Bella started to make her way back along the path that led to the beach huts. Alice, following a few steps behind, turned for a last look at the fire, only to see a stretcher being carried into the back of the ambulance. On it was a body covered entirely in a blanket. She had no way of knowing if it was Mrs Hailsham or her daughter, but it must be one of them. She wanted to wait, to see if a second body was brought out, but she didn't want Bella to see, and she felt a little ashamed, too, as if she were a spectator at a public execution where choosing to watch was in very poor taste, and so she hurried to catch up with her sister, tears pricking her eyes.

They walked slowly and silently back the way they had come, having nothing to say that could add to what they both so clearly felt about the terrible fire.

When they came to the row of beach huts, it was almost a surprise to them both to see their own looking as shiny as new, with pristine stripes of deep sky blue and white, the strong aroma of new paint evident, even with the ashy smell in the air.

'I'd nearly forgotten about the hut,' said Bella. 'It seems like hours since we decided to come to see it.'

'I feel the same,' said Alice.

Their eyes moved sideways to Mrs Hailsham's hut, now looking shabbier than ever compared to their own, and with boards nailed over the broken windows. Alice thought that the sad-looking beach hut would not be used again.

'We should look carefully so we can say to Millie how nice ours is and how pleased we are,' said Bella quietly, swallowing back tears. 'It does look lovely.' But her heart wasn't in anything to do with the beach hut now, and soon the sisters walked on towards home, taking the path alongside the Promenade.

After a minute or two, they heard the parp of a car horn and a vehicle neither of them had seen before drew up beside them. It was a very smart Morris Minor saloon, and Bobbie Reeves was waving from the driver's seat.

Alice went to the window, and Bobbie leaned over and wound it down.

'Hello, Alice. And Bella. I thought it was you. Would you like a lift home?'

'Oh yes, please,' said Alice, cheering up.

She got in the front, and Bella sat in the back.

'That fire!' began Bobbie. 'I was seeing someone who knows my father at the hotel, and I left the car at this end. I couldn't believe how bad the smoke was. Did you see anything of it?'

Alice recounted what they knew and what they had seen. She didn't mention the body she had witnessed being brought out to the ambulance.

'How simply awful,' said Bobbie. She put out a hand and squeezed Alice's. 'I do hope your friends are all right. Certainly, it doesn't sound as if their house will be.'

'No,' said Bella sadly. 'Mebbe we'll learn more about what's happened in a few days. There's nowt we can do.'

'If I hear anything in Baybury I'll let you know, shall I?' offered Bobbie.

'Well, we haven't got a telephone,' Alice reminded her. 'But I can speak on the shop phone. There!'

They were just passing E. & G. Patterson Books as she spoke, and she pointed across to it.

'So that's where you work,' said Bobbie. 'I was trying to think where it was when you said it was a bookshop on Theddleton High Street. D'you know, I always thought that place was . . . well, I'm sorry to be rude, but I know it's not your own shop . . . I always thought it was a junk shop. I know that's silly of me, but I think it has something to do with that window.'

Bella, despite the horrible evening so far, was smiling from the backseat. 'Oh, Alice, isn't that just what Millie said? Really, the Pattersons should know how folk regard it, and mebbe they'd see it with fresh eyes themselves.'

'I think Mr Patterson already knows, but Miss P doesn't like change, especially if the idea is someone else's or involves spending money.'

'Perhaps I should come in one day soon and make a bit of a point about it,' suggested Bobbie, with a twinkle in her eye. 'I'll pretend I've never met you and I just happen to be passing – what do you think?'

'I think if an impressively smart and well-heeled woman came in and just happened to remark to Miss Patterson about how her window was letting her shop down, she might take some notice, whereas she never takes notice of owt I say,' said Alice.

'Aha! A little play-acting and a touch of mischief – the spice of life, in my book. Gosh, what an awful pun! Now it's this turning, isn't it? Right, I shall see you at the shop, Alice, to carry out this act of intrigue. I shall bring Father's car – this one's my own – and park it right outside, shall I? At least the car's impressively smart and well-heeled, even if I'm not.'

Alice laughed. She was so pleased to have met Bobbie again and to have enjoyed a few minutes of charming amusement on what was otherwise a horrible evening. 'I shall look forward to that, Bobbie.'

Bobbie drew up outside number 8 Chapel Lane and then turned the beam of her beautiful smile on Alice.

'So shall I,' she said.

# CHAPTER TWELVE

FROM THE FRONT door, Alice and Bella watched Bobbie turn her car and drive away with a little wave. Their spirits had been lifted briefly by the vivacious young woman, with her confident air of independence. Bella thought her sensible, capable, yet not at all strait-laced or dull. She wished she was more like her.

When Bella and Alice went inside, however, gloom settled on them both again.

'We'll have to tell Dad and Millie about the fire,' said Alice quietly, as they took off their outdoor shoes in the hall. 'It'll be in the newspapers, and besides, they've both met Mrs Hailsham, and Dad was well acquainted with her husband. They should hear it from us first.'

'You're right, of course, Alice, but, oh dear . . . I really don't want to go over it in detail. It was just awful. I wish now that we hadn't gone to see.'

'So do I,' said Alice heavily.

Millie, however, was not at home.

'I haven't seen her since I got back from the Three-Mile,' said Thomas. 'I thought she was painting the beach hut.'

'She has been, and it looks lovely. We went along to see it, hoping to find her there, but she had obviously finished already and gone. But, Dad, while we were out that way, we saw summat really horrible,' began Bella, distress bubbling up inside her as she recalled what she had seen of the ferocity of the fire.

The girls went on to tell him what they knew: how bad the fire had looked, how many engines had attended, and that the neighbours, including the Chalfonts, had had to leave their houses for their own safety.

Thomas, who had seen the distant smoke but knew nothing about the fire, was horrified.

'Oh, that poor woman, Rosemary Hailsham. As if she hasn't had enough cares in her life, and she unable to find the strength to manage. I just hope she and Marjory escaped the blaze, but . . . well, where will they live? What will happen to them now?'

Further gloom descended on the household, and Alice was glad she hadn't said anything about the tragic sight she had seen as she and Bella were leaving. She didn't know who had died in the fire, and it would be wrong to guess and make everyone else feel even more unhappy. Bella, particularly, took everything to heart, and Thomas wasn't much better. They would all learn the truth soon enough.

They were just having a restorative cup of tea when Millie came in, singing loudly and seemingly in a very good mood indeed.

She gave one look at the family, congregated miserably in the sitting room, and asked, 'What?'

Bella recounted what they had seen again.

Millie listened very carefully, and the look on her face was difficult for Bella to interpret. It wasn't satisfaction exactly, but she certainly wasn't upset.

'That's bad luck on them,' she said, with a little frown, more puzzlement than unhappiness. 'Perhaps Mrs Hailsham was a little clumsy with a cigarette or something.'

'It's not for us to speculate, Millie,' said Thomas. 'If she was, she's paid dearly for a moment's carelessness.'

'Was the house quite destroyed?' Millie asked. Her face showed only curiosity, not pity or sadness at the terrible event.

'I doubt it's more than a shell now,' said Alice quietly. 'We didn't stay to see. Such a fine house, and such a big blaze.'

'We were up at that end of the beach to catch you after work,' Bella explained. 'I thought you might just be finishing your painting.'

'No, I was all done earlier this afternoon. Did you see it? Do you like it?' Millie was apparently well able to shrug off the subject of the destruction of the Hailshams' home.

'We'll go again and have a proper look. We were a bit distracted by the fire today. But the beach hut did look as good as new, from what I saw,' said Bella, not wanting Millie to feel they didn't care about her efforts. 'Thank you for doing it, and if anyone asks, we'll be very keen to recommend you.'

'Thank you,' said Millie, beaming. 'Now, shall I start on the cooking?'

The others looked at each other. Millie certainly was full of energy this evening.

'I'll do it – you can help,' said Bella, getting up slowly.

While they were standing at the table, side by side, cutting up vegetables, Bella noticed that Millie's clothes and hair smelled of smoke. Previously, she'd smelled of paint and sea air while she'd been working on the beach hut.

'So what did you do after you'd finished painting?' Bella asked tentatively, continuing peeling carrots and not looking at Millie.

'I went down to the allotments.'

'Oh, yes? Who did you see there?'

'Mrs Cook and Edwin were on their plot. And old Mr Wilkinson.'

'That's good. What had they got to say?'

'Not much really,' said Millie, with a shrug. 'Now, are you going to let me cook these carrots with some butter, or do we have to have boring old plain boiled?'

'We're having them boiled. Millie, was there, mebbe, a bonfire at the allotments?' asked Bella, trying not to let a very bad thought that had entered her mind grow into any kind of possibility, trying to keep her tone casual and light.

*Surely not . . . No, not such destruction, such hatred . . .*

Millie stopped chopping carrots and turned to look at her. Bella met Millie's eyes and saw a strange and unnerving light in them that she couldn't interpret. There was a long moment when neither of them moved and Bella hardly dared to breathe. She felt a rush of nerves to her stomach, a *frisson* of fear.

'You've guessed right, Bella,' Millie said calmly. 'In fact, it was me that lit it.'

'What!' Bella could feel the blood draining from her face, and she sank into a kitchen chair.

'Yes, Slow William was clearing an unused plot and there was stuff to burn. The smoke was terrible as it was all too damp to burn nicely . . . not like Mrs Hailsham's house,' she added, almost under her breath.

Bella's stomach did a complete flip. 'Millie, don't ever make a joke of anyone's terrible misfortune again. That's not funny or clever: it's just horrible. I don't like you hanging around the allotments with Slow William, and I don't like you being uncaring about people in Theddleton. This is a nice place to live, and most folk know summat of many of the others and care about them. So, please, just be kind, can't you?'

'I don't see anyone caring much about Slow William,' said Millie. 'Why shouldn't I be friends with him? I thought he was scary at first, but he isn't once you get to know him. You don't mind me being friends with Edwin Cook.'

'Millie, stop being difficult,' snapped Bella. 'You know

perfectly well what the difference is between Slow William and Edwin.'

'Well, they're both people, so don't they deserve the same consideration?'

Bella slumped forward and put her hands over her face. 'Millie,' she said eventually, 'will you please just stop it? It was very upsetting, seeing Mrs Hailsham's house going up in flames, and I really am not in the mood to field your daft arguments. Now, I'd prefer to do the tea by myself, so please just go up and change out of those smoky clothes, and don't come down until you have snapped out of whatever it is that's making you awkward.'

With a sudden and violent fling of her arm, Millie drove the point of the kitchen knife into the wooden tabletop a few inches from Bella's arm and stomped out of the kitchen, leaving the knife handle quivering upright with her anger. Bella heard her feet drumming up the stairs, then the next flight, then the distant slam of her attic-room door.

Thomas came in to see Bella visibly wilting over the kitchen table. Silently he pulled the knife from the table and laid it safely to one side.

'I heard the end of that. Don't fret, love. She's just upset about the Hailshams, I reckon, and it's put her in an odd mood. I think what our Millie needs is summat to occupy her. There's one of the girls at the Three-Mile about to leave, and I'll ask Mr Fairbanks if he'll take on Millie in her place. She'll be pleased of the money –

truth is, we'll all be pleased of a bit more coming in – and I'm sure she will manage the work. If owt doesn't suit her, she'll just have to learn to say nowt about it. It'll only be until she's got some cash to buy her painting things and the commissions start coming in.'

'I don't know if she's upset about the Hailshams, Dad, and I don't know what she thinks about the fire,' said Bella tiredly. 'I *hope* she's upset, as any right-thinking person would be, but she has a strange way of showing it, if so. But I agree that she's not got enough to occupy her, and there's a danger of her wasting this precious time while she's so young by misbehaving and getting into the wrong company. Slow William, I ask you! As for the job at the inn – well, she's wayward, and she won't do it if she doesn't want to. But yes, why not ask Mr Fairbanks?' She stood up and straightened her back, pulling herself together. 'Perhaps she'll love it, working there . . .'

'Oh, love, I doubt I'd go that far.'

'. . . And mebbe the discipline of a regular job is exactly what Millie needs.'

The following day, Bella felt drained, and her eyes were still prickly from the smoke from the fire. The talk at the toyshop was all about that. The Warminsters had heard about it, of course, and were stricken to think an acquaintance of Bella's had suffered such a misfortune.

'Oh, Bella, love . . . here, have another custard cream,' said Cassie, passing her an opened packet. It was all she could think of to offer immediate comfort – that and extra sugar in Bella's tea. 'What you need is summat to take your mind off yesterday. Now, I'd give you the morning off, but I don't want you wasting time wandering about aimlessly because you're in a tizz about Mrs Hailsham, so I'd like you to get on with those babies' rompers and see how many of those dolls you can dress by the end of the morning.'

Bella appreciated Mrs Warminster's good sense – and her business sense – and she set to work at the cutting table and the sewing machine, managing to make clothes for several of the naked baby dolls that were bought in and then enhanced with the cute and pretty outfits for which the Warminster dolls were well known, as well as serving in the shop and selling a whole box of tin soldiers, a child-size badminton set and three board games.

By midday, Bella was feeling more cheerful.

The shop closed at lunchtime. Sometimes she liked to meet Sidney then, but lately he'd been busy, he said, and so she stayed in and ate her sandwich in the workroom. While she was eating, Bella pulled a magazine out of her bag and opened it at a page she'd marked.

'What do you think of these flowers?' she asked her employers, who also sat in the workroom to eat their lunch.

'For your wedding bouquet?' asked Cassie.

'Yes, of course,' smiled Bella. 'I don't often buy flowers, I'm afraid.'

'Well, I can see they're very dainty,' said Alfred. 'But have you thought if these will be available in September?'

'No,' said Bella. 'Oh dear, you're right, of course. These lilies-of-the-valley are spring flowers.' She put the magazine away with a sigh. 'I can't afford hothouse or special out-of-season flowers.'

'Well, that needn't be a problem,' said Cassie. 'Choose summat that's in season in September and go and see Iris Cook. You know she does the flowers in church, don't you?'

'I'd forgotten that. I'm not much of a one for church on a weekly basis.'

'Ask Iris if she'll help you with the bouquets – I'm sure she'll agree to. And didn't you tell me that your father grows flowers?'

'He does. The front garden is beginning to look lovely, and he's got a patch at the back for flowers for the house. Mam loved to have flowers indoors; he started growing them for her and has just carried on in her memory.'

'There you are, then,' said Cassie. 'Pretty English garden flowers. In September, there'll be roses and asters and mebbe some delphiniums in season. Ask your dad and I reckon he'll be pleased to make sure there's summat lovely for you and your bridesmaid. They won't cost you owt, and with a bit of arranging by Iris, they'll look better than any bought from the shops.'

'Mrs Warminster, you are clever,' said Bella.

'Oh, you'd have thought of it yourself in time,' said

Cassie. 'And have you persuaded Alice into a pretty bridesmaid frock yet?'

'No, I think summat plain and elegant might suit her better. Alice doesn't really go in for "pretty".'

'With your skills, I'm sure you can make a beautiful dress for her that you'll both be pleased with. But you'll need to be starting now, if you haven't already. And what about your cousin, Millie? Is she also to be a bridesmaid?'

It was then that Bella realised she hadn't even thought of a role for Millie in her wedding. It wasn't a deliberate omission, just an oversight. She tried to imagine Millie in a dress that would match the kind that Alice might wear – and failed. Then she tried to think of her in something younger and prettier in style – and failed there, too. After their disagreement yesterday, and the horrible suspicion Bella had had about the fire, which she was still trying to forget, she didn't know what to think about Millie. All she knew was that her young cousin, far from being one of the Marchant family now, as her father thought, was largely unknown to them. First the smashed windows at Mrs Hailsham's beach hut and then the house fire – Bella felt almost ashamed thinking either incident had anything to do with Millie, but she just could not entirely lay to rest her last tiny nagging suspicions. It was, to Bella's mind, as if she was acknowledging that Millie could deliberately step out of their embrace and away into dark and murky shadows. How could she ask someone she really didn't know or understand to be her bridesmaid?

'Bella?' It was Cassie, prompting her for an answer.

'I'll see,' said Bella. It was the most truthful answer she felt she could give.

Bella was so busy with the after-school mayhem at the toyshop – bold little boys grabbing marbles and pop-guns, and shy little girls wanting cut-out books of paper dolls – that she managed to avoid any unwelcome thoughts distracting her.

'Off you go early, Bella, and don't forget to ask your father and Iris Cook about the wedding flowers,' said Cassie, as Bella tidied up after the rush of children had subsided at about four o'clock. 'It will be summat sorted out, and then you can tick it off your list, and that will cheer you up. If you've an hour or two spare, you might want to think about making a start fitting those pattern pieces for your dress, too. You haven't got bags of time. If Alice isn't any help, bring the pattern here and I'll give you a hand, if you like? I promise your dress will remain a secret.'

'Thank you,' said Bella. 'You are so kind, Mrs Warminster.'

'Nonsense. I shall never be a mother-of-the-bride, not having a daughter of my own, so I hope you don't mind if I take an interest in your wedding preparations, love. It'll be a pleasure for me to help if I can.'

'You've been helpful already.' Bella smiled.

She and Cassie looked round as the shop bell rang again.

Standing on the threshold was a tall, thin young man

with neat dark hair and little round glasses. He had tiny upward creases at the corners of his eyes, suggesting he often smiled, as he was doing now. It took Bella a moment to recognise who it was.

'Toby!' Cassie swooped to hug her boy, and Alfred, hearing their son's name, came through from the back room to shake his hand.

'We weren't expecting you until tomorrow.'

'Finished everything early – with the incentive of seeing my olds to spur me on – and got the first train I could. How are you both?'

'Fine, thank you, love,' Cassie answered for them. 'Now, do you remember Bella Marchant, our employee and treasure? I'm sure you two have met before.'

'Of course,' said Toby with a wider smile. 'Bella, it's a long while since I saw you – just bad luck that I've missed you more recently, p'raps – but I'm pleased to see you looking so well today.' He gazed at her with open admiration.

Bella felt shy for a moment as she offered her hand. 'How lovely to see you again, Toby. How are you?'

'Oh, very well, thank you. All the better for getting back to Theddleton. For all that my folks are incomers from Scarborough way, Theddleton feels like home. It certainly beats London and its filthy air, hands down.'

Bella was pleased to hear this, being a Theddleton girl, born and bred.

'Incomers?' laughed Alfred. 'Why, we've lived here for years.'

232

'About six,' said Toby. 'So only another fifty to go before you're classed as locals. Unfortunately, I never will be, living and working in the Smoke.'

'Remind me what it is you do,' Bella said. 'I'm sure I've been told and ought to know.'

'I'm a tailor. It's not just women who can sew, is it, Mam?'

'Our Toby's far more talented than I am,' said his proud mother. 'Suits for toffs, fancy waistcoats – the lot.'

'Not talent, Mam, just training. But it was you who started me off with the sewing, don't forget.'

'Well, I hope you enjoy your stay,' said Bella. 'I'm off now, but I hope I'll see you tomorrow.'

'So do I,' said Toby. 'Have a nice evening.'

She went to the workroom door to put on her coat and take up her bag.

As she turned to leave, she gave a little wave goodbye at the door, but the Warminster parents were fussing round their son like nesting birds with one chick, and they didn't notice her.

For a moment, Bella felt strangely excluded. How silly, when she had her father and Alice, who loved her every bit as much as Cassie and Alfred Warminster loved Toby.

But then, she thought, as she let herself out into the High Street, what of Millie? How did they fit together? They had struck up an immediate affection, but now Bella felt it was being undermined by . . . what, exactly? Mistrust? Millie's wayward disregard for other people?

The dynamic at home had shifted since Millie's arrival. Bella allowed herself the indulgence of thinking, for the briefest of moments, that it had been better before Millie came. Then she mentally slapped herself. Millie had no one; Bella had her family and friends, and she had Sidney.

Chastising herself for her mean thought, Bella decided to go to have another, proper look at the beach hut and see if anyone was around who might want theirs repainted for the coming summer.

She set off towards the beach, passing the bookshop. There was no sign of Alice when she glanced through the door – or anyone else – and no sign of Bobbie Reeves's father's monumental car parked outside. Bella hoped Bobbie wouldn't forget what she had said about supporting Alice over changing the dismal window. Bobbie didn't seem like the kind of person who would offer to do something and then forget or not bother, and she and Alice clearly liked each other.

At the hotel, instead of crossing the road straight away, Bella continued along by the front of the grand building. Looking up between the pillars into the foyer, she saw people milling around, possibly waiting to be shown into the dining room for afternoon tea. The dining-room windows, very tall, with swags of crimson velvet around them, looked out onto the Promenade from behind some railings and tubs of manicured little trees. It did look rather formal, not very relaxed, with tablecloths so stiff they stuck out around the table legs,

and lots of crimson and gold-edged crockery. And . . .
good heavens! Wasn't that Sidney?

Bella screwed up her eyes and peered up into the
window. Yes, it was Sidney, without any doubt, looking
dapper and wearing that very striking tie he'd first
worn to the fundraising do. He clearly had expected
to be visiting the Imperial Hotel today and not just
going to his desk at the town hall, yet he'd been too
busy to meet her at lunchtime. And who was he with?
By now, Bella was unconsciously making a spectacle
of herself on the pavement, craning her neck, pulling
herself up on the railings to see who was partially hidden
by the fall of the curtain.

Sidney must have noticed the movement down in the
street, outside the window where he was sitting, because
he looked round and – for one very brief moment – the
expression on his face was almost a caricature of guilt,
like a cartoon with the caption *Caught Out.*

Then Muriel Chalfont leaned across towards him,
putting her hand on his arm, and she, too, turned to
look outside. The expression on her face was, just for
a second or two, unguarded triumph. Words were
exchanged, and then Sidney made a rather awkward
beckoning gesture to Bella to join them.

Bella realised she'd been almost climbing the railings,
her mouth open, and she hurriedly tried to regain her
dignity, straightening the sleeves of her coat while
thinking what on earth to do. She didn't really want to
have tea with them in the stuffy hotel, but she was very

interested to know why Sidney and Muriel Chalfont were sitting there together on a Friday afternoon.

The doorman opened the door for her without much of a flourish, and Bella set off across the foyer to the dining room like a woman on a mission.

'May I help you, madam?' asked the head waiter, guarding the dining room.

'I am joining Miss Chalfont and Mr Bennett for tea,' said Bella. 'They are expecting me.'

She was shown to their table, another chair was brought, and Sidney at least had the manners to stand up and greet her with a kiss on the cheek.

'Oh, Bella, we thought it was you,' said Muriel. 'I was just saying to Sidney, wouldn't it be funny if Bella came by and saw us having tea together?'

'And I said I expected you were at the toyshop.'

'But, what a surprise, there you were, craning your neck like you've never seen owt as smart as the hotel dining room. And we couldn't let you think we were having an assignation of some illegal kind,' said Muriel, trilling a merry laugh.

'Illicit,' said Bella.

'What?'

'An illicit assignation.'

'Not one of them either,' said Sidney.

'Do sit down, Bella, and have a cup of tea,' said Muriel. She waved her hand imperiously, and a waiter came over with a place setting for Bella. Another waiter followed with a fresh pot of tea.

'Well, this is nice,' said Sidney awkwardly, rubbing his hands together nervously. Whatever he and Muriel had been talking about before Bella arrived, they weren't going back to the subject now.

'I'm glad to see you are all right, Muriel, after the terrible fire yesterday,' said Bella politely. 'I hope there was no damage to your parents' house.'

'Not to ours, thank goodness. Sidney very kindly came round here when he heard about the fire and our having to evacuate our home, to see if I was all right.'

'Yes,' said Sidney. 'Everyone was worried about you . . . and your parents, of course.'

That at least explained what Sidney was doing here, although why his enquiry about the Chalfonts should involve having afternoon tea, Bella didn't know. It was kind of Sidney to come and see that they were all right, yet Bella couldn't forget the look on his face when he'd seen her through the window. Probably he just thought she might misinterpret his being here, which was exactly what she was doing, of course.

'But what of the Hailshams?' asked Bella. 'I haven't heard owt since I saw their house was burning down.'

'You saw it?' asked Sidney.

'Yes, Alice and I were on the beach when we saw the smoke, and we went to see if there was owt we could do, but the fire brigade were just arriving, and the fire was massive already.'

'Well, I'm afraid the Hailshams are both dead,'

announced Muriel boldly, her voice betraying her pride in being the one with the prime information.

'Oh, no!' gasped Bella. 'I did fear that – the fire was so fierce – but I just hoped . . . Oh, what a terrible thing to happen. I am sorry.' She felt tears prick her eyes. Rosemary Hailsham had been little more than an acquaintance in the neighbouring beach hut, and Bella knew Marjory only by sight and reputation, but it was tragic that they had both died before their time, and in such a horrible way.

Muriel shrugged and leaned in, pouring tea into Bella's cup, then adding too much milk without asking her. 'Bit too fond of the drink, Rosemary Hailsham,' she said, her eyes sparkling with relish at the gossip. 'It wouldn't surprise me if there hadn't been a little *carelessness* and that caused the fire.'

Bella was about to shut off this line of conversation when Muriel added, 'Very sad for them, of course, but lucky for us. Dad's thinking of buying up their plot of land, knocking down the ruined house and building summat even bigger. Folk pay a lot for nice houses like ours, overlooking the sea, or it could be a business opportunity.'

Bella could not believe what she was hearing. Had the woman no shame, no respect? She turned to see how Sidney was taking these words in such outrageously poor taste, but he was still looking strangely nervous. Surely he had heard what Muriel just said? How could he possibly condone her selfishness, her lack of shame?

'Well, at least Rosemary and Marjory Hailshams' deaths have some advantage *to you*,' said Bella, getting up. 'So the whole sorry episode is not entirely tragic. I won't stop for tea, thank you. Mebbe I'll see you tomorrow, Sidney.'

She got up and left quickly, hoping no one there actually mistook her for a friend of the ghastly Muriel Chalfont. She felt tainted to be in this hotel, owned by a man who had already speculated about how he might profit from such a tragedy. And she was surprised that Sidney obviously didn't feel the same.

# CHAPTER THIRTEEN

WHEN BELLA GOT home that afternoon, she felt more desolate about the fire than ever. It had been a mistake to go to look at the beach hut again so soon. The air at that end of Theddleton was still heavy with the smell of smoke, and there was hardly anyone on the beach or walking along the Promenade, as if the townspeople had an unspoken agreement to stay away as a mark of respect for the Hailshams. There was no one to show off the newly painted stripes to, no one to whom she could recommend Millie's skills. It didn't matter: in the circumstances, the subject of painted beach huts was too frivolous to mention anyway.

Bella broke the sad news of the deaths of Rosemary and Marjory Hailsham to her father, who was back from the Three-Mile and pottering around in the garden. Thomas took off his cap and bowed his head. When he looked up, his face was etched with sadness.

'Ah, what a terrible thing. I wonder when the funeral will be and who is to organise it. I'll ask at the *Informer* office when I'm next passing, see if anyone knows, but if you hear owt, please be sure to tell me, Bella.'

'Of course, Dad.'

Bella decided a discussion about her father growing flowers for her wedding bouquets could wait until another day. Now was not the time for such things. Nor would she be doing anything about her wedding dress this evening.

'You're back a bit earlier than usual, love,' said Thomas. 'Or have I lost track of time?' He glanced up at the sky, trying to gauge the hour by the level of light.

'It's not long after five o'clock now. Mrs Warminster let me have the rest of the afternoon off after we'd dealt with the rush of children. That's how I came to see Muriel Chalfont, who told me about the Hailshams. The Warminsters' son, Toby, turned up as I was leaving work.'

'They'll be pleased to see him. Doesn't he work in London?'

Bella related what she knew of Toby Warminster. She recalled his smiling eyes and thought that her encounter with him, brief and full of social conventions though it had been, had been something of a high point today, especially set against the terrible news about the Hailshams and the unpleasantness of Muriel Chalfont. And quite why Sidney was having tea with Muriel when he said he'd only gone to enquire about her welfare after the fire was still a mystery. Probably she had just invited him to show off, playing the hostess in her father's grand hotel. That would be typical.

Bella went indoors, swapped her work shoes for older ones, and her coat for two ancient cardigans, and came back out to help weed around the rose bushes in the last of the afternoon light.

'Did you ask Mr Fairbanks if he'd consider Millie when the girl who's leaving goes?' asked Bella.

'Ah, yes,' said Thomas. 'The job's hers if she wants it. Of course, it'll be up to Millie, but I think she ought to take it. She needs to feel she can do summat, can contribute and make her own way. I'd love her to do as she wants: to paint pictures, or murals in folk's houses. That will come in time, with talent and good fortune, I'm sure, but she can't just wait for that good fortune to find her, because it won't. She needs to get out and meet folk. You get to meet all kinds at the Three-Mile and, you never know, it could lead to an unforeseen opening for Millie.'

'Well, we'll see,' said Bella, thinking that her father's job as a potman hadn't opened up any opportunities for him. He hadn't mentioned meeting anyone interesting, either – just anonymous customers who passed through, never to be seen again. Still, he'd only been there a couple of months.

And there she was, hoping and wishing for him again, when he never made the slightest effort to pull himself up. So much work for so little pay, Mr Fairbanks's

legendary impatience to deal with, and not a chance of
the wretched job leading to anything better. Sometimes
it was hard work being optimistic, especially about her
father and his prospects.

Millie, however, had expressed her determination to
find her place in the world, Bella remembered. Bella
only hoped she'd learn that sometimes you needed to
take a circuitous route to your goal, if the direct one
was too difficult to achieve, otherwise she might be
disappointed. She might be waiting for ever for an
opening as an artist, when all she'd done so far was
paint the outside of the beach hut and illustrate
Thomas's stories.

When Millie came in, having spent the afternoon
doing nothing more than messing about in the *Hope
and Peace* with Edwin, she didn't seem to be at all
saddened by the news of the death of the Hailshams.

'Well, I'm sorry that you're both upset,' she said, 'but
I'd hardly met them.'

And she certainly wasn't enthusiastic about the pro-
spect of the job at the Three-Mile.

'Can't I think about it?' she asked, frowning. 'It's not
what I want to do. Something more in keeping might
come up.'

'I realise that, but you have to start somewhere,' said
Thomas.

'And honestly, Millie, nowt will "come up" if you don't
actively look,' Bella felt she had to point out. 'I could
be telling you the same, Dad,' she added, then turned

her attention back to Millie. 'Really, sweetheart, you've done very little about finding yourself any employment, haven't you?'

'Mr Fairbanks needs to know he's got sufficient staff, and if you don't take the job straight away, he'll have to offer it elsewhere,' Thomas explained. 'But I shall be there, too, of course, so it's not like you'll be in a place full of strangers. I'll keep an eye on you, love.'

'Give it a go, Millie,' persuaded Bella patiently. 'It needn't be for long, just until you've earned some money: a bit for your keep and the rest for yourself. As it is, we can't afford to kit you out with lots of painting materials. You'll soon make friends with the other staff, and then mebbe it won't seem so daunting.'

'I'm not a baby; I don't need friends like a child in a playground,' Millie snapped back at her. 'I shall let you know tomorrow, Uncle Thomas, when I've had time to consider it,' she added imperiously.

Thomas and Bella exchanged glances. Bella rolled her eyes.

'All right then, Millie,' said Thomas. 'But I thought you'd be glad of the pay. And there will be a share of the tips, too. Still, if you haven't told me by the time I leave in the morning, I shall have to tell Mr Fairbanks you don't want the job.'

Millie sighed dramatically. 'I probably don't, anyway.'

'Look, Millie,' said Bella, 'I know things haven't been easy for you, but you're here with us now. You have a home and a family, and we've done our best to make you feel that you're one of us. Now you have to start playing your part. We all have to go to work and earn some money to pay for the things that make this place a home, for the food and clothes, for lighting and coal, all the boring bills. Dad, Alice and I do that, and we are pleased to share it with you, but you need to contribute, too, as you're no longer at school, and mebbe it's time you started.'

'But I will when I find someone who wants to pay me to paint their rooms with beautiful murals, or maybe their portrait. I've got all sorts of ideas.'

'I'm sure you have, sweetheart, but how are you going to find this person? And what about in the meantime? It might be months – years – before you earn any money from commissions. You haven't even started looking for any, have you? You haven't even got any paints. I know it's lovely to have a dream to aim for, but you have to live in the real world, too.'

'But when I'm a world-famous artist, I'll be able to support you all, and you'll be glad then that you didn't make me do some boring old job at the Three-Mile or anywhere else.'

'Millie, I'm the last person to tread on your dreams, but I really think you should give this job a go and not close your mind to it as "boring" before you've even tried it. Dad thinks you'll be able to do it, and you'll have your days off to do whatever else you want to do. When you've earned some money, you can even save up to put an advertisement for your painting – portraits, murals or whatever you want – in the newspaper. I'm sure Alice will help you word it appropriately.'

Millie put her hands over her ears. 'All right, all right, don't go on!' she yelled. 'I'll take the stupid job. It's not what I want to waste my life doing, but if you really think that's all I'm worth then I'll do it.' She flung herself down full length on the sofa, as if she were exhausted just thinking about working at the Three-Mile.

Bella sighed. Really, Millie could be very childish sometimes.

'Well, I'm not going to bribe you to go,' Bella said, crossly.

'Neither am I,' said Thomas, but more gently. 'As I said, just let me know, finally and sensibly, if you've decided to take the job by the time I leave tomorrow.'

Thomas left the cottage for work the following morning with no word from Millie about accepting the job at the Three-Mile Bottom.

Well, he thought, wheeling his bicycle through the garden gate, he'd done his best. He'd thought better of Millie than that she would get worked up and refuse to engage with regular employment, but she had set her heart on this painting lark and nothing else would do. The trouble was, she was an additional person in the house and none of those who worked earned very much. He didn't want to force her into work, but he could see a time fast approaching when she really would have to pull her weight. There was Bella's wedding to pay for.

Bella had paid her way happily since she'd first gone to work at the toyshop, and it wasn't fair if her wedding had to be on an even tighter budget than it was already while Millie lived a life of idleness.

He'd just closed the garden gate when the front door opened, and there was Millie, standing on the doormat in the early morning light.

'Uncle Thomas, I've decided to give the Three-Mile a trial,' she said with solemn dignity. 'Thank you for mentioning me to Mr Fairbanks. I shall start next week, when this Susan has left.'

'Next Friday,' said Thomas. 'Good girl, Millie. I'm glad you've seen sense, love.'

He got on his bicycle and pedalled away down the lane, his spirits lifting. Heaven knew, there were better places to work, but at least he would be able to keep an eye on Millie. Lately, she'd become rather evasive about what she was doing all day while he and his daughters were working. Probably it was just hanging around at the allotments, chatting with Mrs Cook, sailing her boat with Edwin, and perhaps getting up to a bit of innocent mischief, but he needed to be sure she wasn't going off the rails. She had been indulged for long enough.

Nanette had been wilful and naughty, he remembered. There had been some accusations of stealing from various shopkeepers and some evenings when she couldn't be found at home, where she was supposed to be.

And, of course, unforgettably, that time she had attempted to run away, which had ended with Frank, presenting himself as 'head of the household', taking it on himself to bring her back and give her 'a good hiding'.

Remembering his sister's terrible screaming and Frank's shouting, Thomas felt his good mood start to dissipate. *Was* there such a thing as 'a good hiding', he mused. Surely all hidings were bad: barbaric to one party and brutalising for the other. How strange that he and his brother should have such opposing views on physical punishments . . . Certainly the punishment Frank had given his siblings had gone against their mother's wishes, but Frank had been a lot bigger, healthier and stronger than their mother, and there had been no reasoning with him when a temper was on him. Perhaps, given the way the girls said Millie had been treated at Frank and Mona's, Frank had been punishing Nanette still, through her daughter. Again, Thomas wished with all his heart that he had intervened that time in London, instead of being taken in by the childless couple purporting to want the girl. He should have known better . . .

By now, Thomas had reached the long straight road, and there was the inn, the chimneys already showing smoke. He rode round to the back and went to tell Mr Fairbanks that his niece, Millie, would be available to start work on Friday.

At the toyshop, Toby was keen to lend a hand, although his parents didn't like to think of him working on his weekend off.

'Honestly, Dad, it's not like work when it's not *my* work,' he said, carefully wallpapering a miniature parlour. 'How am I doing?'

'What do you think, Bella?' Alfred called through to the shop. 'Does our Toby get many marks out of ten?'

Bella came into the back room to look and pretended to consider. 'Ooh,' she said slowly, sucking her teeth, 'at least a four, I reckon.'

Alfred and Toby laughed, confident that the work was worth full marks, as it was so neat.

At lunchtime, when Alfred closed the shop, he took them all down to the seafront to the Fish and Ship café, as a treat.

'Proper Yorkshire fish and chips by the sea, lad. Summat for you to remember when you're back down south,' said Alfred. 'We'll sit in, in the window, like visitors, and watch folk battling the breeze with their windbreaks.'

Afterwards, everyone felt rather too full to face going back to work.

'We need to get back and open the shop, don't we, Alfred,' said Cassie, easing herself up slowly from her seat as if she had eaten too much, 'but why don't you two youngsters take a stroll along the beach?'

'Oh, Mam, I reckon that's what I need,' said Toby. 'I feel like a snake that's swallowed its prey whole.' He patted his stomach. 'How about it, Bella? I'll enjoy the exercise all the more with your company.'

'Yes, please,' Bella agreed, and she led Toby down to

the beach and turned south, wanting to avoid the other end, with its smoky smell, this afternoon. She didn't want even to think about the fire.

As they walked, Toby asked Bella about her family and her life in Theddleton. She didn't know why, but she didn't mention Sidney or anything to do with her plans for the wedding. Instead, she talked about how much she liked her work, her enthusiasm for knitting and sewing, and about her cousin, Millie, and Thomas and his garden, and about Alice and the bookshop. He, in turn, talked about his life in London, where he rented a room in a house 'out east', and about his ambition to have his own tailoring business one day.

'I'm a keen reader myself,' said Toby, picking up on Alice and the bookshop. 'If I go in this afternoon, do you think your sister will be able to recommend me some wonderful novel for the train journey back to London?'

'Without a doubt,' said Bella. 'And not just one.'

Heading back up the High Street, however, they saw – parked outside the bookshop – the most beautiful grand car.

'It's Bobbie's,' said Bella, delighted. 'I knew Bobbie wouldn't let Alice down.'

'Is Bobbie her boyfriend?' asked Toby.

'Oh, no, Bobbie – Bobbie Reeves – is a really nice woman, and this is really her father's car.' Bella explained about winning the ride out in the car and Alice going instead. 'Bobbie said she'd support Alice over the refurbishment of the shop window. Miss Patterson likes it the way it is, but Alice thinks it needs turning out completely and then a good clean and a fresh look. She's got some lovely ideas. I think Bobbie has in mind some role-playing to persuade Miss Patterson.'

'Aha! Intrigue,' said Toby. 'C'mon, let's go in and see if we can be bit-part players. It'll be fun.'

Actually, thought Bella, the whole afternoon had been fun: the delicious and filling lunch in the gentle and considerate company of all the Warminsters, and the walk in the fresh air with Toby, who was so open and amusing. Now she had the chance to see Bobbie working on changing Eileen Patterson's intractable opinion about the window.

However, she had work to do, and Miss Patterson might suspect a conspiracy if Bella suddenly turned up to support Alice's ideas for the window when Bobbie was there undercover, so to speak, and undoubtedly doing a very good job on her own. So Bella went back to the toyshop while Toby, promising to tell her everything that happened, went into the bookshop.

'I saw a copy of *Mrs Dalloway* in the window,' Bobbie said to Eileen Patterson. 'I wonder if I might have a look at it, please?'

'*Mrs Dalloway*? Hmm, we don't get much call for Virginia Woolf in Theddleton,' said Eileen.

She looked carefully at Bobbie, possibly trying to place her or to reconcile this unusual request with the tall and elegant woman in a smart spring coat and a hat with a jaunty feather. Alice wondered if Bobbie had actually come dressed as Mrs Dalloway, as a kind of joke, but how would she know in advance that there was a copy of the book in the window?

Through the glass in the shop door, Eileen's eyes slid to the huge car parked at the kerb. 'I shall ask my assistant to get it for you. Alice, would you be able to get the Woolf out of the window, please?'

'Yes, Miss Patterson.'

Alice's face twitched with amusement as she lifted the catches of the screen at the back of the window and prepared to climb in and work towards retrieving the book.

At that moment, a tall, thin young man, wearing glasses, came in, gave Alice and Eileen a big smile and said he'd come to browse novels.

'All these downstairs rooms are fiction,' said Eileen. 'Please feel free to look around and let me know if I can help.'

'Thank you,' he said, and went to look on a shelf not far away.

'May I ask which, um, heap . . . whereabouts in the window you saw the book, madam?' asked Alice.

'Oh, I'm not absolutely sure,' said Bobbie. 'I think it was over to the right – no, your left from in here – and somewhere near the bottom of one of those piles.'

'Thank you,' said Alice. 'I wonder, Miss Patterson, if I might pass out to you some of these books, please, so that I can get in to have a look?'

'Of course,' said Eileen. There had been no need for anyone to go into the window for some months.

Alice began carefully lifting out heavily bound books, two or three at a time, giving them to her employer. This slow passing from hand to hand went on for a few minutes. In the meantime, Bobbie waited patiently, with a serene look on her face, seemingly unbothered by the work she was causing. Alice wanted to laugh, but she managed to compose her face and carry on for the greater good of the window.

'Do you remember the colour of the jacket, madam?' Alice asked Bobbie.

'A reddish brown, I think – just boards, no jacket. Shall I go out to the front and direct you to it?' said Bobbie.

'No, no, I shall go,' said Eileen. 'We're sorry to delay you, madam.'

'It's really no trouble for me to wait,' said Bobbie. 'I can see that your window has even more in it than I had thought.'

Books were heaped up in piles on the floor in the main room. It was amazing that the window could have held so many, now removed, and yet could still seem to be almost full.

Eileen offered Bobbie a chair while she waited and then hurried out to the street and peered into the window, trying to see the book, and eventually directed Alice to it by pointing. Then Alice began moving other books so that she could get it without risking an avalanche of heavy volumes falling onto her feet.

Suddenly the young man who had been browsing was leaning into the window area.

'Let me give you a hand,' he said, smiling up at Alice. 'Toby Warminster,' he whispered. 'Bella has told me about the window.' He tapped his nose like a bad actor and grinned.

'Thank you, sir, but there's really no need,' said Alice loudly, just as Eileen re-entered the shop.

Just then, a huge black spider ran out from one corner of the window, and Alice leaped out onto the shop floor with a genuine cry of surprise and revulsion.

'Allow me,' said Toby gallantly. He gathered the creature up in his handkerchief and went to the door to shake it out into the street.

'Wildlife, too,' said Bobbie, loud enough for Eileen to hear. 'Whatever next?'

'Thank you, sir,' Eileen said. 'I do apologise that you were faced with that.'

'I don't mind,' said Toby. 'Where there are cobwebs, there are spiders.'

'It is all a little Miss Havisham,' laughed Bobbie, as if just making an observation.

'Oh, very good,' said Toby. 'Now you've put me in mind of what I might read next.'

Alice had to turn away to hide her smile. The whole scenario was starting to get out of hand, especially with Toby joining in. It didn't look as if Toby and Bobbie were acquainted, but Alice wasn't sure, so well were they playing their complementary roles.

'Here you are, madam,' said Alice, making to hand the book over to Bobbie. 'Oh dear, just a moment . . .' She went to the counter, rummaged behind, and produced a duster to wipe away the cobwebs and general grime.

'Thank you – and for all your effort,' said Bobbie. 'I think if I'd known it was going to be so difficult to access the books in the window, I really wouldn't have asked. You have worked very hard, and all just for one book.'

'It's no trouble,' said Alice. 'Now, please take your time to have a look at it. And do please let me know if there are any others that caught your eye.'

'While you have them out,' laughed Toby, 'I shall take this copy of *Great Expectations*, which this lady so cleverly alluded to in passing.'

'Thank you, sir,' said Eileen, and went to the counter to wrap it in brown paper.

'And I shall take *Mrs Dalloway*,' said Bobbie to Alice.

'Are you sure?' asked Alice quietly. 'You don't have to, just because of the window.'

'Oh, but I want to. I shall think of you struggling with those dusty old volumes while I read it.' Bobbie looked into Alice's face with genuine warmth and amusement in her dark-blue eyes. 'What time do you finish?' she whispered.

'Five thirty,' murmured Alice.

'I'll be parked on the Promenade.'

'I'm sure I'll be able to spot the car.' Then Alice raised her voice: 'Thank you, madam. Is there owt else I can help you with?'

'No, thank you, not today,' said Bobbie.

By now, Toby had left with his book, calling a merry 'Good afternoon, everyone,' from the door, and Alice went round the counter to wrap the book while Eileen wrote out the receipt.

'You know,' said Bobbie to Eileen, as if it had just occurred to her, 'you are missing a trick with your window. I hope you don't mind me saying, but this is a really interesting shop – with attentive staff' – she looked at Eileen, then at Alice, beaming – 'and it seems a shame not to make a feature of the window. You have all that space looking out on the High Street, and yet what is presented to customers looks almost as if it's your storeroom, which you'd never normally allow them to see.'

'We used to have another screen and just a few choice books at the front, but I don't know what happened to that,' said Eileen, suddenly showing a vague side to herself that Alice didn't recognise. 'But the window's got potential that we're wasting, and I have been putting my mind to refurbishing it.'

Alice struggled to compose her face. She dared not try to catch Bobbie's eye.

'Some enjoyable reading is such a big part of being on holiday, isn't it?' said Bobbie. 'I'm sure visitors must throng here in the summer, and a lovely window display would be such an attraction.'

Eileen didn't respond to this but said instead, 'It's good to have the opinion of, well, the kind of customer we are aiming to attract. I shall certainly put some thought to it and see if I can persuade my brother and partner in the business to be a little more inventive with the window display. Thank you, Mrs . . . ?'

'Miss Reeves,' said Bobbie.

'Miss Reeves,' repeated Eileen, writing Bobbie's name on the receipt. 'Thank you for your custom.' She folded the receipt and handed it to Bobbie, while Alice finished tying string around the brown paper wrapping and then handed over the parcel.

'Good afternoon, Miss Reeves,' said Alice, and Bobbie, her eyes twinkling, thanked her and swept out, the feather on her hat flying like her battle colours.

Toby Warminster was hovering just out of sight of the bookshop window in the hope of seeing Bobbie Reeves leaving. After a few minutes, the young woman came out of the shop, unlocked the amazing car and leaned in to put down the book.

'So *Mrs Dalloway* is to be your passenger?' said Toby.

Bobbie straightened up and turned to him with a wide smile. 'Hello again,' she said. 'I'm sorry I didn't catch your name when you were speaking to Alice, but I realise you were somehow in on our little plan.'

'Toby Warminster. Bella, Alice's sister, told me about you, and that you were supporting Alice over the window. Bobbie Reeves, right?'

'Right. Well done with the spider, Mr Warminster. I'm not sure I was up to dealing with that, but I'm pleased to say I think we've achieved what we set out to do this afternoon. Your turning up added a depth to our plot that made it all the more authentic to Miss Patterson.'

'Then I'm pleased, too, Miss Reeves. It was fun.'

'Do you work at the toyshop, too, with Bella? That is Warminster's, isn't it?'

'It is, but it's owned by my parents. I don't work there. I'm only here for the weekend. I'm a tailor, and I work in London.'

'Really?' Bobbie sounded genuinely interested. 'Mr Warminster, you could be just the man I'm looking for. They serve tea at the Imperial Hotel – shall we go and have a cup, and I'll explain?'

'Why not?' said Toby.

Well, that did sound promising. This confident, clever woman, with her poise and social standing, had not only invited him to have tea with her but was alluding to something that sounded like a work opportunity. First the sweet, gentle and extremely pretty Bella Marchant, and now the impressive and assured Bobbie Reeves – it was just a shame, thought Toby, that he would have to be on a train back to London the following afternoon. Perhaps he'd have reason to be visiting his parents more frequently from now on . . .

# CHAPTER FOURTEEN

EARLY THAT EVENING, Bella met Sidney on the Promenade. She was wearing her hair up in an elegant style, wanting to look nice for him. He always made an effort for her, she thought, and sure enough, he was wearing a sports jacket she couldn't remember seeing before, but which fitted his broad shoulders perfectly. They caught the bus to Baybury, where there was a cinema. Neither had thought to look up what was showing, but they decided to take pot luck.

'So why *were* you having tea with Muriel yesterday?' asked Bella when they were sitting side by side on the bus. 'You didn't look very pleased to see me.'

'Well, it was, er, a work thing, really. Not a social occasion. That is, I wasn't really there to enjoy myself . . .'

'Work? Tea with Muriel Chalfont?'

'Yes, it's, um – it's this floral clock.' Sidney lowered his voice, leaning into her so that she would hear him above the sound of the engine while he kept his voice low. 'She's trying to persuade me, in my role in Planning, that her father should pay for it in return for it being an advertisement for the hotel.'

'And so the tea was to . . . er, butter you up?'

'Er, yes . . . yes, I suppose it was.'

'Why didn't she ask Mr Penrose instead, as head of Planning?' Bella knew she was being difficult here. She had met Mr Penrose, Sidney's boss, and she didn't think he was the kind of man who would ever go to a hotel to drink tea. Or lay himself open to bribes.

'I don't know. Perhaps she realises I have the ear of Mr Penrose, and she knows me already, like.'

'So you went to tea with Muriel Chalfont so that she could bribe you about her father sponsoring the floral clock.'

'No! No, it wasn't like that. You see, I heard about the fire, so I just nipped out of the office and went to the hotel to see if she – if *they* – were all OK.'

'Well, you clearly planned to go to the hotel in advance, or have you started wearing your best tie to work? Sidney, none of this makes any sense. Either you went there to ask how the Chalfonts were, or Muriel invited you to tea to talk business about the floral clock, but you going to the hotel was definitely pre-planned.'

'I . . . er . . .'

'So which was it?'

'Bella, stop being difficult. I hope you don't reckon I'm the kind of fella who would hear that people he knew had been evacuated from a burning building and not go to enquire if they were all right.'

'No, I don't, but I wasn't aware the Chalfonts' house had been alight,' said Bella. 'I saw the fire, and it was the Hailshams' that was burning down, not their neighbours'.'

'I just wanted to see that . . . that they were . . .'

'All right – yes, you said. So you turned up at the hotel, to see if the hotel's owner and his family were being looked after properly, you wearing your new tie, and Muriel invited you to have tea with her and then she, totally out of the blue, started spouting on about her father sponsoring this wretched floral clock?'

'Summat like that, yes.' Sidney looked sheepish.

Bella remembered what Muriel had said: 'I was just saying to Sidney, wouldn't it be funny if Bella came by and saw us having tea together?'

'I don't believe it was quite like that, Sidney. I think you planned all along to turn up there, hoping to see Muriel, p'raps push yourself forward with the Chalfonts. Then she took the opportunity to invite you to have tea at a very prominent window table, where, if I happened to pass, as she hoped, I would see you together. Or, possibly, other folk would see you both and report it to me.'

'And why would she do that?'

'Why do you think, Sidney? Isn't it just like Muriel Chalfont to stir up trouble? She wanted me to see her, or other folk to see her and tell me about her, with my fiancé. She wanted to show off to you about her daddy owning the hotel, and for me to know that she's rich and pretty and can have owt she wants, including the man I'm going to marry sitting like a lapdog at her table.'

'Bella, I don't think that's quite fair,' said Sidney, sounding hurt.

'So I'm wrong, am I? It's just my imagination?'

'I think you've got it all wrong,' said Sidney. 'Poor Muriel was all aflutter about the Hailshams being killed in the fire. I could hardly refuse to keep her company when she said she was so upset.'

'But, Sidney, you yourself said she was on about this blessed clock. She didn't sound in the least bothered about the poor Hailshams. She was playing Lady Muck in her father's hotel, patronising me – patronising *you* – and probably trying to bribe you with a cup of tea and a scone, then speculating on how much her father might pay for the plot where the burned-down building is – where Mrs Hailsham and her daughter died.'

Sidney smiled indulgently. 'She can be a little thoughtless, I suppose, but she means well.'

'In what way, exactly?' asked Bella, her tone full of disgust.

'Oh, Bella, you know Muriel.'

'Unfortunately, I do,' said Bella. 'And you'd do well to bear in mind she'll do nowt without some motive that pleases her.'

'There's no need to speak to me as if I'm daft,' said Sidney. 'I can cope with Muriel Chalfont and her ways.'

'Can you, indeed? And in what regard are you so friendly with Muriel that "her ways" have any bearing on you?'

'Well, I'm not . . . really. But Theddleton is quite a small place, and I do get around town, as you know, and the Chalfonts are important people here, so our paths are always going to cross.'

Bella said nothing, just looked at him a long moment. They hadn't reached Baybury yet and already the evening had developed a brittle, argumentative air.

It did not improve when they arrived outside the cinema. The film showing this week was *Sabrina*, which Bella was keen to see, but Sidney said he thought it would be 'soft' and he'd rather miss it than see it.

'Oh . . . all right, then,' Bella said, disappointed to miss watching the glamorous love story with the man she was going to marry, and also that he wasn't prepared to see it just to please her. 'I'll go another time with Alice and Millie, or mebbe with Vera or Iris.'

'I'll buy you some chips, and we can walk along the front instead,' said Sidney.

'I had chips earlier.'

'You didn't tell me.'

'Well, I didn't know until now that you were going to turn your nose up at the film and offer me chips instead,' said Bella, exasperated.

'Who did you have chips with?' demanded Sidney, combatively.

'Mr and Mrs Warminster and their son, Toby.'

'Toby? Toby Warminster? The name sounds familiar. Do I know him?'

'I don't know, Sidney. Do you?'

Bella was beginning to wish she had stayed at home and begun fitting the paper pattern pieces for her wedding dress, instead of coming all the way to Baybury, just to be offered chips and to field Sidney's evasions about Muriel Chalfont.

'Toby didn't say owt about knowing you, if that's what you mean,' said Bella, well aware that she'd avoided all mention of Sidney, although she still didn't know why. 'I've met him before, a while ago. He's a few years older than I am . . . than we are, and he works in London.'

'P'raps I've just heard the name. Some bigwig, is he? Works for the government or summat?'

'Why would you think that? Not everyone in London has an important job. He's a tailor, actually.'

'Oh, aye? A man who sews for a living.'

'Sidney,' said Bella, pulling him round to face her as he turned to move away. They were still outside the cinema, and couples, arm in arm, were skirting round them, eager to go in and claim good seats for the film. 'Why are you being so horrible and sneery? It seems there's nowt I can say that will please you this evening. Toby Warminster is here for the weekend to visit his parents, and so he was around while we were working. Mr Warminster took us all out for fish and chips on the Promenade, and then Toby went to the bookshop. That's all there is to tell.'

They started to walk down the street together.

Bella had deliberately omitted to mention the walk with Toby on the beach, but then there wasn't much to say except that it had been very pleasant. She didn't want Sidney questioning her about that, too. Toby hadn't returned to the toyshop before Bella left that evening. No doubt she'd hear all about what had happened at the bookshop from Alice later.

'Now, are you going to tell me how the match went this morning? Did you score any goals?' asked Bella. Oh dear, she thought, why do I always broach this topic of conversation with Sidney when I want to shut him up, like a parent bringing out a teething ring for a fractious baby?

'I don't "score goals" every week, Bella. It's all about playing as a team, giving everyone the chance to play his best,' said Sidney, looking noble.

'So did you win?'

'No, we lost three nil.'

'Oh, what a shame. So that didn't work then: giving them all the chance to play their best?'

What had got into her this evening? What had got into him?

Sidney stopped walking. 'Bella, do you want some chips or not?'

'No, thank you. But you have some.'

'I will.'

'Good.'

He set off again in the direction of the seafront, and

Bella, feeling low, was wondering whether to follow him when a female voice called, 'Bella!'

It was Vera Hoskins, who had known Alice since their schooldays and was now a good friend of both sisters. Bella felt that she had conjured her up somehow, having mentioned her name just a minute or two before.

'Alice not with you?' asked Vera.

'No, I came here with Sidney. I want to see the film, but he's not keen and has gone to get some chips instead. I'm just wondering whether to go home.'

'Chips instead of Audrey Hepburn! Is the man mad?' Vera linked her arm through Bella's. 'I was going to bring Mam, but she's got a bad cold. She insisted I come anyway and not miss the film while it's on. It's a piece of luck seeing you. You will join me, won't you, Bella?'

'Yes, please,' said Bella. 'Only, let me just tell Sidney before he disappears. Here . . .' She thrust a florin into Vera's hand. 'Please get me a ticket, and I'll see you in the foyer.' She rushed off to catch up with Sidney, who was halfway down the road by now, his shoulders hunched in his smart jacket.

Perhaps he expected me to be following behind him like his dog, thought Bella.

'Sidney, I've just seen Vera, and we're going to see the film together. I'll get the bus back,' she told him.

'Oh! Oh, all right . . . if that's what you want.' He sounded sulky.

'Well, you did say you didn't want to see it, so you're

not missing out, are you?' she answered, trying to appease him. 'And mebbe I'll see you tomorrow.'

'If you like,' said Sidney, turning his back on her, and he sloped off, hands shoved deep into his trouser pockets.

Goodness, what a strange mood they were both in. Should she run after him and say sorry? But for what? For not putting up with his selfishness and his bad mood? And why was he in a bad mood anyway – because The Seafarers had lost three nil? Why did that matter? There would be another match next Saturday and they might win. Maybe he felt caught out about Muriel, but she was clearly using him for her own ends – the floral clock plans or to make Bella jealous, or both – and Sidney was being stupid if he didn't realise that.

Bella shrugged and turned back towards the cinema. She was going to see a very promising film in Vera's delightful company, so the evening was not at all wasted.

Vera was waiting in the foyer, grinning with anticipation.

'Oh, I'm so glad you're able to join me, Bella. Here's your change. I've got seats in the one and nines – I hope that's OK – and, ta-da! Chocolate!'

'I can't wait,' said Bella, grinning back.

Bella got off the bus on Theddleton Promenade, crossed the road by the hotel and started to walk home. It was a balmy evening, and she strolled slowly up the High Street, thinking about the gorgeous film she'd just seen.

When she got to the bookshop she saw, as she had earlier, on her way out, that the dusty heaps of books had been disrupted and reduced, possibly for the first time in years. Even this chaotic change made it more eye-catching than usual, simply because it was different.

She walked on and was just passing the Victory public house, at the top of the High Street, when the door opened, and Alfred and Toby Warminster came out.

'Bella,' said Alfred. 'Not on your own, love?'

'I'm only going home,' said Bella. 'I've just got off the bus from Baybury. I've been to the pictures.'

'Well, we can't have you walking home by yourself in the dark,' said Toby. 'And I reckon as Dad can find his own way home,' he added, laughing. 'I'll see you back safely.'

'Good lad,' said Alfred. 'And I'll see you on Monday, Bella, love.'

'Good night, Mr Warminster,' said Bella, and Toby courteously stepped to the outside of the pavement as they turned to walk on.

'What was the film?' asked Toby. 'I hope you didn't go to see it alone?'

'*Sabrina*, and no, I saw it with my friend Vera.'

'Good choice of picture, especially for anyone who likes to look at beautiful clothes. Or view wonderful locations. I saw it in London, and not just once.'

They smiled at each other, thinking of their favourite moments in the film.

'So what happened at the bookshop?' asked Bella. 'I

noticed when I went past that the window is now untidy chaos, but I suspect it's a work in progress.'

'It surely is. Bobbie Reeves is summat of an unstoppable force, isn't she?'

'She's very impressive – what little I've seen of her. I almost feel sorry for Miss Patterson, except when I think of the way she tries to keep Alice under her thumb. Now, I take it, she's more than met her match.'

'A three-pronged offensive, although mine was only a bit part,' said Toby. 'Mainly ridding the bookshop of a spider. You must ask Alice about the details. Modesty forbids me to tell you how huge . . . I mean, the size of the beast.'

Bella laughed. 'I can imagine Alice's face.' She pulled an exaggerated expression of pure horror. 'Alice isn't afraid of owt except spiders.'

'I was happy to play the rescuer of the fair ladies, Alice, Bobbie *and* the redoubtable Miss Patterson. Anyway, afterwards I saw Bobbie in the High Street and we had tea in the hotel.'

Bella's mind was immediately filled with the picture of Sidney looking guilty in the hotel window, and Muriel smirking and being patronising. She hurriedly dismissed this.

'I told Bobbie I'm a tailor, and she's commissioned me to make a jacket for her father, copying the design of an old, worn-out one of which he's very fond. It's got an unusual number of useful pockets, which is what makes it unique. It should be easy enough to copy once

I've checked Mr Reeves's measurements. But you see, Bella, this is a wonderful opportunity for me: my first solo commission. It's what I've been dreaming of, ultimately, although of course I'll have to have more than just one copied jacket under my belt before I can set up my own business. Still, it's a start.'

'That's marvellous, Toby,' said Bella and, before she realised what she was doing, she had moved close to squeeze his arm in excited support.

Toby, in turn, put his arm around her shoulders and they walked on companionably, their shared thoughts of the splendid film they both loved, their admiration for Bobbie Reeves and the opportunity she was giving him, and the triumph of common sense in the bookshop linking them in happiness.

When they got to Chapel Lane and number 8, Bella found Toby's arm was still around her, and she gently extricated herself.

'Thank you for seeing me safely home,' she said. 'Would you like to come in for a cup of tea? I'm sure Alice will be pleased to support your claim as to the immense size of the spider.'

Toby smiled. 'Thanks, but I'd better get home to Mam and Dad. I don't see them as much as I'd like to, and in fact, I won't have seen them very much this weekend, but that's my fault. Another reason, along with the jacket commission, to be up here again soon.'

'That would be nice,' said Bella, meaning it.

'Yes, it would,' said Toby, looking into her eyes, then

bent and gently kissed her on the lips. 'Thank you for your company today, Bella. I'll see you very soon, I hope.'

'I hope so, too,' said Bella, her heart pounding because the kiss had been lovely, but it was so wrong, and she wasn't going to tell him about Sidney right now, she simply *wasn't*.

'Goodbye for now, then,' he said, turning away with a huge show of reluctance.

'Oh, but Toby . . .'

'Yes?'

'Please, borrow my torch. You'll never find your way safely back to the High Street in the dark without it.'

Bella looked at the paper pattern for her wedding dress and felt despondent. Until this morning, she'd sneaked little peeks at the illustration on the front of the envelope and been filled with thrilling anticipation. This morning, examining it again, she thought the design staid, unimaginative, even old-fashioned. Was that because of that wonderful film yesterday? The costumes had been gorgeous, and Audrey Hepburn had looked divine. Ordinary women could never compete with her glowing, fragile beauty. But Bella was quite sensible enough to know the difference between Hollywood and real life.

No, it was something else that was making her feel disgruntled, and she knew exactly what it was: her conscience. She decided to go for a walk and see if she felt better.

'You coming, Alice?'

'No, thanks. I reckon I'd better tackle the ironing, and while I'm doing that I can think about the bookshop window . . . now Miss Patterson has come up with the brilliant idea of clearing it out and making it a feature.' Alice added the last bit with an ironic lift of her eyebrows.

The previous evening, Alice had told her family all about Bobbie's tactic at the bookshop, and how Toby Warminster had joined in. After work, Alice had met Bobbie, and they had celebrated the success of their plan with dinner at Bobbie's house.

'What was it like?' Bella had asked.

'Delicious. Bobbie is a good cook,' said Alice. She smiled at Millie. 'You'd have liked it: lots of roast potatoes and a nice pudding.'

'I meant the house,' said Bella.

'I wasn't really taking a lot of notice,' said Alice, evasively. 'I met Bobbie's father, though, and he's quite a character. Pretends to be gruff and no-nonsense, but he's very kind really, and he absolutely dotes on Bobbie. He's been widowed for many years, I gather. Bobbie's got an older brother who I think lives somewhere further north. She's asked Toby Warminster to make her father a jacket. It's to be a present.'

'Heavens, that was quick work. I thought you said they hadn't met before today.' Bella knew this, and yet she couldn't admit it without revealing that she'd seen Toby again. And she wanted to keep quiet about that. *Oh dear, the lies! How they grow and grow.*

'They hadn't. I think they're both the kind of people who just get along with everyone,' Alice had said.

Now she told Bella: 'I might come to the beach hut later, if that's where you're going to finish your walk? I'll bring food, and we can have a little picnic. Millie's gone sailing with Edwin – did you know?'

'She seems to have accepted that she can't swan around week in, week out without a job,' said Bella. 'I think Edwin has helped there, with his commitment to the bakery and his generally sound attitude.'

'I was thinking the same. Once she has some money saved up, Millie will be able to buy her paints and whatever else she needs, and then her plans might take off. As it is, we can't afford to help her get started when she's making no effort herself,' said Alice.

'I'm afraid that's what I had to tell her on Friday,' Bella replied. 'But it will all turn out for the best, especially as Dad will be able to keep an eye on Millie at the Three-Mile.'

'Yes. I can't help feeling that Millie does need someone to keep an eye on her.'

Bella's walk took her down the High Street, past the toyshop. She thought about Toby's kiss, and her stomach did a thrilling little kick. She couldn't resist looking through the door in the hope that she might catch a glimpse of him before he left, but the shop had a closed Sunday look. The Warminsters lived in a flat over the shop, which had a separate entrance at the side.

At E. & G. Patterson Books, the window looked, if anything, in even more disarray, the piles of books toppled and chaotic, as if they'd keeled over with old age. Alice would be busy tomorrow.

Bella walked on, round the corner by the hotel. Today, there was no Muriel Chalfont sitting in the window, flirting with someone else's handsome fiancé. Bella felt cross about that still, but she thought she'd worked out what Muriel's game was. The really upsetting thing had been Muriel's shameless speculating about her father buying up the land where the ruins of the Hailshams' house stood. That had been far more shocking than any thought of Muriel flirting with Sidney.

But what about *her*, flirting with Toby? *Had* she been flirting? In all conscience, not really. She thought they were being friendly, finding things in common as he walked her home. But she had known he had had his arm around her, and she hadn't been entirely surprised by the kiss. And she hadn't objected to either in any way, nor had she spoken one word about her engagement to Sidney.

That had been wrong. It was all right to be friends with Toby, but only like she was friends with Colin Wilkinson or Vera's brother, Mike. She would have to tell Toby next time he came up from London that she was engaged and getting married in a few months.

If Sidney himself was still up for the idea of their being married, that was. Bella felt herself slumping. She'd had a lovely evening in the company of Vera, but afterwards, alone on a bus full of couples on the way back to Theddleton, she had gone over and over the argument, trying not to think it was all Sidney's fault and what a thoughtless idiot he'd been, sitting in the hotel dining room, dancing to Muriel Chalfont's tune.

Perhaps I was too snappy, thought Bella. Perhaps I shouldn't have questioned him so much. He was probably feeling defensive and a bit foolish, being Muriel's lapdog, and I made everything much worse. I shouldn't have trodden on his feelings. I shouldn't have called him a lapdog, even if he was behaving like one.

She crossed the Promenade then, and went down to the beach. A little way out to sea, a small boat with a sail was heading towards Baybury. Bella wondered if it was Mrs Cook's boat, crewed by Edwin and Millie. It was too far away to see.

Her thoughts stayed on Millie. She still hadn't admitted to sneaking into Bella's room and looking at the illustration for her wedding dress on the pattern envelope, but how else did she know what the dress was going to look like? Were there other things she hadn't admitted to? Breaking Mrs Hailsham's beach hut windows? Worse – much worse?

*No, don't even think that. Millie was at the allotments. She said so. The fire was nothing to do with her. She's little more than a child, not some dangerous arsonist.*

Feeling her mood lowering further, Bella put her hands to her face, willing herself to snap out of her dark thoughts. When she looked up, there was Sidney coming towards her, wearing a very fine pair of flannel trousers and a Fair Isle pullover.

'Bella? Are you all right?'

'Yes, thank you, Sidney. I hoped I might see you. Did you . . . did you enjoy your chips?'

'Not really.'

'Oh, Sidney, I'm sorry I was cross with you.'

'I reckon I should have gone to see that picture with you. I don't suppose it would have hurt me.'

'Vera and I had a nice time, but I'm not sure you'd have enjoyed it.'

He wrapped his arms around Bella then, and she leaned in to him, inhaling the scent of new wool.

'Lovely pullover. New?'

'Present from Mum. She likes to spoil me.'

'Mm . . .' Bella stood on tiptoe and kissed Sidney, who kissed her back absent-mindedly. 'All forgiven and forgotten?' she asked, trying to look into his face, but he was gazing distractedly out to sea.

'Of course.'

'Where have you been, coming from the Baybury end?'

'Oh, I went to see if you were at the beach hut. When you weren't, I went to look at the Hailshams' house.'

'I expect it's a ruin.'

'It is. Black and horrible. Smouldering still.'

'I shan't go and look again. It was awful, seeing the flames shooting out of the upstairs windows. Did you see Muriel?'

'No. I reckon the Chalfonts are still at the hotel.'

'So you did go to see her?'

'I never said that,' Sidney said quietly. 'I said I went to see if you were at the hut.'

They walked on in that direction.

'Bella,' began Sidney, after a minute or two in which she could feel him becoming fidgety, 'I went to the beach hut 'cos I wanted to ask you summat . . . about the wedding.'

''Course. What?' She smiled, but her stomach fluttered with misgiving. He wasn't about to tell her he didn't want to marry her, was he? He's been less than attentive lately and had often said he was too busy to meet up with her at lunchtimes or after work – the kind of casual time together that they had enjoyed so much in the past.

'Do you think it might be better to wait a while . . . mebbe till next spring . . . or however long it takes to get our own place?'

It was what Dad and Alice had been suggesting. Bella wished it were different, but it was the sensible option, after all.

'You know I do. But I thought your mam's feelings would be hurt if we didn't go to live at her house, after she's offered. That's what you said, and that's why I thought there was no reason not to marry sooner.'

'Well, I was thinking about this last night, and I reckon she'll just have to put her feelings to one side. What do you say? Shall we wait a bit?'

Bella felt a totally unexpected rush of relief. It was as if a burden were being lifted from her shoulders, and she realised this was mainly to do with starting her married life living at Mrs Bennett's house. She knew that nothing she did would be right in her mother-in-law's opinion. All her encounters with Mrs Bennett had pointed to this, but it was much easier to cope with the woman for short visits than to live with her on what would inevitably end up being entirely her own terms. She had, Bella now realised, dreaded that, but she'd unconsciously offset her dread with wanting to be married, wanting to be the bride, the fairy on top of the tree, the girl in the lovely dress, the woman who was adored by a handsome man – the man she loved. She had been ridiculous. Why not wait and start their new life together on a far better footing, in their own home? What was the hurry?

'Yes, Sidney. I think you're right: that would be best. But, please, if we're saving up, let's save up properly. Let's put our money away safely in our building society accounts as often as we can, so that it grows with interest – really make a point of doing so, not just meaning to do so. Otherwise, come next spring, we'll be in exactly the same position.'

'Good idea. I'll tell Mam that's what we've decided. And she'll be able to go to her sister's for her holiday in September. At least she'll be pleased about that.'

'Good,' said Bella. 'All settled then.' She smiled up at Sidney. 'There's a lot to arranging a wedding, and it's hard to get organised, especially when I'm at work most days, and I haven't even started on my dress yet.'

Sidney looked relieved. 'No need to set a date yet,' he said. 'Let's just wait until we're ready.'

# CHAPTER FIFTEEN

MILLIE WENT TO see Mr Fairbanks, to learn what her job entailed – which was basically being a general dogsbody at everyone's beck and call – and to see if he thought she would be suited to the work. Afterwards, Millie didn't know what Mr Fairbanks thought of her, except that he'd given her the job, but she thought him bossy and rude.

'He seems to like to make everyone unhappy,' she said to Thomas as they walked home from her interview. 'He could be much nicer. I saw him chivvying Susan and Pam along very rudely when it was plain to see that they were getting on fine. It's as if he needs to keep making sure they all know who's in charge. As if they'd forget for one minute.'

'I don't think he reckons being "nice" is part of his job, love.'

'Then why do you want me to work at the Three-Mile?' demanded Millie. 'Do you want me to be unhappy, too?'

'No, of course not. But it's a job, Millie, and you do need to go to work. And I'll be there. You'll be able to save up for things you want, once you get a bit of money.'

'That's a bit rich, coming from you,' she said. 'Haven't you had a hundred jobs and still haven't managed to save up for Bella's wedding?'

Thomas looked stricken by this blunt accusation. The really hurtful thing was that it was essentially true. He *hadn't* managed to save up much towards Bella's wedding, and now she and Sidney were putting it off until they could afford their own home. Was the postponement partly his fault? He hoped not, but there was a nagging feeling in his mind that it was.

Why did he always let everyone down? *Why?*

They walked on in silence for a while, Millie looking cross, swinging her bag at the weeds in the hedgerows as they passed, Thomas looking sad and thoughtful.

'So do you think you'll be able to do the work, Millie?' he asked eventually.

'I shall see when I start. If I don't, I shall leave.'

'Give it a chance, love,' advised Thomas. 'It's just not what you're used to.'

'P'raps not what I want to be used to,' snapped Millie.


Thomas had arranged that Millie would borrow Iris Cook's daughter Joan's bicycle, which Joan didn't use herself. So the two of them set off that Friday in the cool of a late April morning, Bella and Alice, at the front door, calling goodbye and good luck in loud whispers.

Thomas felt his heart fill with gratitude to be riding to work with this lovely girl beside him. With plenty of nutritious food and sea air, Millie had grown noticeably taller since she'd come to live here. One day this little imp might be as tall as Alice. This morning, she'd done her hair in a plait, the way Bella did hers for work. Millie really did look like Bella and Alice's little sister today . . . like his own daughter. She was volatile and cheeky, but then she'd been through so much. She was like a missing piece in his life, found at last.

Millie was out of practice at cycling and found it hard work, so she was concentrating and, for once, not voicing an opinion. This gave Thomas the chance to reflect, to daydream, as he usually did on this journey, making today just like every other day, only better.

It would be good to have Millie working alongside him, where he could keep an eye on her and know she was not wasting her time and getting up to who knew what. Of course she wouldn't want to stay at the inn for ever. Who would? Once she'd saved up for the things she needed to get her painting career underway, and she'd got a bit of that kind of work lined up, she'd want to leave as soon as she could . . .

In the meantime, there was the postponement of Bella's wedding to get used to. Bella had said little about it, but as she tended to wear her heart on her sleeve, Thomas thought this meant that she wasn't completely stricken with disappointment about the delay. He hardly dared allow himself to think it, but perhaps this would give her time to see sense. The lad was all right but selfish and a bit stupid, and Bella really could do better. Perhaps she could find greater happiness with someone less shallow, someone with more about him. Still, Sidney was her choice. He was good-looking, right enough, and perhaps at Bella's age, that mattered. But then what would she think of him when they were both in their forties, and possibly he was not such a handsome fella? All the more reason for Bella to wait, to grow up a bit. She was, in some ways, a little girl, wanting to be in a fairy tale with a beautiful wedding, in love with the idea of being in love.

And what of Alice? Still no boyfriend, although she had plenty of friends. This new friendship, with Bobbie Reeves, was obviously making Alice happy, but then Bobbie was such an impressive woman, being intelligent and charming as well as beautiful, by all accounts. Thomas hadn't yet met her, but Bella and Millie thought much of her, too.

By now, Millie was weaving about on the bike as if she'd reached the end of her strength.

'Honestly, Uncle Thomas,' she panted, 'when we get there, I will just fall straight off this bike, my legs too wobbly to hold me up. They have never been more tired. I feel quite ill with the effort.'

'You just need a bit of practice, Millie; get used to pushing the pedals. Now, look, not far to go.' He pointed out the inn, the solitary building on the road ahead. 'When we're there, pull up to that verge where the grass is long, and you can clamber off without hurting yourself.'

Millie did as he suggested and tipped herself onto the grass, where she lay breathless but unhurt. After a few seconds, she slowly sat up.

'Please, you'll have to help me to my feet. My legs are like jelly. I'm so weak, I doubt they'll hold me.'

Thomas, laughing, hauled her upright, and she held onto him for a moment.

'I can hardly move.' She tried a few steps. 'I need a cup of tea and a lie-down.'

'It's breakfasts first thing, love, and Fridays are always busy. C'mon, I'll get you a cup of tea, but there won't be a lie-down, that's for sure.'

They wheeled their bicycles round the back, Millie stumbling and dragging her feet, and then went in through the kitchen door.

'Glad you could make it, Thomas,' said Mr Fairbanks sarcastically. 'Two minutes late – not a good example to set the girl.'

'I'm sorry, Mr Fairbanks.' Thomas didn't say that it was Millie who had held them up.

'Millie, get that apron on and start setting those tables. Follow what Pam has done with the others.'

Pam, just a little older than Millie, was the other general help at the inn, the one Millie had seen Mr Fairbanks bossing around, alongside Susan, who Millie now replaced. Millie had met Pam briefly already and thought they would probably get on.

'Yes, Mr Fairbanks. But may I just have a drink of water, please? My legs are nearly giving way with the bike ride.'

'I told you to get on with those tables – didn't you hear me?'

'Yes, Mr Fairbanks.'

'Then why are you still standing here?'

Millie, remembering just in time that Thomas had warned her against answering back, went to do as she was ordered, laying more breakfast tables. Gradually her legs found their strength, but she was gasping for a cup of tea.

'Here,' said Thomas, as she came into the kitchen, handing her a mug. 'Keep it on the side there, out of the way, and take a sip whenever you come in. That's what we all do.'

Millie took the tea gratefully, had a quick sip and then reached for some plates of cooked breakfast.

'Aah! Oh, my gosh . . . oh, good grief, that's burning hot.'

'Use the *gloves*, Millie,' said Pam, coming in behind her. 'Of course the plates are hot.'

'I think I'm burned. My hands are ruined!'

'Show me. No, it's not too bad. Quick, take these plates and then rinse your hands under a cold tap while I do the others. But hurry up!'

'Toast for table three,' called Fabio, the cook.

'Yes, Fabio,' said Thomas, grabbing the filled toast rack and hurrying out, while Millie, now wearing oven mittens, took up the two fiercely hot plates of bacon and eggs and followed him.

'Clear these tables now, Millie,' said Mr Fairbanks, as Millie hurried past him in the hope of being able to cool her burns without delay.

'I just need to rinse my hands – look,' she said, holding up one red palm.

'We haven't time for mollycoddling, girl! These good folk have paid to have their breakfasts before they get back on the road. They can't be waiting around for you.'

Millie gave her boss a defiant glare but said nothing. She started collecting up dirty plates and took them through to the kitchen, where Jane Regan, a tiny woman, like an urchin of indeterminate age, stood at a sink of steaming, soapy water.

'Hurry up with these clearings,' she snapped at Millie. 'Just 'cos you fell off your bike doesn't mean you get the morning off work.'

*Morning off work?* What was she talking about? Millie felt as if, despite the weariness in her legs from the unaccustomed bike ride, her feet hadn't stopped moving since she had come in through the door. And now even the skivvy was giving her a hard time.

'Don't stack 'em like that, you daft bugger. Now I have to wash the undersides as well,' snapped Jane.

'Sorry,' said Millie. 'I didn't know.'

'Well, seems you know nowt,' said Jane with a sneer and a toss of her head. 'Get a move on, and don't stand there with your mouth gaping, otherwise I'm likely to stick a bar of soap in it.'

Millie rushed out to fetch more dirty plates, while

Pam straightened the gingham tablecloths and reset the cleared tables.

'Grab one of those teacloths and start on this lot, will you?' said Jane when Millie arrived back with the washing up. 'I've nowhere to put the clean 'uns down.'

'Sorry,' said Millie, 'but Mr Fairbanks has just asked me to bring in the next lot,' and she went off to fetch some more used crockery, feeling pleased to be able to answer Jane back in a perfectly justified way. But she had a feeling Jane Regan was not a woman to forget a slight.

In the meantime, Thomas and Pam were running in and out of the kitchen, shouting 'Yes, Fabio,' every few seconds, while Mr Fairbanks alternated between shouting at his employees about the next most urgent tasks and beaming smarmily over his customers, offering them more tea, more toast, more marmalade . . .

At last, the rush died down. The travellers were now settling their bills over the bar counter, and Millie had the chance to take herself off to the lavatories and rinse her face and hands in cool water.

'Well done,' said Pam, coming in as Millie dried her face. 'You did well.'

'Apart from the burns and Mr snappy Fairbanks snapping his snappy head off at me every five seconds. And who the hell does that Jane Regan think she is? She's like some poisonous dwarf from one of Uncle Thomas's stories.'

'Millie, I don't know what you're talking about with the stories,' said Pam, pushing dead-straight mousy hair, which had escaped from her ponytail, back behind her ears. She put a finger to her lips and tiptoed over to look under the cubicle doors. All were empty. 'Always check before saying owt,' she said. 'You never know who's listening.'

'Thanks,' said Millie. 'Basic advice. I didn't think.'

'You'll remember if you get the wrong side of Jane,' said Pam, lowering her voice and glancing over her shoulder towards the door. 'She used to work in a circus: the world's smallest strong woman or summat. You wouldn't think to look at her, but I gather she's been in prison for beating up some fella. Steer clear of her is my advice. She's not a nice person.'

'What's she doing working here? It's a long way from the circus.'

Pam looked askance. 'She lives here, in one of the rooms upstairs at the top. Her job comes with board and lodging because she never leaves,' she said. 'She doesn't like to go outside; some sort of fear she developed in prison. She may be a dangerous lunatic, but she's still got a right to earn her living, same as we have. If I were you, I'd keep very quiet around her. Summat tells me you've got a manner of answering that she'll find annoying, and she'll let you know about it.'

'I'll remember that, Pam,' said Millie.

'Why didn't you warn me about Jane Regan, Uncle Thomas?' Millie asked crossly as they left the inn together through the back door.

'I'm sorry, Millie, I simply forgot. I generally try to steer clear of her. I suggest you do, too.'

'That's what Pam said.'

They got on their bikes and set out for home, Millie nervous about being able to make the distance before she'd had sufficient practice to develop her 'bike legs'.

'Pam's all right,' went on Thomas. 'You'd do well to listen to her. But Jane has got some kind of hold over Mr Fairbanks – don't ask me what – and he seems obliged to employ her and put up with her, so she always gets away with everything she says and does, however unpleasant she is.'

'Seems to me that Fairbanks himself thinks he can get away with anything, too.'

'But he owns the place. It's his role to tell folk what to do.'

'There's telling people what to do and there's bullying,' said Millie. 'He doesn't know where one ends and the other starts.'

'It's a job, Millie. You haven't got an alternative that will pay you owt this week, so I suggest you keep your head down, lass, and just put up with it. And keep quiet about it at home, too. I don't want Bella and Alice to start fretting.'

Millie pedalled on a few turns, her progress slowing. 'You know, Uncle Thomas, you shouldn't have to put up with it either,' she said. He appeared not to have heard her, so she continued. 'I said you shouldn't have to put up with it. It's paid work, not punishment.'

'Well, Millie, I've been around a fair few years longer than you, so I hope you'll allow me to know what's what,' he said.

'You mean allow myself to be bullied? I'd no idea it would be like this.'

'Just stick it out until you've enough money to do as you like, then you can leave,' Thomas reminded her. 'Honestly, Millie, you'd be lucky to find owt else with your lack of experience. You have to start at the bottom of the heap when you're young.'

'And what about you, Uncle Thomas?' she retorted. 'Why are you still at "the bottom of the heap"?'

Thomas said nothing but looked hurt, and she deliberately fell behind, then eventually got off the bicycle and pushed it the rest of the way home, walking by herself.

Millie was in a bad mood all evening, refusing to help Bella cook the dinner and not speaking to Thomas as the four of them sat around the kitchen table eating it.

Eventually Bella suggested that Millie was overtired after her first day at work and she had better go to bed early and have a good night's sleep.

'What's the matter with her, Dad?' Alice asked when the sound of Millie's feet thumping up the stairs had faded. 'I know she wasn't that keen to start a real job, but she's old enough not to behave like this about it.'

'I reckon it was harder than she expected,' he said evasively, 'and she's blaming me for that.'

'But you took her to meet Mr Fairbanks before she started,' said Bella. 'And you're there to keep an eye on her, smooth things along while she's getting to know the job.'

'Mm . . . I think she finds it hard to deal with owt that doesn't go her way,' he said. 'But she'll soon get the idea.'

Millie had taken her notebook up to her bedroom. She sat on her bed and thought about her first day at work and how much she had disliked it. She didn't want to go to the Three-Mile again, but she needed the pay. If she didn't turn up tomorrow, she thought it unlikely Mr Fairbanks would give her the money he owed her for today. He was the kind to think up some reason not to pay her, and there wouldn't be a thing she could do about it.

Well, there was, but any revenge she thought up would not get her the money.

Best to save up as much as she could for her paints, drawing paper, and canvases, then leave at the earliest opportunity. If Uncle Thomas was spineless enough to put up with the bullying at the Three-Mile, then let him. This was – as if she had doubted it – just the way Thomas must have been when Uncle Frank had thrashed his siblings, playing the big boy, the 'head of the family', making younger, smaller people his victims and relishing it. Well, Millie would not be playing the victim at work – or anywhere else.

She did some rough calculations in the back of the notebook but then decided they were probably worthless; she didn't know how much her paints and canvases would cost, and she hadn't any commissions just yet, so it was impossible to know when she would be able to leave the Three-Mile. She had hoped to be able to count the days there, even from now, like a prisoner awaiting release. The reality was that she would be working there for the foreseeable future. She'd noticed the food here at home was getting plainer – more boiled vegetables and less meat, no puddings – and Alice sighed more loudly over her household accounts. Millie knew she couldn't just abandon paid work, without having more work to go to, and leave them struggling even more.

She flung herself back on her bed, anger igniting in her and growing with every passing moment and every dark thought.

In a little while, she felt the urge to sketch what she felt about the Three-Mile Bottom and Mr Fairbanks and the ferocious Jane Regan. Once she started, images shot into her head, into her hand, as if the drawing were directing itself at a furious speed, with slashing pencil strokes and violent colours: red, orange, and black.

When her picture was finished, Millie lay back on her pillow, drained, and closed her eyes. When she opened them and looked again at her sketch, she was surprised at the detail, at the strength of feeling, at the very clear depiction of Mr Fairbanks and Jane Regan, locked in an embrace like a dance of death amid the chaos. It felt to Millie as if someone else had drawn that picture; that it had come from some unknown outside element, through her hand and onto the paper. She did not feel that she owned it, but she did like it.

There was a gentle tap on her door and Bella's voice called, 'Millie, are you awake? Would you like some cocoa, sweetheart?'

'No . . . no, thanks, Bella. Good night.'

With Bella's interruption, the violent anger – so strong that it felt like some powerful force – dissipated, leaving Millie just a tired, disappointed girl, lying on her bed with her sketchbook.

If Millie was having a hard time at the Three-Mile Bottom, Alice could not be happier at the bookshop. By midweek, she'd cleared out and sorted all the old books from the window, some of which were so foxed with age or so impregnated with damp black dust that they could never be displayed on shelves in the shop. The rest had gone to the storeroom at the back of the shop, awaiting shelf space.

Godfrey and Alice were all for throwing the damaged books out, but Eileen wouldn't hear of it.

'No one will want them, Eileen,' reasoned Godfrey. 'It must be years since they came in, and I fear they are fated never to leave except by the back door. We bought them in so long ago that we're hardly losing money on them by dumping them now. Let's just cut our loses as we won't notice them.'

'Well, you never know. I'm not going to give up on them yet,' said Eileen, as if this were the nobler choice. 'We could put them in a box labelled "Reduced". There's always someone who wants a bargain, and we'd get at least something, as opposed to nothing, for them.'

'I suppose we could put the box outside by the door, distance them from the regular stock so folk don't think they really represent the shop,' suggested Alice, 'but then, Miss Patterson, I think they'd just end up being a nuisance, having to be brought it when it rains. They're not in keeping with the new look to the window we're intending at all, are they?'

'But it's against my principles not to try to make something from them,' Eileen moaned.

Honestly, did Miss Patterson never listen to reason? Alice thought that Godfrey really was saintly to put up with her stubbornness and her penny-pinching.

Just as this thought passed through Alice's mind, Godfrey finally reached the limit of his renowned patience.

'Oh, for goodness' sake, woman,' he erupted, startling both Eileen and Alice, 'if no one's bought them in the last ten years, they're not likely to do so in the next ten, are they? Well, *are* they? They've given up being books anyone wants to read and have become rubbish. Sorry, but there it is. There is no money to be made – at all, *ever again* – from these books, and this is where they're going!'

To the open-mouthed astonishment of both his sister

and Alice, he picked up the box of decrepit books under one arm, strode across with it to the back door at the far corner of the main room, yanked open the door and, with all his strength, hurled the box out into the yard. Eileen and Alice heard it land with a resounding thud.

Eileen had her hands over her face and was visibly shaking, while Alice was struggling with the terrible temptation to laugh. It must be hysteria. Oh, no, poor Eileen would be so upset if she thought Alice was mocking her. And Godfrey had been so decisive, so masterful, that Alice was seeing him in a new light. She really hadn't thought he had that much backbone in him.

By the time Godfrey had returned, slapping his hands together to show he felt that was a job all done and dusted, Alice just couldn't hold in her mirth any longer.

'Oh, I'm sorry,' she gasped, her face red with the failed effort of not laughing, 'but . . .' She struggled to get the words out. '. . . oh, Mr Patterson . . .'

Eileen uncovered her face. Far from looking furious, she was rosy with hilarity. 'Your face, Godfrey! You should have seen your face . . .' She guffawed, and doubled over, laughing and gasping and fanning herself.

All three were soon roaring with laughter, Godfrey slapping his thighs and trying to say something he was laughing too hard to get out.

The shop doorbell rang and a man in late middle age came in to find the bookshop staff in a state of hysteria, so far as he could see.

Alice pressed her hands to her face to try to subdue her laughter, and managed to address the man on the second attempt.

'Good afternoon, sir. Mr Penrose, isn't it? How can I help you?' Her voice was only slightly wobbling.

'Yes: Penrose. I see the window is empty. That's quite a surprise. You're not closing down, are you?'

'Oh, no, far from it. We're just making some changes. It's going to be better than ever,' said Alice, enthusiastically but nonsensically – and then wanted to laugh again.

'Closing down? Where did you get that idea? If there are rumours abounding about the shop, I hope I can rely on you, Mr Penrose, to dispel them,' said Eileen, immediately prickly, her mirth shut off like a tap.

'I've not heard any rumours, Miss Patterson,' replied Mr Penrose, now on his dignity. 'I merely enquired, what with the window being empty, like.'

'It's as Alice said,' said Eileen. 'Now, can I help, or are you browsing?'

'I'm wondering if you have a copy of *The Picture of Dorian Gray.*'

'Oh, yes,' answered Eileen, pointing. 'That shelf there is completely Wilde.'

There was a moment's silence, and then all three of the bookshop staff erupted into loud laughter again.

Mr Penrose looked affronted. 'I can see I've come at a bad time if I want a sensible conversation,' he said.

'Oh dear,' said Godfrey, 'it must be some joyous spirit

we've released from imprisonment in the dismal window, and it's now inhabiting the shop.'

Alice thought this was just the kind of fanciful thing Bella might say. No wonder she herself was so fond of Godfrey; he and Bella had some similar characteristics, for all he was so bookish and Bella rarely read.

'Let me look you out what we have, Mr Penrose,' Alice said. 'I'm sure we have several copies.'

'And then, Alice, I think you'll need to get cracking on fixing up that window with a new display,' said Eileen. 'We can't have people thinking the business has failed.'

'Especially,' added Godfrey, 'when it's going to be so much busier now we're instigating Alice's brilliant idea.'

Heck, thought Alice, as she kneeled to search the Oscar Wilde shelf, is this a new Godfrey – a no-nonsense, plain-speaking version of the formerly over-cautious, painfully diplomatic bookseller? Things were definitely looking up.

# CHAPTER SIXTEEN

I T WAS ONLY the pay that kept Millie going to work at the Three-Mile Bottom in the following weeks. She could see that Thomas didn't like working there either – why would he? – but he put up with it. Millie knew that Thomas had seldom kept a job for very long at all – sometimes only a few months – and had yet to find anything that really suited him, but he was sticking with this to help pay for Bella's wedding. Millie had overheard Bella saying to Alice that she was worried their father was getting a reputation for being unreliable, but he was a likeable man, popular in Theddleton and – she regretted this as much as understood it – people felt sorry for him.

His was undoubtedly a low-grade job, but perhaps he liked to have no responsibilities and a job he could just ride away from on his bike every day and not give a thought to until the next morning. Certainly, Millie soon noticed, he enjoyed the bike rides and the daydreaming time they afforded him. Perhaps this was when he thought up the stories he told his family on a Sunday evening.

She knew that, with no proper education and no experience, this was the kind of employment she might expect to have until she had enough saved up to be able to start making her living as an artist. No one was going to do her any favours and offer her anything better. She had not heard from the hotel about any cleaning or laundry jobs there, but she wasn't really surprised. There must be a lot of people with no qualifications asking for work there.

Millie handed over most of her wages to Alice each week. Alice budgeted the household and made sure all the bills were paid on time, although, of course, those bills were always addressed to Thomas, not his daughter.

What small portion of her pay Millie retained, she squirrelled away in an old biscuit tin under her bed. As soon as she had saved enough for what she needed, she would have a shopping trip to Baybury, where she had discovered there was an art shop. By now, she had priced up the things she wanted to buy. Each week, she carefully counted up her savings and, labouring over the sums, calculated how much more she had to put aside, how much longer she must cycle to the Three-Mile six days a week.

In the meantime, she'd bought herself a cheap sketchbook and some more coloured pencils from the newsagent's in Theddleton. On her days off, she made sketches of the beach and the seafront buildings. She even did a sketch of Edwin, sitting in the *Hope and Peace*. He was so delighted with it that Millie gave it to him to give to his mother.

'I'll show it to Mr Harcourt at the bakery, too,' he said, as they walked back to Chapel Lane together after a Monday afternoon on the beach. 'It's such a good likeness – and really charming and attractive – that, you never know, if word gets round how talented you are, it might lead to summat for you.'

'Charming and attractive, that's you.' Millie laughed, nudging him with her elbow.

'Go on with you. I meant the style, you daft bat,' said Edwin, looking coy. 'By the way, there's a vacancy in the bakery coming up. You'll have to be committed, though; get up early, work hard in the heat.'

'Thanks for telling me, but I know I couldn't do it. It's hard enough getting up to go to the inn. I wouldn't last a week getting up earlier.'

'Lightweight,' smiled Edwin.

Millie was pleased that Edwin was willing to spread the word about her artistic ability, but she wasn't going to hold her breath that it would come to anything. Bella and Alice's beach hut was by far the smartest in the little row, but no one had asked them who had painted it or said they wanted theirs done. It was a pity: that kind of painting would have made a very acceptable job while she saved up to launch herself as a proper artist.

The hardest thing about working at the inn was

keeping quiet at home about Mr Fairbanks's attitude to his staff. Millie was not one to keep quiet about anything, really, but her uncle Thomas, while not looking happy about his work, never grumbled openly. Millie understood there was no point in upsetting Bella and Alice, and sowing anguish. Their father's moods of self-pity were a part of his character as much as the result of his discontent at work, so the girls thought nothing of them. Bella and Alice's happiness in their work was, they recognised, perhaps something of a rarity. When Millie wanted to let rip about Mr Fairbanks or Jane Regan, she went down to the beach and hurled stones into the sea. There were, she imagined, places she could be employed that were a lot worse than the Three-Mile, but that didn't mean she liked it any better.

There were just two good things about working at the inn. One was that sometimes the customers were generous with their tips. Equally important was that Millie, Thomas, Pam and Fabio instinctively stuck together and watched each other's backs, so far as they could, in the face of Mr Fairbanks's ill-temper and lack of regard for them, and Jane Regan's wild and random hostility to everyone and everything.

Now, in May, the inn was noticeably busier than it had been when Millie first started working there, with people coming in to break their journeys or staying overnight as they passed through Yorkshire. In a few weeks it would be the summer holidays and there would be more day-trippers stopping by for food and drinks. Millie thought all this business might have improved Mr Fairbanks's mood, but he was as curt and as sarcastic with his staff as ever . . . more than ever, really, as there were more tables to serve, more food to cook, more clearing to be done, and nothing anyone did was quick enough or good enough.

Millie was friends of a sort with Pam Braithwaite, although Pam was naturally cautious and suspicious around other people. Perhaps working at the Three-Mile had made her so. Pam had a few survival tactics she had passed on to Millie, but probably this was just so they both had quieter lives. No one benefited if anyone got on the wrong side of Fairbanks. He liked to target his sarcasms and his put-downs at all his employees equally.

As for Jane Regan, it was impossible to keep on the right side of her. Millie could well believe that the tiny woman had beaten up someone much bigger than herself and gone to prison for it. She was frighteningly aggressive, angry about everything, and would launch an unprovoked attack on anyone except Fairbanks himself. There were rumours about why he kept her on, although Millie and Pam were excluded from the gossip – it was 'not for innocent young ears', Fabio told them with a grin. Millie had already half guessed, based as much on the drawing that had formed in her notebook as the hints among the other staff.

Jane took exception to Millie from the outset.

'Don't you talk to me in that la-di-da voice, putting

on airs and graces,' she would snap at Millie whenever Millie couldn't avoid having to speak to her.

But how could she talk to anyone except in her own voice? It wasn't her fault she didn't sound local. The woman was clearly an idiot.

Millie swallowed down her anger and took her cue from Pam, who never answered back. There would be no winning in an open confrontation with Jane. If the woman thought Millie was cowed and defeated by her sharp tongue and dirty tricks, however, she was mistaken. In time, Millie vowed, Jane would get what she deserved.

Jane's mean acts took the form of throwing cups of greasy washing-up water in Millie and Pam's faces, or hurling cutlery at them on some violent whim. The woman was crazy and dangerous. Once, she smashed a pile of plates, simply hurling them to the ground in a temper because she was overwhelmed with the number of them heaped up to be washed. A shard of pottery shot across the floor and caught Pam on the leg, the wound bleeding profusely. Thomas cleaned it up for her, while Mr Fairbanks chivvied them to 'get a move on'. Then he deducted the cost of the broken plates from everyone's pay, even Pam's, although he knew it was Jane who was solely responsible.

She was a lot less aggressive with Thomas and Fabio than she was with the girls. Her confrontations with them generally took the form of vicious tongue-lashings rather than physical violence, although there was a frightening incident one day.

Jane, reaching out with her dripping rubber gloves, grabbed the bacon off one of the guest's breakfast plates, which Fabio had just finished, ready to go out, leaving a trail of filthy dishwater across the poached eggs. The usually jovial cook turned on her, furious, as she chewed the bacon with a self-satisfied look on her face.

'You ever do that again, woman, and I shall pick you up bodily and take you out into that car park, and then into those fields, and leave you there – outside!'

Panic crossed Jane's face briefly, but she squared up to the big fella. 'You can try, matey, but I reckon you'll die in the attempt.' She grabbed one of the broad-bladed kitchen knives off the workbench and waved it in front of him threateningly. 'Come on then, let's see what you're made of.'

Fabio wisely backed off and, while Millie and Pam retreated from the kitchen, fearing for their lives, Thomas hurried to fetch Mr Fairbanks to calm Jane down. He was the only one she would listen to. Her temper would ignite for no reason that the others could understand, and she would threaten violence if anyone so much as looked at her in what she considered to be a disrespectful way.

Early one lunchtime, William Gladstone came to the inn. He'd never been there before, and it was unclear why he was there now. He was known to live in a tiny, run-down cottage at the other side of the allotments from Chapel Lane, and the Victory was his local, but perhaps he just fancied a change of scene.

'Hello, William,' said Millie, who was setting tables in the dining room, seeing him wandering about the place, looking lost. 'Are you eating?'

'Dunno. I might if I'm hungry,' he said slowly.

'Then why don't you sit in the bar and have a drink, and then decide?'

'All right, M . . .'

Millie found him a seat in a corner, where he would not be repelling other customers, and where there were newspapers to hand, although she was unsure whether or not he could read.

'What's he doing here?' asked Mr Fairbanks, a little too loudly, appearing behind the bar.

'Mr Gladstone has come for a drink, Mr Fairbanks,' said Millie.

'Well, what's he having?'

'I haven't asked him.' Millie was too young to serve drinks.

'Well, ask him now.'

'I don't think I'm allowed to serve alcohol,' said Millie pointedly.

'I said, ask him!' snapped Fairbanks.

Millie went to do as she was ordered, then came back and requested a half of mild.

'Hardly worth him bothering us,' sneered Fairbanks.

'He's a customer. He might want to eat later.'

'I hope not. He looks like a tramp and smells like one, too.' Fairbanks poured the beer carelessly, deliberately spilling it over the side of the glass. 'Here, give him this, take the money and tell him to get a move on drinking it and then leave.'

Millie was feeling cross now. It was true that William was not the most presentable of customers, but if he could pay for his beer, there was no reason to be hostile towards him. And after all, she had seated him well out of the other customers' way in his cosy corner, where he would be happy and other people could easily ignore him if they wanted. Usually, Fairbanks was very strict about Millie and Pam not serving in the bar, but now he seemed to have forgotten the law. But, as the landlord and owner of the place, he could at least show some hospitality towards William, Millie thought. The customers at the inn were not always the kind many people might want to meet socially. All sorts stopped here, some of them shabby or shifty. Some proved themselves to be drunks, and both she and Pam had discovered a few had wandering hands. 'Perverts', Pam called them. 'If you tell Fabio, he'll make sure they get what they deserve,' she advised Millie. 'Just be careful you don't get the plates muddled up.'

Now, Millie took the beer over, told William the price, helped him count out his money correctly, and forbore to say what Fairbanks had asked her to.

Mr Fairbanks was serving some customers in the smaller space to the side of the bar, so Millie went to put the money in the wooden cash drawer. Bills for the food were written down and presented at the tables, a copy put on a spike, but no record was kept of the bar sales, which were mostly paid for in small change.

She had never seen inside this drawer, not having served in the bar before now. It contained quite a lot of money. Most of it was in coins, sorted into separate compartments, but there were notes neatly stacked on their edges at the front, as well. Millie put William's coins in the correct places, then, quick as a blink, took two shillings out and slipped them into her skirt pocket, under her pinafore.

'Price of rudeness,' she told herself.

This small act of dishonesty was a little triumph for justice, Millie thought, as she was almost certain she had seen Fairbanks pocketing some of the tips that had been left on the tables for herself, Pam and Thomas as customers departed that morning.

Then Millie went back into the kitchen, where she told Thomas about William Gladstone's unwelcome presence in the bar.

'Mr Fairchild hasn't spoken to Slow William. He insisted *I* serve him and then tell him to drink up quickly and go,' said Millie. 'I didn't say that, of course.'

'You've every right to refuse to serve drinks to anyone, love,' said Thomas quietly. 'You're not old enough, and Mr Fairchild knows that. I'll go and see how things are. I've got glasses to collect anyway, and I don't want Slow William getting upset.'

He went out and Millie followed quietly behind, bringing with her a teacloth as a prop so she could pretend to look busy, if need be, although she intended to stay out of sight. She was curious to see what would happen. She didn't think her uncle Thomas would stand up to Fairbanks. He never had before. She didn't really want to witness the miserable scene of Thomas getting shouted at by their boss, but it would be a test. She needed to know, once and for all, if Thomas was still the same as when he had let his little sister get the thrashing of her life.

In the bar, William Gladstone was far from upset. He was contentedly drinking his half in a leisurely way, making it last, and looking at the pictures in the *Daily Express*. When he heard the clink of empties being collected, he looked up slowly and gave Thomas a big grin, his terrible teeth not reining in his smile at all. Clearly, he was unaware of their effect on other people.

''Lo, Mr Thomas,' he said.

'Hello, William,' said Thomas. 'You all right there?'

Thomas was hoping William would drink up and go, and that would be the end of the matter without any unpleasantness, but he wasn't going to ask him to do so.

'Yes, mister, I's all right.'

'Have you finished?' asked Thomas, seeing the glass contained little more than foam now. 'Shall I take that?'

William tipped his head back, drank the residue and put the glass down firmly on the table.

'I might have summat to eat now,' he announced.

Thomas's heart sank. 'There are sausage rolls and pickled eggs,' he said, hoping to keep William in the bar. He didn't think the rat-catcher's budget would stretch to a slap-up lunch at one of the set tables. William was always alone and never went beyond the public bar at the Victory, so far as Thomas knew.

'Pickled eggs,' said William. 'Two of 'em, please.' He put some coins on the table, and Thomas took the right amount and pushed the rest back towards the old man.

'I'll bring them over.'

Thomas was scooping the pickles out of a gigantic jar onto a plate when Mr Fairbanks came round the bar corner, added some money to the drawer and then saw what Thomas was doing.

'Who's ordered those?'

'Mr Gladstone.'

'Well, he's not having them. He's not welcome to stay, sitting there, smelling like the great unwashed and looking like he's been dragged through a mire. I've already told Millie to get rid of him. He's putting other customers off.'

'What other customers?' asked Thomas. 'It's fairly quiet here so far. The fella's all right where he is,' he added mildly. 'He's paid, and he's doing no harm.'

He picked up the plate and a knife and fork, and started to walk over to William.

Mr Fairbanks came out from behind the bar and stood in front of him so he couldn't pass, looking hot and angry. Thomas put the plate down carefully on a table, to avoid the eggs rolling off. He looked up at Fairbanks calmly.

'Why do you think it's this quiet, you daft bugger?' snarled Fairbanks. ''Cos that tramp is sitting in my bar, keeping other folk away! It's not for you to decide who stays and who goes, Marchant. Now I suggest you ask that filthy-looking fella to leave immediately. Either that or it's *you* who leaves immediately.'

Millie had by now placed herself silently, invisibly, behind the bar, out of the eyeline of both her uncle and Fairbanks. When she heard the way the conversation was heading, she saw her opportunity. If Uncle Thomas didn't finish this, she was going to.

First things first, however. She silently opened the cash drawer a fraction, scooped out all the notes, and put them in the pocket in the side seam of the gathered skirt Bella had made for her. She disappeared silently back into the lobby through the staff door, then burst back through the main door into the bar, making her presence known.

Thomas had evidently been considering his options because he hadn't moved.

'What's the matter?' she asked.

'That ruddy tramp in my bar!' said Fairbanks, loud enough that William must have heard. 'I told you to chuck him out – told both of you – so why's he still here? Eh?'

'You really are the most appalling bully, Fairbanks,' said Thomas, clearly and quite loudly, looking his boss straight in the eye. 'I hate the way you pick on the girls.'

'You make me sick the way you pick on *all* your staff, except Jane – people who you're supposed to be responsible for while they're here,' said Millie, approaching. She stopped when she was standing at the other side of Fairbanks from Thomas so that the publican had to turn his head between his two accusers.

'This is supposed to be paid work, not some kind of punishment,' said Thomas.

'And you couldn't pay us enough to put up with you and that violent, lunatic lover of yours, Jane Regan,' said Millie.

It was conjecture, informed only by what she had observed and half heard over the past weeks, and the strange vision that had flown through her hand and into her drawing. But, without any doubt, she had hit the mark.

Fairbanks turned puce and stood with his mouth moving, but no sound coming out, for a few seconds.

Then: 'How dare—' he started.

'A coward and a bully – that's what you are,' said Thomas. 'I should have told you that weeks ago, but I'm damned well telling you now. You're just a pathetic loudmouth, not very bright and with a vicious temper, who likes to exercise his power over folk he reckons won't answer back. Since Millie came to work here, you've shown your true colours. I thought we could all put up with you, but I was wrong. I've had enough of you.'

'Go to hell, Marchant. Get out, the both of you, and don't expect to be paid.'

'We're going,' snapped Millie, raising her voice and preparing to let rip. She was determined to have her say now, never mind the sacrifice of her dignity in front of the gathering audience, and nothing was going to stop her. 'And we don't expect to be paid fairly for the work we have done. After all, why would you do that when I saw you stealing our tips, left on the tables for us by satisfied customers? I was wondering why the tips had been so few recently, and this morning I saw for myself.'

There was a murmur of shock from the assembled customers.

'And when that madwoman Jane Regan broke all those plates and Pam got hurt, you didn't care one bit about her,' Millie went on. 'All you minded about was making us – not Mad Jane – pay for the plates! You are, without a doubt, the worst employer anyone could possibly have.'

'Get out! Get out! Get out!' yelled Fairbanks, no longer caring that more and more customers were congregating in the bar to observe the row between the landlord and his staff.

'You couldn't keep us here,' said Thomas, with dignity. 'And if I hear one word of you bad-mouthing Millie or me or Pam or Fabio, I will lose no opportunity to tell the whole of Theddleton about you. After all, you're not from round here: no one knows owt about you, and mebbe it's time they were warned. We're all local, and the town is filled with our friends and families.'

This was a slight exaggeration, he knew, but Millie's outburst had opened the floodgates for accusations and insults to be lobbed at Fairbanks.

'I said, get out!'

'Oh, we're going,' said Millie. She turned to the audience of customers. 'Anyone care to come with us? I doubt you'll want to stay now you know what this . . .' The word 'whippersnapper' passed through her mind from her ill-tempered encounter with Marjory Hailsham, but, no, that wasn't the right insult at all. She settled for something more obvious and accurate. '. . . this vile bully is like. Who'd want to give *him* their business?'

'Well, not me,' spoke up a fella in a suit, who looked like a travelling salesman.

'Me neither. Can't stand that kind of behaviour,' said another.

'C'mon, let's go,' said a young man to the woman he had been lunching with.

Others agreed, and there was a hubbub as people took up their jackets and bags, many hurriedly downing their drinks before going, and made for the main door.

'But some of you haven't paid!' yelled Fairbanks, rushing after them into the lobby.

'What's happening?' said Pam, coming through the far door with some plates of ham, egg, and chips and finding the customers were making for the car park. 'Where's everyone going?'

'Leaving,' said Millie. 'Uncle Thomas and I are leaving, too.'

'When?'

'Now! Are you coming?'

'I can't. I can't afford to lose this job. I've three younger sisters at home, Mum's got another little 'un on the way, and it's only me and Dad earning. I can't just go. I'd like to, but I can't.' But indecision was written all over her face. She was clearly desperate not to be left with Mad Jane, and only Fabio to mind her back.

'Then come now. There's a vacancy at the bakery on the High Street. Just leave those plates, and go and tell Fabio we're leaving before Fairbanks comes back.'

That galvanised her into action, and she sprinted out the way she'd come in, Thomas and Millie following quickly behind her.

The four collected their bicycles and rode away while Fairbanks was still remonstrating with the customers who were leaving without paying.

Half a mile down the road, Fabio signalled that he wanted to stop.

'Will someone tell me what's going on?' he asked. 'Pam said you'd had a row and were leaving, and I wasn't going to stay there alone with Mad Jane Regan. But, by heck, I'm hoping I've not made the wrong choice.'

'It would be far less safe to stay there,' said Pam. 'But I am worried I'll be without a job now. Dad will go crazy when I tell him.'

'I told you,' said Millie. 'My friend Edwin works at the bakery, and he says there's a vacancy.'

'Why don't you want it?' asked Pam suspiciously.

'Because I don't want to get up in the middle of the night to go to work. It's an even earlier start than it is at the Three-Mile. Besides, I've got other ideas,' said Millie. 'So off you go and get your new job. Go on. The baker's called Mr Harcourt, and Edwin says he's a good man.'

Pam nodded, turned away and rode off towards Theddleton as fast as she could.

'What about me?' asked Fabio. 'I don't suppose the bakery wants a cook, does it?'

'I haven't heard so,' said Millie, 'but won't there be lots of jobs in catering very soon, when the holiday season starts and the place is thronging with visitors? Here' – she took a pen from her bag and held out her arm – 'write your address on my arm, and if I hear of anything, I promise to let you know.'

Fabio did so. Then he, Millie, and Thomas rode on towards their homes.

Mr Fairbanks managed to extract some payments from departing customers, but nothing like as much as he was owed. Furious, cursing Thomas and Millie, he went back inside, only to find the place deserted except for William Gladstone, sitting waiting patiently in the corner of the bar.

'What are you doing here still?' said Fairbanks. 'I thought I asked you to leave.'

'No one said owt about me leaving,' said William. 'T'others it is who've left. I's waiting for my eggs. I's paid for 'em, like,' he explained, and then added with a sudden flash of apparent comprehension, 'Which is more than most folk have.'

Fairbanks turned to where Thomas had left the pickled eggs on a plate, and there they were: the only things that remained as they had been just fifteen minutes before. He brought them over to William.

'There. And don't ever show your ugly face here again.'

William said nothing. He had the pickles he'd paid for, and he was used to being insulted.

Fairbanks went to put what money he had managed to extract from the fleeing customers into the cash drawer. When he opened it, he found it contained nothing but small change.

'You filthy tramp, you've stolen my cash!' he accused William. 'Hand it over, or I'll call the police.'

'I never took owt,' said William. 'I's got a respectable job. I don't need your brass, mister.'

'I said, hand it over.'

'I don't have nowt of yours. I paid for my eggs. And my beer.'

'I don't believe you. Turn out your pockets. Go on, show me.'

William, grumbling under his breath, stood up and turned out the pockets of his trousers, the linings grey with dirt and a red-brown colour, which looked like dried blood. One pocket had a hole in it and held nothing; the other contained sevenpence, which was the change from his lunch, and the severed front foot of a rat, which explained the blood.

'I tell you what,' said William. 'I shall tell folk not to come here.'

Then he sidled out from the corner table and left, taking the dog-eared copy of the *Daily Express* with him.

# CHAPTER SEVENTEEN

MILLIE HADN'T BEEN at all sure of Thomas's support against Fairbanks, and even now they were back home, she still couldn't quite believe what had happened. Zinging with belligerent energy, she felt jubilant that the inn staff had achieved a victory over Fairbanks's tyranny, but, at the same time, angry that she had had to put up with Fairbanks and Mad Jane at all – and had had to keep quiet to her cousins about what she was enduring.

Thomas, however, had other concerns.

'We'll just have to tell the girls straight out that we've left,' he said, bringing a restorative cup of tea outside for Millie. He still looked shaken about the row, despite his resolute words.

He sat on the wall of the low raised bed to one side of the little garden, while Millie paced up and down, huffing and muttering and spilling her tea.

'I just thought, all this while, that I'd keep quiet about

what it was like and try to stick with the Three-Mile so I could save up to pay for Bella's wedding,' Thomas resumed, sounding subdued.

'I know,' barked Millie. 'Yet you thought it was good enough for me, being shouted at all the time by Fairbanks and dodging Mad Jane's violence! Would you have wanted Alice or Bella to work there? No, you wouldn't!'

'I reckon you're right, Millie. But then Alice and Bella have jobs, and so I didn't need to consider that. I can see I should have thought it through more carefully.'

'Aah! What kind of excuse is that?' yelled Millie, now properly angry. 'I haven't got my own father to guide me and a fat lot of use you've turned out to be as a stand-in! I should never have trusted you about the job. In fact, I don't think I should trust you about anything. Mum was right: you're weak and cowardly and completely hopeless. Even Aunt Moaner said you were hopeless, and I think it's the only time she's ever been right about anything!'

'Oh, come now, Millie—'

'Well, the girls think you are. Always rolling their eyes and shaking their heads at you being pathetic, while putting up with it. It's a wonder Alice isn't going to get married too, just to get away from you.'

'No . . . oh, no, Millie, love. Don't say that. I couldn't bear it if both my girls left me.'

'Why? Because you'd be left with me, who you don't care about? Who you think is only good enough to be bullied all day at that awful inn?'

'No, love. Listen. It was all a mistake, a misjudgement.'

'My misjudgement was ever listening to you, Uncle Thomas. I can see now exactly how it was when you let Uncle Frank half kill Mum!' Millie yelled. 'I hate you!'

She hurled her tea, mug and all, to the paving at Thomas's feet, and rushed inside and up to her room, leaving him alone, shaken and tearful, which is how Bella and Alice found him when they came in from work.

Bella persuaded Millie to come down and eat her dinner with the family.

'We need to include you, Millie,' she said. 'The situation affects us all, it was partly of your making, and we don't want you to be left out. You are one of us now: I told you that.'

Alice knew how much money needed to be coming in to keep them afloat at even the usual level of respectable thriftiness, and it wouldn't be enough with what she and Bella earned.

'Couldn't you have just given your notice and stayed for your references, if you really felt you had to go?' she asked. 'It's one thing to leave a job; quite another to make a scene, walk out without your pay and take the rest of the staff with you. Honestly, Dad, I thought better of you. We're suddenly cast adrift financially, and no one will employ you if they hear you're a rabble-rouser.' She glared at her father, who looked sheepish in return. 'As for you, Millie, well, I can hardly say I'm surprised, but I really wish you'd just grow up and start behaving like a responsible human being.'

'That's not fair, Alice!' shouted Millie, stamping her foot. 'It was awful at the Three-Mile. Uncle Thomas hated the job, but stayed because you and Bella were so keen for him to stick at something. I'm only sorry he roped me into it, too.'

'We wouldn't want Dad or you to be unhappy when the job was horrible,' Alice answered. 'But . . . well, we do have to live, you know, Millie. You'll have to find another job soon, Dad. We won't manage long on what Bella and I earn at the shops. It'll be difficult for us two to support all four of us.'

'I intend to, love. I just need to have a look around, see what's suitable.'

'Oh, Dad, when have I heard that before?' Alice sighed. 'Sometimes I just wish you'd knuckle down, get a job that suits you and stick with it. Other folk manage that – why can't you?'

Bella was looking increasingly upset. 'It's different for you, Millie,' she said. 'No one expects owt of you, which is good because at least they're not going to be disappointed. You just swan around, dreaming of being a painter and doing nowt about it, but there are bills to pay and food to buy, and it's about time you faced up to that. I know it's nice to have a dream – I have dreams, too – but we have to live as well. And . . . and I am really trying my hardest to save up to get married. Sidney and I, we decided to make a big effort and save up properly, everything we can, in our building society accounts, so that we can have our own house. And now . . .' Her voice broke, and she dashed away sudden tears. 'We'll *never* get married, the way things are going. We'll *never* be able to afford to.' She started crying in earnest.

'Oh, love, don't take on so,' said Thomas soothingly.

'Would you rather we were both downtrodden by Fairbanks and threatened with violence by Mad Jane Regan at the Three-Mile every day, just so you can marry Sidney Bennett?' Millie asked Bella. 'Perhaps you don't care about me – after all, I'm not your sister – but I'd have thought you would have set Uncle Thomas's welfare above your wanting to rush into marrying that imbecile.'

'Who are you calling an imbecile?' snapped Bella.

'Sidney Bennett, of course,' retorted Millie.

'Why don't you just shut up?' shouted Bella. 'Just don't speak to me again until you've got yourself a proper job that pays regularly. You've been taking and not giving owt back for far too long.'

'Bella!' gasped Alice. 'I can't believe you said that.'

'Well, I did,' said Bella, and went out, slamming the sitting-room door behind her.

Thomas, Alice, and Millie looked at each other.

'She'll come round,' said Thomas.

'She's just disappointed,' said Alice. 'And that wasn't very kind of you either, Millie.'

'She doesn't like to hear the truth sometimes,' said Millie.

\* \* \*

Bella, furious and tearful, put on her jacket and decided to go for a walk in the mild spring evening and think about what to do. With every passing week, it seemed to her that the prospect of her and Sidney marrying retreated further into the future.

What was worrying her, too, was that he had been less affectionate of late and not so keen to take her out for a drink or to a dance or the cinema. He'd said he was going to be busy – 'Stuff to do with work,' he'd said vaguely. It was as if, now the wedding wasn't to be so soon, he felt he could make less of an effort. He'd always been generous with little presents of chocolate or a few flowers, but now there were none of these.

Despite this, by the time she got to the High Street, Bella had decided to go to see Sidney and share her worries with him. This was, after all, big family news.

Just as she was passing the toyshop, the door to the side – which gave access to the upstairs flat – opened, and there was Toby Warminster, carrying a large canvas bag.

Bella's heart gave a little skip of pleasure to see him. He hadn't been in the shop earlier, so perhaps he'd only just arrived from London.

'Toby! I didn't know you were back in Theddleton.'

'Hello, Bella,' he said politely, smiling hesitantly. 'Are you all right?' He was looking at her face and Bella thought it must be blotchy with her crying. Too late now to do anything about that.

'I'm fine, thank you.' She smiled, pretending it was true.

'I'm making a flying visit with the finished jacket that Bobbie commissioned for her father,' explained Toby. 'I'm just going to meet Bobbie on the Promenade now, and she'll take me over to Baybury. I really hope she and her father are pleased with what I've done.'

'I'm sure they will be. When do you have to go back to London?' asked Bella, hoping Toby would be at the shop the next day, joking with his father and letting his mother fuss around him while he wallpapered doll's-house parlours and chatted about his life in London.

'I'm catching the early train. I have to get to work.'

'That's a shame.'

'Well, we've all got stuff to do,' he said, then looked uncomfortable. 'Look, Bella, I'm really sorry about last time. I didn't know you are engaged to be married. I didn't mean to overstep the mark, make a nuisance of myself . . .'

Bella was taken aback for a mere second. Of course, Mr and Mrs Warminster would have told Toby that their assistant was planning to be married, if he had mentioned her name at all. In fact, it was quite natural that the topic would have come up, Mrs Warminster being so excited about the wedding preparations, and both of them taking a kindly interest in Bella.

'You didn't. You weren't a nuisance,' said Bella, blushing. 'I should have told you. I didn't mean to mislead you.'

'Yes, I reckon you should have,' said Toby, mildly. 'But anyway, I know now, and I hope there's no harm done.

Right, I'd better get on. I mustn't keep Bobbie waiting. Bye, Bella.' He gave her another little smile, turned towards the Promenade and strode away.

Bella felt she'd disappointed him, that she'd been deceitful. Probably she had. She remembered she had had numerous opportunities to mention Sidney and had failed to do so.

She stood for a moment, her hands to her face, disappointed in herself, then decided she needed to continue her walk.

Toby had disappeared round the corner by the hotel. Bella took the same route but at a distance. When she reached the Promenade, she saw, parked a little way past the Imperial, Bobbie's car, and Bobbie standing on the pavement, in the process of greeting Toby with a radiant smile. Then she opened the passenger door for him and he got in, while she went round to the driver's side.

Bella realised she was staring and, not wanting to be noticed, she quickly turned the other way, to go to Sidney's house.

She decided to cross over, to walk along the path overlooking the beach. She felt miserable and fed up. Toby thought she was flighty and unreliable. She didn't want anyone to think badly of her, and Toby was such a nice man, as well as being the son of her employers. Maybe he'd tell Bobbie, and then Bobbie would think she was a flirt, too. Bella and Alice both liked and admired Bobbie. Her friendship meant a lot to them. Maybe Toby and Bobbie would fall in love, and he'd come back to Theddleton to marry her, and Bella wouldn't be able to be friends with them because she had kissed Toby once and not told him about Sidney, and everyone would be scornful of her behaviour and think she was fast and deceitful . . .

She was just about to recross the road further down when she saw Sidney walking along on that side, towards the centre of the town, dressed very smartly in his suit, his features set in concentration. Where on earth could he be going? He'd said he was too busy to see her.

'Sidney,' she called. 'Sidney, hello!'

He looked up, and an expression of pure annoyance crossed his face. There was no mistaking it.

'Bella,' he said, without enthusiasm, when she was beside him on the pavement. 'What a nice surprise. I didn't expect to see you here.'

'I was just coming to see you, to tell you what's happened,' she said. 'But where are you going, looking so smart? Am I invited?' She spoke lightly, not thinking for one moment he would take her seriously.

Sidney looked at her cotton skirt and her lace-up shoes. Then his eyes ran over her hair, fine strands around her face escaping from her plait. The look on his face spoke volumes.

'No,' he said.

'It was a joke,' Bella said in a little voice, feeling foolish and very hurt.

'I should hope so,' said Sidney. 'Look, Bella, what's the matter? What's happened that you want to tell me about?'

'It's nowt,' said Bella quietly. 'I just . . . No, it'll keep. It's not important.'

'Then I'd better be getting on.' He made to move away.

'But, Sidney, you still haven't told me where you're going, looking so smart. Is it the hotel?'

'No, it isn't,' he said. 'If you must know, I'm having dinner . . . with friends.'

'Dinner? Sounds posh. Who? If they're friends of yours, I must know them, too.'

'Not necessarily,' said Sidney. 'I'll be seeing you.' And he strode away so quickly that she couldn't even think about continuing the conversation.


Bella wandered slowly home, cross and disappointed. No one wanted to know her, not even her own fiancé. She had been needy, silly, and cowed, not the strong woman who could give as good as she got – and more – with Sidney.

Goodness, today really had been a disaster. Half the household were now out of work, and there'd been the horrible row with Millie because of that. Then the disappointed look Toby Warminster had been unable to hide at her behaviour. And now Sidney, being superior and secretive. Perhaps it was just some event to do with the football team . . . Even as the thought crossed her mind, Bella knew she was being stupid. When had Sidney ever not mentioned anything to do with the football team? He'd been very evasive about Muriel Chalfont lately, but when she'd asked him, he'd always had an excuse. She could hardly follow him to wherever it was he was going.

She wondered what she could do to help her father find another job. The answer was: nothing. He would just have to manage that for himself. He had always found something in the end, although now there were four of them to live off the two wages in the meantime.

But what about Millie? She was determined on this painting business, and she did seem to be wonderfully talented, but how could she make that pay? And how long would it be before it took off and became viable as a way to make a living? Millie was so young and had to start from scratch. It could be ages . . . years. Bella remembered the story Millie had told of how Aunt Nanette had had to sell Uncle Harry's paintings because she wasn't making enough to support the little family alone. It didn't bode well for commercial success in Theddleton.

# CHAPTER EIGHTEEN

'So, Sidney, love, how was your dinner with Joseph Chalfont?' asked Nancy Bennett, dishing up eggs and bacon to her son, who sat at the breakfast table while his mother bobbed up and down between her chair and various sizzling pans, fussing around him. 'You looked right smart yesterday evening, love. I'm that proud to see you're moving in the right circles these days.'

'It was good,' said Sidney. 'We talked a lot about Mr Chalfont's plans for Theddleton. The man has got real vision, you know. Now he's seeing me as the kind who can smooth things along for him, his "man at the town hall", so to speak.' He looked smug.

'I'm so proud he recognises your worth,' said his mother. 'What sort of plans? Summat exciting?'

'Obviously,' said Sidney, as if he thought his mother was being dim. 'Nowt I can really tell you about – confidentiality, and all that . . .'

Nancy mouthed 'confidentiality' carefully. It was an

important-sounding word, and one she might have opportunity to repeat.

'. . . but let's just say, it's useful that Keith Forester, who plays full-back for The Seafarers, is also in Planning – at the district council in Baybury – and he has been made aware of certain plans to rebuild a certain place in the form of a fine, new cliff-top hotel. I reckon he might look favourably on those plans if I were to introduce him personally to my friend Joseph, and mebbe they could come to some agreement.'

'Oh, yes,' said Nancy knowledgeably. 'It's always more agreeable if you know folk, like. Keep it all friendly. Best way to get business done.'

'Quite right, Mam. Like the floral clock. Once I managed to persuade Mr Penrose what a good thing it would be for Theddleton, it went through a lot quicker. Planning were umming and ahing about it summat daft before that. Plus, we've still got the funds you and the Committee helped raise, which we're now going to put towards some bedding plants along the Promenade, so it's a gain all round for Theddleton.'

'That'll be nice.'

'It will. I reckon if we have them in the same colours as the Imperial's crest and the hotel's window boxes, it will all look lovely.'

'And what about Muriel, love? Was she at this posh dinner?'

'Of course. Her and her mam. After all, it was at their home. Muriel was looking lovely, as usual.'

Nancy nodded. 'I'm glad you're getting to know them all so much better. Perhaps I should ask Muriel to tea,' she said.

Sidney looked taken aback. 'I don't think so, Mam.'

'Oh? Why not?'

'Well . . . she's a busy woman. And I don't want to look pushy. We're keeping it low-key between us at the moment.'

Nancy looked thrilled. 'So you and Muriel . . . ? I take it you've told Bella Marchant that the engagement is off . . . if it was ever on in the first place.'

Sidney, now he thought of it, had seen a lot less of Bella since they'd decided to postpone the wedding until next year; so much so that yesterday, he'd noticed that she was looking far from her best, a bit homespun. It hadn't helped that it also looked as if she'd been crying. The more Sidney saw of glossy, blonde, fashionable Muriel, the more shabby and ordinary Bella looked, like someone from a time he was growing out of. And, truth be told, Bella had looked relieved about the wedding postponement, so perhaps she saw that soon she might be a little out of her depth with him. He was beginning to think that the whole engagement had been a bit of a young-love fantasy, some foolish scheme they'd both grown out of and which was best forgotten. The sooner the better.

'No, I've said nowt to Bella, but I reckon she knows. I'll make it clear when I next see her, just so there's no misunderstanding.'

'That'll be a relief, love. You're a good lad. I can always rely on you to do the right thing.'

Thomas was up early, out of habit as much as wanting to get on and find another job. Still feeling upset by the rows of the previous day, and then Bella coming back from her walk with her spirits lower than ever, he pottered around a while and then decided to go over to Baybury to see if there were any jobs going.

He wheeled his bicycle through the front gate – no Bella up early to wave him off today – and pedalled slowly away. The lane was full of birdsong, rabbits grazing in the meadow opposite, and the sun was radiating a soft warmth already.

Old habits die hard, and Thomas was soon daydreaming about his girls and about Lottie, and vaguely thinking about ideas for stories. He'd known the route to Baybury for much of his life and didn't need to concentrate on that.

He spent the day in Baybury, visiting business he knew and several he didn't, but without any luck. Never mind; he'd made a start and there was always tomorrow.

He was cycling home, his thoughts wandering, and had just turned onto the Baybury Road, which led eventually to the end of the Promenade, when a dog shot across in front of him. Thomas hardly registered what it was, saw only a small, fast-moving creature. He applied his brakes with such force that the back of the bike rose up, sending him straight over the handlebars and into the road, where he landed in a heap with the bike half on top of him.

Thomas could hear voices – a woman, distraught, and then a man, and then more. He lay still for as long as he could before he felt people crowding round and then hands helping him. He just wanted to gather himself and think how badly he was hurt and then decide what was to be done about it.

'Oh my goodness! Oh, I'm so sorry. Rufus just slipped his lead and made off. You poor man – let me help you,' fussed the woman's voice.

Thomas opened his eyes and saw a middle-aged woman with a kind face.

'What a relief you're not dead,' she said.

'I feel the same,' said Thomas. 'Just give me room, and I reckon I'll be all right.'

'Here, mate,' said a man. 'Let me give you a hand. I reckon you're just winded, like.'

'Oh, do go carefully. Sit up slowly first and see how you are,' advised the woman. She turned to one of the men. 'Here, would you mind catching the dog? Just put this on his collar.' She handed over the unreliable lead and turned back to Thomas, asking if he'd hit his head, and what was hurting, and did he think he could move to the pavement if these fellas helped him up . . . ?

Thomas was bruised but not broken, and, mercifully, his bicycle had escaped damage altogether. Soon, he was reassuring the bystanders that he was well enough to pedal home.

'Yes, home's where you should be after such a nasty fall,' said the woman. 'Are you sure you can manage?'

'I'll be fine,' said Thomas, anxious to get away from the fuss and be patched up by his kind and sensible daughters, if that was necessary.

Then, with thanks to all his helpers, he set off back to Chapel Lane, his scraped knees and bruised shoulder hurting like blazes.

Millie was glad everyone had gone out. She had the cottage to herself and could mooch about. Gradually her anger of the previous day dissipated, although her conscience was pricked by the accusations she'd flung at Thomas.

Her mood bucked up when she found the large fold of stolen banknotes in her skirt pocket. She'd forgotten about those, what with all the arguments that had followed her taking them.

She put them in the biscuit tin under her bed with her savings, delighted at the possibilities that such riches afforded. Of course, she couldn't just produce a whole lot of money to help out Alice with the housekeeping – that would be asking for trouble – but she could gradually hand over a little of it, whenever she'd earned anything. Which would start to happen very soon . . . as soon as she'd bought her paints and got her first commission.

Eventually Alice and Bella came home from work, tired, Bella subdued still, and set about cooking. Millie joined them but hadn't much to say for herself.

'Where's Dad?' asked Alice.

'Gone out. To Baybury, I think he said.'

'Hmm.'

Right on cue, the front door opened and there was Thomas, with a scrape on his cheekbone, limping.

'What's happened?' gasped Bella. 'Oh, Dad, have you fallen off your bike? Are you badly hurt?'

'Just a bit of an accident, love. A dog ran out in front of me. I've got a few bruises, but there's no real damage done.'

To his surprise, Millie, who had appeared at the kitchen door, looked horror-stricken. She charged over and flung her arms around him, while he winced with his aches.

'Oh, thank God you're all right,' she gasped. 'I couldn't bear it if I'd killed you as well.'

Thomas, used by now to Millie's dramatics, led her into the sitting room, while Alice turned off the pans, found some sticking plasters, and she and Bella followed.

'Here, Millie, let me sit down – my shoulder feels like it must be black with bruising – and tell me what you're thinking,' said Thomas. 'I can't think what being tipped off my bike has to do with you. It was a dog that pulled me up, that's all.'

However Millie would not be calm. 'But it was me. Yesterday, when I was so angry, I hated you.' She wrung her hands, and tears rolled down her anguished face. 'I'm so sorry. It was my hate that caused you to be hurt. It's all my fault.'

'Nonsense, lass. It was just crossness. Little harm done, and what harm there is, is nowt to do with you – it really isn't. Now, where did you get this queer idea from?'

'It was just a bike accident, Millie, no more than that,' said Alice.

Sobbing and mopping her eyes, Millie explained what had happened to her parents.

'I wished them dead – I told them that – and then I painted this picture full of my anger and hatred, which was like a horrible crash all over them, and then Mags and a policeman came and told me that they were dead.' She put her face in her hands and sobbed loudly.

'Oh, Millie, don't take on so, lass. Surely you can see you didn't cause the accident?'

'But I did, I really did. It's a bit like the drawings – you know, that I did of Grandma Marchant, and the one of your wedding dress, Bella, which you were so angry about. I couldn't help doing those – the image kind of flies into my head and my hand and it's what I have to draw – and I think . . .' She dashed away her tears again. '. . . I think if I wish for something to happen, then it's part of the same thing, a force that I conjure up: it happens.'

Bella and Alice looked at each other, astonished.

'I can't explain about the drawings you did for the stories, Millie. It seems to me to be a strange kind of gift. But they've not been bad things, have they?' said Alice.

'I admit I was unsettled about the picture of my mother, but only because I loved her, and I couldn't explain how you knew how she looked to me. And Bella – well, no harm done. It was a lovely dress. She was upset you hadn't included Sidney, I seem to remember, but we all thought you'd just imagined Bella as the princess but not Sidney as the King's robe-maker. It doesn't really matter.'

'No, it doesn't, it really doesn't, Millie,' said Bella. 'I know I was cross then, but if I'd known that you were full of all this guilt about your parents dying – and had got this strange idea that is really all wrong – then I wouldn't have been cross for even a second, I promise, because some things *are* odd and can't be explained, and some things are . . . just stuff that happens, and bad stuff happens to everyone from time to time.'

'But I wished Mum and Dad dead – only for a bit, but they were. And then, Uncle Thomas, I said I hated you, and you were nearly killed, too. I should have learned not to wish for bad things, to not be so angry, but sometimes I can't help it and then . . . bad things do happen, and it's my fault.'

'No, Millie—' began Alice.

'But you don't understand: I *wanted* some horrible thing to happen, and it did. I can't help making bad wishes – I just fly into a fury and I can't help it – but then they come true, and then I really, really wish I hadn't said or thought what I had, but it's too late!'

She threw herself down on the sofa, bawling loudly.

Eventually Thomas got up and limped out to the kitchen, and made a pot of tea.

'Poor Millie,' Bella said, mopping Millie's tears with

her own handkerchief. 'All this time you've been thinking that, and it's truly not your fault. How can it be? Nanette and Harry died because they didn't drive their car carefully enough, and Dad fell off his bike because a dog ran out in front of him and he had to brake hard. That's all there is to it.'

Millie sniffed. 'I was so cross – with everyone, but with myself most of all. I've done this terrible thing, and now nothing will ever be right for me. First I had to endure Uncle Frank and Aunt Moaner, and now I've been rescued from there only to bring bad things here.' She started crying again.

'Well, life takes some getting through sometimes, Millie, but there's nowt for it but to carry on,' said Thomas, coming back with a cup of tea for her. 'I've been side-tracked myself for a long time – by grief, by a lack of resolution, probably by selfishness: relying on my girls too much and not taking the lead. None of us is blameless, Millie, but we can't control other folk's fate, that's for certain.'

She nodded, although she didn't entirely agree with that.

'Now, let's decide to get rid of all that anger and hatred and start again in a more positive frame of mind. What do you say?'

Millie nodded again. She thought of the picture she had drawn of Richard Fairbanks and Jane Regan, but decided to keep quiet. She couldn't do anything about it now anyway. And she still hated them.

Bella hugged her and stroked her tangled hair. 'You just need lots of love, Millie, and you know you've got it here, don't you?'

Millie nodded.

The following day, a police constable came to 8 Chapel Lane and told Thomas and Millie that a large amount of cash in notes had gone missing from the Three-Mile Bottom, and asked if they knew anything about that?

Of course, both denied all knowledge. Thomas was genuinely baffled. He said he knew Millie had had no opportunity to take any money because he had been in the bar all the time she had. He'd seen Mr Fairbanks putting cash in the till not long before his staff left, and Fairbanks would have noticed if the takings had been missing then. Millie vouched for her uncle and pointed out that Mr Fairbanks had been with Thomas in the bar.

'Have you any thoughts as to who might have taken the money, then?' asked the constable.

'Have you questioned Jane Regan?' said Millie. 'She's a law unto herself. Everyone's afraid of her: her nasty tricks and her violent outbursts. I didn't see her take anything, but she's the one with the chance to do so, living at the inn as she does.'

'I've met Miss Regan,' said the constable, the memory of that encounter writ large on his face.

'Well, then,' said Millie. 'Or it could be that Mr Fairbanks is pointing an accusing finger at his staff who have left to stir up trouble for them. Possibly he knows all about where the supposedly missing cash is himself.'

Thomas nodded. 'He's not a good man, Constable. I think you might be wasting your time if you're looking for the guilty party outside the inn.'

Millie took the bus to Baybury to buy what she needed from the art shop. The Baybury Artist was on the main shopping street, a smart shop with a big window displaying professional painting materials, as well as sketchbooks, paintboxes, and coloured pencils more suited to amateurs. With Mr Fairbanks's money in her handbag, Millie decided she'd better set a small budget and stick to it on this first shopping expedition, so as not to arouse any suspicions at home or in the shop. A young woman with a thick fold of banknotes would be memorable, and Millie wanted to be noticed only on her own terms.

She would stick to just five basic colours of paint in tubes, a couple of brushes and two small canvases to start with. She could improvise a palette with a sheet of glass.

She was about to enter the shop when she noticed someone she recognised walking down the street in a purposeful way.

It was Muriel Chalfont.

Muriel had never knowingly set eyes on Millie, so Millie knew that if she kept a discreet distance she might be able to see, just out of interest, what had brought Muriel to Baybury in a hat with a flirty little veil on it and very high-heeled shoes. It was clear to Millie that Muriel was not a woman who liked to go unnoticed.

Muriel's heels clack-clacked along to the first turning off to the right, another street of shops and other businesses, and she turned down it and soon reached a tearoom. The doorbell jangled merrily as she went in, and who should be sitting in the window, rising to greet her, but Sidney Bennett.

Millie crossed the road to where she could see into the tearoom window clearly without hovering outside. It was obvious that Muriel and Sidney had arranged in advance to meet there. They were flirting quite openly, laughing and leaning in to listen to each other, sending the waitress away because they hadn't even got round to looking at the menu, and each letting a hand rest on the other's hand, arm, shoulder . . .

It was only mid-morning, and Millie had all day. When she decided she'd been there long enough, she wandered up the road a short way, crossed over and then slowly walked back down the other side. There were benches along the side of this wide street, positioned under cherry trees so that visitors to the pretty town could enjoy a sit-down. Millie nipped into a bakery where there was no queue and bought herself a doughnut. Then she went to eat it on a bench just along from the tearoom, where she could see who came and went, but not be easily seen.

After about half an hour, Sidney and Muriel emerged into the street. They were laughing and holding hands now, as they strolled back to the main street. Out of sight of the tearoom window, they stopped, and Sidney appeared to brush a crumb or a smudge off Muriel's face. Then he leaned towards her and boldly kissed her, right there, in the street, while people carrying shopping baskets walked by them and looked.

Laughing, they strolled on, and Millie got up from her bench and followed at a distance, casually stopping to look in shop windows but keeping them in sight.

At the end of the street, they turned for the seafront, crossed over the wide road and walked along to one of the shelters that sat at intervals there, open to the sea but with glass sides to keep out the wind. They snuggled up together on the wooden bench and kissed some more.

Millie went down onto the beach and walked towards the sea so that the shelter was in sight above her. It was tricky to watch from here because she had no business to be standing staring into a wind shelter at a courting couple, but Sidney and Muriel were very much occupied with each other, and Millie watched them flirting and kissing for a couple of minutes before she decided she'd seen enough.

Bella needed to know about this. There was no way Millie couldn't tell her what she had seen all too plainly: that Sidney Bennett was not only an imbecile, but a two-timing bounder as well!

# CHAPTER NINETEEN

WALKING HOME FROM the bus stop, carrying her art materials in a carrier bag, Millie passed the bookshop. Usually she hardly noticed it, but today a very shiny car was parked right outside, which drew her attention. Or maybe she was just trying to fill the time before the inevitable moment when she would have to tell Bella that Sidney was two-timing her. Perhaps Alice should be the one to tell Bella . . . But no, it wasn't Alice who had seen Sidney and Muriel.

The bookshop window was now set out with a display suggestive of a garden, with a central deck chair, a trug and a trowel beside it, and gardening books artfully displayed around, some open at attractive pictures, other presented with their titles and authors prominent. A couple of potted geraniums finished the scene.

It looked very pretty, although somehow not entirely right – not quite as good as it could be. Millie gazed at it, assessing what could improve it. An idea began to form in her head.

When she peered through the glass of the bookshop door, she saw Bobbie Reeves, looking like a fashion plate in a very tailored two-piece, chatting with Alice and the Pattersons. That explained the car. Millie knew that the Rolls-Royce belonged to Bobbie's father, so this Morris Minor must be her own.

Millie liked and admired Bobbie, who was friendly and amusing, from what Millie had seen of her. Millie even thought Bobbie looked a little bit like a younger, blonde version of Nanette, if Nanette had been able to afford what she had called 'good' clothes. So, far from feeling that the bookshop was none of her business, Millie went in to say hello. Besides, a chat with friendly people would take her mind off Sidney Bennett and Muriel Chalfont until she really had to speak about them.

Everyone turned and greeted her as the doorbell rang, Alice, Bobbie and Godfrey smiling broadly. Millie knew by now that Eileen Patterson wasn't much of a smiler.

'I've just come by to admire the window now it's been refurbished, Millie,' said Bobbie. 'I must say, Miss Patterson, you really do have vision. The little scene is very eye-catching.'

'Thank you. I'm glad you like it, Miss Reeves. Alice has worked hard to clear out the old books and set up the display. We had to harden our hearts and part with some very sad-looking volumes, but needs must . . .'

Millie saw Godfrey winking at Alice behind Eileen's back, and Alice suppressing a grin in return.

'What do you think, Millie?' asked Godfrey, in a tone

344

that suggested he was politely humouring Alice's young cousin by asking her opinion.

'It's fine,' said Millie, with a carefully calibrated shrug. 'But it could be better.'

'Oh?' said Eileen, immediately sharp. 'Are you an expert on shop windows, Millie Boyd?'

Alice, more used to Miss Patterson's manner, quickly answered for her. 'Actually, Miss Patterson, Millie is summat of an artist and has an exceptional eye for a well-constructed scene. Perhaps you can tell us what you reckon would improve it, Millie.'

'It's the screen at the back,' said Millie. 'It's all nice and clean now, but it looks too plain, like the back of a shop window.'

'Which is what it is,' said Eileen.

Everyone ignored her.

'In what way could it be improved?' Godfrey asked Millie.

'Well, it's just painted wood – and rather old-looking paint, at that. The hardware shop has much the same in their window. It would look much better here if it was, say, a mural: the kind of design that you could use for any window display you choose, but that adds to every one of them.'

'I'm not quite sure I understand what kind of thing you mean,' said Bobbie carefully. She cast her eyes to the canvases in Millie's carrier bag. 'If Miss Patterson and Mr Patterson don't mind . . .' She looked at them to gain their approval. '. . . could you perhaps sketch it out for me . . . ?' She beamed at Alice and understanding passed between them.

Godfrey fetched a sheet of the brown paper in which purchases were wrapped at the front desk, while Eileen and Alice moved some books aside to make space on the central display table. Then Millie sat on a stool at the table and sketched out an idea with a rather blunt pencil, which, apart from a fountain pen, was the only drawing implement available.

Alice broke off watching to serve two customers, including one who had noticed the book she wanted to buy in the window, and which Alice was able to reach for her in seconds.

'Nice window display,' said the book-buyer. 'I'd no idea you had this. I've never felt tempted to come in here before.'

'There are shelves of gardening books in the little room along the corridor there and up the stairs on the right,' said Alice. 'If you'd like to browse, I'll keep this book safely here for you in the meantime.'

'Yes, please,' said the woman, and disappeared down the corridor.

Godfrey smiled his approval at Alice.

Millie finished her sketch and explained it to the Pattersons. Even Eileen saw straight away that what Millie had come up with would look better than the plain screen.

It was the illusion of a bookcase containing some books, a vase, some potted plants and a couple of little framed paintings on its shelves. Wild roses and bindweed grew around and over it so that the scene was both indoors and outdoors at the same time. It could be the backdrop to almost any theme for displaying books.

'It's very clever,' said Godfrey.

'And so attractive,' said Bobbie, 'like a kind of *Sleeping Beauty* fantasy. I think if your window contained such a work of art, Miss Patterson, it would be quite an attraction in itself, for locals as well as visitors.'

'Mm, I can see that. But how much would it cost, Millie? And how do I know that you can work this up from the sketch successfully?'

'I can vouch for Millie's talent,' said Alice. 'Her mother, my aunt, was an artist who painted many murals in the West Country, and she taught Millie herself. Her father taught her portrait painting. I've seen some beautiful illustrations she's done.' She smiled encouragingly at Millie.

'It would cost two shillings an hour for me to paint it,' said Millie.

'Is that all?' asked Bobbie, taking command of suitable reactions to this news. 'That's a very reasonable price for an original work of art.'

'Well . . .' said Eileen, still not convinced. 'What if I don't like it when it's done? And what if it takes you months to do and the bill is enormous?'

'It won't be,' said Millie. 'Even allowing for the under-layers to dry so I can paint over to build up the picture, it will all be done in a few days.'

'I'll have to think about it,' said Eileen.

Alice knew that if Eileen considered it for any length of time, she would do what she always did, which was to decide to leave everything as it was. The commission must be agreed now.

Bobbie had obviously realised the same thing because she said, 'Miss Patterson, how would it be if I took the risk for you? If Millie paints your mural and you don't like it, I shall pay her for her work, so the only expense you'll have will be to paint over it. If you do like it, you can pay her what you owe. I have every confidence you will love it and you'll have got yourself a work of art permanently in your window at an astonishingly reasonable price.'

This last sentence must have been the clincher, because Eileen promptly agreed. Millie would produce a coloured sketch of the design for final approval, and then work from that, starting as soon as she could.

Millie left the bookshop in a far better mood than she'd entered it. Bobbie followed her out.

'Thank you, Bobbie,' said Millie. 'It was kind of you to persuade Miss Patterson.'

'Nonsense,' said Bobbie briskly. 'I'm glad to help you out. And Alice will be pleased. She's been worried about you, you know, and . . . well, I don't want Alice to be worried.' She beamed her lovely smile at Millie and stepped towards her car. 'I shall be in to see what you've done, and I can hardly wait,' she said.

'I absolutely promise to do my very best, Bobbie. This means so much to me – thank you.'

'It means a lot to me, too,' said Bobbie and, with a little wave, got into her car.

By the time Millie got home with her painting purchases, she felt a strange mixture of excitement about her commission and her new paints and canvases, and foreboding about telling Bella what she had seen earlier: the best and the worst of news all in one day.

Remembering how Bella had verbally lashed out at her over her and Thomas leaving their jobs, Millie was tempted, for the merest moment, not to tell Bella that Sidney was betraying her. It would serve her right. But no, of course it wouldn't! Bella didn't deserve that. It would be siding with the ghastly Sidney Bennett, too. And anyway, the only person who really wanted Bella to marry Sidney Bennett was Bella herself. Everyone else thought it was a rotten idea; they weren't saying it in so many words, but Millie had no doubt about it. Even Sidney didn't like the idea any more, if he was now canoodling with Muriel Chalfont so publicly. The man was a disgrace. Anyone could have seen them kissing in the street and in that seafront shelter. He should have told Bella he'd changed his mind before moving his affections to that shameless flirt, who knew he was engaged to Bella. Muriel and Sidney had both behaved appallingly, and they deserved each other.

Thomas, Alice and Bella all arrived home at the same time, giving Millie no chance to tell Thomas or Alice about Sidney's two-timing and relieve her of the burden of breaking the news. Thomas had been to see if he could find any seasonal jobs in the shops and cafés along the Promenade, and had met the girls coming out of the bookshop and the toyshop on the way home.

Alice was sparkling with excitement about the window commission for Millie, and had Millie tell Thomas and Bella all about it straight away, interrupting with observations about Bobbie's part in the conversation.

Thomas had had no luck with his job search, but wasn't too down-hearted. 'Summat will turn up,' he said. 'I just know it. It's early for the seaside holiday businesses to be fully up and running yet.'

'Perhaps you can sell buckets and spades at that kiosk overlooking the beach,' said Bella heavily. 'Or take the money for deck chairs.'

'Bella, you're obviously still cross with Dad, but don't you reckon you've made your point?' said Alice. 'You've been mardy with him for days, even though you know Dad's been out looking for a job every day since he left the inn, despite having that frightening little accident.'

'Which is why I'm still cross,' Bella answered. 'I'd have thought you might have found summat by now, Dad. After all, beggars can't be choosers, and it's beggars we'll be if you're too fussy about where you work.'

'Nonsense,' said Alice briskly. 'We're all doing our bit to be thrifty – we'll be all right if we're careful. And look at Millie! A commission already and guaranteed to be paid for, either by the bookshop or by Bobbie if Miss

Patterson really doesn't like the mural – which she will, I'm certain.'

'What's in it for Bobbie?' asked Bella suspiciously. 'Why would she do that for Millie?'

'Because she's a generous woman and can afford it, mebbe,' reasoned Alice. 'She doesn't have to have a reason to be generous, does she?'

'No, I suppose not. It's just a bit odd that she should offer to lavish money on Millie. She hardly knows her.'

'Bella, you really are in a bad mood, aren't you?' said Alice mildly. 'Why would you begrudge Millie having her first real commission when the one from Mrs Hailsham fell through so horribly? It's what we all want, isn't it – Millie to be employed doing summat she's really good at and enjoys? It's the start of her painting career, and that's to be applauded, not resented.'

'Yes, you're right. Oh, I'm sorry, I didn't mean to be mean. It's just that . . . everything seems so hopeless to me. All these months of planning the wedding and saving up for my dress fabric, because I can only afford a home-made dress, and Dad's growing the flowers, which will be lovely, but other brides get to choose theirs from a florist and have them made into bouquets by professionals, and I don't think we'll even be able to afford to have the town hall room for the reception, never mind the music I'd have liked, even though the wedding's postponed so we can save up some more. And we probably won't be able to afford our own house now, either, and so we'll still end up at Mrs Bennett's, the way things are going. And Sidney's been in a very odd mood lately, but mebbe he's feeling mardy, too.'

Millie felt a rush of panic. She couldn't *not* say anything now – couldn't let Bella think everything between her and Sidney Bennett was just as it had always been, and that she was actually going to marry him – but she knew that telling Bella was not going to go well. How could it? However, if she kept quiet, she would be colluding with Sidney and deceiving Bella, and that was unthinkable, now she'd considered it. She took a deep breath.

'Bella, there's something I need to tell you.'

She'd spoken quite loudly, and everyone looked at her expectantly.

'What?' asked Bella. She had picked up on Millie's tone and her eyes were wide with foreboding, as if she was in a car and about hit a wall at speed, and there was nothing she could do to prevent it. 'Tell me,' she croaked.

Millie stood up from what had become her favourite chair in the sitting room and started pacing, flapping her hands.

*Just say it. Say it after three: one, two, three.*

'Sidney and Muriel Chalfont. I saw them kissing.'

'What! When did you see that? When?'

'This morning, in Baybury.'

'No, you must be mistaken. Are you sure it was Sidney? Why wasn't he at work? And how do you know who Muriel Chalfont is?'

'Yes, it *was* Sidney Bennett, and it *was* Muriel Chalfont. I know it was. I heard her being called by her name one time when she went into the hotel. They met at a tearoom, and then they left and . . . I saw them plainly in the street.'

'Sit down, Millie,' said Alice. 'Tell us calmly.'

'Aye, I remember you said you'd seen them together walking on the beach one time, but I thought nowt of it,' said Thomas. 'But kissing in the street, you say? In front of folk? Then anyone could have seen.'

'Yes. I'm sorry, but yes, they were. And *I* saw. And then they went down to the seafront, to sit in one of the shelters, and they were kissing again.'

'No . . .' whispered Bella, her face completely white.

Alice reached out and tried to take Bella's hand to comfort her, but Bella snatched it away, beyond being comforted.

'It's true,' said Millie. 'I followed them to make sure I wasn't mistaken – that it wasn't somehow innocent and I'd got it all wrong, although I knew straight away it was them – and it's true. I wouldn't lie to you about this, Bella.'

'No! Oh, I can't bear it!' Bella started to cry very loudly, huge sobs, and Alice leaned over and put her arms around her.

'Poor love,' she murmured. 'Don't cry, Bella. Please don't cry . . .'

'Muriel Chalfont!' gasped Bella, furiously, pushing Alice away. 'That vile, spoiled hussy. She was nasty at school, and she's even nastier now. Hasn't she got enough of her own to not need to take from me? To steal my fiancé?' She flung herself down on a sofa cushion, howling.

The others all looked at each other, helpless.

'You can't steal people, my love,' said Thomas. 'If Muriel Chalfont wanted to flirt and Sidney didn't, he'd have told her to sling her hook. Oh, I'm sorry, Bella. I'm so sorry.'

'Don't speak to me, any of you!' screamed Bella, her face now red, tears flowing unchecked. 'Please, don't say owt more to me!' She got up and ran from the room, and they heard her feet drumming on the stairs.

Alice had her hands to her face now and looked in shock. 'Oh, Millie . . .' She sighed. 'I wish you'd told me first. We might have found a way to break it to her more gently.'

'I don't think we could have done,' sighed Thomas. 'It's not your fault, Millie. It's a cruel blow, however it falls, to learn of such a betrayal.'

'I couldn't let her continue to think she was saving for a wedding and a home with that man when it isn't going to happen,' said Millie, 'could I?'

'No, love,' said Thomas. 'She had to know sooner rather than later. Not saying wasn't an option.'

'Even so . . .' said Alice with a huge sigh. 'Oh, I could kill Sidney Bennett. It's absolutely typical of him to ruin everything with his clumsiness and his selfishness and his stupidity. Couldn't he see that a wife like Bella would be the making of him? She's more than he deserves, and he's passed her over in the cruellest and most careless fashion for that worthless cat Muriel. I've a mind to go round to his mother's house now and tell him exactly what I think of him.'

'You don't owe him the shoe leather,' said Thomas, looking absolutely furious. He stood up and squared his shoulders. 'I'll be the one to do it. And, by God, I shall make sure he knows how disgusting he is in my eyes.'

Thomas hammered loudly on Nancy Bennett's front door. After a couple of minutes, in which she slowly drew back the heavy curtain and fiddled with the lock, she peeped out, almost as if she feared she was about to face a horde of Viking invaders on her doorstep.

'Oh, Thomas Marchant, it's you.' She sounded as if she would have preferred it to be the Vikings.

'It is indeed, Mrs Bennett. I'm here to speak to Sidney.'

'He's not here. He has an engagement at the hotel this evening,' she couldn't resist adding smugly.

'He had an *engagement* with my Bella – an engagement to be married – but he seems to have forgotten that,' said Thomas angrily.

'Bella? What's she got to do with owt?' asked Nancy, slow to understand. 'My Sidney's dining with some very important people. He's moving in the best circles now, you know.'

'Is he, indeed? Would that be the Chalfonts?' asked Thomas.

Nancy looked even smugger. 'And what if it is? You can't blame the lad for wanting to get on in life.'

'No, I can't,' said Thomas, thinking this awful woman was as slow on the uptake as her son. 'But I can blame him for two-timing my daughter. I can blame him for lying to her, promising to marry her, and then flirting openly – in public, actually kissing in the street, where anyone could have seen him – with Muriel Chalfont.'

Nancy looked taken aback for a moment. She clearly had no idea that the relationship between Sidney and Muriel had developed this far. She fought to control her mouth from forming a wide smile, which made Thomas even angrier. He wouldn't be surprised if that mammy's boy hadn't been encouraged by this ridiculous, social-climbing woman.

'Well now, I'm not so sure my Sidney was ever really engaged to Bella,' she began.

'Rubbish! The poor girl has been saving up for months for the stuff to make into her wedding dress. She'd been planning for ages for the wedding to be in September, but then they decided to wait a while longer so they could save the deposit for their own home. You know all this!'

'But he never gave her a ring, did he?' crowed Nancy triumphantly. 'It's not a proper engagement if she's not wearing his ring.'

'Who says so?'

'I do.'

'Well, you can say what you like, Nancy Bennett, but all Bella's talked about for months is the wedding, and now her heart is broken. Your son hadn't even the decency or the courage to come and tell her he'd changed his mind. Disgraceful!'

'Well, she knows now, and I doubt he'll change it back,' said Nancy, with the air of someone having the final word.

'If he does, I will personally wring his bloomin' neck,' shouted Thomas. 'The lad's a two-timing louse, a bounder, a spineless idiot without honour or integrity. And if he so much as speaks to my precious girl again, I will kick him down the steps of that hotel. And now I'm going round there to tell him so to his face.'

Nancy looked shocked, possibly at the names Sidney was being called, possibly because the last thing he would want when he was dining at the hotel with the local bigwigs was the irate father of the girl he had betrayed turning up and causing a disturbance.

'I think if you fetch up there making a noise like you are doing, you'll not even get to the dining room,' she said.

'Do you now?' said Thomas. 'Well, we'll see about that, won't we?'

He turned and stalked away in the direction of the hotel, leaving Nancy standing helplessly on her doorstep with her mouth open.


At the hotel, Thomas decided that Nancy was probably right: if he went in making a row from the outset, he wouldn't get far.

He took a few deep breaths to steady his temper, then walked along the Promenade, past the tall windows of the Imperial's dining room, and saw a table occupied by the Chalfonts and Sidney Bennett. There the lad was, smarming and kowtowing, and there was Muriel, simpering and sitting very close to him. Well, it was as well to be sure of the facts of the situation before he made his move.

He went up the front steps and the commissionaire opened the door for him. There were a few people in the foyer occupying the sofas and possibly waiting for their friends. Good. Thomas didn't like an audience, as a rule, but this was different. This was for Bella. He swallowed down his natural timidity and squared his shoulders.

He went to the reception desk.

'I wonder, please, would it be possible to write a note to be delivered to Mr Bennett, who is dining with Mr Chalfont this evening?'

'Yes, of course, sir,' said the smart young woman on reception. She produced a sheet of paper headed with the hotel's crest, and an envelope, also with the crest on the back. 'Here, sir – use this pen if you like,' she said, offering him a ballpoint with a smile.

'Thank you.'

Thomas took the stationery and the pen and went to sit at a little table to one side of the large and luxurious room, aware that he was shortly to shatter the peaceful murmur of civilised conversation. He wrote:

# THE LETTER

*Sidney Bennett,*
   *I am in the hotel foyer. I have important information,
very much to your advantage.*
   *T. Marchant*

He sealed the brief letter in the envelope and then
asked the head waiter, who was at the dining-room door,
if he would please deliver this urgent message to Mr
Bennett. Then he saw an empty sofa right in the centre
of the room and went to sit down on it. This would do
perfectly.

After a minute or two, Sidney appeared, looking
puzzled and clutching the note Thomas had just written
to him. He looked around and saw Thomas.

'Mr Marchant?' He came over to where Thomas was
sitting. 'What information? What do you know that's to
my advantage?'

Thomas stood, took a step towards Sidney, and looked
him up and down.

'It is to your advantage, Sidney Bennett, that you
keep away from my daughter Bella and, indeed, never
try to speak to her again,' he said loudly. He was pleased
to hear that his voice was quite steady and that he was
entirely in control. His anger was ice cold. Remembering
the scene of his and Millie's confrontation with
Fairbanks on the day they left the inn, he paused to
allow a quiet to fall in the foyer. 'Because if you do,
you two-timing scum, you cowardly, social-climbing
nobody, I will come here and I will drag you away from

your important friends and kick you down those steps into the street. I will also make sure that everyone in Theddleton knows that you are not to be trusted, that you cannot keep your word and that you have neither decency nor integrity. I've always thought you were stupid and selfish, and I have been proved right. I thank God that Bella now realises what kind of a man she might have married. Fortunately, it is not too late for her, but I pity any woman unlucky enough to be taken in by you. Remember, Bennett, if I hear that you have spoken one word to Bella, I will damn well make sure you wish you hadn't.'

The people sitting around in the plush foyer were agog and had completely given up pretending that they weren't eavesdropping and fascinated by what they were hearing.

Sidney had gone completely white, as if he might faint. 'I . . . I . . .' he began, but he didn't know how to continue. He had nothing to say, not even lame excuses to stammer.

Thomas stood looking at him in disgust for a moment and then, without another word, he pushed him out of the way with both arms to the chest, so that Sidney stumbled back and sat down heavily in an undignified heap on the deep carpet. Without even looking at him again, Thomas turned and left. The doorman was very prompt to open the door for him.

Thomas set off for home, now shaking with anger. Of course, he'd got what he had secretly wanted: Bella wasn't going to marry Sidney Bennett after all. But, oh dear God, how long would it be before poor Bella saw the broken engagement as anything but the complete wrecking of her carefully planned future?

Bella found it hard to sleep that night. Her eyes were sore with crying, swollen and heavy. Her little bedroom felt stuffy, her bed felt hot and hard, the sheets rumpled and scratchy. Sometimes she slept briefly and then woke suddenly, disturbed by some terrible dream, which quickly faded from her mind but left her feeling even more unsettled.

She opened the window, but there was no breeze to air the room, so she straightened her bedclothes as best she could in the dark and lay down again . . .

There was a strange noise overhead, coming from Millie's room. It sounded like the wind blowing, like a gale whipping up, a kind of roaring sound, elemental. After a minute or two, Bella got up to see what was happening. Her bare feet were silent on the floor and, strangely, she could not feel the hard floorboards or the softness of the rag rug in her room. She went up the narrow stairs to the attic and stood outside Millie's door, listening.

The gusting of the wind was louder here, moaning and hissing almost audible words, and the door was shaking with the draught, gently tap-tapping. Perhaps Millie had left her window open, but why then did Bella's own room feel so airless?

'Millie?' she called, keeping her voice low. 'Millie, are you all right?'

No answer.

'Millie?'

Bella reached out her hand for the doorknob. She felt afraid, although she didn't know of what, and her hand was shaking as she grasped the Bakelite and turned it. The door was heavy but slowly it yielded, and she stood on the threshold of Millie's bedroom.

The whole room was vibrating gently with some invisible force. Millie was sitting on her bed with her back to Bella, looking out of the open window. Bella could see the shape of her silhouetted against a strange, orange light coming in at the window, and it was the energy radiating from Millie herself that Bella felt. It was as if Millie was zinging with some pent-up force, which it was hard to think could be contained in so small a person.

*Millie?*

Bella couldn't speak the name – she was too afraid – but the sound, the question, was in her head.

*Millie? Millie?*

Slowly Millie turned her head to look at Bella, and then, it was as if the energy was suddenly switched off, the power cut, and she faded away where she sat, becoming transparent, her image growing ever fainter until she was invisible. In moments she was gone, leaving the room empty.

*Millie! Millie! Please . . .*

Bella tried to call her back, but it was hopeless. She wanted so much to save her, to bring her back, to tell her how much she was loved, but no words came out. Instead, her thoughts were crowded with chaotic images of Sidney kissing Muriel Chalfont, Dad being sacked from his job . . . falling from his bicycle, Mrs Hailsham's vandalised beach hut, a huge fire, a car crash, and a knife blade stabbing and quivering just inches from her hand.

She woke, screaming and shouting, with Alice holding her and stroking her hair.

# CHAPTER TWENTY

BELLA CAME DOWNSTAIRS feeling terrible. Her head ached and her eyes were puffy. She was completely exhausted after a night of partial sleep filled with weird and terrifying dreams.

In the way of all dreams, their sharp and frightening details had faded, so that now only an impression of vague but disturbing images lingered.

'Oh, poor love. It's all the upset about Sidney that's to blame,' said Thomas.

Alice had heard Bella screaming in the night and had gone to comfort her. Millie had gone, too, but Millie seemed to have been part of the dreams, and Bella became upset all over again.

'I know how it can be: summat bad happens and then your subconscious mind plays it up into a very exaggerated version of reality that is far, far worse. I reckon it's a way we have of coping with horrible things: nowt is as bad as the worst nightmares, so we gain a bit of perspective.'

He poured Bella a cup of tea and passed her a piece of toast. There was no marmalade this week, just a scrape of margarine.

'Where's Alice?' asked Bella, huddling into her dressing gown.

'She's gone to the bookshop. Millie went with her. It's gone nine o'clock, love. Alice said she'd drop by the toyshop and tell Mr and Mrs Warminster that you're not well today.'

Bella nodded. 'That's kind of her. I didn't realise it was so late. I'm glad Millie's gone. I don't want . . . I'd just rather she wasn't here today.' She slumped down in her chair. 'Oh, Dad, I can't bear everyone knowing what's happened. That Sidney found someone else because he thought I wasn't good enough for him.' She started to cry again.

'There, there, love. Don't take on so. Anyone who knows Sidney Bennett will realise that can't possibly be true,' said Thomas, putting his arm around her. 'Rather, they'll wonder what on earth you ever saw in him and think that you got out before it was too late.'

'Oh, Dad . . .' sobbed Bella, pushing her toast away. She put her head down on her arms and gave herself up to another bout of heartfelt weeping. 'I almost wish I didn't know, that Millie hadn't told me . . .'

'Millie's not to blame. She did the right thing. Go back up to bed, Bella,' said Thomas eventually, 'and I'll bring you another cup of tea and some aspirins for your headache. How would that be, eh?'

Bella nodded and dragged herself back upstairs.

There was a knock at the cottage door early in the afternoon. Edwin Cook was on the doorstep, bursting with news.

'Come in, lad,' said Thomas, who had stayed in all day with Bella instead of going to look for a job. 'Millie's working at the bookshop, but I can give her a message if it's her you're after.'

Edwin followed him into the sitting room. 'The bookshop? I never saw that happening.' He grinned.

'Oh, nowt to do with books. She's painting the window screen. She's gone to sketch it out and see if what she's planning suits the Pattersons.'

'Hurray!' said Edwin. 'It'll be amazing. Millie's brilliant at art. We'll have to have a trip in the boat to celebrate when she's got time. No, it was you as much as Millie I came to tell, Mr Marchant, you having worked at the Three-Mile Bottom until recently.'

'Oh, yes?'

'Got burned down, didn't it?'

'No! When was this?'

'Last night. Big fire in the middle of the night. It's too far off to see from here if you're not looking that way, but Pam lives nearer, and she and her folks heard the fire engines. Her dad went out to see if there was owt he could do – you know, tea for the firemen and that – and he got to hear. Pam told us at the bakery all about it.'

'So what happened?'

Edwin lowered his head in respect. 'I'm afraid it's bad news, Mr Marchant. That bloke Fairbanks and the one Pam calls Mad Jane . . . burned to death.'

For a moment, Thomas stared at the young man, hardly able to believe what he'd heard. He felt as if his blood was running cold.

'Oh . . . oh, that's terrible. I know he was a nasty piece of work, and Jane Regan was . . . well, I'm sorry to speak ill of the dead, but I'd be very surprised if there's anyone mourning her passing. Even so' – he swallowed – 'it's a bad end to them.'

Edwin nodded. 'True. Apparently, it's not known yet what caused the fire, but it looks like it started in the kitchen. Fairbanks and Jane Regan were found together in the room above. The whole place is destroyed. It was lucky there were hardly any folk staying and they all got out safely.'

'Thank goodness for that. I do wonder . . .'

'Yes, Mr Marchant?'

'Well, Jane had this phobia she developed in prison. She was too scared to go outside.'

'What, at all?'

'I never saw her leave the building. When the place was alight, I think mebbe she was trapped by her fear of open spaces. She was a tough woman, brutal in many ways, but that was her weakness, and she wouldn't have

367

been able to leave. Perhaps Fairbanks was trying to help her and neither could escape the flames in the end.'

Edwin exhaled heavily. 'That is sad. Poor woman. Pam says she was a holy terror, but I'm beginning to pity her.'

'Mm . . . you're a kind lad, Edwin. I'm not sure I'll be shedding tears over Jane. Tell you what, though, let *me* tell Millie this news when she comes in. She can be a little bit cruel about folk who have crossed her and . . . well . . .'

'Oh, aye, I understand. I remember she wasn't too cut up about Mrs Hailsham and her daughter, although most folk at least liked the missus, felt sorry for her, really. Strangely enough, that was a fire, too, wasn't it?'

'I believe so,' said Thomas, who knew full well it was.

When Edwin had gone, Thomas went to check how Bella was and found her sleeping, exhausted. Then he sat down at his kitchen table with a strong cup of tea and had a really hard think about the two fire tragedies and how they could ever be connected. At the end of the afternoon, he had reached absolutely no conclusion that made any sense to him.

When Thomas broke the news of the inn fire and the deaths of Fairbanks and Jane, Millie looked neither surprised nor sorry.

'Why should I care?' she said. 'I disliked them both, and it would be hypocritical to pretend I'm sorry.'

'But they were human beings, for all their faults,' said Alice gently.

'They were horrible and the world's a better place without people like them,' said Millie. 'Now, is Bella getting up for her dinner, or am I taking it up to her . . . ?'

'I'll take it up,' said Alice. 'Sometimes, Millie, your mood is not in keeping with the situation, and now is one of those times. Bella's upset and we don't want her to be even more upset. Do we?'

Days passed, and Bella still felt too low to go to work. She had eaten hardly anything since she'd learned of Sidney's betrayal, and she barely had the strength to come downstairs or to go back up after a few minutes of sitting around listlessly. She remained wary of Millie, as if the bad dream, which she hadn't wanted to relate in detail, was upsetting her still. She was growing thinner by the day and her face was very pale, except for the deep shadows under her eyes. Her hair was lank and greasy as she had neither the inclination nor the strength to wash it.

Alice tried to interest her in a bracing walk to the beach hut for a picnic, but it was very soon clear that this idea was a non-starter. So Alice went with Millie, thinking the fresh air would do them good. The book-shop window was nearly finished, and they were very excited about this, their pleasure in Millie's success and their working together uniting them in a more sisterly bond than they had felt so far.

Cassie and Alfred Warminster were just about managing without their assistant but were anxious that Bella should

369

soon feel well enough to come back to work. Cassie took a little box of chocolates and a few back copies of *Woman's Weekly* round to the Marchants', thinking the magazines would entertain Bella when she felt well enough to read, but, although Bella thanked her nicely, she soon went back to bed, leaving the magazines downstairs and the chocolates unopened.

Bobbie appeared one evening to take Alice over to her father's house for dinner. She brought Bella a bouquet of glorious pink roses, the heady perfume of which scented the entire cottage. Bella was pleased, but the kindness of Bobbie's gesture made her cry, and she ended up feeling sorrier for herself than ever.

'Have you seen the mural?' Millie asked Bobbie, when Bella had crept tearfully back upstairs in her drooping dressing gown. 'It's all but finished.'

'Not yet. I'm waiting for the great reveal. But are you pleased with it?' asked Bobbie very seriously.

Millie's eyes were shining as she nodded. 'I am, but will Miss Patterson be? I know you're going to pay me if she doesn't want it, but the bookshop window will also be *my* shop window if the mural stays. People will come by and see it, and I'm hoping it will be a talking point for visitors, but not if Miss Patterson emulsions over it! This commission will have led to nothing then, and I'll be back at square one.'

'That's not going to happen, Millie,' said Alice. 'Miss Patterson would be shooting herself in the foot if she painted over your beautiful work. If there wasn't a good chance she'd accept it, she would never have agreed to your doing it in the first place.'

'Just what I was going to say,' said Thomas.

'Don't worry, Millie. If you are pleased with it, if you know it's as good as you can make it, then you have nothing to fear,' said Bobbie. 'Now, when are you finishing? Tomorrow?'

'Yes, I will be all done by mid-afternoon; I'm sure of it.'

'Well, then, it's time to arrange a grand window opening event, don't you think, Alice? I'll come by tomorrow, take a look, lead the cheers, and perhaps we can have a little party, say, on Friday evening, if the Pattersons agree. I'll provide some drinks if they would like to invite their friends up and down the High Street. It'll unite everyone just as the summer holiday season gets underway – cement the feeling of community – and launch Millie as the new young local artist of talent. You never know when you need people batting on your team.' Bobbie smiled at Alice, suddenly looking less sure. 'Do you think that would be all right? Sorry, am I bulldozing you all? I hate myself when I do that.'

Alice laughed. 'No, Bobbie, dear. You are just what the bookshop needs – some strong-arm tactics to wrestle it into the 1950s.'

Eileen and Godfrey Patterson had never had a party at the bookshop before.

'It's a good job Miss Reeves is supplying us with all

these bottles of fancy wine,' said Eileen, holding one up and inspecting the label. 'We'd have been bankrupted buying that little lot ourselves.'

'It's very generous of her,' said Godfrey. 'And I'm pleasantly surprised that so many of our High Street neighbours want to come by. Of course, it's an open invitation. We may well have a few people coming that we haven't invited personally. But that's fine. They might even turn out to be future customers, if not customers already.'

'Just so long as they're not here entirely for the free drinks,' said Eileen.

The mural was draped in a sheet but the Pattersons, Alice and Bobbie had, of course, had a good look at it already. It was everything Alice had hoped Millie could achieve, and she felt ready to explode with pride at her cousin's talent. Surely Millie's career as an artist was about to take off.

The window had been emptied of props while Millie had been working on the screen, and it remained empty now, just for the evening, so that everyone could have an uninterrupted view of the mural in all its beautiful detail.

The Warminsters and the Wilkinsons closed their shops early and turned up looking smart in their best clothes. Cassie and Alfred brought Toby, who had just arrived for the weekend. He went over to greet Bobbie.

'Toby, I'm delighted to see you again,' said Bobbie, taking his hand. 'How could I forget your part in the charade?' she added, making sure Eileen wasn't close enough to hear. 'And my father will be so pleased you're here.' She pointed out to Toby where Mr Reeves was sitting on a chair to the side of the room, his walking stick hooked over its back.

'Of course! I'll go and pay my respects now,' said Toby.

'Please do. He loves the jacket you made. See, he's wearing it now. Actually' – she laughed – 'he wears it all the time.'

'I couldn't be more pleased,' said Toby. 'I think I told you, I'd like to set up my own business making bespoke clothes for gentlemen, but I'm a way off being able to do that yet.'

'Well, you've made a wonderful start. My father's friends have been admiring the jacket. I know he'll be pleased to recommend you.'

Toby remembered the evening that Bobbie had taken him to their home, just outside Baybury, with the jacket he had been so proud to have made for her father. Toby had hardly been able to keep back his gasp of astonishment at the beauty and character of the perfect little castle with two turrets and a crenellated roof terrace, as Bobbie had driven up the drive.

'It's just a fancy farmhouse really,' she had said. 'I help my father run the farm now he finds it more difficult to get about. I also keep the books and all the records, which means some days it's just desk work, pretty much as if I worked in any clerical job.'

'But what a truly lovely office,' Toby had replied, gazing at the castle's façade.

The Reeveses, despite their grand house, could not have been more friendly, however, and Toby was delighted to greet again now the redoubtable old man, who clearly doted on his daughter.

Thomas, meanwhile, was fussing about having had to leave Bella at home alone.

'Alice, love, she wouldn't come. I think she's afraid that that scoundrel Bennett might turn up.'

'If he does, he'll not be welcome,' she said. 'But I think that whole wretched business has so rocked Bella's confidence that it'll be a while before she wants to go out and socialise. She needs to get her strength back, and then she'll feel better able to face folk. Everyone's been asking how she is, though, and so sympathetically. The feeling among our friends gathered here is all for Bella and all against Sidney Bennett.'

'Isn't that Mr Penrose, from the town hall, Bennett's superior in the Planning department? I didn't know he knew the Pattersons.'

'Oh, Dad, he's becoming a bookshop regular since the clearing of the window made it plain that the place is not a junk shop. We got off to a slightly rocky start – Eileen had just understood her first joke and there was much hilarity – but he's extremely well read, and we do have some very interesting bookish conversations. Now, I must take round the wine and refill everyone's glasses so they can toast Millie when her work is finally revealed.'

Alice had just moved away when Sidney Bennett

entered the shop with Muriel Chalfont on his arm. He was wearing a double-breasted suit in a very loud check, and Muriel was in a shiny pink dress with a flirty hem and, ridiculously on such a warm evening, a fur tippet with the poor dead creature's tail still evident at one side.

Thomas drew in his breath in shock at seeing the lad blatantly flaunting his romance with that woman so soon after being caught betraying Bella, but Alice had turned and seen them and strode over confidently.

She did not greet them. She drew herself up to her full height, which made her as tall as Sidney, and rather taller than Muriel, and she said, without raising her voice, 'Sidney, you and Muriel are not welcome here. Please leave now.'

'I gather it's an open invitation,' said Sidney, looking round to see where the drinks were. 'I can see my colleague Mr Penrose over there – look.' He raised a hand to hail his superior in a chummy fashion.

Alice did not turn to see the effect of this familiarity on the strait-laced Mr Penrose. 'It's not an invitation open to you and Muriel, Sidney. Please leave now.'

'Oh, come now, Lady Alice. Always on your high horse, aren't you? We've every right to be at a bookshop opening or whatever it is. Free drinks, I gather.'

'Sidney Bennett, I thank God that Bella isn't marrying you. I loathe your stupidity and your fatuous self-importance. Bella is worth fifty of you, and I hope she will never stoop so low as to speak to you again. In fact, Muriel, she thinks it most fitting that you've taken up with this low-bred nincompoop because you deserve each other.'

Muriel went very red in the face, which was unfortunate beside the shiny fuchsia-pink dress, and she pulled at Sidney's arm.

'I reckon we should leave, Sidney. We'll go and have a drink at the hotel instead. Who wants to stand around in a dusty old bookshop with a lot of boring old book readers anyway?'

'Yes, off you go and don't ever come back,' said Alice evenly, and herded them out of the door into the street.

Toby and Bobbie were beside her by then.

'Who was that spivvy-looking man in the ghastly suit?' Toby asked.

'Ah, no one to worry about,' said Alice, not wanting to mention Bella's troubles if Toby wasn't aware what had happened.

'Are you all right?' murmured Bobbie.

'Yes, dear Bobbie, just fine,' said Alice quietly, and squeezed Bobbie's hand. 'I've been wanting to tell Sidney Bennett what I think of him for months. Now, where's Millie? I think Miss Patterson's ready to do the honours . . .'

The party spilled out onto the High Street, where people could get a proper view of Millie's mural in the shop window, revealed at last in all its glory.

'I never want to stop looking at it, Millie,' said Alice. 'It's even better than I thought it would be, and I know the Pattersons are both thrilled. You've turned the book-shop from some dusty old shambles that got mistaken for a junk shop into a place everyone will want to visit,' she said.

'No, you did that, Alice. But I'm so glad you like the screen.' Millie was standing between Alice and Bobbie, and she took one of their hands in each of hers. 'It's you two who have made this dream of mine come true. There'll be no stopping me now!'

'We'd better look out, then,' laughed Bobbie. 'Well done, Millie. Now, there's a photographer from the *Theddleton Informer*, and I believe there should be another from the *Baybury Gazette* here, so nice big smiles for the camera, girls.'

'You arranged this, didn't you?' said Alice. 'Oh, Bobbie, that's so thoughtful.'

'Well, it's no use knowing people if you can't phone them up and tell them where the news is, is it?' said Bobbie.

Everyone had an opinion of Millie's mural, and all the opinions were good. Millie was the centre of atten-tion, which of course she loved. Alice tried to keep an eye on her but, by the time the party guests started to drift away, Millie and Edwin were sitting on the floor in one of the little rooms, sharing the last of a bottle of Bobbie's champagne and giggling and hiccuping.

'Leave those bottles and glasses, Alice,' instructed Godfrey. 'We'll have a tidy-up tomorrow and then you can have the honour of dressing the stunning new window. I think we'll leave opening until ten thirty, give everyone a chance to recover from the excitement.'

He gave a sidelong look at Eileen, who was pouring the dregs from a bottle of wine into her glass.

'Time for you to shepherd the young people home – before they consume more than they should,' he added pointedly to Alice.

She smiled and gathered up her family and Edwin for the walk home. Bobbie had already departed with her father.

The meandering walk home was full of tired excitement and observations about whom everyone had seen and whom they had spoken to, and all the praise for Millie. Alice didn't mention Sidney Bennett and Muriel Chalfont – she hoped never to have to speak their names again – but she was glad that, after all, Bella had not been at the party to be upset by them.

She had been deeply missed, however. Alice just hoped it would not be long before her poor sister rallied. She was beginning to worry that her disappointment in love had set Bella back for good.

# CHAPTER TWENTY-ONE

Toby Warminster knew next to nothing about flowers, but he thought the sweet peas in the florist's window were pretty. They were like Bella: gentle-looking. There were flowers far more expensive – his budget was only small – and blooms that made a terrific statement of elegance, which were more like Bobbie Reeves, but the sweet peas were exactly right for Bella.

He thought about the party the previous evening and wished Bella had been there. She would have made the evening complete for him.

Cassie had explained in full Bella's absence from the bookshop party over breakfast this morning.

'Disgraceful, that Sidney Bennett,' she said to Toby. 'He knew how Bella was planning that wedding, saving up, wishing and hoping, and looking at bridal things in magazines, and then having to rein in her ideas and make the best of it in her cheerful way. And all that time he hadn't even bought her a ring! I don't think that sweet girl is the sort to start demanding diamond rings, but now I reckon it's plain that he was hedging his bets all along. I think his mother might have had summat to do with the broken engagement.'

'We don't know that, love,' said Alfred, pouring Cassie another cup of tea.

'We know what that Nancy Bennett's like, though, don't we?'

Alfred said nothing, and Toby turned to his mother with a questioning look.

'The kind to be impressed by Muriel Chalfont,' said Cassie, as if that explained everything.

'Right,' said Alfred, getting up to end the conversation. 'Time to open the shop. We've more on our plates since Bella's been ill. I'm hoping she'll be feeling well enough to come in next week. I reckon she'll feel better for the distraction of work, myself, but it's no use expecting to see her if she's too brokenhearted to rise from her bed.'

'That bad?' asked Toby.

'Terrible,' said Cassie. 'Poor lamb. I took her some chocolate and an old magazine or two, but she was clearly feeling too depressed to bother with them. Such a shame. I wish I knew what to do to help.'

'Do you think she'd mind if I went to see her?' asked Toby. 'I'll tell her how much you're looking forward to having her back in the shop.'

'You could go and try,' Cassie answered. 'Her folks will send you away if they think a visit is too much for her, but she might feel up to it. Just don't say owt about Sidney bloomin' Bennett, that's all.'

'As if I would,' said Toby.

Now Toby was making his way to 8 Chapel Lane carrying a bunch of delicate, fragrant sweet peas and wondering if he was doing the right thing or if he would just make matters worse. He had not forgotten the last time he'd seen Bella, and he thought he might have been a little unkind.

His knock at the door of the cottage was answered by Millie. Toby had met her for the first time at last night's party, where she'd been the centre of attention. How talented she was for one so young. The bookshop's window was now a real work of art.

'Hello, Toby,' said Millie. She looked at the flowers. 'I expect you've come to see Bella, haven't you?'

'Hello, Millie. Yes, please. If she's in.'

'Oh, she's in all right. If you wait in the sitting room, I'll tell her you're here, but I don't know if she'll come down.' She showed Toby to the sitting-room sofa, then turned away to go to tell Bella but stopped at the door with an afterthought. 'By the way, she looks terrible. Just so you don't get a nasty surprise.'

Toby almost laughed until he realised this was Millie trying to be helpful.

'Bella? Bella, you've got a visitor,' Millie stage-whispered outside Bella's bedroom door.

'Who? Oh, please don't tell me it's Sidney.'

'Of course not. I wouldn't let *him* in the house. It's Toby, Toby Warminster, and he's brought you some flowers.'

There was a silence. Then Bella said, 'Please tell him thank you, Millie, but . . . Just say I said thank you.'

Millie put her head round the door. 'Please, Bella, make an effort. He's in the sitting room, waiting, and I think he really wants to see you.'

'No, he doesn't. Not like this.'

She did indeed look a sight, with dirty, tangled hair and a sweaty and crumpled nightie. Her face was pallid and unwashed, shadowed and hollow-looking, her eyes puffy and red.

Millie assessed the damage of more than a week's heartbreak, and then thought of Toby, undoubtedly waiting for Bella to appear looking as pretty as she always did, even though Millie had tried to warn him.

'You're right,' she said. 'You can't possibly see him looking like that. What if I were to ask him to come back this afternoon? That will give you time to get washed and dressed and do something about your hair.'

'No. No, thank you, Millie. Just leave me alone. Thank him for the flowers but tell him I'm poorly.'

Millie took a deep breath and put her hands on her hips. 'But you aren't really, are you, Bella? You're just feeling very, very sorry for yourself and very disappointed that Sidney Bennett turned out to be a rotter. I can understand that, but that's not the same as poorly, is it? You're not *dying*, are you?'

'Go away.'

'Not about to peg out in your bed, too ill to manage the stairs, even.'

'I said, go away.'

'Oh, come on, Bella – don't be pathetic. The poor man didn't have to bring you flowers. Is this the way to treat your friends? I'm going to go and tell him to come back this afternoon, and that will give you a chance to make yourself decent. I'll go and bring the bath in then, and you'd better not be wasting the hot water.'

'No, Millie. I can't face anyone.'

'Nonsense. What have you got to hide away from? None of what happened is your fault. At the party last night, everyone was sending you good wishes and asking about you and wondering when they'd see you again.'

'Oh, Millie . . .'

'Honestly, Bella, everyone who matters cares about you and sees Sidney and Muriel for the vile deceivers that they are. And – and this is the best thing of all – you'll never have to go and live with Mrs Bennett, either!'

Bella laughed, despite the tears that were now running down her face, which Millie saw as progress.

'Right,' she added, 'I'm going to tell Toby to come back this afternoon. You've got plenty of time to be ready if you get a move on.'

Bella nodded, and Millie was about to return downstairs when Bella called her back.

'But, Millie, please would you *ask* Toby to come back this afternoon and not *tell* him?'

\* \* \*

Bella was almost nervous waiting for Toby to return. He'd left the pretty flowers, which she'd put in a vase of water on the mantelpiece in the sitting room, but she wondered if he'd want to be bothered to come back since Millie had sent him away.

Now Millie had gone to the bookshop ('I've an idea to discuss with Miss Patterson'), and with Alice also at the bookshop and Thomas in Baybury, as he had been all day, Bella was alone, bathed and with washed hair and even a touch of makeup. She didn't look quite as good as the old Bella, but considerably better than she had an hour and a half ago.

There was a knock at the door, and Bella composed herself and went to answer it.

'Toby, come in. Thank you for coming back and thank you for the beautiful flowers.'

'Bella, I was so sorry to hear you were . . . poorly.'

'Thank you, Toby, but I'm not really ill,' said Bella, taking her cue from Millie earlier and finding that the change of attitude was easier now she had made an effort with her appearance. 'I have just had a bit of a setback and taken it, well, actually too hard. I shall feel better soon, I'm sure.'

'Mam told me summat of what has happened. I'm sorry. It is so hard to be crossed in love, I know.'

'Do you?'

'Oh, yes. I didn't get to be twenty-eight without some disappointments of that sort. But we're not talking about me. I'm here to try to cheer you and show how much your friends, of which I am just one of many, care about you, not to join you in a pit of misery.'

'Yes, you're right, that's what I've been doing: digging myself into a pit; indulging in self-pity. Millie says I should rise above it all, and I can see that that would be better all round – for me and for the folk who have to put up with me. But it's such a hard thing to do.'

'I don't think anyone thinks they're putting up with you, as if on sufferance, Bella. Rather, they're just concerned. As friends are for each other.'

'Are we really . . . friends? It's just that I was so silly that time, and I didn't mean to lead you on, Toby. I was just . . . caught up in the moment.'

'Of course we're friends. I told you, that's why I'm here. And it's for me to apologise. I overstepped the mark, and it was my fault. I shouldn't have been cool with you the last time I saw you. That was a mistake, and I'm sorry.'

'Shall we just draw a line and say no more about it?' said Bella. 'Tell me, does Mr Reeves like the jacket you made for him? And who did you meet at the party yesterday? Dad, Alice, and Millie told me about it from all different viewpoints, and I'd love to know what you thought . . .'

So the afternoon passed in happy chatting and, soon, laughter. Bella made a pot of tea and they went into the garden to sit and drink it, side by side on the raised bed wall, enjoying the early summer sunshine.

At length, Toby said he ought to go.

'I don't want to outstay my welcome, and I expect the house will be filled with Marchants soon, full of today's news.'

'And Millie. She's a Boyd, not a Marchant.'

'Oh, I keep forgetting. She just seems like your younger sister to me. I hope you don't mind me saying that.'

'Not at all. Mostly she seems like that to me, too. And then . . . I don't know, there's summat . . . different about her.'

'Well, yes, I suppose if she wasn't brought up with you and Alice, she's bound to be different in many ways.'

'I meant that there's a part of her I don't understand. Sometimes I catch glimpses of it, and it's all a bit . . . strange, really *different*. Oh, forget I said that. I'm just being silly. Dad definitely thinks of her as his third daughter.'

'And that's good, isn't it?'

'It is,' Bella agreed wholeheartedly. 'Dad has become a lot more cheerful since Millie came to live with us. And Millie and Alice have both been working at the bookshop, which has brought them closer.'

'Alice was certainly looking in her element yesterday at the party. Positively sparkling. Almost like a woman in love, I would say, if I knew her better and was forward enough to voice such an opinion.'

Bella laughed. 'You just have. Goodness, though, do you think so? I can't think who it is, if so. Alice always looks lovely, I reckon, but I'd be so pleased to think she had met someone worthy of her specialness. Odd she hasn't mentioned anyone, though . . .'

Toby cleared his throat. 'Well . . . time for me to go, as I said.'

'Are you going back to London tomorrow, Toby?'

''Fraid so. I'll have to leave in the afternoon, but I'll be back in Theddleton soon.'

'Good. I hope I'll see you then?'

'So do I. And I told Mam and Dad that I'd ask if you might be ready to return to work on Monday. They won't rush you, but Dad thinks it would be a good distraction, and Mam is bursting with things she wants to tell you about. Plus, they are missing you, and so are the dolls and teddies.'

'Please thank your parents for their kind concern and tell them I shall be back on Monday.'

When Toby had gone, with a cheery wave but no kiss goodbye this time, Bella tidied away the tea things and decided she'd manage to make a salad for everyone's tea. While she set about boiling eggs and slicing tomatoes, she thought about what Toby had said about Alice.

Alice in love? Why not? But who could it be, and was whoever it was also in love with Alice? Possibly so, if she was looking so happy with life . . .

The following week, Millie took the bus into Baybury. There was a big stationer's and office equipment shop next to the art shop, and she knew just what she wanted to buy.

Half an hour after entering the shop, she came out with a rather heavy typewriter, which was described as 'portable', in a carrying case, and a box of typing paper.

The money she'd stolen from the till at the Three-Mile Bottom had been very carefully hidden away, but now Miss Patterson had paid her for painting the bookshop window screen, it was easy to add a little of the loot to her earnings and so begin to spend the money without drawing attention to it. If her painting career took off as she hoped, the stolen funds would soon just disappear completely into her income. Anyway, there was only her family to hide the money from now, and she would be very glad to reach the situation of being able to hand some of it over to Alice with no questions being raised. With the death of Mr Fairbanks, no one was enquiring any longer about the theft from the till. Establishing the cause of the fire had eclipsed all thought of that crime in anyone's mind.

Millie was hefting the typewriter to the bus stop on the seafront when she met Bobbie.

'Good heavens, Millie, that looks heavy. Would you like me to give you a hand?'

'Oh, yes, please, Bobbie. It's supposed to be portable, but it gains weight with every yard I carry it, and I'm wishing I'd left buying the paper for another day.'

'Well, let me take it. We'll go and put your purchases in the car, and I'll give you a lift home. I'm parked just over there. But I'm really pleased I've bumped into you because I've got a bit of an idea.'

'Yes?'

'Have you time to come back to my house or do you have to be somewhere?'

The thought of 'having to be somewhere' sounded very grown-up to Millie. She'd have liked to be that kind of woman, but unfortunately she was unemployed again and had all day to do whatever she liked.

'I'm not in a hurry to be home, except to get the typewriter there,' she said.

'You're not thinking of taking up journalism, are you? After your triumph with the mural last week, I'd have thought your career as a painter was assured.'

'I had hoped so,' said Millie. 'I thought people would see the mural and my life would be instantly changed for the better, but here I am with nothing to do again. I think it's 'cos I don't really know anyone who is the kind to want a picture or have a fantasy design painted on their bedroom wall.'

'Don't you?' asked Bobbie in a way that made Millie look carefully at her. 'You know me, Millie.'

'Oh, but . . . What, really? You want to commission a painting?'

Bobbie opened the boot of her car and put the type-writer carefully inside. Then she took the heavy ream of foolscap from Millie, who was standing wide-eyed and amazed, and put that in, too.

'And why not? My father will be sixty next year, and I'd like to mark the occasion with something more substantial than a tea party. I think a portrait of him,

389

wearing his favourite jacket and looking distinguished but paternal, would be a very nice present. If he doesn't want to sit for his portrait, or if sitting still would make his bad leg ache too much, you could do a portrait of the house instead. I'm sure he'd like that.'

'Oh, Bobbie, I'd be so pleased to paint your father. Or your house.'

'I know you'd do a brilliant job. Alice has told me all about the illustrations you've done for her father's stories on Sunday evenings. I'd love to see them. And my father very much admired the mural at the party last week. So let's go and talk about it, shall we?'

Millie couldn't think of anything she'd rather do. Perhaps she had been wrong, and her life was now changing for the better after all.

'Millie, what is that, and what are you doing with it?'

'It's a typewriter, Uncle Thomas, and I'm not doing a lot with it, but you are.'

'What do you mean?'

'You're going to be a writer. It's your new job.'

'Millie, what are you talking about? And where did this come from?'

Millie opened up the case and displayed the typewriter. 'It came from the stationer's and office place in Baybury, and I bought it. I have some money now Miss Patterson has paid me.' This was not actually a lie, she told herself, just a slight swerve from the real facts. 'And – the most brilliant news – Bobbie wants me to paint a portrait of

Mr Reeves. And the other good news is that I mentioned Fabio to her, and she says she has a friend who needs a cook, so she's going to sort out the job for him.'

'What? That's wonderful!' Thomas sank down onto a kitchen chair. 'But I can hardly take all this in. What has Mr Reeves's portrait got to do with the typewriter? Or Fabio?'

'Nothing! The typewriter is for you, to type up a collection of your wonderful Sunday evening stories. Then someone is bound to want to publish them, and lots of people will buy them, especially when word gets round how entertaining they are. You don't seem to have got on too well with working at jobs for other people, so I thought the best thing would be if you worked for yourself. And then I realised exactly what you are brilliant at doing already and, oh, Uncle Thomas, you will be a *huge* success as a writer. I just know it.'

Thomas looked a little shellshocked. 'I don't know, love. It seems a risky business to me. I'd never have said I was that good at writing, for all I used to write features for the newspaper.'

'That's not the same as the stories you tell. You know how much Bella, Alice, and I love them. They're really good. Don't doubt yourself – just do it and see what happens.'

'But what if I can't remember them? If I sit down at that machine, all I'll be thinking about is the typing, not the story.'

'Oh, Uncle Thomas, will you stop standing in your

own way? I've got the drawings I did of the characters, which will remind you, and you can write the stories out in longhand first, just as if you were telling them, if you think the typing will block your thoughts.'

'Yes . . . yes, I could. You're right. And you've even got me some paper to type on. Bless you, Millie. But are you sure you can afford all this? It's so generous.'

'I wouldn't have bought it if I couldn't.'

'Dear child, you really are a blessing to me,' said Thomas, giving Millie a hug. 'All the struggles with hopeless jobs and putting up with the likes of Fairbanks, just because it was paid work, though my heart was never in any of it, and all the time the work I really want to do was relegated to a little Sunday evening fun to entertain my girls. And I couldn't even see it.'

'I think you should start straight away, tomorrow morning.'

'Yes. I don't want Bella and Alice to think I'm just messing about at home when they go out to work. I need to show them that I can do this. And now you have an exciting new commission to be getting on with, so we're all going to be doing what we love. You know, Millie, for years I've felt as much down as up, but since you came here, well . . . all I can say is that you've made a huge difference, and all for the best.'

'Good,' said Millie. 'I like to shake things up a bit.' She laughed.

'You are so like your mother in that way,' said Thomas. Bella and Alice came home from work soon after.

# THE LETTER

Bella was looking tired, finding her strength was failing after three long days in the toyshop.

When Millie announced the news of her commission for Mr Reeves's portrait, her cousins were delighted for her.

'You didn't tell us that Bobbie lives in a castle, Alice,' said Millie, when she'd related how she had gone there with Bobbie.

'A castle!' said Bella and Thomas in unison.

'Well, I didn't know if anyone would be interested,' said Alice quietly. 'It just seems the right house for Bobbie, and I didn't want to boast of our friendship.'

'Are you joking? Who wouldn't be interested in a castle, even a tiny one? It's amazing,' said Millie. 'When I've painted Mr Reeves's portrait, perhaps I'll get to paint a picture of Baybury Grange. I'm sure I could persuade Mr Reeves to commission it.'

'You could try,' said Alice, laughing. 'He won't be persuaded if he doesn't really want it, though.'

'He'll want it,' said Millie confidently. 'And even Miss Patterson, who I think is quite hard to please, has agreed to display a little notice in one corner of the bookshop window saying that the mural is "The work of local artist Millie Boyd. Please enquire within." I just know it's all going to work out once word gets round.'

'I hope so,' said Bella.

'I'm sure so,' said Alice. 'Bobbie has a way of making everything work out well.'

Bella gave her a long, enquiring look.

Then Thomas took his girls through to the kitchen, where the typewriter was still sitting in its case on the table, and explained why Millie had bought it.

'But how will we manage while you're writing the stories and Millie's painting Mr Reeves's portrait?' asked Bella, looking anxious. 'These are not the kinds of jobs that pay regularly. And now, Millie, you've gone and spent a whole load of money on this contraption.' Suddenly she sounded very down.

'You're just feeling a bit tired after a few days back at work,' said Alice. 'We might have to tighten our belts some more for a little while, but we will manage. Don't worry. Let Dad take this chance now Millie has seen what we all failed to see before now.'

'I'm fed up of tightening my belt,' said Bella, on the verge of tears, as she had been so often lately. 'It was tightening my belt and saving up that delayed me marrying Sidney. If we'd just got on with it, we'd have been married by now, instead of waiting until September and then until next spring. I reckon he got fed up of waiting and that's why he took up with Muriel.'

Everyone looked amazed that she should think this.

'Bella, love, I don't think it would have been like that at all,' said Thomas. 'Sidney is selfish and foolish, and that sort never know when they've struck pure gold. He was taken in by the brassy glitter of the Chalfont girl because he's that kind of man. It's nowt to do with waiting to marry you. He might have married you and still betrayed you, and that would have been even worse.'

Bella nodded mutely, looking exhausted. 'I don't know. I don't know owt any more. I'm too tired to want owt to eat. I'm going to lie down.'

She dragged herself upstairs, leaving the cheerful mood of optimism shattered.

'I'll take her summat to eat later,' said Alice. 'I thought she was feeling better, but apparently not. I'm sure she didn't mean to tread on your dreams, Dad. It's just that she's so down about Sidney Bennett. He's knocked her confidence terribly.'

'It'll take time,' said Thomas.

There was a knock at the door. When he answered it, Iris Cook was on the doorstep, looking distraught.

'Such terrible news, Thomas,' she said. 'I can hardly believe it. The police have arrested Slow William for burning down the inn, and for the deaths of Richard Fairbanks and that mad woman.'

# CHAPTER TWENTY-TWO

Harold Penrose had observed the little confrontation between Alice Marchant and his junior in Planning, Sidney Bennett, at the party at E. & G. Patterson Books. He had noted the unpleasantly over-familiar wave Bennett had given him, as if, away from the office, they were friends. Which they weren't. He had observed that Miss Marchant had, rather impressively, seen off Bennett without raising her voice or causing a stir. He had also noticed the overdressed young woman on Bennett's arm and recognised her as the daughter of Joseph Chalfont. In a place the size of Theddleton, rumours circulated like wasps in a summer orchard, and Harold had heard that Bennett had let down a sweet girl to whom he had been engaged. Now he had learned that that girl was the sister of the redoubtable Alice Marchant. It was his own opinion that if Bennett's former fiancée was anything like her sister, she was well out of his league and had had a lucky escape.

# THE LETTER

Joseph Chalfont and Harold Penrose were old sparring partners, acquaintances who would never be friends, but had a grudging mutual respect, and who were only too glad to score victories against each other, with no hard feelings. Harold was head of Planning, but he needed the support of the Planning Committee when it came to voting for or against applications, and he strongly suspected that Bennett was a fifth columnist, always in favour of Chalfont's schemes and persuading some of the other Committee members to vote for Chalfont, too. If Harold had a poor opinion of Bennett's intellect, he didn't rate the rest of the Committee as any brighter. Things had been going Chalfont's way more often than not lately, and Sidney Bennett had been on the side of Chalfont's interests every time. There was usually some inducement, some bribe, at the root of such a volume of support, and Harold meant to find out if this was the case here.

Some of Harold's suspicions were based on the very obvious fact that Bennett had been away from his desk frequently these last few weeks, and the start of these absences had coincided with the raising of various planning applications. Harold had noted Bennett's supposed reasons: that he had 'a meeting' with someone who had been in touch with the office – there were a remarkable number of 'meetings'; that he had to go to inspect the site of some proposed change of use in the town – perfectly plausible, but, again, there were a lot of these; even – and this was possibly the only one that was completely true and certainly made the connection that Harold suspected was common to them all – that a friend of his had suffered a house fire and was staying at the hotel in a distressed state. Harold knew all about the fire that had killed poor Mrs Hailsham, had destroyed her house, and had caused the Chalfonts to evacuate to the hotel for a while. That incident remained in his mind because Joseph Chalfont was wanting to buy the burned-out house and build a hotel on the site. The application for that had gone up to the district Planning office in Baybury, where the smart young go-getter in charge was a man called Keith Forester. In the meantime, Chalfont had got his way over that floral clock monstrosity opposite the railway station, and over a huge sign hanging over the pavement outside the hotel announcing its name, and now all the town flowerbeds and the municipal hanging baskets along the Promenade were planted in the colours of the Imperial Hotel's livery. True, Joseph Chalfont had put his hand deep into his pocket for the flowers that were enhancing the seafront and station parades, but it was beginning to look as if he thought he owned the whole of Theddleton, when the main beneficiary of all this was Chalfont and the raised profile of his business.

Bennett was gallivanting about the town like some cock of the walk, with Muriel Chalfont on his arm, and it didn't take a genius to connect the success of Joseph Chalfont's schemes with Bennett's new girlfriend and the lad's elevated opinion of himself.

Harold Penrose had made a very useful friend at the hotel. The commissionaire in the smart green coat was called Norman, and he and Harold Penrose had bonded at a cat show in Baybury one rainy Saturday. Norman had an astonishingly good memory for who was coming and going at the hotel, and he was a shameless gossip, too.

So it was that Harold discovered just how often Bennett was dining with the Chalfonts in the hotel dining room, and it was a great many times. It was perfectly obvious that Bennett wasn't paying for all this wining and dining himself, not on his town hall salary and not at this venue.

Norman had also told Harold about Thomas Marchant turning up in the foyer one evening and telling Sidney Bennett exactly what he thought of him.

'Made a bit of a scene, did the father of the cast-off girl,' said Norman. 'Bennett couldn't find a word in his defence and crept back to his dinner afterwards with his tail between his legs.'

Harold kept his opinion to himself, but he was pleased to hear of Bennett being taken down a peg or two. It was about time, and he had a growing feeling that he, Harold Penrose, would be finishing that job himself.

Sidney Bennett was out of the office on one of his frequent site inspection sorties when Harold decided to telephone Keith Forester and find out how the hotel planning application was going.

'The proposed Chalfont business at the edge of

Theddleton? Oh, we're considering it, Mr Penrose,' said Keith Forester. 'In fact, I've been meaning to telephone you for a couple of days now. Thing is, I'm not taking too kindly to interference from your man. We'll make our own minds up when we've considered all aspects, both for and against.'

'My man? I don't know who you mean, Mr Forester. I have certainly not sanctioned anyone to interfere with district Planning business.'

'Sidney Bennett, of course. Arrogant fella. In the pay of Chalfont, I suspect, although don't quote me on that. We both play for The Seafarers, and I just wish Bennett would stick to discussing football tactics and not try smarming round me over Planning business. It's a blessing the football season's over, truth be told, but he's forever in Baybury, offering to take me for a drink. I don't even like the fella. I told him to back off, and it went quiet for a week or two, but now he's trying to be friendly again, as if I can't see straight through him.'

Harold Penrose was furious. 'I'm extremely sorry to hear you've been bothered, Mr Forester. I do not approve of such behaviour at all. I had no idea about any of it, and I shall put a stop to it immediately.'

'Thank you, Mr Penrose. I do appreciate that, and I trust we won't need to revisit this topic of conversation.'

'So do I,' said Harold firmly.

He did a little more digging among the Planning Committee, and soon found out who did and who didn't like Sidney Bennett. It was always better to hear from both sides, he thought, to get the full picture before deciding what to do.

'Mr Bennett, Mr Penrose is asking to see you,' said Miss Sullivan, putting her head round the door of the little office that Sidney shared with another young man called Cyril Bishop, whom he disliked. In Sidney's opinion, Cyril was not only too clever by half but was judgemental and po-faced, too.

'Better run along, hadn't you, Sid?' said Cyril, looking up from some plans only long enough to raise an eyebrow.

'Yes, thank you, Cyril. I don't need you adding to the instruction,' said Sidney, getting up.

He followed Miss Sullivan down the corridor to Mr Penrose's outer office. He wondered what this could be about. He didn't like to admit, even now, even to himself, that he might have been rumbled.

'Just knock and go in,' Miss Sullivan said, seating herself behind her desk. 'But be warned,' she added, lowering her voice, 'he isn't in a good mood this morning.'

'Oh, I expect I can deal with him,' said Sidney, affecting a confidence that he was no longer feeling. He rapped on the door.

'Ah, Bennett,' said Mr Penrose, who was of the old school of departmental boss. 'Please close the door. This won't take long.'

He was sitting behind his desk, but he did not invite Sidney to sit down in the chair opposite.

'Right, let's start with the floral clock – although heaven knows I've prayed we'd not need to have any more discussions about that – and then move on to the window boxes, the municipal flowerbeds, the sign outside the Imperial Hotel and last, but by no means least, the proposed redevelopment of the cliff-top site formerly owned by Mrs Rosemary Hailsham. I see by your fading colour that you anticipate my line of enquiry, that you make a connection between all these enhancements to Theddleton – or should I say to Joseph Chalfont's profile in Theddleton and the profits of his businesses?

'Ah . . .'

'Ah, indeed, Bennett. So maybe, with the connection established, there is no need to draw this out with separate questions about each. What do you say?'

Sidney said nothing. He just wished he could either die here, on the spot, or somehow magically wake up from this nightmare and find himself in his bed at home.

'I didn't hear,' said Mr Penrose. 'Was that a "yes"?'

Sidney managed to nod. He had broken out in a terrible sweat and thought he might actually faint right here, on Mr Penrose's office carpet.

'In which case, I'll ask you just once. Are you, or have you been at any time, in the pay of Joseph Chalfont while Planning have been considering the applications for these concerns of his, either for sums of money or for any benefits such as hospitality, entertainment, or gifts?'

Sidney felt his stomach turn right over. He was rumbled all right, well and truly found out, and there would be no wriggling out of it now. He opened his mouth to answer, but was so totally unprepared that still no words came out.

'I . . .' he croaked eventually.

'Yes, Bennett?' Mr Penrose looked thunderous.

'I . . . I h-have,' he admitted. 'But Mr Chalfont has such a way of making things sound all right that I hardly really thought—'

'Silence! Joseph Chalfont has his methods of doing business, and it's up to you to maintain professional standards at all times. A bribe is a bribe, plain and simple, Bennett, and I won't have anyone in my department stooping so low as to accept bribes. Ever! And then saying that it sounded "all right"! Are you a complete ass, Bennett? Well?'

'No, Mr Penrose, sir.'

'I beg to differ. You have one last task before you leave the council's employ. Please write on this piece of paper the names of everyone who you, in your turn, bribed to vote for Chalfont's plans alongside you. Then you may clear your desk and leave.'

Without doubt, those were the worst ten minutes of his life, Sidney thought, clearing his desk in moments, while Cyril Bishop looked down his nose from the moral high ground, and stopping only via Personnel to collect the necessary documents. He had looked to say goodbye to a couple of colleagues, but the other Planning department offices were suddenly strangely deserted.

He didn't remember how he made his way to the front door, but he found himself out on the street, carrying his few personal belongings in a paper carrier bag. It was a dull, grey day, the breeze off the sea gusting coldly and whipping up the waves. The beach was largely empty of holidaymakers, for all it was summer.

He walked in the direction of home in a daze, barely noticing when it started to drizzle, that fine English rain that looked as if it didn't amount to much, but soon added up to a thorough soaking.

Sidney was just passing the Imperial Hotel, bedecked with abundant red and purple flowers in baskets and tubs – as were the lamp-posts and pavement nearly all the way down the Promenade along the seafront side – when he decided to stop and see if Muriel was there. She didn't have a job – didn't need to have one – and was often sitting decoratively in the hotel's lofty foyer, waiting to see if people she knew came in, and reading the newspapers and fashion magazines to which the hotel subscribed. He was due to dine with the Chalfonts this evening anyway, but at least he'd have the comfort of gazing on Muriel's pretty face and keeping out of the rain while she sympathised with his decision to leave Planning and promised to remind her father about job vacancies at Chalfont Property.

Sure enough, there she was, looking lovely in a peach-coloured dress with a corsage of artificial orchids. She was posing on one of the sofas with her legs crossed elegantly, reading *Vogue*.

'Sidney? What are you doing here, and why are you so wet?'

'Hello, Muriel. I came by to see you, didn't I?'

'Did you? How sweet. But have you lost your umbrella? You looked half drowned.'

'What? Oh, no, I . . .'

She peered closely at him, giving him her full attention. 'What's the matter? There's summat wrong, isn't there?'

Sidney sank down onto the sofa beside her. 'I've left Planning,' he said.

'Why?' She looked genuinely puzzled.

'Well, I was invited to . . .'

'Yes?'

'. . . clear my desk.'

A multitude of thoughts seemed to pass through Muriel's mind, if the changes in her kittenish little face were any indication. 'You mean you've been sacked,' she stated, rather more loudly than Sidney would have liked.

People within hearing distance were looking up with interest.

'Well, I wouldn't put it quite like that,' said Sidney, quietly, trying to dial down the volume of the conversation and hoping against hope to save face.

'So how would you put it?' she snapped.

'Er . . .'

'Well, poor you. I expect you'll have to find another job, won't you?'

'I expect so. I'm . . . I'm sure I'll get summat, no trouble.'

'Good . . . that's good,' said Muriel, looking down, casually flipping the pages of her magazine now. 'Well, better get looking, then. Don't let me keep you.'

'Oh, yes . . . of course. So, Muriel, I'll see you this evening, seven o'clock.' He briefly envisaged Joseph Chalfont slapping him on the back and offering him a position in his office. Everyone would commiserate about the town hall job – now that he'd had to admit the truth about his leaving – and say he was far too clever to be wasted in local government, that all the best people were sacked at least once in their lives, which freed them to go on to better things.

'This evening? I don't think so,' she said. 'What do you think my dad is, some sort of provider of charity? Why on earth would he be giving you dinner?'

Sidney was flummoxed. 'I thought I'd been invited.'

'What would be the point? You're no use to Dad wandering around with the dole collectors,' she said cruelly, laying her cards on the table. 'Really, Sidney, you are such a stupid man sometimes,' she added, shaking her head in mock exasperation.

'But, Muriel,' he said, trying to take her hand, which she snatched away, and dripping rainwater onto her peach-coloured dress, 'I thought we were together. I thought we cared for each other and, I hoped, one day we—'

'Stop right there, Sidney. Don't say one single word more. You've got it all wrong. I don't know where you get your ideas from, but you and I have never been, nor ever can be, "together".' She trilled one of her shrill giggles. 'Don't you see how absurd that would be? You're even dafter than I thought you were if you reckon you could ever mean owt to me. Off you go, and stop dripping on the carpet. And take that wet paper sack with you.' She put out one of her tiny feet in her pointy shoes and kicked at his carrier bag of belongings, then turned to her magazine, feigning full attention on a picture of a woman with an eighteen-inch waist, pulling in her own middle in imitation.

'Muriel, please . . .'

She looked up disinterestedly. 'What, still here?' Then she raised her hand to attract the attention of the doorman. 'Norman, dear, do you think you could show Mr Bennett out, please?'

Asked to leave two buildings in quick succession! It really was the worst day of his life, Sidney thought.

It was raining harder now, really set in, and he had neither a coat nor an umbrella. There was nothing for it but to hurry home, getting soaked. He stepped out from under the hotel portico, ran down the steps and into the wet street, head down against the fine rain sweeping across from the sea in waves.

On the corner of the Promenade and the High Street, he ran straight into someone carrying a large tartan umbrella, nearly sending her into the road.

'Oh, I'm sorry, I . . . Bella!'

'Sidney!'

She made to step aside and continue on her way, but he waylaid her with a hand on her arm, which she shrugged off, a look of distaste on her face.

'Let me get on, please, Sidney. I have errand to do for Mrs Warminster.'

'Please, Bella . . .'

'What do you want, Sidney?'

For a moment, Sidney was tempted to answer her with the truth. *I want you, Bella. I was a fool to betray you. It's you I love and only you.* But he knew she wouldn't rush into his arms now. This was no fairy tale. He'd burned his boats with Bella.

'I'm sorry,' he said instead, while Bella held the umbrella over her head and Sidney stood outside its shelter, getting wetter. 'I'm sorry I hurt you, Bella. I was a fool.'

'Well, that makes two of us,' said Bella. She took a deep breath, clearly gathering herself. Then she gave him both barrels. 'I was a fool, too: a fool ever to take up with you. I can see now that I just loved the idea of being in love with a handsome man who I thought loved me, who I thought I was lucky to have even noticing me, never mind engaged to me. I wanted a wedding, where I was the fairy queen in a lovely new dress, the centre of attention, and a party with music and dancing to brighten my life. I painted a lot of doll's houses and dreamed of having such a lovely house of my own, but real. Just like the little girls do whose parents buy them those houses as presents. Perhaps I *will* have a pretty house of my own one day, but not with you. I'd rather be an old spinster among people who *really* love me, who tell me the truth because they recognise I deserve that, than be with a deceitful, lying, social-climbing nobody. A handsome face is worth nowt, Sidney, if the heart is not true.'

'Bella, I—'

'Please let me pass, Sidney. I have summat to do, even if you don't.'

'Bella, please! I'm sorry. I was wrong, and I'll make it up to you, I promise.'

'Make it up to me? What are you talking about? It's far too late to go back now. No, I was wrong not to see through you from the start, to allow myself to be taken in by someone so utterly selfish. Thank goodness I now see you for what you are, and I'm glad to have escaped before it was too late. Goodbye, Sidney.'

She swerved past him and carried on down the Promenade, not looking back.

Sidney stood, watching her go, until a car, travelling too close to the teeming gutter, sent a wave of filthy water over his trouser legs. Then his sagging carrier bag finally gave way, tipping his prized fountain pen, his favourite tie, and his framed photograph of Muriel Chalfont onto the pavement.

He gathered his things up as best he could and dragged himself home. *God, Mam's going to kill me,* he thought.

The doorbell rang mid-morning at number 14 Wellington Road. Nancy slowly got to her feet, easing her rheumaticky legs, and limped down the little hallway to see who was there. Eventually she had the door unlocked and opened it just wide enough to see out.

'Sidney! What are you doing here?'

'Are you going to let me in, Mam, or do I have to stand here while I drown?'

'Come in, love.' He really did look very wet.

Sidney stood dripping on the doormat, his hair plastered to his head. He took off his sodden jacket, the wool smelling like a wet dog, and shook it pathetically. Nancy saw his shirt was also soaked in large patches.

'Tell me what's happened, love,' she said. 'Come in where it's warm. You're not ill, are you, love? You do look a bit peaky.'

'No, Mam, not ill. Worse . . .'

'Not a falling-out with Muriel? Surely not, and her such a good sort. But it'll only be a lovers' tiff. It'll soon blow over, love – don't you worry.'

Sidney shook his head, looking as if he was about to cry.

'Sidney . . . ? You're frightening me now, lad. You're *not* ill, are you? Oh, love, you can tell me – I'm your mam and—'

'Mam, will you please be quiet and let me speak? I've been sacked.'

'Sacked?' Nancy felt confused; surely she'd misheard.

'Yes, sacked, Mam. Mr Penrose took exception to me favouring Mr Chalfont's schemes, did some digging, and then asked me to leave. Straight away.'

Nancy rose to her full five foot and in a sudden rush of anger she grabbed the *Theddleton Informer* off the table, rolled it and hit Sidney around the head with it as hard as she could.

'You daft ha'p'orth,' she yelled. 'Trust you to mess it all up. You haven't the sense you were born with some-times, Sidney. Why couldn't you keep it all low-key, you and Muriel? I reckon folk got jealous of your influence with the Chalfonts and went poking their noses in. Folk who don't know the ways of the real world.'

'What do you know about it, Mam? I took Chalfont's money, and I was found out. Now I've lost my job, and I doubt I'll get another if word gets round – certainly not at the town hall.'

'But what about Mr Chalfont? He'll stick by you, won't he, especially as you and Muriel are courting?'

'She's ditched me. Said I was no good to her or her father without my job in Planning.'

Nancy sat down heavily, looking as if her stuffing had been removed. 'The madam! I knew there was summat not quite right about her, for all she was being so friendly. You were taken in by a pretty face, Sidney, but you would rush in . . .'

JOSEPHINE COX

'Mam, will you just shut up?' said Sidney wearily. 'We were both taken in by Muriel. I'd have hoped Chalfont would have stuck by me, but Muriel says he won't want to know me if I'm no use to him.'

'No use – *used* – that's what folk like them do to us little people. One rule for them and one for the rest of us. Well, lad, you should have watched your back instead of blundering into this situation. Been a bit more savvy than you were. Sacked indeed!'

'I'm sorry, Mam.'

'That's easily said, but actions speak louder than words, my lad. Put on some dry clothes, and then you can go straight over to that Labour Exchange in Baybury and look for a new job.'

'What, now?'

'Yes, now. And don't come back here until you've found one.'


'Are you all right, Bella?' asked Alice that evening, while they sat in front of the fire, stuffing their wet shoes with newspaper. 'You look a bit . . . pensive.'

'Oh, I met Sidney in the street this morning. It was inevitable that I'd see him at some point, but it was rather horrible this first time, when I had to say what needed saying.' She gave a brave little smile. 'At least I was the one with the umbrella, whereas he was completely soaked.'

'Good-oh. I hope you didn't offer shelter.'

'I did not.'

# THE LETTER

Bella told Alice something of the conversation, and Alice gave her a hug and told her how courageous she was.

'As you say, you're bound to bump into him sometimes, but it will be easier from now on. I'm glad you've come through to thinking straight about Sidney.'

'Well, our relationship is quite over and in the past, so there's no point in dwelling on it. I'm learning to harden my heart about that ridiculous man. But what about you, Alice? What are you going to do?'

'About what?'

'About Bobbie, of course.'

Alice went completely white. 'Oh, good grief, Bella,' she whispered, 'have people noticed?'

'If they have, they've said nowt to me,' said Bella, 'but I know you better than most, and I want to be sure that you're going to be happy, whatever you do.'

Alice got up and paced the room for a few moments. Then she quietly closed the door to the passage so that Thomas, who was typing busily at the kitchen table, would not overhear. She sat back down.

'That's what Bobbie says. She wants me to go to live at Baybury Grange with her.'

'And are you going to?'

'I'd really like to,' said Alice. 'We could pretend that it doesn't matter what folk think, but that wouldn't be true.'

'I fear you'll find you've chosen a difficult road.'

'I can bear it if Bobbie can. And I reckon, if I do go to her, the road I'll have chosen will be easier than it might have been if Bobbie were not Bobbie Reeves.'

'Mebbe . . . And what about Mr Reeves? It sounds to me as if Bobbie's father might be a bit old-fashioned, and it *is* his house – his castle – after all.'

'Well, there's the thing, Bella,' said Alice, taking her sister's hands and squeezing them. 'Mr Reeves adores Bobbie and will do owt to make her happy. Bobbie says she broached the idea of my going to live there and he said summat like . . .' Alice sat up straight and put on a gruff voice in imitation of the old man: '. . . "You can have as many friends as you like to live here. It isn't as if we haven't got the room."'

Bella laughed. 'But do you think he understood what Bobbie was saying?'

'Of course he did! Bobbie says nowt surprises him, and that people only think he's strait-laced because he's an elderly gentleman. That's their perception, but it's not reality. And that's good. Folk will be thinking a lot less about us if Mr Reeves is making it clear there's nowt to gossip about.'

Bella hugged her sister. 'When will you tell Dad?'

'When I must. Now, do you think we dare disturb him from his typing? He does seem to be putting his back into it, but I'm getting quite hungry, and Millie will be back soon.'

'How's the painting going?'

'You know as much as I do. Bobbie isn't allowed to see it until it's done. Apparently, Millie and Mr Reeves are getting on brilliantly. Bobbie says she interrupted the other day to see if they'd like summat to eat and,

414

far from working on and sitting for the painting, they were playing Ludo.'

'Mm, Millie is such a child sometimes, but she will have to get on with the portrait if she wants to be paid for it.'

'She knows that. I think she's having fun, though. She deserves that. She likes to have her own money, so I reckon she'll get it finished soon, and, anyway, Bobbie will make sure she does.'

With a smile, Bella got up to disturb Thomas, kissing the top of Alice's head as she passed.

Slow William was blamed for the fire at the Three-Mile Bottom. Someone had to be blamed – people always had to find a scapegoat – and Slow William was easy to accuse and hard to defend, having no family to support him and few words in his head. He could try to say what he liked, but the authorities had already made up their minds and weren't listening. Poor old William Gladstone was expendable.

Iris Cook had tried to intervene and explain that William was a harmless sort, whom she could vouch for, but the police dismissed her as a do-gooder and a busy-body housewife with time on her hands. It was better that the crime was solved than not, and the local constabulary could not begin to imagine how so intense a fire had burned up to an inferno in the empty kitchen in the early hours of the morning and consumed Richard Fairbanks and Jane Regan to ashes. Far easier to take note that some folk had seen William Gladstone at the inn not many days before then and he had not been made welcome. He had a motive for a grudge, he had no words in his defence, and so the investigation had a neat solution.

'Mam's really down about William being sent to prison,' said Edwin one Sunday in September, as he and Millie rowed the *Hope and Peace* along to Baybury on a flat, calm sea.

'I'm sorry to hear that,' said Millie. 'I like your mum. She'll have to find someone else to work on the compost heaps and rid the allotments of rats.'

'What about William?' asked Edwin. 'I thought you were friendly with him. Don't you also feel sorry he's in prison, and for a long time? Arson and manslaughter are very serious charges. I doubt he'll ever see freedom again, he's so old. It's the only reason they haven't hanged him, I reckon: that he's old and daft.'

'You're right, and I don't like him being blamed for the fire at the inn, but I'm afraid there's nothing to be done about it, even though it wasn't his fault.'

Edwin looked carefully at Millie. 'Millie, you don't know who did set the fire at the Three-Mile, do you?'

'No.'

'Well, it sounds as if you definitely know it wasn't Gladstone.'

Millie shrugged. 'Well, your mum knows it wasn't Slow William – have you asked her if *she* knows who it was?'

'Don't be soft, lass. Of course Mum doesn't know. It's just that you sounded so sure it wasn't Gladstone and I thought you . . . you might have heard summat.'

Millie rowed a few strokes, her face set with misery. 'I would say if I knew. I wouldn't let Slow William take the blame if I could set things right, but . . . I'm glad Fairbanks and Mad Jane are dead. I loathed them both.'

Edwin looked at her, seeing her unhappiness. He stopped rowing so she had to, too.

'Millie? Promise me you didn't do owt.'

'I promise, Edwin. I hated them so much that I wished they would die, but it was a wish, in my head, and nothing more. Surely you've hated someone that much?'

'I can't say I have. I'm not much of a hater. I'd prefer it if you weren't either. There are always going to be folk you dislike, but you have to shrug them off and choose others to keep you company.'

'It's hard to do.'

'You were a bit the same about Mrs Hailsham and her daughter dying in that awful house fire. Another fire . . . You didn't seem to care much about them either. Sometimes, Millie, I think you would be nicer if you showed a bit more humanity.'

'Thanks a lot, Edwin,' said Millie crossly.

'C'mon, let's row back to Theddleton jetty,' Edwin said, suddenly fed up with her.

'But I thought we were going to Baybury. That's what you said.'

'I've changed my mind. And I've remembered, I said I'd be back in time to give Mam a hand with the compost heaps at the allotments.'

'So you're the new Slow William, are you?' said Millie mockingly.

'I'm glad to help Mam, if that's what you mean,' said Edwin. 'Now, just shut up and row.'

Millie made little effort with her oars, leaving Edwin to do nearly all the work. She said nothing, but her face showed intense anger. Within a couple of minutes, a squall blew up out of nowhere, impeding progress, the wind gusting and buffeting, and the waves billowing up around the little boat. Millie, sitting in the bow, started laughing, enjoying the rough ride and her hair blowing about her face. She looked as if she were in her element, while Edwin struggled with the sail, hot and tired by the time he manoeuvred the boat alongside the jetty at last, and tied it up safely.

'I enjoyed the ride home,' said Millie, stepping carefully out of the boat. The wind had dropped as quickly as it had got up.

'I'm sure you did, as you made no effort to help,' said Edwin, flexing his tired arms, his hair wet with salty water. 'Right, I'm off now.' He turned away and began walking as quickly as his tiredness would allow, along the wooden jetty towards the top of the beach.

'See you soon,' said Millie, but Edwin didn't answer.

She watched him go. Why had she said she'd see him soon? She knew she wouldn't. After she'd drawn the picture of Edwin in the *Hope and Peace*, with which Iris had been so pleased, all those months ago, Millie had tried to replicate it, but to include herself in the boat. But however hard she tried to make the second figure the image of Millie Boyd, her hand drew Pam Braithwaite. Edwin was not fated to share his journey with Millie. Better to set him at a distance, put a stop to her growing affection now, than risk heartbreak. Besides, she wasn't sure her future was here in Theddleton. She couldn't see the way forward yet. There was something she had to do – a promise she'd made to herself – and then all might become clearer. She wasn't ready yet, but she would be soon.

# CHAPTER TWENTY-THREE

*Some months later*

FOR MONTHS, MILLIE had waited to fulfil the promise she had made to herself in her cold, dimly lit bedroom in Beaucroft Road, Blackburn: that Uncle Frank and Aunt Mona would get exactly what they deserved.

Uncle Frank would pay for making Nanette's life such a misery that she had preferred to attempt to run away when she was little more than a child rather than put up with his bullying. When that failed and she had been forever scarred in the ensuing violence of Frank's temper, she had left as soon as she was old enough to take responsibility for herself. It was time to pay back Frank, both for that and for the relish with which he had wielded his whippy ruler and the flat of his hand against Millie herself, years later.

Aunt Mona would also pay for her cruelty, for her meanness of spirit, her sly violence, her coldness of heart.

# THE LETTER

The Blackburn Marchants had only pretended to want to give a loving home to their orphaned niece, where a child was much longed for but had not been granted to them. What they had really wanted was a victim, an outlet for their cruelty. They were clearly incapable of being loving parents.

Millie had despised them too much to wreak the havoc she wished on them without a sound plan in place. And it had been vital to get away from them first. Now, a year older, as a precocious young woman who had left childhood behind, with her own money in her pocket, plus the confidence that – and the growing success of her painting – gave her, she knew her moment had come. It was as well she had waited. She was ready now. She would light the blue touchpaper, then enjoy the fireworks.

One Saturday morning in spring, she left the cottage in Theddleton early, taking with her a letter she had typed in secret on Thomas's typewriter. It was only short but, even so, it had taken her a couple of attempts to type it without mistakes. She set out quickly for the station. It was barely light, and the birds were singing joyfully. She had told neither Bella nor Thomas where she was going, just left a note on the kitchen table that said she'd be back later.

As she reached the end of Chapel Lane, she heard quick footsteps behind her, and there was Edwin, on his way to work at the bakery.

'Millie.'

'Edwin.'

'You all right?'

'Yes, thank you. I'm fine.'

'I see you around – of course I do; we live next door to each other – but I can't believe we've barely spoken more than "Hello" since that day last autumn. I'm glad I've seen you now.'

'Well, I expect you've been busy. I certainly have,' said Millie.

'So, where are you off to so early, if you don't mind me asking? I seem to think you aren't generally a lark.'

'Nor an owl. I like a comfy bed. It's a good place to think things through. But I've got some business in Lancashire today, and I want to catch an early train.'

'Oh, aye? Painting, are you? Going to shake up the art world of Manchester?'

'Shake things up,' mused Millie, smiling. 'Yes, that's exactly what I'm going to do, Edwin.'

'You're doing well, I hear,' he went on. 'Fine folk asking you to paint their portraits. I'm glad you're making a go of it. You've got a real talent, anyone can see.'

'Thank you.'

'Mam still treasures that drawing you did of me in the *Hope and Peace*, last year . . . when we were still friends.'

'We *are* still friends,' said Millie, looking into his face. 'I can't even remember now why I was cross with you.'

'Nor can I, but I'm glad you're not cross any longer. Strange how that wind got up, kind of matching your mood, I remember. Weird, like you'd conjured it. I couldn't stop thinking of it.'

Millie shrugged. 'So how is Pam? I gather you are to marry,' she said.

Edwin's face lit up at the thought of his fiancée. 'She's grand. You know, she's forever grateful that you told her about the job at the bakery.'

'Ha, one of my rare good turns,' said Millie. 'I'm not usually so nice.'

'Go on with you, you daft lass,' said Edwin fondly.

They were outside the bakery on the High Street now, and he stopped to knock to be let in.

'Have a good time in Manchester,' he said.

Millie smiled. Let him think she was going there if he wanted. 'I'm pleased to have seen you, Edwin,' she said.

She hurried on to the station, where she bought a return ticket to Blackburn.

Blackburn looked exactly as it had that day Millie had left it. It was even raining just the same, although now Millie had both a hat and an umbrella of her own to keep the wet off.

When she left the station, she turned left, taking the route towards Beaucroft Road, but then veered off before she got to the park and walked along to some streets of tiny terraced houses. The roads were cobbled and the houses had no gardens, the front doors opening straight onto the street. People turned in interest to see a stranger. It was the kind of area where everyone knew each other and their lives revolved entirely around these streets.

Millie looked for the numbers, remembering when she had been here before, when she had lived with Uncle Frank and Aunt Mona. Then she had come just to look and to learn. Now she was intending to use what she had found out that day.

She stopped at the house she was seeking, remembering the number – remembering her conversation with the woman in the house next door but one, who had provided some very helpful information – and relieved to recognise the dark red paint of the front door. She had been anxious that she might not find the place again, but this was definitely the right house. She pulled the letter she had typed out of her bag. She just hoped the woman was in. Her whole plan rested on everyone being at home.

She took a deep breath and knocked on the door. There was no answer.

She waited a couple of minutes, fighting down impatience and disappointment, then knocked again.

After another minute, there was the sound of a key turning in the lock and the door opened.

A young woman peered out. She was in her twenties, thin and a little tired-looking. A very sturdy toddler was clutching her skirt, a toddler with a large head and a very large hooked nose.

'Hello.'

'Good morning. Mrs Marchant?' asked Millie.

'That's right.'

'I have a message from you. The gentleman asked me to deliver it to you by hand.'

She offered the envelope to the woman, whose name was typed on the front.

The woman took the envelope and looked at it as if she might somehow discern the contents without opening it.

Millie waited. However keen she was to get her plan underway, she had to stick to her role of messenger. If she betrayed any impatience, she might make the woman suspicious.

It was a relief to Millie when Mrs Marchant opened the envelope and read the letter. Millie, of course, knew exactly what it said.

*My dear Gloria,*

*I have good news! I have found a new home for us. The address is 20 Beaucroft Road. This young woman from the estate agent will bring you to see it this morning so we can look round together. Bring the lad with you. I am waiting there now.*

*Frank*

'Is everything all right?' asked Millie. 'Mr Marchant seems very keen on the house.'

'I'm wondering, why has he sent me a letter – a typed one, at that – and not come himself, like? It seems a bit queer.' Mrs Marchant's face was puzzled but also hopeful. 'Why wasn't he here with us, if he's in town now?'

*Damn.* Millie had hoped the woman would just grab her coat and the child and set out for Beaucroft Road.

'I typed the letter, Mrs Marchant. It was dictated to me down the telephone. But the gentleman is at that house now with the estate agent I work for. If he left to come here, he'd then have to make an appointment to view the house again another day. It's nearby, so you can be there in a few minutes.'

This seemed to have the desired effect.

Gloria said, 'Wait there, please. I'll just get our coats and my handbag.' She disappeared into the house and returned within moments, buttoning her coat. The little boy was already wearing his, and a stout pair of shoes that were rather too big for him.

'C'mon, Frankie,' said his mother.

So, Uncle Frank had named his son after himself. Well, that was no great surprise.

They set off, Millie sharing her umbrella with Gloria. Gloria chatted about her life as the wife of a travelling salesman who was so rarely at home but doted on his son.

''Cept when he's cross,' interrupted the little lad. 'Then I's get a smack.'

'Shush now, Frankie. Only if you're naughty. You know to be good when your dad's home, don't you?'

Frankie nodded solemnly. Millie felt sorry for him. She didn't have to imagine the scenario.

By the time they got to Beaucroft Road, she was almost feeling sorry for Gloria, who turned out to be both blameless and a decent woman, just wanting the best for her son, with his father so often absent. It was a shame to have to sacrifice the future happiness of these two innocents, but, Millie reflected, that was life. People just got caught up in matters that were not their fault. The thought of William Gladstone, languishing in prison for the rest of his life, passed through her mind . . .

Millie was almost certain that Uncle Frank and Aunt Mona would be in, as they were creatures of habit and stuck to rigid routines. There were no surprises in their lives – apart from Gloria and Frankie, who were about to be a very big surprise indeed, as Millie could hardly wait to see.

She knocked on the door, then stood well back to allow Gloria and Frankie to occupy the centre ground.

After a few seconds, Uncle Frank opened the door. His jaw dropped open and his face turned completely white. He was literally speechless. He didn't seem to notice Millie, standing to one side, so astounded was he to see his other wife and their son.

'Frank, I got your note,' said Gloria, but, seeing his face, she was already beginning to falter. 'You said we was to come straight away.' She clearly hoped to overcome the awkwardness by keeping talking. 'And I've brought Frankie, see? So, this is the house, then? C'mon, love, are you going to let us in for a look?'

By then, Frank had gathered himself sufficiently to regain the power of speech. 'Gloria, what are you doing here? With *him*?' He pointed a trembling finger at little Frankie, so obviously a two-year-old version of himself.

'Who's there?' said Aunt Mona's voice from inside. 'Frank, who is it?'

'Oh God,' said Frank desperately, as Mona emerged to stand beside him on the threshold.

'Frank? Who's this?' She caught sight of Millie. 'And what's *she* doing here?' Then she looked properly at the child and her eyes grew huge and round with shock. 'And who the hell is *he*?'

'This is your doing, Millie Boyd, isn't it?' gasped Frank.

'I thought it was time the truth came out, yes,' said Millie.

'But who is this woman?' asked Gloria, indicating Mona. 'And why is she questioning me? And where's the estate agent?'

'Estate agent?' asked Frank. 'What are you talking about, woman?'

Gloria's voice completely betrayed her draining confidence now. 'You know, the one you told me about. Aren't you wanting to buy this house?'

'This is our house,' barked Mona. 'I don't know who you are, but I reckon I can guess. How dare you, Frank? How dare you bring your hussy here? And with a child! Oh, how could you do this to me?'

'Just a minute,' said Gloria, rallying at what she saw as the unfairness of this. 'Who are you calling a hussy, you sour-faced old baggage? This is my husband' – she pointed a trembling finger at Frank – 'and little Frankie is our son.'

'Aah! Your wife! Your son! And you've even called him Frank! Oh, you . . . you bigamist! You monster!' Mona raised her hand and gave Frank's face a furious slap. 'Hateful! Horrible! Your wife! Was I not a good wife to you? Did I not try to give you everything I could? And now you repay me like this? It wasn't my fault we had no children of our own.'

'Well, it looks as if it was,' said Gloria, quick as an alligator's snap.

'Aah, you betrayer!' Mona shrieked. 'And now you bring your floozie to my door, and this . . . this by-blow, to mock me. Was ever an innocent woman so treated? And you, Millie Boyd, I can guess your part in all this.'

'Then you'll know why you deserve everything you're getting, the pair of you,' said Millie. 'I've longed for this day, to see you being paid back, mostly for what you did to my mother, Frank – the violence, the bullying – yes, and to Uncle Thomas, too, and for what you both did to me: pretending to want to give me a loving home, and then not showing one single moment of any kind of love or generosity of heart.'

'No!' yelled Frank, 'that's not true. Whatever Nanette told you, she was lying. She always was unstable.'

'Lying? Unstable?' shrieked Mona. 'You'd know all about that, I reckon. You must be off your head to think you can have two wives!'

By now, the shouting and the accusations had reached an ear-splitting volume and the poor toddler was terrified. He sat down heavily on the doorstep and started wailing at the top of his voice, big fat tears flowing down his round red face.

The Marchants' next-door neighbour opened her front door to see what the disturbance was. She was a hatchet-faced middle-aged woman who didn't take kindly to having her Saturday morning disturbed.

'What's going on?' she demanded.

'I'm married to a bigamist,' bellowed Mona, 'and this woman's come round to move into my home. To throw me out! The nerve of her! Brought her son with her and thinks she's coming to live here.' She turned back to poor Gloria, spitting venom. 'Well, I'll show you, you young madam. Frank's been married to me since before you were born, so you're the false wife, not me. So you can just get off my doorstep and take your bastard with you before I come out there and kick you off.'

Aunt Moaner is definitely showing her true colours, thought Millie.

She was beginning to feel a bit sorry that she had caused Gloria to be subjected to this onslaught of vitriol, and the whole unfortunate situation, but what else could she do? If Uncle Frank's crime were to be revealed, the evidence had to be shown.

'Bigamist?' demanded Mrs Bossy Boots next door. 'Disgusting! A perversion of God's laws, and criminal, too. I'm going to call the police now. And you can all shut up and tell it to the constables instead of shouting about it in the garden.' She went back into her house and slammed the door.

'This is the worst day of my life,' wept Gloria. 'I thought you loved me, and it turns out it's all lies, Frank, even our marriage. I reckon you're not even a travelling salesman at all, but have been shacked up all along with this woman who's also your wife, and only a short way across town from me.'

'There's only one wife, and that's me,' said Mona. 'And my Frank works at a bank.'

'Not for long after this,' muttered Millie. Maybe the moment had come to leave them all to it. There was really only one thing she could add. 'I doubt I'll see you again, Uncle Frank,' she said, 'but you might want to bear in mind: "He that covereth his sins shall not prosper."'

'Wait a minute,' said Gloria, outraged. 'Did you say this fella is your uncle? Why have you done this? He's Frankie's father. Couldn't you have left us in peace? We were just about going on all right until you came and played this horrible trick on us.'

'It wasn't idle mischief-making, Gloria. It was time for the truth to come out. I've been waiting to do this for a long time. I'm sorry you and young Frankie are the innocent victims in my revenge on these two monsters, but I can't help that.'

'Monsters!' yelled Mona. 'You're the monster, Millie Boyd. You're a fiend from hell, a devil in human clothing! You are to blame.'

'No, you and Frank are to blame,' said Millie. 'And now Frank's going to get his punishment, and so are you.'

She turned and walked quickly away, the shouting and yelling continuing behind her.

Round the corner from Beaucroft Road, she met two police constables heading in the direction of the Marchants' house to question and possibly arrest the bigamist. She stepped to the side of the pavement to let them hurry on their way.

At Blackburn Station, Bella was just coming out onto the street when she saw Millie walking quickly towards her, holding her umbrella to one side against the rain.

'Millie! Oh, thank goodness I've met you here. I was thinking I'd have to go to Uncle Frank and Aunt Mona's, and I had hoped never to have to go there again after last time.'

They moved into the station out of the rain. Bella saw Millie was looking a little hectic. Her eyes were darting this way and that, and there were two patches of high colour on her cheeks. Whatever she had been up to, it had involved drama.

'What's happened?' Bella demanded, fearing some kind of violence. There had been a few terrible incidents around people who had crossed Millie, and although those had surely been just coincidences, they were difficult to forget.

'How did you know I was here?' asked Millie.

'Dad and I saw you'd left early, which suggested a

long journey. We found the rejected letters you'd typed in the waste-paper basket, which pointed to your coming here. Then I asked at the station and the man there told me a young person had bought a ticket to Blackburn, and described you. So here I am, to make sure you're all right. But you don't look *completely* all right to me. Please, tell me what's happened.' She was fearful now.

'Oh, Bella, don't look so worried. It's all going to be sorted out. The police were on their way when I left.'

'Police! Millie, what have you done?'

'Just revealed a truth that needed telling,' Millie said. Already she was beginning to look calmer. 'And if we get a move on, we can get that train to York.' She pointed towards the departure board.

'I can't get on a train until I know what's been happening. Millie, I have to know you've not done owt awful. You're scaring me, and I need to know Uncle Frank and Aunt Mona are OK.'

'I promise they're not physically harmed,' said Millie. 'Not unless they've harmed each other. Now come on, or we'll have to wait for ages for the next train.'

She set off towards the platform, dragging Bella with her.

When they were sitting comfortably in third class, or as comfortably as third class would allow, Millie told Bella the whole story of her revenge against Uncle Frank. How she'd seen him with the woman who turned out to be Gloria and her baby, Frankie, in the street one day when she was playing truant from school. The baby so very obviously looked exactly like Frank, with his big round head and his large and characteristic nose, that she'd followed them home, making a mental note of the address. Then she had knocked on the door of the house next door but one, asking about a woman with a baby, saying she'd found a baby's rattle in the street and wanted to return it. Gloria's neighbour had provided quite a lot of information, interested as she was in the woman who claimed to have a husband but whose husband was mostly not there. How keen people were to share their disapproval. Mrs Marchant, the young mother was called.

'Good grief,' said Bella, but quietly. She lowered her voice still further. 'So Uncle Frank was married to two women. I'm astounded.'

'I thought it was about time to bring this to light,' said Millie. 'My goodness, you should have heard the shouting. It was the woman next door who called the police when it all got a bit . . . heated.' She grinned at her deliberate euphemism. 'You know what hypocrites those two were, always so strait-laced and holier-than-thou. It serves them right that everyone now knows all about them. As I said, people are very keen to share their disapproval. Aunt Moaner will have quite a lot of anxiety about what the neighbours think when Uncle Frank is banged up in prison. I'm really sorry for Gloria, though. I'm sure Uncle Frank took her in, and their baby is perfectly hideous to look at: the very image of

Uncle Frank, but aged two. Something the little one said makes me think Uncle Frank smacks him, so perhaps he's better off without his father in his life. Shame about his looks, though. He's stuck with those.'

Bella felt quite shocked that Millie could find anything funny in any of this. Sometimes, still, it was difficult to fit Millie's behaviour into the accepted norm. She seemed to have her own rules, although Bella had noticed more humanity creeping into her dramas since Thomas's bicycle accident and Millie's revelation about her guilt over her parents' deaths. It was as if she were allowing herself to feel. She no longer had to harden her heart in case her anguish broke her. 'Shush, Millie. Please. It's not funny.'

'It is a bit,' said Millie, but she looked chastened.

The train on the last leg of their journey was quiet and they had two seats each to themselves. Both Millie and Bella were tired.

'Reminds me of that first journey, when Alice and I rescued you from Uncle Frank and Aunt Mona, and brought you home with us,' said Bella.

Millie smiled. 'Yes, *home*. At first I didn't know if it would become my home but now I know it is.'

'It's your home for as long as you want it. You do know that, don't you? Dad and I – well, you've made a difference to us. He's so much happier, so much more . . . fulfilled. You found his job for him, his vocation. Now he's having his book of stories published, and with those lovely pictures of yours on the jacket and as a frontispiece – Alice tells me that's what it's called. We're all so excited for both of you. Dad's a success in his work at last, and we are so proud of him. We owe that to you, Millie.'

Millie nodded. 'Thank you,' she said quietly. 'But he just needed a little help finding what he wanted to do, that's all.'

'And you're really making a success of your work, too. I'm so happy for you. It's what you deserve. I thought you'd lost your way at one time, but I realise now you were just waiting for your opportunity. It wasn't that long in coming.'

'Ha, I'm good at that,' said Millie. 'Waiting for my chance. I think my big opportunity came with Bobbie, as did Alice's, but in a different way.'

'Yes, dear Bobbie. Alice is happier than she's ever been. And Bobbie's father adores Alice. I'm pleased for both Alice and Bobbie that each is with the person she loves.'

There were some minutes of silence between them. Then Millie said, 'And what about you, Bella? Are you going to leave the nest?'

'I'm in no hurry this time,' said Bella carefully. 'You know, I was very upset with you for finding out about Sidney. I was silly – I had to know the truth – but I thought at first that you'd ruined my life, and I wasn't sure how much I wanted you as my sister just then. I had a terrible nightmare in which you were . . . well, never mind. Oh, forgive me, Millie. I was foolish about so many things, and Sidney was just one. Dad and Alice didn't want to . . . redirect me onto a saner path because they thought they were respecting my choice, however daft I was, but you had no reservations about speaking the truth. I'm so glad you did.'

'So am I. Honestly, Bella, imagine being married to that half-wit Sidney Bennett. And his mother seemed to come as part of the deal, from what I could see. What a nightmare!'

'I hear Mrs B isn't boasting about her marvellous boy quite so much since he lost his job at the town hall. You might have seen, he spent the rest of last summer hiring out deck chairs, and now he's selling newspapers and chocolate at the newsagent's. I don't mind seeing him in there – I've nowt to be ashamed of – but I've noticed him sneaking away round the back if he sees me coming in.'

'Not much use for his fancy suits there.' Millie giggled. 'I wonder what he does when Muriel Chalfont goes in.'

'Ha, probably the same. I saw her in the High Street shortly after Sidney got the sack, when I was with Vera. Well, of course, Vera knew all the details, and she said in a big loud voice, "Isn't that the ghastly woman Sidney Bennett got taken in by?" And I said, "Yes: Muriel Chalfont. It's hardly surprising that she's never seen with any friends. Folk know to avoid her." Of course, everyone around heard, including Muriel herself, and they turned to look at her as she hurried away.'

Millie laughed. 'So what about Toby? Seems a shame he's in London and you get to see him only every so often.'

'Well, we'll have to see what happens,' Bella replied. 'He's hoping to start up his own business soon, and he'll want to avoid being in competition with Mr Meyer, his employer. That wouldn't be fair after Mr Meyer has taught him all he knows. So mebbe Toby will move back up to Yorkshire, perhaps open a tailoring business in Baybury, where there's a bit more money and more folk to buy smart clothes than in Theddleton. He's thinking about it. Certainly, Mr and Mrs Warminster will be pleased if he does.'

'As will you.'

'Yes . . .'

They leaned back in their seats. Millie took off her shoes and tucked her legs up beside her.

After a while she said, 'Bella . . .'

'Mm?'

'I've learned now, thanks to you, that making my own way doesn't mean having to do it all on my own, shouldering all the bad things alone.'

'No, of course it doesn't. You've got us to help you.'

'Exactly. Alice told me that, too. And we are all far better off together than apart.'

Millie leaned back and closed her eyes. Soon she was asleep.

Bella watched her, free to examine the face that so closely resembled her own. In many obvious ways, Millie Boyd fitted in perfectly as the third Marchant sister. But in other ways, she was not an ordinary, predictable, comfortable person at all. Some strange things had happened in this last year, good and bad; the lives of the entire family had changed and taken new paths, and some secrets had been revealed. Much of this was clearly down to Millie but, thank goodness, the belief that Millie had had, that her fury had power and could influence events and that she was in some horrible way responsible, had been well and truly overcome.

Just as this thought passed through Bella's mind, the clouds parted for the first time that day and the low sun blazed through the train window onto Millie's face, transforming her instantly, her head lit and haloed like a madonna's, her blue dress glowing as if it were painted with precious lapis lazuli.

Yes, that's what she is, thought Bella. Our naughty angel, the missing sister. How thankful they all were that she had written that heartbreaking, misspelled letter, begging to be rescued. How far Millie had come in a year.

Millie opened her eyes. 'What are you thinking, Bella?'

'What a difference you have made to us and how lucky we are to have you, Millie.'

'That's strange,' she said. 'I was thinking exactly the same – about you and Uncle Thomas, and Alice and Bobbie.'

The radiant light shifted, and Millie smiled her Marchant sister smile.

# Josephine Cox's classic novels of family drama have sold over 20 million copies worldwide!

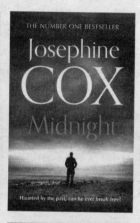

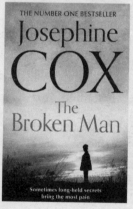

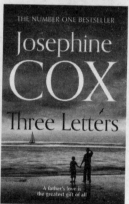

# Have you read them all?

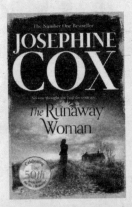

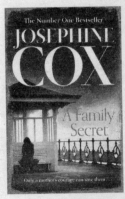

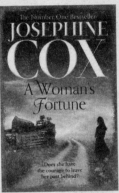

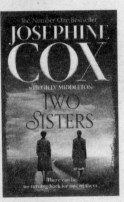

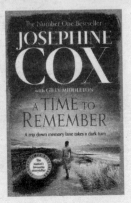

# JOSEPHINE COX

## with GILLY MIDDLETON

Sign up for the Josephine Cox Chatterbox email newsletter to hear about new books from Josephine Cox, written with Gilly Middleton, plus news, competitions and ebook offers!

**Sign up here**:
https://bit.ly/SignUpToJoCox

Or use this QR code: